For ~~Isabella~~

Greg's "shining" novel which will ~~hopefully~~ keep the memory of his rare intellectual wealth ever pertinent and vital.

Gloria Lauri-Lucente

OVER THE MOUNTAIN

Gregory Lucente

Copyright © 1996 Gregory Lucente.
All rights reserved.
ISBN 0-9653968-0-0

Front cover by Philip Chircop, 1995.

This manuscript was prepared for printing by
Dingo Publishing Services, Ann Arbor, Michigan.

Manufactured in the United States of America.

For my mother and father

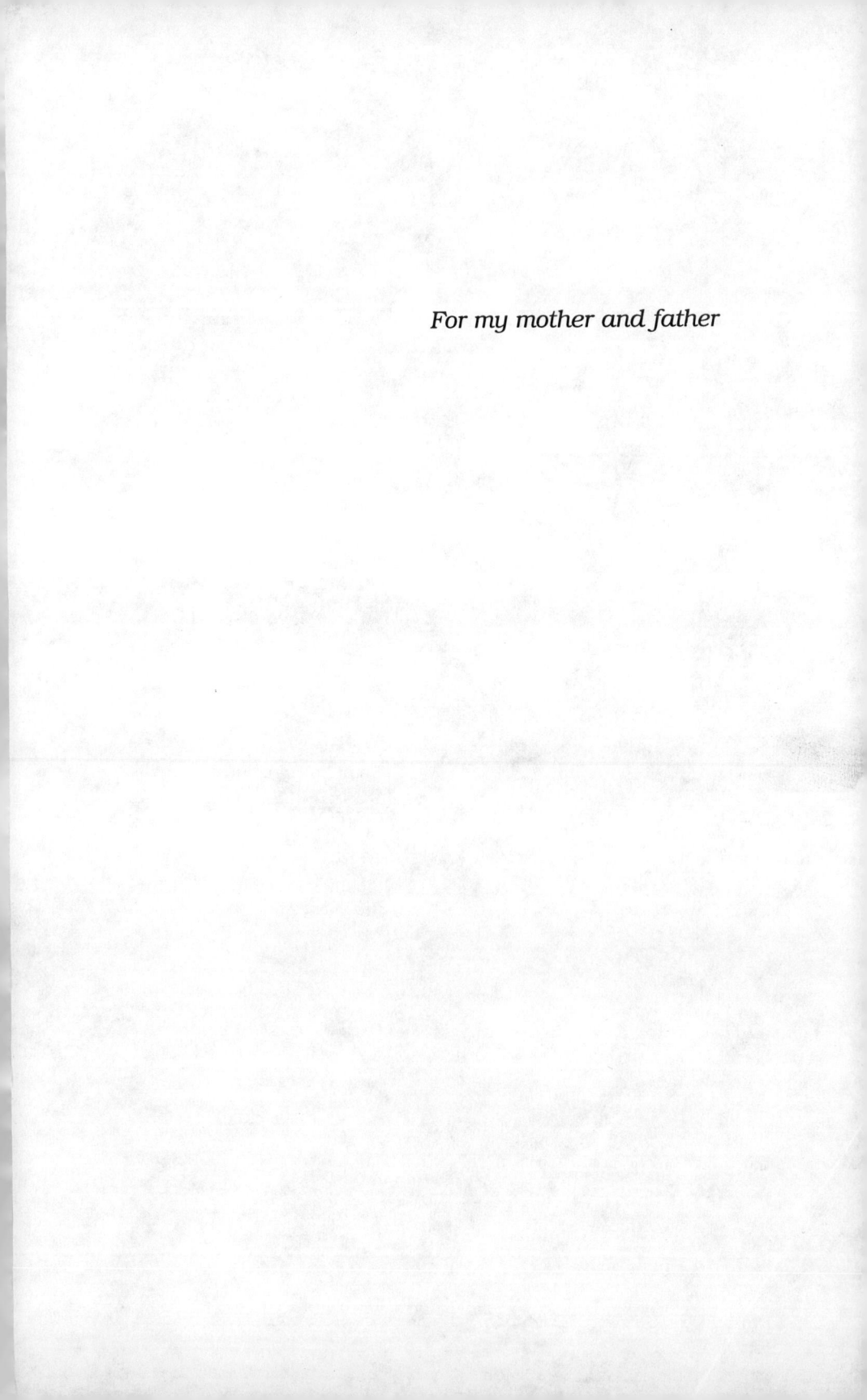

Oh —
The bear went over the mountain
The bear went over the mountain
The bear went over the mountain
To see what he could see.

To see what he could see,
To see what he could see
Oh —
The bear went over the mountain
To see what he could see.

Oh —
The other side of the mountain
The other side of the mountain
The other side of the mountain
Was all that he could see.

All that he could see,
All that he could see
Oh —
The other side of the mountain
Was all that he could see.

Oh —
He went back over the mountain
He went back over the mountain
He went back over the mountain —
To see what he could see....
— Child's song

*   *   *

Meanwhile the mind, from pleasure less,
Withdraws into its happiness:
The mind, that ocean where each kind
Does straight its own resemblance find;
Yet it creates, transcending these,
Far other worlds, and other seas;
Annihilating all that's made
To a green thought in a green shade.
— Andrew Marvell

Contents

Chapter 1. A Promise   *1*

Chapter 2. The Summers   *49*

Chapter 3. Hunt   *109*

Chapter 4. Fugitive   *175*

I.   A Promise

There is always time to have more time.
— A. Roa Bastos

Then they were on the green lake. The sky was white and blue.
"*Curiosity killed the cat—satisfaction brought him back: Now you go on.*" *That's what his Grandma Britzen, glaring down and waving them off, had said.* But this is the way it was at first:
"Toss it over there." Grandpa gave his smile and leaned into the sun, waving the brace of spatulate, crooked fingers—a lumberman's fingers, Gianni learned afterwards, from what the others told him—the middle two, since the space for the first was bare, the skin on that knuckle's end smooth across and indented, like the hole where a little stump has been dug out. The smooth-creased, yellowed face turned down to him, hard and distant in the frame of forehead and jaw, and nodded toward the shore. The eyes, from that angle, shone blue-grey.
"Over where your brother's been putting it," he said. "Where the light's shining and then some, a bit further. If you can toss it up to that patch of lilies, you might get one…" The voice came, quiet and distant as the face was distant. "That is…if you live right." The old man shifted, and Gianni felt the prod of the fingers at his shoulder.
The boat rocked them on the little waves, up and down. He glanced across the water at the other boat, white like theirs but with broad green bands, where his father and O.B. seemed to rise

and recede one after the other above the glistening water in a motion that all at once made him want to laugh. But then he lifted his chest. His father knew about things, too, but not like Grandpa knew. No one knew like that.

He gazed at the spot, green and gleaming in the shafts of light and the nodding willows.

He cast.

It was not going to be far enough, and Grandpa turned away. He waited for the splash and then started to work the reel, knowing now that nothing could possibly come of it, then all at once he began reeling furiously, despite what he had been taught, till the rod jerked up and the reel's handle jammed in his hands.

He hadn't got it right, not at all. It might not have been so bad, except that it seemed O.B. always got it right, every time. It wasn't fair. He ached to know the reason—if O.B. could get it, why couldn't he? If only he could know just that. He remembered what they said: Wait. But he would not, of that, at least, he was sure. As he sat there, his fists gathered tightly before him and he could feel his breath coming fast. He could not have said what he felt, but he knew that the time would come when he would show them—once good, sometime, Grandpa, too, once and for all. In that instant, he could have wished them all dead. Again he ached with the feeling of it, until his mind raced and his neck and shoulders burned with the heat of his revenge.

Then he heard the voice once more. This time it said his name. "Just a little further, Gianni, that's all. A bit more, and then you'll have it."

He listened to the words, and he felt the touch at his shoulder again. In the next moment, he heard the rustling sound among the trees on shore. Out of the reeds a blackbird slid along the swell of breeze, down the little bay, scooping the light with gay red bands, rose off. Its song came to him. He lifted the rod, willowy like a green branch springing in his hands, and cast again.

When Gianni looked up later on, the sun was already gone. Then he heard the dog's bark. It seemed to come from a long ways off. It was the woman's dog. It had run out and barked when they drove in, too, so he thought maybe somebody else was coming. But when he looked, there was no one, only the hill ascending to the white house and the shed in back and the line in back of that where the white rug hung—still now, except for the breeze. When they had first come up, she had been beating it, hitting it so that, approaching, they could hear the thud, thud, as though she were angry at it, with only the mat of the broom visible above the dust that billowed around her, like the witch in the story who gets surrounded by the good wind and blown away.

But she was not a witch. Because after the car had bumped to a halt and their father had gotten out and walked the brown ruts to where she was raising the broom, she came out of the dust and put the broom down, smoothing her dress, and smiled hello to them. Then she made the dog stop barking. That was when he had looked the first time. But that time there was just the woman, there wasn't any man yet, at least not to see or to talk to. So the woman smiled again and went back to hitting the rug, and they took their fishing rods out of the car and started down the hill, along the twisting path toward the thick weeds that, far below, bordered the green lake.

From the boat now, Gianni could see the empty path, descending the hill away from where the rug was still hanging.

As they started down the path his father had gone first, Grandpa behind, with him and O.B. in the middle. He followed O.B. O.B. called back his challenge and started to run, so Gianni started too. O.B. always yelled back that way when he was already in front. Halfway down Gianni felt his foot miss and he could hear the lures jingling inside the box and getting all tangled, but he held the rod up as he fell and it didn't break. O.B. kept running, and he got up and started after him, running harder.

He ran all the way down the hill, past their father's blue shirt, till he could see the group of little boats at the end of the path, in the weeds amidst the willows and the dragonflies. Most of the boats were already half-sunk in the water. Once, when he had been younger, he had thought he would like to try one of those sometime. But their father had said no, they were no good, and even if the people would let you take them they wouldn't work. Then Grandpa had laughed and kicked his boot through the dark stained wood. "Fit for Swedes!" Grandpa chuckled, grinning at the rotted wood that had caved in without so much as a groan. Still, he thought, he wouldn't mind trying one sometime, even if they were suited for Swedes. It seemed to him that you could always see just how far you get before you went down with your ship and swam in to shore.

When he finally got down to where O.B. was, O.B. turned and made a sign for him to stop. O.B. held one hand in front of his mouth for him to keep quiet. In the other hand he had a stick. His eyes went dark beneath the shock of hair falling over his forehead, and the white scar above his eye was jumping up and down, like when he was mad. Gianni didn't know why, but O.B. made the sign with the stick again, only harder, his eyes darker yet, and whispered—but loud—"Watch out!" Then he nodded for Gianni to come, and so he saw it, coiled at the edge of the weeds.

He jerked back.

He thought "coiled," but it was not—it was not that kind of snake, you could see that. But you could pretend that it was, because instead of sliding off when O.B. yelled and poked the stick at it, it raised its head to open its mouth, with its tongue going, and hissed and looped its body to one side in the grass. But even so, it was yellow and black and the neck was not too thick, so it was all right.

Still, Gianni would have preferred that it just slid off. The time before when they had found one of them, Nero had bit it in two. But that had been lucky, the men said who had come across the field to the fencepost to look, because even though it had been small, that was the kind you had to watch out for. Nero had held himself back with his hind legs tensed and lowered his head to growl, pawing at its brown and black coils with one paw outstretched—the way you try the breakfast food Grandma sets down in front of you, to see if it's still too hot, and just what it is, and all—and then it lunged.

Nero dodged, and they all laughed and shouted choruses of "Hurray! Hurray for Nero!" The next time, Nero jumped first, and when the snake tried to dodge, he bit it in two.

When the men came toward the fence to look, they asked them where it had come from. And they told them not to touch the glistening head because even when they've been cut in two, or whatever happens to them, the head can still bite. So they dug a hole for it and put the head in and buried it.

But this one was not that kind (and this was not the place where you'd ever find that kind, Gianni knew that). So when it turned and hissed, starting for them, O.B. slid the stick under it and scooped it up. He raised it way over his head and cried out and held it there while the snake writhed on the stick, before he shook it triumphantly and heaved it out into the water. Then O.B. tossed the stick back toward the reeds. So Gianni and O.B. laughed out loud and went on through the damp, green weeds to get in the boat.

After a moment their father and Grandpa came up. They looked at the two of them already sitting in the boat and then turned away, and Gianni and O.B. could hear them talking to each other and see them nodding. Then Grandpa looked back and boomed out, "All right—who's coming with me?" So one of them would have to get out and get in another boat, because they were going to take two. Grandpa looked again. "All right," he repeated. "Who then? Who's coming with me?" But Gianni already knew he was, because he had grabbed the heavy box before O.B. had even noticed, and he squeezed the smooth metal handle and listened to the lures jingling happily inside. So they headed out in the two boats, one behind the other, out onto the green lake.

Then Grandpa was looking up so Gianni looked up too and saw the sun again, gliding among the thick white clouds that spilled into each other like the cream puffs their mother said not to have too many of. He looked down and saw the water shining, with the sky in it, and felt the breeze moving them. All at once it seemed they had been out a long time. O.B. had already caught a fish; but he hadn't caught anything.

"Drew'll be coming pretty soon now," Grandpa said. "According to Sol, it's getting on." Old Sol was time. Grandpa said he never changed. And still he hadn't got anything.

Then O.B. had another one. "Ho—whee!" O.B. yelled, and their father yelled and O.B. was standing, his shirt flying in the wind and the rod alive in his hands hooking down into the water, as their father started up from the back of the boat with the net, shouting instructions. When at last the shouting and the lunging had ended, they lifted the net over the side of the boat, with the fish setting crossways like a log in the bottom, so you could already see how big it was.

Their father put it down on the stringer and O.B. called over and raised it up for them to see better, dark and shining beside the other one at the end of the rope. Grandpa yelled so he yelled too. It was a good one all right, even a birthday fish, anybody could see that. But it wasn't all that big; at least, it wasn't the biggest O.B. had ever caught.

Still, it was a lot better than nothing.

That was before he saw it there, waiting for him.

He had shifted sideways along the smooth plank of the seat to get out one of the sour candies that their father had stuffed into their pockets when they left Grandma's house, the ones that make your mouth taste like the inside of a lemon. Then he was raising the rod and working the reel, trying to concentrate on the spot Grandpa had said to aim for. And he kept concentrating, trying to get his lure as near as possible each time.

So when he first came aware of it, it had already been there a while, shimmering beneath the water's surface, with only the occasional twitch of the back fins to let him know it was real, and not just a figurine (like the ones they stuck inside the little glass balls in the display case in the dimestore), suspended between the layers of light as though resting in just that spot, waiting patiently for him to come along and lean over and see.

But then he knew that that was wrong. Because from where he watched, it was facing sideways, not toward him, about twenty feet off in the shallows. For the moment, at least, it seemed to take no notice of him whatever. He'd seen lots of them, but this was different. He watched, hardly breathing, the way it is when you're off by yourself in an empty field, or in the deep woods, and all at once you come onto a butterfly sitting in the sun on a log in a clearing. And even if you don't know just what kind it is, you don't think of that—the dark wings diaphanous in the light with perhaps a white or yellowed border around the outer edges, opening and closing with a motion that is as gradual and effortless as your own breathing, but that doesn't disturb or even depend on the air about it, or on you, either, resting there as though completely unaware of your presence and just expecting you to come along too, both at the same time, to watch it there in the light and the stillness. So you stand stock still, transfixed, without thinking of catching or even surprising it, as though one good breath or just the motion of thought itself would be enough to lose it forever. And all you want is to stand there that way, perfectly still and watching, and never move again. But in the end, of course, you do move, because you have to move. That, he learned later, was time.

Gianni watched, utterly still, while the fins twitched. Then he lifted the rod, with his arms so light he could feel them tingling, and he flicked the lure. It went a ways past, hit the water above and behind, and as he brought it in nothing happened at all. He lifted the rod again; and now Grandpa had turned to watch as he re-set the reel.

Then Grandpa was raising the gun. He lifted it to his shoulder, leaning to shoot, the trees behind him rising up dark, with only the tip of the bluff behind pressing into the grey light, as they stood in the clearing and watched and he pressed against O.B., their hands tight against the cold. To their side, the dogs rummaged among the damp leaves, jumping back and forth and kicking up the earth so they could smell the river in it amidst the other smell, like something burning, and Grandpa was raising the gun, and O.B.'s hand tightened until Gianni's ached, and Grandpa turned just a little. But still no shot came.

He cast and watched once more. The lure splashed into the water and then trailed up so close in front that nothing could ever have missed it—and so he took it. Gianni saw the dark figure dart at the red lure, and he felt the jerk and tried to set the hook good and then not go too fast, but he did and couldn't help it.

"I've got one!" he shouted. It was coming right in and not fighting, but only a little, and he yelled and kept reeling, too fast and couldn't help it.

But Grandpa already knew that he had one, and he had the net.

It was coming up through the water at the side of the boat, then it was in the net and over the side onto the bottom flopping over and over, with the white belly twisting wildly in the netting on the wooden planks. Gianni knew he shouldn't but he leaned back and tried to hold it down beneath the rubber sole of his shoe. But it slipped away. Then finally Grandpa told him to wait and reached down and got it, and he held it up for him.

When at last he could see it, he felt suddenly like the time once before, when he had hooked something in the shallows and knew it was a fish and father had said no, it was just weeds, but he had felt the tug, tug, and knew that it wasn't weeds, but was a fish and said so, but his father said no, since it was weeds it was useless to get the net, and Gianni brought it in through the weeds to the boat and felt it all the way, tug-tugging like a fish. At last the green mass of weeds rose and flowered on the surface of the water, and in the middle of the mass was the fish. He remembered it in a flash exactly as though he could see it again. The fish had slipped sideways once and was gone, as the weeds sank away. So he had sat in silence by himself for the rest of the morning.

But this was worse, he could see that, too. He wished this time it had just been weeds, and he didn't want to yell out or to say anything. Because it was too small.

As the two of them stood waiting the smell of the leaves had grown so strong it seemed they'd been covered with them, and the damp ground was sinking beneath their shoes. They could feel Grandpa heave and relax, then he let the gun down and turned fully around to them: "There now," he said. "That's how you'd do it—if you were going to do it." They asked and he put his head back and laughed, and even the dogs stopped their rummaging and looked up.

So Grandpa told them they couldn't, not then, but maybe sometime. There would always be time. That's what he said. It was a promise. That had been the first time, that summer amidst the leaves in the clearing with the dogs going again like crazy and the smell already burning, the first he could remember. But it didn't occur to

Gregory Lucente

them then to ask or even to wonder just what it meant to promise that.

So instead they asked him: When?

"Don't worry," Grandpa said. But he was just trying to be nice. Maybe he had seen the expression on his face. "Don't worry," he repeated. "You'll get another one," and he worked at the hook.

But it had taken the hook way down, like they always do, Gianni thought, because it was in too deep. Grandpa had already taken the pliers from their place in the box, and he could hear him trying to whistle as he dug at the hook. But the back had stopped wiggling and an instant later the gills stopped, too, behind the eyes that bulged and shone now like glass.

Gianni looked away. The smell had begun to spread, and despite the sound of the whistling Gianni could feel the heat in his chest again as he looked into the bottom of the boat and saw the fine vermilion threads trailing through the muddy water.

But it was not his fault. You can't tell how big a thing is when you just see it that way—everyone knows that. It's the same as when you put your hand under water in order to see your fingers look swollen and fat. And besides, the lure was a big one—too big for a little fish like that to take. Grandpa had even said that sometimes, so Gianni knew he was right. It was not his fault.

Then with a jerk and a twist, the hook came free

Grandpa lifted the fish over the side into the water that had gone black as pitch. Gianni looked after it floating away, belly-up, white and slick amidst the darkness. As he watched it go, he felt his throat draw and his nose begin to feel tight, like when you are going to sneeze, but he wasn't going to sneeze. And then he knew it was going to happen.

And so they asked again, and Grandpa smiled. But this time the dogs didn't stop, they just kept on fooling. Grandpa said "No." But they both insisted, and finally Grandpa shrugged and said, "Well, all right, then. Come on."

Grandpa took the oar from the oarlock and lifted it, reaching out, *then he was bending down on one knee and telling them to get behind again, one to each side,* and he eased the blade under the fish as it floated away, *and he and O.B. put their hands to Grandpa's shoulders while he glanced each way to make sure,* and nudged it just a little, *and Grandpa looked again, raising the gun,* till the water began to splash ever so lightly, *and Gianni felt the tremor beneath his hand, because he had that side,* with the ripples building so that all at once the fish appeared to shake as it floated away, *and he tightened, too, and through the stiffened shoulder he*

8

felt the shock and heard the "Boom!... Boom!..." And the fish rolled over and gave a little splash, like a swimmer in a race, and swam off. Gianni stretched to look after it, over the deep water, trying to find it again now that Grandpa had made it live. The boat rocked and he sat back, looking at Grandpa, the calm, distant face, and the smile in those eyes, confident, inscrutable.

Grandpa put the oar back in the oarlock. "Now see if you can't get something a little bigger—something for my breakfast anyway," he said. "And you better be quick about it, too, 'cause Drew'll be coming on now."

So after that he got them, a pair of them, exactly as Grandpa had said to. Twice Grandpa said: "Now with that cast, you'll get a fish." And sure enough, when he started to reel it in, he had one. It was almost as though Grandpa had caught them through him. His arms and chest tingled as first he and then Grandpa called out, and Grandpa lifted them to show his father and O.B.

"How did you know?" he should have asked. But he didn't. Perhaps the question didn't even occur to him. And even if it had, he would have known the answer, predictable, confident, inscrutable like the eyes and the smile: "Because we live right," he would have said. "That's why."

Then on shore the barking started up again, angry now, like a warning, and when Gianni looked to the strip of sand, there was Drew, the hired hand, calling out to them and waving his black hat with the hole in it that even Grandpa laughed at, and Nero, too, barking and running up and down through the long grass. They were together again, and Nero was swimming out to meet them. So Gianni was ready, and it was time.

They rowed in, and Nero raised his head to make his noise hello, his eyes passing from one boat to the other as he turned himself in the water to lead them in, the balls of his shoulders bobbing above the water and his black head shining. Nero sounded his noise for him and O.B., but especially for Grandpa. "Nero and I understand each other," Grandpa always said with his smile. Nero climbed on shore and shook himself so the spray shone bright in the sun, although up close it smelled like the half-worms in the bottom of the boat. But Gianni and O.B. didn't care, and when they clambered out they rubbed Nero's head to say hello, and Nero barked and made his noise back. They went up the path, Nero running in front. Then Nero stopped, all at once, with the ridge of his neck suddenly erect. He had heard the other dog's barking. But something must have happened in the woman's house, because a moment later the barking and all the other noise ceased, and it got so quiet that, as Grandpa would say, even the dead were still. They got in the cars, O.B. and Drew in the pick-up, Gianni and Grandpa and his father in the car, with Gianni's place in the back seat hot from the sun, so it felt like the pan must feel for the turkey inside the oven on Thanksgiving or Christmas Day; and they started off down the same winding trail they had come in on, bumping past the big rocks on either side, and as they went Gianni thought to look for the woman again, to wave to her. But when he turned all he could see were the trees behind them tinged with rust and the dust and the pickup following, since the house was already lost.

    It was when he turned back again—they had just rounded a bend, sharp with the trees straggled and down all along one side—that they saw the man. It was the first they'd seen of him. He was standing at the back of the turn among a cluster of rocks beside one of the downed trees. He had a branch in his hand, and he stood waving at them. At first Gianni wanted to lift up in the seat and wave back, but then their father was stopping the car because the man was not waving hello. He was holding the branch out and waving it the other way, for them to stop.

    They pulled close and Gianni could see how dark and bent-over he looked as he stood there, with only the whiteness of his face beneath the black stubble of whiskers for a light in the darkness. Their father rolled down the window on that side and the man came around and leaned forward, balancing himself with his hands on the door and shoving that face into the open window. Gianni watched his eyes—sunken and dark, then all at once brightening, as though discovering something about them that they would never have noticed, even if they'd seen it themselves a million times. When he spoke, Gianni could smell the breath, like a goat's, as he watched the eyes brightening amidst the pallor and the darkness.

    "You folks already pay for them boats?" the man asked.

    It seemed such an odd thing to ask, Gianni thought. Had they paid too soon, then?

    "You pay—" *The sound rang through the iron trees rising all around them, then Grandpa shifted again and they were all still, with even the dogs poised silently above the leaves to see what it had been. Then the dogs had started back and forth again in the middle of the clearing with their heads down, and when he and O.B. looked they could see he was smiling that smile that was just his. He broke the barrel to look and opened the case and put the gun inside, calling to the dogs and to them, too, though they'd stood right there watching and hadn't moved at all the whole time: "Well, come* on then! You don't want to stay around here forever, do you?" He nodded to Nero, and they all marched off, over the wet leaves.

"Well, I guess you could say so," their father nodded, with his voice so calm you couldn't tell a thing by it, except if you knew him. When their father leaned to roll up the window the man stood back.

"You mean—"

"Yes," their father shot out once, fast.

"Well, all right then," the man said, still holding the branch but lowering it now. "Just looking to make sure."

Their father rolled the window tight and they started off. But Grandpa didn't have to roll up his side—he had never opened it for the man or even turned to look at him for all Gianni could see. He had simply sat the same way, bolt upright, the whole time without paying heed to the man in any way.

After a time they came to the blacktop road and the fields opening beyond it and the little red house beside the bridge over the stream, where their mother said the troll lived. A big cream-colored car sped by in front of them along the black curve, and then another. The second one honked its horn and their father had to turn the car in with a jerk, and he cursed, honking back. In the distance the car honked again, far away but even louder. So their father honked back again, too, sharp and louder, too.

Then they started up along the smooth road. Since the dust was behind them now, it was all right to crack the windows a bit to get a taste of breeze as they drove along. Gianni sat back into the felt cushion imagining what it would be like when they got to Grandma's house again and their mother and everybody would crowd around to see what they had brought back with them for O.B.'s birthday. But then when he sat up to look, it felt funny to him to see all the green fields massed one after the other, as if their edges were piled up on top of each other as far as he could see, because he couldn't tell anymore where they were.

Once, in order to avoid forgetting, he had tried giving names to all the fields and houses as they passed. But that hadn't worked, since almost immediately he had forgotten which went with which, so that all the designations he had assigned were useless, because he couldn't remember; and that was how he learned that names without memory were pointless.

"Knee high by the Fourth of July!" their father said, looking at the corn as they passed the fields. "I think it's made it this year," he said. "The sun's been good, I hear, but you've had your measure of rain, too."

Grandpa agreed and gazed out.

"Even the Stoddard place looks all right this year," their father said right on time.

Grandpa nodded. "The old fellow must have got his wife out to work the fields for him. You can see he hasn't got around to fixing his front porch yet, though." Grandpa gestured toward the yellow and grey house with the broken-down porch as though he were offering it for their inspection.

Gianni had thought that the Stoddard place seemed familiar. In fact he was acquainted with one of the Stoddard boys, George (acquainted in a manner of speaking: O.B. had beat George up once when he called Gianni something, he didn't remember exactly what, and Mrs. Stoddard had said that they were responsible for straightening his teeth and that she was going to send the bill to their father. But his teeth had been crooked in the first place and even looked a little better afterwards, Gianni thought—and their father had thought so, too). Gianni sat back again, tracing the rest of the route in his mind, home from the green lake, landmark by landmark. Now he didn't have to look out anymore or wonder where they were as the car rolled down the little hills that made his stomach drop and they drove into the sunny morning. Because at last he knew where they had got back to again, as they had been now without him knowing it for a while: they were in the world.

* * *

Later that morning they walked down the drive past the shed and the barn in the heat that rose from the ground like liquid. It seemed much hotter than it had been on the lake, almost too hot even for mid-summer. Grandpa stopped to open the gate and went through and shut it after them. Gianni could see the other fence, way off, at the side of the big pasture, and beyond that the rows of bushes marching up the little hill, neat and green with the sun on them, the light moving, too, like one of the gods their father read to them about, marching up the rows. That was Grandma's berry patch, where they were not supposed to go, because it wasn't theirs— or even Grandpa's for that matter. Beneath the hill stood the clump of trees around the spring, and past that the narrow strip that Grandpa had fenced in for the new horses and ponies to run, the ones he'd bought from Henry Stillwell, who Grandma said smelled like three-day-old cabbage. His mother had taught him how to say what kind of ponies they were, repeating each sound separately with him: Shetland. She'd told him what it meant and where it came from. He'd catch one sometime, he had thought, and trot it all the way in, holding its head high, as they do in the Calvary, and surprise everyone. He'd already thought that even then.

At the top of the house, from the bed in the north room where he and O.B. lay huddled together, whispering in the dark about the wolves in the pasture, both red and white, as the rain fell against the wooden shingles to make the cold, hollow sounds on the places that were worn away (he had seen Drew cock his head once to listen, and Drew had told him what to listen for, so he'd know), in the stillness of the night, except for the rain and their whispering they could hear, far below, the footsteps crossing and recrossing the floorboards, time and again.

Then he told O.B. the way to say it: Shetland.

O.B. raised up on one elbow and snickered. "I know," he said. So already Gianni felt that feeling again, as his grand design vanished before him. "And it's 'cavalry,'" O.B. added with a sneer in his voice, "not 'Calvary.' But never mind about that." Then he told Gianni something even better than Gianni's plans. "Listen: They're Grandpa's—I know. But we could try 'em sometime, the big ones, too, if we wanted. I'm not saying for certain yet, but we could raid in, you know." O.B. grabbed his arm and shook it hard. "We could try 'em, the two of us. You know? Together. We could do it." The eyes looked so bright in that light, dark like little coals, as though O.B., too, were burning with the idea of their adventures. Gianni nodded quickly once and that was all, he was so startled. "All right," O.B. said. "Just be careful not to say anything, that's all. We could make a raid, we could raid right in, if we wanted to. Just us—don't forget. I bet we could. Don't forget—and for chrissake, be careful and don't say anything, not to anyone."

Then it was late, so late that the footsteps had stopped, too—so Gianni must have been asleep and come awake again. He lay listening to the whirring of the wind all around the house like birds' wings—because the rain had stopped then—waiting for it to start up again, as it always did if he could just wait long enough, the sound that he could recognize but never understand for sure, the tread, tread, tread echo and resound.

In the morning when Grandma came to wake them up, it was always the same: the firm grip grabbing him up out of the greyness, as though he were being pulled up, rising towards the light and air at the water's surface. Just as he reached it the grip would tighten and he would hear the voice—but strange, not Grandpa's, or not like Grandpa's, anyway, because it said "Goodby, Gianni....I've got to go....Goodby....It's time now....It's time....Goodby." And then: "It's

Gregory Lucente

time to go!" So then Gianni knew it was true, and he had not been dreaming, though even if he had, that could have been true too, because Grandpa said that a dream was a dream, but if you dreamed it twice or more it became as good as true. But by then the greyness was gone and they'd be scrambling about trying to get out of bed, yet never in time, because before they could really get free of the tangle of covers the figure would be through the door and gone, leaving only the voice behind, Grandpa's now for sure: "Well don't just lie there you two, like a pair of old stick-in-the-muds. Get up!" Then the voice was gone too.

On the days when Grandpa didn't go to the sawmill, he would be waiting for them at the foot of the stairs when they came down, his hat already on his head—the grey homburg that never looked right—and the case in his hand. So he and O.B. would rush to the kitchen, bolt the pancakes Grandma had made, and hurry back, ready to start off.

They went on past the pen in the heat where the cows were coming in to bend their heads to the trough and look their slow looks at one another—as though they had nothing at all to do and nothing would ever come to touch them (but it would, he knew, because he knew the ending, how when the big mallet swung they didn't run away, like turkeys and even chickens do, but just went right down like your broken buckle. Still, he wondered if they wouldn't at least lower their heads and make that sound at the end, or if they really did go right down, as Drew had said). They hurried to follow him, as he pushed forward without a halt, like a General on the move before his troops, in the dark pants and pale shirt, carefully ironed but loose at the shoulders and fluttering lightly in the breeze, toward the back pasture where the flickers rose and swooped and flew off. When Grandpa got to the clumps of grass at the top of the rise, he paused and looked back. He turned again and walked to the fence and dug around in the long grass till he found what he was looking for, lying, as usual, behind the cracked post. He put the can on top of the post and walked back to where they stood watching.

"There now," he said as he always did, and he opened the case. "At least they can't bother us here." Then came the crack and the "ping!" and the can flew away. Three times more in succession, as always, the crack and the "ping!", until the last time O.B. didn't even look.

As they rose out of the ravine off the road to the level spot, the fall wind cut to their bones, damp and numbing like the knife that slips in the cold water. They started out over the barren field, edged by trees like a half-moon, with only the chopped-off stalks left as a reminder of what had been there before. Grandpa set his hands on his and O.B.'s shoulders to push them forward. Drew came up quickly with the dogs straining and barking, but he held onto their leashes until the brown cases were undone. "They're about ready now," Drew said with a flash of the jagged smile, the pride strong in his voice as he set them free, and they started off. Gianni and O.B. followed now, just behind Grandpa and Drew, with Nero off to one side on his own as usual and the other dogs out front working back and forth over the field according to the design known to them alone: to them and Grandpa, Gianni thought, and perhaps Drew.

Grandpa yelled to Drew across the wind: "Don't let 'em get too far in front. They'll just keep going on you 'less you take 'em in a little." So Drew looked back, his face downcast. He straightened up and yelled loud, once, and the dogs stopped dead. They turned to look, waiting with that surprise and disappointment in their faces, too, as though someone had made to throw a stick but didn't. They all got up a little closer and then Drew yelled once more and Grandpa did, too, and the dogs started off, happy again, and they all kept on, across the field.

The mud was deep despite the top crust from the cold, and Gianni's boots got caught in it, but he kept on as fast as he could, bringing his knees up high each time so as not to get the soles clogged too badly, and to keep up. Then there were big clods of dirt and he stumbled and his knees hit hard. He got up, breathing fast and gulping the cold wind that seared inside as he began to trot, and they all kept on.

But when he next looked, he could see that up in front they had all stopped. He saw Drew's head peeking over the jumble of brush and the low, swaying shoots at the edge of the field, where the stalks were thickest, and where Grandpa had said was a good place. They all stood waiting, while the dogs held still as a bowstring just before you let the arrow fly. Then the air rushed away. Not one, as he had expected, but a bunch rising all at the same time. He heard the "boom!" "boom!" "boom!" "boom!" and saw them fall.

The dogs brought the birds back and laid them at Drew's feet and looked up. "Both mine!" he shouted. Drew rubbed the dogs' heads and they yelped with pleasure as he gave each of them a swat—hard enough so you could hear it, but not hard enough to hurt. Mr. Red Man and Copenhagen were Drew's special dogs. Then Drew bent to get the birds and put them in his coat, in the pack, so he looked funny, as though he were all swollen back there. At almost the same time, off behind, Grandpa broke his gun open in disgust and tossed the shells away and started to reach for more; but then Grandpa looked over at O.B., standing beside him in the red coat that was too loose, and he said—not smiling but dark now, with his face looking as though the ridge of dark clouds were in it, but the flint in his eye and his voice sharp against the wind—"Here, now, give that thing to me." O.B. handed him the case. For the first time Gianni saw the gun that was there. He hadn't even noticed it before. Grandpa put the first one away and drew out the other one. He gave the case back to O.B. and started off, and Gianni waited to see what would happen, as Grandpa moved along the edge of the field, his coat brown and black in front of the trees, beneath the falling grey sky.

Grandpa was raising the gun. *It was the other one.* Because when the dog jerked and the birds flew up and Grandpa rose up in the coat against the thick sky that was rising too, and the sound came, it was the "crack!"—like the sound had been before, but no "ping!", just the first part. Then in the next moment, the other sound came, the "boom!" "boom!" which was Drew. And then the "crack!" once more. The birds plummeted down, brown and green and purple in the grey light, and the dogs ran out. But when Mr. Red Man and Copenhagen brought them back, they laid them at Grandpa's feet, their heads tilting up with the tongues hanging out like bright ribbons along their mouths.

"No!" Drew yelled in protest. "One's mine!" Grandpa leaned down and turned the two birds carefully in his hands, brushing back their feathers and then he shook his head and yelled "Here!" So he had been right, Gianni thought, they were his and not Drew's.

But Grandpa wasn't even looking across at Drew. He was looking at O.B., who came over and stood before him, as Grandpa had meant for him to do. "Here, boy!" Grandpa said. "Hold still now." And he reached around and put both the birds inside the back of O.B.'s coat and touched O.B.'s shoulder. So O.B. looked that way, too, like Drew did, swollen like that behind. They started again, and Gianni watched them moving off, in their red and brown coats, until in the distance the pair of them looked almost like Grandpa and Drew (who, he knew, was still off to the side, walking by himself down the other track of the field; besides, it couldn't be Drew because Nero was with them), the red and brown and grey of the two of them fading and bleeding together like a strange new being, united as one beneath the dark trees.

Grandpa nodded, and this time O.B. lifted the gun. Gianni held his breath, waiting, then shuddered at the "crack!"—the same as usual—and then the "ping!"

The can flew down.

Grandpa started to say something, but he seemed to think better of it and walked off before Gianni could guess what it had been. Grandpa went and searched in the grass and put the can up again before turning back. "Once more," he directed.

Gianni smelled the burnt smell now and saw how dark O.B.'s eyes had become as he turned to look. The black barrel flashed. Not far off, a bird rose up flapping, but O.B. was not aiming for that yet, because amidst the noise and the flutter Gianni heard the "ping!" and again the can flew down. This time when Grandpa smiled and nodded that way, Gianni heard what he said: "Yes," Grandpa said. "They were right. I believe it's time." He leaned back to open his shirt pocket and get out the little packet of snuff with the Indian on it, taking the pinch and putting it away. He rocked back on his heels. Then, as though in an afterthought, he made the gesture they had been waiting for. "Well now," he held the packet out to them. "How about you fellows?"

Grandpa stood there with that look: happy, assured, conspiratorial, but it didn't last. As his gaze began to wander, the smile flickered and then died altogether. He was looking past them down the hill. They turned and saw what he had seen: the black dot chasing Henry Stillwell's ponies around the little pasture like the riders in the picture show chasing the cattle that rush in to clot up, then move off slow but tense, or like the little metal balls in the pinball machine when you've shot too many too fast and for an instant, before they break apart again, it seems they've run out of places to go. Then the pack broke and they headed every which way, with Nero chasing wildly behind each and every one of them individually, it seemed, yet all at once, and Grandpa cursed, which surprised them even more than the sudden look had. In the next moment Grandpa was running, shouting at the top of his lungs, and they were coming behind, running, too.

Grandpa had been opening the gate when Gianni asked, but at first he had said nothing and now he stood looking down at the two of them in silence as though they both should have known better. At last he spoke: "Why no, of course not," he said, as his eyebrows danced along his forehead. "They couldn't catch us," he said. "Never in a million years. Because." He stooped low toward them, amidst the sweet, drifting ether of the tobacco. "Because we live right," he smiled. "That's why."

So they entered the berry patch, going up and down the rows of green bushes (where they were not supposed to go, because it was not theirs, or even Grandpa's: it was Grandma's and they were supposed to keep out), picking the bright berries that peeked out as they went by, and eating them right then, as fast as they could get them down.

Far away they heard the kitchen screen slam.

He and O.B. looked up, but Grandpa was already nodding toward the house—as if to say, yes, I've heard, we've all heard—where now the bell was ringing loud and steady but not urgent.

So they hadn't been seen yet.

They circled around, through the back gate, and before Gianni had even stopped to think about it, they were heading up the drive, kicking the soft brown earth from their boots and trying not to smile, with Grandpa walking a little out in front, just as though there were nothing strange at all—or ever would or could be—up the graveled lane toward the white house that rose before them, beckoning to them beneath the noon sun.

So when Gianni asked if he could gather berries, Grandma Britzen hesitated, moving her shoulder as if the big apron were too hot for her, and put the rolling pin aside, smoothing her front. She heaved a sigh, naturally, but in the end she gave in, looking down and waving him off as she always did. "Well, I guess it's all right," she nodded, "seeing as how you can't find them. It's a special day, anyway. I suppose I can't say no to you either." As he started out he could hear her words coming after him more like stones than orders. "But just this once, mind you. And only one bowlful, no more, you hear me? Only *one*!"

Far off, across the fields and the hollow of the valley in the quickly fading light of early summer, half-way up the hill, in the neatly (and newly) fenced side-pasture, he and O.B. alone could see him— from their window in the top room—Nero looking like a black ball rolling after the ponies over the crazy-quilt of the pasture, in which Nero, too, was inscribed in his own frantic motion. And they cheered, but as quietly as possible, so as not to alert the others, who would have to run to fetch him: "Hurray!" they whispered loudly to each other, the two of them together. "Hurray for Nero!"

He moved alone up and down the green rows, filling the white bowl with the bright red berries and imagining how she would smile when he brought them in for her. Now and then he would glance over at the horses, but he did not think of his pact of the year before with O.B. to raid in and ride them. Rather, he thought of how Grandpa had looked that first time they had seen him, some time before, breaking the horse in the snow, amidst the drifts and the rising steam. He remembered, later, watching Grandpa fence the pasture by himself, taking time for it in the afternoons, without

Drew, and the strange look on his face—what he knew afterwards as peace perhaps, pleasure certainly—as the old man sat on the porch, looking off, watching the first batch of horses run, like toys endlessly crisscrossing a green board without any apparent purpose or design, at least not that Gianni could see, then or ever.

When the bowl was full, Gianni wiped the white rim clean, and he took it in to Grandma. It would be like it had been earlier that morning, when they had come back from the green lake and crossed the lawn to the porch, with everyone out waiting for them, and O.B. had held up the best of the fat fish in the sun to show to their mother and Grandma and the rest, for them to raise their hands from their aprons and say "Ahh!," with their eyes bright and their faces beaming.

The berries would be his gift, on a day of presents.

Gianni crossed the lawn and mounted the porch, empty now, and he heard Grandma inside busy with the bowls and the towels and things in the kitchen. Despite his excitement, he managed to get in the door without forcing the screen or spilling the berries. He wanted it to be like before, when O.B. had held up his birthday fish and Grandma had beamed her approval.

After that, O.B. and their father had gone off, he wasn't sure where, and he hadn't been able to find Grandpa to ask, either. It seemed no one knew, because when the milk-truck came rumbling in and the man in the big boots stepped down from the running-board to greet Drew, Gianni had asked them if they had seen them or knew where they were. But they hadn't. Instead of telling him, Drew hid his face beneath the brim of his hat. He waved his hand and hurried to help the man. Grandma hadn't known either. Gianni had checked the pastures but found no one. He had even asked old Mr. Trimbell, with the cane and the veiled eyes, whom he usually avoided at all costs. Mr. Trimbell had seen Grandpa, at least, and O.B., too, since he'd seen the white, flowing shirt. "I could tell they must have been going somewhere special," he said. "Maybe Redwing or somewhere, on account of they had the guns, and Jake Arndt and that big black dog was with 'em, too." But they had been too far away to stop, or even to notice him. So no one knew for sure, except that they were gone.

Gianni left the hall and entered the high kitchen, and as he watched his grandmother there, moving among the bowls and dishes and jars of sugar and flour with an aura of excitement and expectation, it struck him that she had been waiting all along for him to bring her the surprise. Now, he told himself, not too fast, and with both hands he lifted the bowl up, offering it to her. "Here you are, Grandma," he said without a tremor, and he held the bowl out.

"Why, Gianni!" she turned to him. She had put her hand to her chest, and he could see her surprise. "I didn't hear you," she said. "You scared me." She looked odd and pale, and it didn't seem right, but it was too late to go back, so Gianni kept coming forward, holding the bowl out.

She began with the rolling pin again, frowning. "I didn't know you had that bowl," she said. "It's the one I've been looking for. Now how do you expect me to be making a cake for your brother if you've taken all my kitchen things outside?"

In the silence, she glanced at him. "Oh, the berries," she said, as though seeing them for the first time. "It looks like you've done all right for yourself," she smiled. "Now put them over there," she nodded toward an empty space on the counter. "And I'll fix them up for you later on."

"No...I..." Gianni searched for the words.

"They're for the cake, then?" her face tilted down to him. "You mean—"

"No," Gianni gathered his courage and reached the bowl out further, almost shoving it toward her. "They're for you, Grandma. I picked them for you."

Her smile receded; the surprise and confusion showed in her eyes. "Well, who would have thought...." Her face began to soften, then all at once the look disappeared and she stood back, composed again. "But not now—you can see how busy I am now," she sighed. "Later—I'll fix them up for us and we can have them later, just the two of us. How will that be? Later on."

Gianni watched as she moved off among the bowls again, hoping that maybe she had forgotten his earlier question, and would not mention it anymore, and would let him go. It was not fair; the berries no longer meant anything to him. But she hadn't forgotten, because a moment later, while he was trying to get to the counter to put the bowl down and get out and away, she glanced at him from the corner of her eye. "Now where did they go off to, anyway?"

He stopped dead. He knew the question that would follow. Because she already knew. He could tell it would come even before she said it, and he looked away. But that didn't help. "And you—Gianni—how come you're still here?" she asked. "All alone."

Gianni felt the breeze, its sickening coolness on his skin—he hadn't noticed before how cool it was—and he let out a breath; there was no need to hide now. They had left without him, without telling him, he didn't know why, nor where they had gone. When she took the bowl from his hands he hardly noticed it. She laid it on the table and he watched the fresh white cloth flutter above it in the air, then descend to cover them. He stared at the cloth resting peacefully on the bowl and tried to think what the berries must look like, buried in the darkness beneath it, and if it wouldn't be nice to be in there with them.

Before he could think of anything more, he heard the question come again, and he heard his response, as though it were not his but had been made for him, and then its reflection, coming back in her voice, the insistent echo of his ignorance: "So you still haven't found out?" He remained where he stood, silent. "Well, if you're not going to move or help, I need room now—You'll have to get out of my kitchen. Can't you go outside and find something to do—at least for a while?"

He felt her hands on his shoulders, pushing, but the pushing had changed, then it left off completely, and when she spoke again, her voice was urgent and demanding, "Well, what now—" before falling silent again. Then he heard the cracks, too, three of them, hard and crisp in the stillness, not right near but not far off, either. He whirled away, through the hollow hall, out the door and down the path, as, behind him, the heavy screen door slammed shut on her words.

By the time the cracks came again, he was almost to the fence. His foot slipped in the dust at the gate, but he went through and then he saw them, all in a line at the back of the pasture, Nero, too, before the rise. Grandpa moved and then O.B.'s white shirt fluttered in the wind, and Drew's black hat moved, too, and the other, who must have been Jake Arndt, and Gianni kept on and didn't even stop to think how odd it looked. Then they were all moving, and he saw the flashes like signals, and he kept on.

He was still a ways off when they turned—all at once, still in a line, as though by agreement among them—and saw him coming. O.B. was the first to acknowledge him with a nod, then Jake Arndt. Drew raised his hat, the one with the hole in it, and called out, "Look, now! It's Gianni!" So they all waved.

As he came nearly even to them Grandpa shrugged, and they all turned back in a line as before.

"Well all right," Grandpa said, pushing back the grey homburg.

"Yes, all right then," their father nodded. "But take your time now."

O.B. nodded, too, standing in the flowing shirt, facing the fence, and he lifted it up till Gianni saw its shine, saw it, fully, for the first time. His heart sank.

It was O.B.'s, damn him, he knew it at once.

The black barrel raised and flashed, glimmering in the sun.

"Now!" Grandpa said, and O.B. shot. Gianni heard the "ping!" and saw the can fly away. They called hurray for O.B., and then, to Gianni's surprise, they turned to him.

"Go ahead," his father urged. "Let Gianni lift it. Go on."

At first the rifle did not seem heavy at all, but as he hefted it to his shoulder his arm began to give way, so finally Grandpa had to come to stand behind him and steady him as he pretended to aim. It was still too wobbly, but all the same, just holding it and feeling the stock at his face made him feel better.

Then he had to give it back. His father took it and lifted it, and they heard the "crack!" and the "ping!" Then came Drew's turn, and then Jake Arndt's, but he only shot once and didn't show off, and then Grandpa's "One more time, now, just for luck," and then they all went in, with O.B. out front, as usual, in his shirt that looked like a flag now, carrying the gun in its case across the pasture and yard to the tall white house.

This time when her gaze looked down, it told them nothing. "There's a full hour till supper," Grandma said. "So you boys can go on if you want. But you be back when you're supposed to be and don't forget and lose track—not tonight, not when everyone's coming special."

They crossed the grass to the spot behind the shed to spin with their arms out, and Gianni dropped first, hitting the flat ground with a thud. Now as he rolled over and felt the cool grass beneath him, he thought of what he would do—he would no longer be going to South America with O.B. and the Castells to join the rebel bands, he knew that. He lay watching the sky, his heart still dizzy, and he felt it beating faster, lying so close to O.B. that, if they had only been among the Indians then, he could have rolled over and raised up without a sound, so swiftly he would have done it, to draw the knife above the throat.

Instead, O.B. rolled over and propped his head up on one hand above the matted grass. As a smile flickered along the hard mouth, O.B. told him what he'd heard Grandma tell their mother, that Jane and them would be coming up soon now, not for his birthday, but soon. "'Jane *and them*,' they said. So Judd will be coming, too." O.B. rolled away and then turned back again, sitting up and grabbing Gianni's arm. "You know that pasture with the ponies in it," he said. "You remember what we agreed. So Judd could come, too. O.K., Gianni?" Then as O.B. rolled away again he repeated: "Gianni—O.K.?—You remember?"

So he dropped back too, watching the sky go and feeling the rush of excitement tingling again, even though he couldn't stand Judd. Now that made no difference at all. Above them, the colors gathered and faded till just the roof of the barn was left rising away from them, splitting away into the haze and wash of the light and the sky. It was all right again, in spite of everything.

A while later they heard the bells and then the last glimmer of pails approaching, Nero following Grandpa, and they saw the figures coming up the yard—Grandpa and their father, lost up to the waist in the dusk, so that just the shoulders and the heads came floating by, accompanied by the vague sounds of the pails again, receding. So the cows were all in. The two figures passed talking, but without a word to them, though it was late now.

Gianni lay and felt the feeling rise again, tight and sweet, beginning again. Beside him, O.B. rose up. Far off, across what was now full darkness, they heard the hand-bell's ring. The last of the cars had come up and stopped amidst the slamming doors and the loud laughing voices long before. So it was time. The women's calls came too now, distant and predictable, Grandma and their mother, the voices adamant across the darkness, paired in antiphony first one and then the other, then the first again rising urgently over the other as though meant to sound just that way, calling them into the blinking lights of the house, calling out across the darkness for them to come on.

But for a while longer they would not.

Hours later, after the dinner, they sat around the huge table that was still loaded with the last of the half-empty platters of white and dark meat and the bowls of stuffing, and all of them, the Connollys and the Snowers and old Mr. Trimbell and everyone, gazed at the cake that now commanded their attention, its ten candles all aglow with their little flames amidst the bright red raspberries that Grandma Britzen or their mother—or someone—must have added as an afterthought, since everyone knew they really didn't go on a chocolate cake. After Gianni's piece had been passed down to him and he had tasted and then, with increasing enjoyment, finished it, the red berries, stained with the flecks of chocolate, lay cast aside at the edge of his plate like so many hand-me-downs, for the time being, his single, mute protest. Yet it had come before that, the moment that, long afterwards, he remembered most vividly: just when the cake was first brought out by their mother and Grandma Britzen with all the excitement and clatter, and Grandpa led the group in singing Happy Birthday as O.B. sat in the middle, glowing in the light from the old chandelier, the sound of the voices rose together louder and louder, until even Gianni was drawn despite himself into the singing of the song, so that he sang too. And that's what he remembered years later, amidst the glow and the bustle and the cheerful faces: he sang, he sang too.

*   *   *

By later that summer, they had learned to use the gun. Or at least O.B. had. In the afternoons they would set out across the pasture and up the hill, through the oaks and the pines, until they came to a clear run closed off at one end for a backdrop to practice. At first they would be under the watchful eye of their father, or, more often, Grandpa and Drew. But eventually they were permitted to go off alone, with Nero, and Gianni would find himself following O.B. through the trees or along the banks of a stream until they (but really O.B.) would spot a branch hanging down at an odd angle, or a stray scrap of paper, or, once, to their chagrin, what turned out, far off and high above, to be the grey bulb of a hornet's nest.

By the summer after that, they were back in the flat pastures since there was no longer need for a backdrop (that had been one of the first things Grandpa had told them about the rifle, and Gianni never forgot the look on his face at that moment, still distant but somehow disturbed, too, perhaps from memory, perhaps from imagination, as he looked down at them both and took O.B.'s shoulder: "A twenty-two can go a mile, son, so you remember, both of you, and be careful"), because by then O.B. didn't miss. They would start out down the ruts at the side of the pasture until all of a sudden O.B. would stop and raise the rifle—fast but not quick: deliberate, sure—and then before Gianni would realize it, usually after he had tripped to a stop but before he would actually see anything to shoot at, the sound would come and the gopher or whatever it was would drop right over like one of the little targets in the booths at the fair.

That summer those were still to come, the booths and the gawking crowds and the hawkers thin as weasels and smelling to match, the boasting and, naturally, the bets. But even when O.B. won, which was always, so that eventually the only interest in it would be not if but when, to see just how long it would take before O.B. had cleaned the other fellow out or had been refused the rifle (if the hawker himself were shooting, as was occasionally the case, or, more likely, if he were betting and had chosen wrong, he would run out of shells, suddenly and absolutely, though just temporarily, too). Even so, with all their excitement and intensity, these fairs were not Gianni's most memorable.

That one had come more than a year before. It had not been in summer nor even a fair, really, but only a contest. Their father had put them on the train coming from Chicago, him and O.B., at their grandparent's request—even though Nero couldn't go along that way—and they had taken it all the way to Redwing, on the river, in early January, with the snow piled pure white all along the tracks, and inside the car the heat broken down so they would see their breath rising every time one or the other of them would turn to speak. The rest of the passengers sat huddled silently together in groups of twos and threes, most of them elderly women, it seemed, taking their daughters or nieces to visit or heading home themselves after visiting away for the holidays. The passengers sat bundled in coats and knitted gloves and wool scarves, their feet booted and held close together and their heads down, with shawls wrapped securely about their faces as part of what appeared to be their agreement not to talk at all. He and O.B. got out once to wait for a passing express at Houton City, where the line joins the river before turning north, and he and O.B. stood shivering with the cold and kicking their boots into the crusted drifts, then waited for only a minute before hurrying to climb back in when the other train roared by.

At Redwing, as they stepped down through the steam onto the bright, snow-colored platform, they were suddenly surrounded by the bustling crowd that had come to meet the other passengers. Gianni held onto O.B. with one hand and with the other he squeezed the wrapper of the hard candy that their father had given them and that he held now against his palm inside his glove. They looked through all the people along the platform for sight of Grandpa and Drew. At first they saw no one, but then all at once the crowd seemed to split apart, and there they were, Grandpa's grey homburg and Drew in his black hat, coming toward them fast, through the others. Suddenly Drew stopped. He had turned, and a knot of people had gathered around him, and then someone yelled, and they couldn't see the grey homburg at all anymore. A moment later Gianni felt O.B. nudge his shoulder to guide him forward, and they started to walk. At the back edge of the crowd, they could see Grandpa standing again, looking off now, not at them, with his hat pulled low and his face ashen in the cold, but Drew was coming on toward them glancing back at Grandpa and looking forward at them through the noisy crowd, his smile broad and serene and his arm raised to wave to them, just as before. So everything was all right.

    They got in the pick-up and started to the farm in Crooked Falls. Drew drove. As they went across the Island, Gianni looked at the funny houses up on stilts resting like strange birds. Drew chattered on and told them about the big snow and the cold snap—then the thaw—and the dead man that had been found in the woods near the road. They had discovered his body just the week before when the snow melted. Someone had seen a hand sticking out of the snow between the trees with a card in it. The people on the Island played cards for money: it was a secret, but everybody knew it. When Grandpa finally spoke he said it couldn't have been much of a game if the fellow had only had a three of spades in his hand. Gianni could imagine the players all sitting back with their cards having a good time and smiling, but Grandpa said it wasn't like that. They played there because it was no-man's-land and there weren't any police on the island, being in the middle of the river and all, and neither side wanted to claim them for their own anyway, not the people in Wisconsin and not the people in Minnesota, either. Drew said they sold whiskey, too, and that was why the man had been shot, not for the card games. But later Grandma said Drew just wanted to believe that so he wouldn't feel bad about playing cards himself. Drew smiled and tipped his hat, but then he shook his head no to deny it. Besides, he said, they played cards different: 'Five Hundred' and euchre weren't the same as poker and blackjack, that's all there was to it, Drew said.

    The adults would play cards too but not right away, because it was too late and the next day was the day of Bay City's icefishing contest. Grandpa usually didn't go, but Drew loved to fish through the ice, even more than he loved the riddlegames with Gianni and O.B., since you never knew what might come up at you through the dark water and the hole in the ice. So that year Grandpa and Drew had invited Gianni and O.B. to go with them. There were prizes to be given out, according to the rules, rods for the winners and tackle for door-prizes, but neither Gianni nor O.B. knew about them yet. They wanted to win, period, regardless of prizes and rules, and Drew was going to help them do it. That's why they had come. That's what everyone said.

    The next morning they slid the pick-up out onto the frozen river among the other cars, and Drew took the auger from the back of the truck and started to drill the holes—one for himself and Gianni and O.B. and another for Grandpa and Jake Arndt. The wind was up, and Gianni watched the grey clouds lifting over the bluffs and the ghostly shoreline of white birch before advancing across the snow-covered curve of the bay, which, if he hadn't known, looked more like a separate snowy lake than just another part of the river. In back of the birch the bluffs rose right up, steep and covered with pines. When Gianni saw the bluffs in that section, no matter in what season, they always seemed foreboding to him, and this was so even now, with the snow on them, because the cover of pines kept them dark. It made him tingle to look at them from a distance, but he did not want to go any closer. He remembered what their mother had told them about those bluffs. That was where their greatgrandfather had gone to build his house when he first came from Sweden, the house taken by the fire on Torson Bluff. In the summertime there were snakes in the woods up there. They would lie sunning themselves on the rocks of the bluff. One time one of their mother's uncles, when he had been just a child, even younger than Gianni and O.B., had been sent by another of the boys, on a bet, under the wooden porch after a stray chicken, and had found it and brought it out—along with a nice fresh egg it had laid under there—and behind the chicken and the boy, who was smiling in his short pants and holding the egg, came the biggest snake they had ever seen. Another of the uncles, one of the older ones, had snatched the boy up, and one of the women had killed the snake with a hoe just as it was entering the garden. After their mother told them the story she showed them the rattle that had been kept in memory for all those years. Their mother had shown them a picture, too, of their greatgrandfather with his daughters: the old man's eyes so clear and bright they seemed to burn into the camera's lens, but the rest of the face bearded, covered and foreboding like the bluff he had picked to live on. It was too high and dark and it was too cold to live up there, Gianni knew. They had found the old man frozen to death in the winter snow, toppled over like a great tree or a Viking into the middle of a drift (in point of fact, keeled over would have been closer to the truth, though neither Gianni nor O.B. knew anything of that yet).

    When their hole in the ice was ready, he and O.B. put their lines in. They stood and waited for a big fish to come along and take their bait. But it was so cold. It was only the second or third time Gianni had been to fish through the ice, and he hadn't realized how cold it would be. Before long he was shuffling his feet and holding his hands tight inside his mittens in an effort to keep warm. It was bad enough to be so cold, but, worse, nothing came to take their lines.

"Come on," O.B. reproached him. "If a good one does bite, you'll lose it holding the rod with your hands all bunched up that way." O.B. was right, and Gianni knew it. By then all he was hoping to do was to keep the rod from falling into the hole from its own weight, pressed as it was between his two fists. For a minute, Gianni tried to hold the rod right, but soon he went back to concentrating on keeping himself warm. It was too cold, and it was a silly way to fish anyway. Then all at once Grandpa had hooked something. As Gianni watched him fight the fish with the short rod, Gianni wondered if he had known all along beforehand, like he always seemed to know, and if that was why he had decided to go that year, or if that only worked in the summer. When Gianni saw the catch come up through the ice, he thought it probably worked all the time, because the fish was a big one. As Drew held it up, all the people crowded around to see and make their comments on how big it was, much bigger than the walleyes they got in the summer, and on how lucky they had been to bring it up (so no one else knew, Gianni thought, only them).

Suddenly everything was still again, except for the wind, and another group of people was moving through the crowd toward them, dressed in overcoats and galoshes, a funny way to dress for fishing, Gianni thought, and looking as cold as Gianni had felt before. Then following the man in the middle came a woman dressed all in white, in a cap and a white fur coat and fur boots with bright red bows, and a beautiful smile, white too, even whiter than their mother's, looking just as comfortable as though it were a summer's day. "It's the Ice Queen," O.B. leaned over and whispered to him. "She's coming to give the prize."

"Who ever caught such a big fish?" The Ice Queen smiled.

Before anyone could answer, Gianni felt Grandpa's grasp through his coat and then saw the twinkle in Jake Arndt's eye and felt something hard in his hand. It was the stringer, frozen solid. At once he felt the weight and the pressure, so he lifted the rope with both hands, as the fish struggled against him. "This boy did!" Grandpa said loudly, while Drew and Jake Arndt looked on, all smiles: "My grandson."

The Ice Queen nodded with surprise. "Such a big fish," she repeated (but then she didn't say the rest of it, like Grandma and the others would have); and she held out her hand toward Gianni. A gold medal hung down on a chain from her mitten, and despite the flush of embarrassment Gianni managed to reach out and take it.

But the matter wasn't finished with that, because all at once one of the men who had come with the Ice Queen yelled, "No, no, wait a minute. That's not right." So Gianni thought he would have to give it back. Then the man said, "Stand over there together. Get in back of him, Trudy, and let the kid stand in front. You know—the medal in one hand and the fish in the other. There—can you hold onto it, partner?" he asked Gianni with a foolish grin. "It'll look better that way in the paper, believe me. I know what I'm doing, even if nobody else around here does."

So they weren't going to take it back. Gianni wished they would hurry up and snap the picture before they changed their minds. But as the man got ready to take the picture there was another voice amidst the noise of the crowd telling them to wait, Grandpa's. Gianni thought that maybe he was going to get mad at the man for saying what he'd said, as their father would have, but he wasn't. Grandpa had removed his big coat, the one sewn from the skins of the foxes he had trapped on his rounds. "Here," he said, and he threw it around Gianni's shoulders. "Now you're set."

All the people got quiet and the Ice Queen held her arms around him from behind as he raised the fish, and she put her face down next to his, so he felt her breath and her lips against his cheek and then her skin, first cold and then warm, almost hot, just as the camera's light flashed, so quickly he'd almost missed it. In that instant, engulfed in the sudden warmth, it seemed to Gianni that he had never been cold at all, or ever could be. That's what he remembered, years afterward, even more than the medal (which he had had to turn over to O.B., anyway, to be fair, so O.B. wouldn't get mad) and more than the yellowed newsclipping and the picture (with his name spelled right and not 'Johnny,' though his father had had to fix it): the warmth and the happy flash of light amidst the motionless white snow.

Of course, things did not always work out that way. Once, in June or July, Gianni had gone to the fair, another one, with his cousin Judd from Houton City. His cousin had invited him specially, so Gianni was happy to go. They rode the ferris wheel and Uncle Henry bought them cotton candy. Their hands got sticky, but Gianni knew he could still pitch all right, so they went to the ring toss. "Step up, boys," the ring-toss man yelled at them in a voice that made him sound like a bulldog. "Who's first?" the man barked at them. "Which one?"

"I am," Gianni spoke up, since O.B. wasn't there. So the man gave him the rings and nodded at the bright yellow pegs.

"Go ahead, then," the man said in his big voice.

Gianni wiped his hands on his pants and aimed. He got four out of the ten rings around the pegs. Then it was Judd's turn. Judd only hit three of them.

"I won," Gianni said, as the man gave them their prize. "The puppet's mine!" and he grabbed it. It was easy, and it made Gianni feel flushed; it was almost as much fun as when he and O.B. and the Johnsons would spend the afternoon popping frogs' stomachs out their mouths with their thumbs and tossing them back into the water to watch them float away on top like little white balloons.

"How about two out of three?" Judd said, his fat cheeks flushed like a beet.

Gianni nodded, and he threw again. This time he only got three; so did Judd. "Once more," Gianni said, and he tossed four. But that time Judd was lucky. He got six (though by then the rings were sticky enough to get caught on the pegs by themselves and not bounce off). So they were tied.

"Three out of five?" Gianni said quickly—that much he had learned from O.B.—and Judd smiled in agreement. This time Gianni knew he would win. And he did, both times. He smiled at Judd. "I killed you," he said, and he took his two new prizes from the barker's hand. "Maybe next time you'll get lucky," Gianni rubbed it in.

Uncle Henry came wading through the crowd with his glasses that looked like goggles. "What's going on?" he asked as he saw the prizes. "Look at all I won," Judd chirped as the three of them started to walk away. "We had a contest," he announced, "and I won. Look at it all, Dad."

Gianni was furious. He couldn't help himself. "Here!" he shouted. "Take your prizes then, you cheater!" He shoved the mass of prizes into his cousin's chest, spilling them all over the cinders. Gianni gave them a good kick, and then he knew he was going to do it, no matter what his mother had told him, and he hit his fist into Judd's soft stomach—it felt so good.

Then Uncle Henry was drawing them apart and scolding him. "He's just lying!" Gianni yelled at the top of his lungs. "I won, not him." But that only made Uncle Henry scold him all the more.

They left right away, even before Judd had been able to stuff another cotton candy in his mouth. They argued almost all the way home to Crooked Falls, Gianni and Judd in the back seat, with Uncle Henry chiming in now and then and only Aunt Jane quiet, looking out the side window in her frilly black hat. Finally, to change the subject, Aunt Jane turned her head around and asked Gianni when he would be going to visit at his other Grandpa's. "Not soon enough!" he wanted to shout back. But instead he told her when and he tried to be nice, since he knew she was trying, too, even though he felt like the soldiers must feel when the Indians surround them and catch them and whoop and holler. "And they'll all be there—O.B., too, and all our cousins." So he figured at least he had made Judd feel bad by comparison if nothing else, since he and O.B. were the only cousins Judd had to speak of.

"How many aunts and uncles do you have on that side, anyway?" Aunt Jane asked, still trying to be nice, it seemed. So Gianni counted them up, warming to his subject, and answered again. "Twelve," he said loudly. But even that didn't do any good, since almost before he had said it, Uncle Henry cut in.

"Twelve?" he bellowed over his shoulder. "Blood relations? No—That's not right now." When he turned back, Gianni could see from behind, how red Aunt Jane's ears had become as she turned her head toward Uncle Henry. "Now, Jane," Uncle Henry continued, speaking to her as though they were suddenly alone in the car. "Not blood relations, he hasn't—He's not figuring right. Why, that's twice too many."

"Hmph!" Aunt Jane replied, and then she leaned over and said something to Uncle Henry that they couldn't hear in the back seat, though they could see the black frills shake as she nodded her head. Whatever it was that she said, it worked, because Uncle Henry sighed and grew silent. So Gianni gave up, too, and they rode in a truce of silence the last few miles, except for the whir of the engine, the sound of the tires on the blacktop, and the wind.

The afternoon when they got back to the farm from the contest on the frozen river, carrying the big fish and their gold prize, Grandma and her friends were busy playing cards in the parlor, as was to be expected on a Sunday afternoon in midwinter.

"Go on in now," she motioned to Grandpa and Drew after she had inspected what they had brought. "We've been playing threehanded rummy 'til now, but Jack and Clare Connolly are coming over later for Five Hundred, so we can have two tables: you're just in time."

"No," Grandpa said. "There's still some light left. I'll be in a little later. I want to work on those two new ponies."

"Now William! Don't be foolish," Grandma protested. "You could pick some other day besides Sunday to fool with those things of yours. And, besides, what about your—"

"Never mind," he said simply. "The snow's fresh now. And I'll need Drew, too, so you just go on with the rummy until Jack and Clare show up or until it gets dark. Then I'll be in," he said, as he smiled his smile and winked at her, "to show you how it's done."

Grandma must have seen there was no use arguing, or maybe it was the tone of Grandpa's voice, because she gave up and nodded curtly. "All right then, do as you please." And she went back to join the others.

Grandpa put his hat back on and started down the hall with Drew, but before he got past the big deer head to the door he turned around and looked Gianni and O.B. over from head to toe, as though just remembering them and waiting to see what their reaction would be. "Well, don't you two want to come then?" So they were going to go, too. It was the first time. Before, the few times they'd been lucky enough to be there when he went to break the horses, they'd only been permitted to watch from inside the house. It could be dangerous, their mother said, even if by then Grandpa seemed so used to it all that it didn't trouble him in the least. Every winter he would break the three or four young horses he had bought from Henry Stillwell the autumn before by riding them in the heavy snow of the pasture below the barn. That way he saved money and—he claimed, despite Grandma's scoffs—broken bones. Grandma said that instead of an arm or a leg he would break his neck one day, so where would he be then with his savings? But Grandpa never even answered that and just went on as he had, two or three times every year; so maybe the savings weren't so important after all.

Gianni remembered the first glimpse he had had of it: one morning several winters before he had been coming through the dining room of the farmhouse with a tray of ornaments for the Christmas tree when all of a sudden O.B. grabbed his shoulders to whirl him around and commanded "Look!" When he spun, he saw, past O.B., Nero jumping wildly back and forth and Grandpa and the horse fused together in the majestic, furious dance, just as they lurched out of sight. Since that time he had always wanted to go out to watch, but both their mother and Grandma had said no. Now they jumped at their good fortune. They went down to the barn past the drifts that rose taller than a man and waited with Drew while Grandpa got everything set. Then Grandpa brought the first one out, and Drew helped him calm the horse and mount. Then it began: the horses lunging wildly in the incomprehensible dance with their nostrils flared through the flying snow and the great drafts of rising steam, first one horse and then the other until they were finally unable to bring their legs up through the weight of the snow any longer or even hold their heads high because of their fatigue. By the end of the last ride, dusk really had come, and, from where they stood watching, they could no longer tell which was the horse and which was the man, so closely were the two joined first in their fury then in their exhaustion, and finally in utter stillness. How strange, it seemed to him years later, recalling the sight they had seen, that what had begun so violently had ended in such quietude, as though beginning and end were separate and unrelated acts rather than both parts of the same motion.

When it was over and the horses had been put away in defeat, Grandpa came to join them, and they walked back up to the house, Grandpa silent and spent, with the look in his eyes as lifeless as ice, so Gianni wondered if the spark were gone then, if it could go out, vanish—even if just for the moment. He found out the truth of it later as he sat in the shadows of the warm parlor and watched Grandma and Grandpa and their friends while they shuffled and dealt and bid and slapped their cards down to take the tricks, with the coffee cups and the plates of homemade cakes pushed off to either side so you could tell the game was serious. The players sat beneath the little overhead lamp, Grandma to one side, constantly clucking, and Grandpa to the other, his neatly pressed shirt open at the neck now and his face relaxed, as the game moved monotonously back and forth, one player to the next, in the rhythm of slow song. Then all at once Grandpa came oddly alert, so quickly that Gianni thought perhaps he was the only one to have seen it, while Grandpa continued to look at his cards and watch the others speaking calmly and playing theirs in turn, the cards gliding back and forth across the shiny table, until Grandpa raised his hand and slapped his card down too hard on the table top, to the consternation of Grandma and the obvious surprise of Mr. and Mrs. Connolly and Drew, who came bolt upright in his seat in the corner. "There!" Grandpa shouted to take the trick, and then, amidst the sudden confusion and Grandma's sputtering, and the clink of cups and saucers, Grandpa's eyes came alive once again, and they danced in the light as he rose up without waiting and slapped down another card and then another. "There's for you!" he cried as he slapped down another and another and another to take not just one but all the tricks. "There! And there again!" he shouted with glee in his voice and the spark in his eye. "There's for you!"

And he was riding the horse.

* * *

That had been in the summer of Gianni's ninth year, when O.B. got the rifle and began to use it, and had rolled over in the dusk to speak to him, and to plan the raid they would make with

Judd, and they had decided what to do. But when in the end nothing went according to their plans, it made no difference really. Because the summer had not been aiming toward that. For all its false starts and uncertainty, it was heading elsewhere. Gianni and O.B. had each sensed as much all summer long, that it was time for some conclusion or turning, or so it seemed to Gianni when he remembered it later. But just the same he felt certain that neither of them had had the least inkling of what it was to be. They only knew that something was missing and that in time the summer would complete the arc of its motion, supply the end to its order which would make everything turn around and appear to have made sense all along, the end which, in retrospect, would make sense of the order. They waited for that moment, after which they would see everything differently, waited without knowing what they were waiting for, or even that they were waiting at all.

So on the day when what they had awaited finally came, it probably should not have been such a surprise. The entire summer had been slowly bending towards it. Still the day did not start out any more remarkably than a thousand others, except, perhaps, for the task of cleaning up the last of the debris from the fire in the small barn two nights before. If anything, the day was almost too quiet, without a cloud in the sky to tarnish the frozen blue, and no breeze coming—or maybe just a whisper from time to time, though even then hardly enough to stir the leaves, rusted now in early September's heat, lining the oak branches that arched and descended over the bright yard of the farm in New Providence as Gianni sat on the porch step at the edge of the brown lawn. It was one of those days when in fact it doesn't seem that anything at all could possibly come, with the sky and the air brittle that way, and the world so still that it throbs with the sudden void, like the hollow ache in your chest when you've been moving fast and all at once stop. Gianni watched, and waited though he didn't know it, as the day settled towards noon and grew quieter still.

It had not been quiet all week. They always had plenty to do at Grandpa and Grandma Mariagrazia's. He and O.B. would go out to the woods—boulders and stumps really, left over from what had been a woods generations earlier, before the oak and elm and then even the maple had been cut for fuel—where they would work for a time on the fort that they had been constructing from stones and logs and whatever stray brush they could find among the rocks. But no matter how they worked on it, it never changed very much. It was one of the projects begun two summers before with great energy and enthusiasm, even to the point of moving three of the boulders with branches fashioned specially for the purpose; but eventually even the pretense of protection against the Indians had begun to seem senseless. By that time O.B. was good enough with the rifle so that their father had given them permission to go off into the woods, alone except for Nero, though they had to promise to stay within the boundaries of the farm and not to scare the stock, and most importantly not to let anyone else shoot (and especially not Terry Elroy, who, according to their father, was too big for his breeches and untrustworthy to boot). In fact they were careful, keeping the gun unloaded most of the time and shooting only at set targets, and only when they were sure no one was near enough to hear them or to care, since they knew that one mistake would probably be all it would take to lose the rifle for the few weeks that were left that summer, without Grandpa Britzen there to argue their side for them.

    They would go fishing every other day, either for trout in the stream behind the woods or for walleyes on the big bay of Round Lake. When they returned in the afternoons, if there were time and if anyone else could be found, they played tag on the rafters in the barn, which was Gianni's favorite game. They had played once at the beginning of the week with their older cousin Richie and the Castells, and they had let Terry Elroy come, too, since he was there alone and seemed just waiting to be asked. They climbed one after the other through the chalk-white door at the side of the barn, beneath the hill, and down the steps inside into the cage where Grandpa Mariagrazia kept the tractor (except that it was gone then) and up to the huge, darkened loft. When they called out their numbers and showed their hands, Gianni was it. They all spread out, and Gianni tried not to look down into the hollow black pit where the hay was—so dry now, he could practically smell the flecks of dust rising slowly through the dim shafts of light as the wind whispered in through the cracks and rose, too. He took off after Terry Elroy right away, clinging to the planks and keeping to the sidebeams along the wall to make time, exactly as he had learned from O.B.

    He caught Terry as soon as he hit the crossbeam and could move freely once more. Gianni pushed off fast and moved away. As Terry started along the rafter to the other side of the loft, heading for O.B., Gianni moved to the wall and pulled himself to the next sidebeam up and kept going. He'd never get caught that way, if he didn't slip or get tired, because he'd been with O.B. and the Castells enough to know how to tag and move off and keep away on his own, even without O.B.'s help. Gianni could see across the barn to where Terry Elroy was following O.B's t-shirt along the planks of the wall, though he knew Terry would never catch O.B. O.B. kept moving fast and steady, looking back from time to time so you could see the little white scar over his brow—from when O.B. had been too small to play but had played anyway, with Richie and the Johnsons, and had been so quick on the crossbeams that he had won, they said, even if he did fall and gash his forehead— the little line bouncing up and down now as he smiled, showing his teeth, so Gianni was sure Terry would never catch him. Finally, Terry could see as much himself, and he stopped dead, turning his head both ways, perplexed, while O.B. and Richie and the Castells, from their perch high up on the end wall, yelled to him, calling to Terry and taunting him just as they used to in the years before. So Gianni joined in and taunted him too. Terry was mad, you could hear it as he yelled back at them even louder, though for the moment he stayed where he was. Then all at once Terry was coming back across the rafter to Gianni's side, chasing after him again.

Gianni took off toward the end-wall where the Castells were. Terry was coming fast, but Gianni was up higher, and he had already passed the double rafter at the middle of the loft and Terry hadn't. Crawling over the double rafter as he had done (Terry could never leap it—not even the Johnsons could do that) would slow Terry down at least enough to let Gianni get close to O.B. and the Castells, who were keeping up the chorus from their perch. Then they could all spread out again and leave Terry at the end wall by himself: that was what Gianni thought. But Terry didn't crawl over the double rafter at all. Instead, he followed the same route Gianni had taken with such care, using the strength in his arms and shoulders (from working those horses of his, Gianni thought too late) not to crawl but actually to swing up to the beam above. So then he was at the same level as Gianni, moving along the wall right behind him, and coming fast.

Gianni thought of moving back down to the level below, but he knew he couldn't do it quickly enough to get away and still keep his balance. He saw the shock of Terry's red hair and the eyes darting. At that moment Gianni heard the other's shout of victory as the hand touched his shoulder.

Then the black air rushed away and he was caught in its current—and so he fell.

Gianni hit, rolled onto his shoulder, tried to spring up from the hot, dusty hay but lost his balance and went down once more. He could smell the dust again in his nostrils and feel the stems scratching his neck and down inside his shirt, prickly with the sweat. He got to his feet, unsteady but angry—because he hadn't just fallen, as a book will lean over onto its side or even as a leaf will drift to earth in the wind. He could see the son of a bitch leaning over in the dimness on the rafter above, with a hand perched firmly on each knee, looking down at him.

"Hey," Terry called to him. "You fell."

Then, behind, Gianni saw the white shirt moving, and the teeth flash.

In his astonishment, he moved barely in time to avoid having Terry fall directly on top of him.

"Looks like you fell, too, you little jerk," O.B. yelled from the rafter, and then he sprang down himself. He pushed Gianni out of the way with his body and grabbed Terry and yanked him up by both arms.

As Gianni and the Castells watched, O.B. slapped him once to bring him up straight—so they could hear the report—and drew his fist back, but then instead of hitting him he swung him around and started him off with a kick toward the shed and the side door. "And see if we ever let you come back, you creep!" O.B. yelled after him while the Castells hooted from above. "Try it, and you'll get the same all over again."

"Don't worry," Terry Elroy answered once he had reached the safety of the door, "I wouldn't come around here again even for the Pope himself—not even for a chance to pinch the Pope's nose!" So O.B. made a start for him, but by then the doorway was already empty, with the shaft of light streaming in, and he was gone.

Terry was back bright and early the next morning, his face all smiles as though nothing had happened at all. He came edging up the sun-dapppled lawn toward the dust of the drive, holding a freshly cut branch in one hand and the tether of the horse in the other. Gianni had started to say something, but O.B. put his hand out for him to keep quiet. O.B. was staring at the horse. It was a big, high-shouldered palomino, white and tan, with a huge white spot in the middle of its forehead—for luck, so they said—which seemed constantly moving, the eyes not exactly wild but hardly calm either, and its coat curried till it shone as though someone had taken a bar of wax to it instead of just a comb. "He's not mine," Terry volunteered. "But my folks let me take him whenever I want, just like he was."

They could not tell immediately if Terry was holding the tether so tightly out of necessity or if he was just being careful. In the other hand he shifted the branch to free two fingers, which he reached into the top of his pocket to produce a cube of sugar. The horse blinked and started, and Terry yelled, pulling the tether down hard, but still without dropping the cube. Then he brought the animal up close, across the lawn, and handed the sugar to O.B.

"Go ahead," he urged. "He's not wild. It's all right now."

O.B. reached up with the cube in his hand and the spot on the horse's head rose, too—it moved so fast they could not follow its motion, the hooves slicing the air almost daintily, like a dancer, until Terry shouted and used the branch, at the same instant that he drew in the tether again. When the horse was still—except for the eyes—he patted the animal's flank and began to make the noises of reassurance in a language both the boy and the horse seemed to understand.

"Try it again," he turned back to O.B. "This time reach your palm out open with the cube sitting flat on it, and just let him do the taking, however he likes."

O.B. did as Terry instructed, and the sugar disappeared.

"So you actually ride him, too?" O.B. asked. "Is that it? I mean, instead of just walking him around."

"Sure." Terry said. "He feels better with someone up—that's his nature. I've ridden him every day the two months we've had him."

"So O.K.," O.B. said skeptically. "Why'd you bring him here?"

"I thought you might like to try him," Terry said. "Just you, though," he grinned. "Gianni's too little. You could even keep him for a while if you wanted to. We're going away for a week to my Mom's folks—my aunt's sick again. So you could even keep him in your barn. That is, if you wanted, and if..."

Before he'd finished, they heard Nero's bark as he came running up to them from the house. The horse pulled back again, whinnying and raising up. Gianni grabbed Nero and held onto his collar, but Nero kept growling low.

"Don't mind Nero," O.B. said. "He won't hurt you."

"I know," Terry smiled as he loosed the tether and the hooves rose up once more, slicing the air. "Whoa there! Whoa! Stay down now!" Terry shouted the commands and the horse calmed. "You see, you've got to be extra careful with him," Terry said.

"And if what?" O.B. asked.

"Huh?"

"You were saying—if I wanted ... and if what?"

"Well, you know, I still haven't got a chance to try that new rifle of yours. Maybe it is just a twenty-two, but it looks pretty nice. I guess a chance to try that would be worth at least one ride."

Gianni glanced at O.B. and thought of what their father had said. But O.B. wasn't paying any attention to him or to Nero. He was staring at the horse again. Gianni wanted to shout at him, remind him or warn him, but he didn't. Terry smiled and again the hooves rose up. "You just have to watch and keep him reined in tight," he said. "That's all."

O.B. looked back at Terry as though suddenly remembering he was there, too, and not just the horse.

"Now Terry—you were saying?" he asked.

*

Robin, their closest neighbor, had come up the dusty gravel drive in the afternoon sun leading the too-fat cow, his head turned straight into the heat of the sun, not glancing even once toward the brown field on the one side or the white house on the other, with the bird swinging in his off hand, already plucked, so even from a ways away you could see what the sun made to look like pock marks all along the colorless flesh. His gaze seemed to shift momentarily when Maria approached the window; nonetheless, he did not smile or give any other sign of having noticed her. He had a hat, wide-brimmed for the sun, but he wasn't wearing it. He held it in his hand, the same one in which he held the bird—on the near side now, toward the house, as he turned from the drive to the walk and shifted his grip. She could see that, too, as he left the cow and came up the neat walk toward the house, still not permitting himself to look to the fields, or anywhere else, as far as she could tell, and approached the screen.

"Hoa, Maria!" he called as she came through the kitchen.

"Robin!" she cried. "What do you mean standing out under the sun that way? Come in." It probably wouldn't hurt if his brains did fry, she thought. But instead she smiled at him and repeated, "Come on in, for land's sake."

He came close enough so she could smell him through the screen. But she knew she would have to open it for him. How can they ever keep their women, she wondered, when they're so slow and clumsy? He entered the kitchen, the long, raw-boned arms and the huge red hands, dangling from the sleeves, smelling already of the barnyard, and stood passively under her gaze. She looked at his lean frame in the pants and freshly-ironed shirt, faded blue, and wondered what he would have been like. But no, she thought, even if he were fit he probably wouldn't know what to do without an awful lot of help.

"Well?" she asked.

"Is Michael here?"

"No, he's not—he's in the fields."

"Well, what I meant to come for," he began to explain, as if in apology, still not looking at her, "was to see Michael." He reached out his arm and laid the bird on the table.

"Oh, how nice," she smiled. "You've brought him a chicken."

"No—no," he protested, as the red bones of the cheeks flared redder and for a second his eyes flashed. But then he looked down again; the anger was gone, or covered. "No—I mean I'm sorry I missed him, but—"

"But he's just in the south field there, by the drive. You must have seen him," she said. "Or anyway, he was a little while ago."

"I didn't see him," he said stubbornly. "I passed by some of the others, but not him." And then again, "I'm sorry I missed him."

"Well, why don't you go ahead and tell me, then," she said, knowing that that was what he wanted but also knowing she would have to draw it out of him. "Since Michael's not here..."

"Well," he hesitated. "All right," and then as though the dam had broken, everything that had been inside of him gushed out. "I came about that cow," he began, glancing outside to where the cow had begun grazing on the front lawn. "We'll be going away for a while now. It's Ethel's sister Harriet, taken sick again, shut in this time, and we have to go to her." There was no one else, he went on. Of course, Ethel didn't drive, so he had to go, too, and Harriet, her older sister, he added, making her sound well past a hundred, really only cheered up when she saw Terry—not him, he had guessed on his own, though Harriet would never admit it—so that left nobody to home for at least four maybe five days. Well—that cow's time had come, it was about to burst from one minute to the next, anybody could see it, she was just being stubborn and holding back—learned it from Harriet, he would've thought, except no, they'd never been around each other. Not that the cow would be trouble, it wouldn't really need care so much as just watching.

"So could I leave the cow in Michael's barn, just in case?" he asked at last. "If nothing else, to let me rest and not worry."

Maria nodded and moved toward the counter to get the piece of cake to offer him, except that he wasn't finished.

"And then there's Terry's horse," he said, almost as an afterthought.

"You brought a horse, too?" she asked in genuine amazement and moved toward the screen to look out.

"No, no," he stopped her. "It's not here—I ain't seen it all day. Truth is, I almost never see the thing, now that the boy's taken to riding it all over the countryside. Anyway—it's a special horse, skittish, and needs a separate stall to itself. Not that it's dangerous or even finicky or anything like that—a little high-strung but nothing serious, just nerves, that's all." He stopped and looked up, with the suggestion of a smile, barely suppressed, already vanishing from his eyes, like a man about to make a wager. "So do you think you could take him, too?"

She nodded agreement, too quickly, but she wanted to get it over with since it was bound to come, and the sidebarn was empty anyway. He took the piece of cake, visibly relieved. "I'll put the cow in now, if that's all right—I know where," he said, as he gulped the cake and started for the door. "I'll bring the horse up sometime this evening—that is, whenever I can get my hands on it again."

After he had finished with the cow he started back down the drive, his steps faster now, lighter, too, since he knew that once the animals were on that property they were certain of the best treatment anywhere for miles around—even all the way to New Auburn, as far as that went, including those fancy German places off south with their big lawns. And although the old man hadn't actually agreed to it by his own word, the deal was as good as made now—even if it did include playing nursemaid to one of the most temperamentally useless pieces of palomino racing stock he'd ever seen, much less had the misfortune to own (in point of fact young rather than useless, since, despite what he'd been told and had actually believed, the horse in question hadn't even passed enough dirt under its hooves yet to be calm enough to breed).

From the house, she watched him go as he had come, past the stretch of lawn where Filomena was hanging out the sheets to dry, not stopping or even slowing his pace to wave, moving so quickly now with his jerky gait that he appeared actually to be fleeing rather than simply heading home. She let the curtain fall and tried to think what she was going to tell Michael when he came in, happy to the extent that she at least had only to deal with Michael and not with the other one anymore, may he rest in peace, and wondering whether he would come up to the house first and make it easier or if he was going to go straight to the barn and make it simply impossible.

*

Gregory Lucente

Nero picked Gianni up half-way down the yard and then trotted at his side; they crossed the gravel together and then Nero had to come back because they were going to cut through the edge of the weeds that bordered the other barn, the small one off to the side of the yard. Gianni pushed open the heavy door, already smelling the oats, and stepped into the dark cool barn, darker still for the one shaft of light coming through the open door, then without stopping for his eyes to adjust went straight to the stall, where it stood waiting as he knew it would, in the dim light at the back of the stall, quiet except for the breathing, but not still, the huge center splotch appearing even purer now, unbelievably white, awash in the layered dimness at the bottom of which it seemed to swim, vibrant, as though even the act of waiting were just another kind of motion, minute, constant. He opened the stall, his head filled with the wonder of what he was going to do mixed with the rank odor (he did not even bother with the saddle—which he wasn't sure how to fit on anyway) and slowly took the tether, then touched the animal's chest to calm it, as he had seen Terry do. He secured the strap and heaved himself up to head out—thinking, the hell if he'd wait for the fish and the gun and everything else, too—and exploded into the dazzling brightness. He heard Nero's barking but that was all and then the wind started up and he gathered all his strength now at last, for once, to show them, all of them and him, too, there to see it or not, and they were off: *And he was riding the horse.* He was riding out across the field, over the rough furrows, and his stomach started to rise but he swallowed hard and his legs clung tighter, as his feet dug into the supple flesh and the jolts came faster, flying over the furrows, the wind so cool now as it rushed at him, filling his ears so he couldn't hear at all except for the roar, and then, against what he had heard them say, he was racing, riding the horse. Far off, beyond the edge of the field, he caught the light of the leaves sparkling at him, and he held himself on tighter with his legs so as not to fall—because he didn't know what would happen then—and suddenly they were going faster, the jolts coming faster still and much harder, as his heels dug in. Then at once Nero was there again, the black spot—he had forgotten all about him—rushing at them, barking and growling, then circling away despite all his shouts and rushing back in again, as they went faster still, the wind magnificent in the galloping rush and torrent of his defiance, as he held tighter still, and below them, all at once, the dog's great black head and shoulders and the tongue red and rushing, too, as he shouted, flying into the wind, and then the horse kicked out.

42

He had forgotten, and the horse kicked out.

Down below him, above the red tongue, on the ridge over the eye, a gash opened suddenly and kept growing. As the wound screamed out to him, Gianni's stomach rolled.

He knew no more about slowing the horse than he had about making it race, and by the time at last that he had gotten the horse stopped, the black spot had reached the far edge of the field. In the next instant it bounded from sight. He knew it was hopeless to call out, or to curse or even to kick the horse as, for a second, he had wanted to do. He had forgotten, it was his fault, that's all he could think of. After dismounting he walked the horse in over the hard furrows, the tether numb in his hand, mute. Because Nero had been there, and he had forgotten.

He closed up the horse in the stall and walked back to the house. He could not see the dog anywhere. In the house Uncle Dominic and some other men he didn't recognize were playing their noisy game of cards, passing the cards in turn and yelling, then making speeches at each other, the ones that always ended in shouting and arguments and Grandpa or Uncle Dominic yelling, and everybody scraping their chairs and leaving all at once. The phone was ringing on the wall between the dining room and the kitchen, but they weren't paying attention. He went past them and past their mother and Grandma Mariagrazia to the room he shared with O.B. and took off his clothes in the quiet, feeling sick and thinking how nice it would be to lie down on the cool sheets. After a while their mother came in to see if he were all right, then Grandma Mariagrazia put her palm to his forehead and lowered her head to his cheek, nuzzling him like the cows nuzzle their young with the huge soft chest pushing warmly against him, and later their mother or Aunt Fil or one of the others must have come back—but not O.B.—because he heard the sounds of women's dresses about the bed and when he came awake for a moment there was a glass and a pitcher of cool water on the table beside him.

When he awoke later no one was there. It wasn't morning yet, he knew, but it wasn't dark, either. The whole side of the room was pink, it was so pretty. He heard the men shouting, but it wasn't the game anymore, he knew that, too, because the noise was coming from outside, and there were more voices, eerie and loud. Then he smelled the smoke. He scrambled out of the bed, dressing himself as he went, and ran to the door. There were people all over the yard, running from the well to the sidebarn and back again. Everyone was shouting, calling out commands and counterorders in the confusion. The slats of the barn were all aglow, and as he stood watching, warmed by the heat, he saw the ball of flame go bouncing up through the roof. Off to one side he could see O.B. holding the horse, but Nero was nowhere to be seen.

Amidst all the shouting and confusion, only Uncle Dominic remained calm, standing with a cigarette perched in his mouth as the scene unfolded before them. "Now it'll go for sure," Gianni heard him say to someone standing nearby. "Nothing left to do but watch. Lucky it was the small one, and that they got that horse out. It should never have been in that barn anyway." Then Gianni saw that Uncle Dominic was looking at him.

"Hey—I heard you were sick," Uncle Dominic called. "Now, you tell me, didn't I see you out with that big black dog of yours this afternoon?" he asked.

Gianni nodded.

"Well, you better go tell your father, if you can find him in this mess," he said. "'Cause he was looking for it all evening. It ain't come back."

The other man turned to watch the sparks flying higher and brighter now than the Fourth of July.

"Hey, Gianni," Uncle Dominic said to him, his face aglow in the ghastly light of the flames. Gianni looked away, feeling sick again, the confusion and the fire and all the people making him feel even worse. "You go on now. Go find your father like I told you. Hey," Gianni heard the deep voice louder, demanding. "Hey, Gianni—you listening to what I'm telling you?"

Almost two days passed before they saw the dog again. That was the first day that Gianni had really been permitted to be up and about, even though the fever was gone and he had insisted he was all right. He had to find the dog, but he couldn't tell them that, or why. He had not even been allowed to help O.B. and their cousin Richie and the others clean up the debris left from the fire. Instead their mother and Grandma Mariagrazia had made him watch the excitement from the window of the room. But no matter how vigilant he was from his post, he had not caught even a glimpse of Nero; and neither had O.B. or anybody else.

Gianni spent the morning of the next day listlessly watching the heat gather over the front lawn. Around midday he got up and crossed the fields and started down the road toward the Lund's property. The day was still quiet, too quiet, really, without any breeze to it. After a while, among the willows along the stream behind the Lund's wheatfield, he caught sight of a black spot moving back and forth between the trees.

He finally got close enough so that he could tell for sure it was Nero (he had felt it instantly: what Gianni hadn't known was whether or not the dog would come to him, which in the end he did willingly, almost joyously), and it was easy to see that he was all right. Although the swelling above the eye shone deep purple, a scab had formed and the wound had already begun to heal. But as they headed over the fields together in the bright heat, back to the farm, Nero would flinch and growl every time another animal came near to them or they to it—a heifer or horse, once even a thoroughly disconcerted mule—and the ridge on the back of his neck would rise in anger. At least for the moment, however, Gianni was too excited and grateful to worry about that or even, really, to take much notice.

Near the edge of the Lund's property they came onto Billy Castells and the Johnsons, who greeted Nero with shouts and hugs like old friends. They began tossing sticks and whatever they could find for him to fetch as they moved over the pasture toward the road that marked the end of the Lund's farm and the beginning of Grandma and Grandpa's. Across the road, Gianni knew, they would be home—he could actually feel it—and everything would be all right again, his foolishness erased, the slate wiped clean just as his mother said happened at such times. As they approached the road they saw Richie and then O.B. running toward them in the dust, over the gravel, yelling at them and shouting hello to Nero to welcome him home.

They all ran faster, shouting back and forth to Nero and to each other. Even when, to their surprise, a big black car came up behind Richie and O.B., coming toward them fast through the clouds of dust and honked and passed, none of them turned to look or slowed down, they were so close to home.

What happened next wasn't ever certain. Gianni remembered yelling at O.B. and running and seeing the car come and pass and then the look on O.B.'s face as he watched in shock and anger. Gianni hadn't even heard the horn, though everyone else had to agree later with the driver and admit that they had heard it—two blasts like blows as the car passed, not slowing. Then O.B. was yelling and running toward them through the dust. O.B. went by him, and as Gianni turned to see what was happening, he saw the car, black, but so covered with dust that if he hadn't known he would have thought it was tan, come to a stop. He couldn't see Nero. In fact, he didn't see him at all till O.B. was already kneeling at his side in the dust of the road, holding on to him, still shouting.

By the time Gianni got there, they were coming across the field from the big white house, and his mother was already there with them, kneeling down in the dust between him and O.B., rubbing Nero's shoulders and talking to him, then patting him with the regularity of a beat. But it didn't do any good. His black body—which had never even seemed a body in that way before—lay motionless, as still as anything Gianni had ever seen, even stiller, like when you hold your breath for too long and the world stops. But then there wasn't any more movement at all, and their mother gave up patting him and sat back on her heels, staring, while Nero lay still as a log in the dust.

"It's a bad road," they heard people say to each other. "There's foreign traffic that comes on this stretch, going God knows where." Richie stood off to the side with their father and Uncle Dominic, looking odd but quiet for once. By then the man, thin and balding with strange red spectacles, had begun to explain, while the woman in the car sat waiting—they could see her sitting straight upright in the front seat.

"The boys were running along one side," the man said to their father and Uncle Dominic.

"Why were you going so fast?" they said.

"To tell you the truth, I didn't think I was," he said. "Who says so? Who says I was going fast?" he asked, and he began describing how it had been. But how could he tell them? They had to understand. He had had to make a choice, he had had to—one side of the road or the other, the boys or the dog, unless he could get between them and somehow squeeze through. He would have made it, too, except that at the last possible moment the dog had turned and barked wildly—he couldn't forget how strange it had looked through the dust, seeing the white teeth bared in the black face—and lunged at the car, as if to attack them, or to guard the boys, if you could imagine. He knew it sounded odd, but that was the truth, so help him. His wife had seen it, too, even in all the confusion on the road, they could ask her if they wished. They were sorry, but there was nothing else they could have done short of driving off the road into the ditch: there was nowhere else to go. Strange as it sounded, instead of the other way around, the dog had actually run into *them*.

While he had been talking, the man held the attention of the others completely. But when he paused for breath and began to go over the events again—slowly and clearly, like a sermon, because he wanted them to understand it just as it had occurred—and none of the boys could contradict any of what he said— the attention of the others, which, until then, had been all his, suddenly turned, and he fell silent. Because someone else was coming out from the house, calling across the fields through the air that was hot and still as a blanket.

As the figure got closer, they could see it was Aunt Fil raising her skirts so she could run better once the path was gone and she had entered the field. But still, even though they could see who it was, the voice didn't sound like hers. She kept shouting but it sounded so odd—like an excited animal or like when you've been scared bad and have to talk anyway. She came toward them across the stubbled field, with the flickers swooping away home in front of her, sounding strange like that. Aunt Fil made her way up the ravine at the side of the road, shouting and gasping for breath, and hurrying toward them, so Gianni thought she was coming to hold him or, perhaps, to hold Nero. But then he could see that she wasn't even looking at them. Instead, she was talking to their mother, who was standing between Aunt Rachel and their father and who seemed just as surprised and unsure as everyone else, since too much was happening at once.

"Helen," she said, "I'm so sorry. They just called—it's your father—"

"But, Fil, what did he want?" their mother began.

"No," Aunt Fil said. "No—he didn't call. It was *about* him. They—" Aunt Fil gasped again. "Oh Helen, I'm so sorry—I don't know what to say. They just called now. I'm so sorry."

Then O.B. was holding onto him, and their father was coming toward them, speaking to them.

The last thing anyone passing by would have seen that afternoon, after the tableau had broken and the remnants had dissolved back into the house, and their father had taken Nero away in the car and returned and gone inside himself, was Gianni, sitting on the stoop between the house and the lawn, in jeans and a soiled undershirt, looking out over the yard and watching the delicate movement of the leaves—faint, but visible—along the branch overhanging. The sky was still clear, but whiter now in the first wash of evening.

This was the way things happened, Gianni knew that now. Things would come and surprise you, frighten you if you had not been ready, and then all the promises didn't count anymore. How could they? There was no time for them to count—or not enough, despite what he had always told them. So what good was it to live right if that didn't make any difference or make things last, if things could come like that, and it didn't help or change things one bit?

What good was it to be able to make things live if it didn't work all the time, or when it mattered most? He had learned that, at least. Now his turn would never come: they had all lied. Time would come, he sensed that much, but not *his* time. Now he was all alone. But it was not his fault, he was certain of that, too. Even Nero wasn't his fault, even if he had wanted to ride that horse, and had forgotten, and Nero had gotten hurt. And even if he had run with him on the road, he was just trying to get back home. Besides, everybody knew that people don't die too, at the same time, just because of things like that. There isn't any connection like that. There can't be. He could prove it if he had to. To hell with all of them. He would take that damn rifle of O.B.'s and shoot that horse and kill it if he ever saw it again, and that man in the black car, too; so they'd better look out. But no, that wouldn't do any good either. He wasn't even sure he could get the gun right anyway. Maybe he'd just poison them instead, or shut them both in a barn and light it on fire and burn them up.

Inside, he could hear O.B.'s voice and then their father's, talking about their mother and the trip to his grandparents' place in Crooked Falls, and he heard them talking on the phone to Drew and Uncle Henry and Jake Arndt. He knew he should feel sorry for her, too, and he did; still, he felt more strange than sorry. He didn't feel like going in yet, so he remained sitting on the stoop looking out over the yard to the yellowed fields and imagining Grandpa and Nero and all of them—him, too—walking over them, happy again, going somewhere. But that just made him feel worse; besides, he had never seen them all there, like that. He hated them anyway, with their talk and dogs and guns. And it wasn't right—not like that, not in those fields. He couldn't even get *that* right.

So he gave up and concentrated on the sky, pale and pure as milk, seemingly unchanging, as the color faded and the clouds came up, and he watched the little movements of the leaves waving in the breeze, the last of the summer it seemed now, and listened to the hollow tattoo of a woodpecker he could hear but couldn't see.

Still, he thought, no matter what happened, and no matter what anyone said or might say, now or ever, he knew at least one thing for certain, that he was right: they couldn't blame him. Because it was not his fault. He wasn't the one who had lied or gone back on his word. And there was no connection anyway. No matter what anyone said, no one could blame him. Anyone could see that. He'd show them someday.

Couldn't they see?
It was not his fault.

II.   The Summers

The two men had met exactly once, after their children's wedding. Some time after, actually, they had shared a quiet afternoon on the back porch of the farmhouse in New Providence, each sitting with an untouched glass of lemonade at his side, each staring across the fields, exchanging comments on the stock and the crops from time to time and little else. In truth, even if they had felt the urge to talk, they would have had little to say to one another. It wasn't that either actively disliked the other or bore a grudge—though the circumstances of the wedding had caused a measure of discomfort for each of them, especially once the other relatives on both sides had become involved—or that they were markedly taciturn by nature, which, appearances to the contrary, neither man really was. It was just that in spite of their overt similarities, both of them large men, noticeably past-middle-aged farmers, heads of families, they were irremediably foreign to one another, and not only or even primarily because of their origins, though that, too, was a part of it. Their differences lay deeper than birth or family or style; the sources were at once more profound and more mysterious. Both could sense the distinctive foreign presence within the other, and each, accordingly, kept his distance.

It is also true that the families were of dissimilar backgrounds. The Mariagrazias had settled in that farmland under circumstances and for reasons that the Britzens, had they known, would have found bizarre to say the least. The Mariagrazia family, or what there was of it then, had come to New Providence over thirty years before from Milwaukee, where Michael's father, Andrea, had owned a tavern. Before that he had been in Chicago, where he had met Michael's mother, in New York, and, as a child and youth, in Italy. Like other Italians from the barren mountains and the parched fields of the south, he had come to America in part to escape starvation and in part to make his fortune in the land where, as he and everyone else he knew believed, all shone of gold. He got half of his wish right away, which was better than some got. For the other half, he was willing to wait.

In New York he worked the docks beside the *padron*'s men, began to learn English—real English, so that when he wished to go up town and had to ask directions, the man on the corner wouldn't laugh at him for saying *stritta* instead of "street" and *carro* instead of car. The *padron* took care of the men's salary in his own way, making a show of helping them while actually robbing them blind—except that he, Andrea, wasn't blind but simply willing, at least for a period, to trade his labor for security and food—and they were in fact regularly fed, with the result that for the first time in his life he ate without worry and abundantly, if not exactly well. After he had been in New York less than a year he saw a flier announcing jobs working on the railroad going west and he took it, signing himself on with his real name—Mariagrazia and not Andrew Marygrace, as the immigration officer had insisted amidst the press and confusion of the crowd, and then had actually written down on the form for him in an attempt to humiliate him into silence—since by then he had learned to write, too.

Inside of two years he was nearing Chicago, the end of the line, with a girlfriend, not Italian, whom he had picked up on the way (so quickly had he taken to what he assumed were American customs) and a sockful of money left over from his wages and from his uncanny skill at cards and at guessing, during the breaks in the work, the number of fingers flung out on the other man's hand. When another man challenged his winnings, or, as happened on occasion, suggested that Andrea was a queer sort of name for a man, Andrea would settle the question with his fists. Once in the city he left the job and the girl behind and kept the money. His fortunes had never looked better.

In Chicago he took a job with a carting company driving a horse and wagon, about which he knew little, and then, when that proved not only hot and filthy but also, to put it mildly, pungent, he left the rutted streets to become a kitchen hand, about which he knew even less. But he learned. After six months he had become the day cook in a small restaurant with a good but, luckily, simple menu (simpler yet once he got there, since at the start the only vegetables he liked and trusted himself to prepare were squash and carrots, only one of which could be found without difficulty). On his behalf, however, it should be said that he did make up for the items he had quietly deleted from the menu by adding several new ones based on his experience and taste: carrot soup, carrot tart, carrot cake, and the newfound object of his delight, carrot soufflé. When one of the regular diners would complain, he told them either that green vegetables were tainted that season or, if he were pressed, that some of them were actually poisonous, like the green mushrooms mixed in with the lettuce and celery that had killed twenty people at the old Lexington before it burned down. If he were *really* pushed, the number grew to forty and the location changed to the Douglass, which was then the most elegant hotel in the city, with the single exception of the Union League Club, which didn't really count since, strictly speaking, it wasn't a hotel. Anyway, the Douglass was safe to mention because no one there had ever heard of him, and fortunately so, since by the end of that year he had become the Douglass's assistant chef.

It was a good job. He cooked whatever they told him to, and when he didn't have any idea at all how to prepare something, he would simply ask the busboys (never the waiters or the diners) how *they* liked the dishes to be done and then followed their recommendations to the letter. He added a few Italian specialties of his own, mostly spurious mixtures of things that they had been fed on the railroad line, with some tomato and a little garlic thrown in, but occasionally authentic if uncomplicated dishes, such as the chicken or lamb with rosemary, from his memory of the land that he missed deeply but that now he had no expectation or desire ever to see again.

He worked six days each week. On Mondays, his day off, he would find himself in the park eating ice cream and strolling, watching the birds flicker past in the sun. One afternoon he saw a group of girls walk by, and one, over her shoulder, looked back, smiling. When he saw her again two weeks later, alone this time amidst the friendly bustle of the crowd, in her pastel dress and lily-white shoes, he spoke to her and offered her an ice cream. She shook her head no but still managed, somehow, to look pleased, so he bought it for her anyway. "Gelato piace," he said, holding it out happily, permitting himself one brief reversion to Italian, just to make sure. He said it as an affirmation rather than as a question, which would have been too easy, and when she smiled again, nodding agreement, he knew he had been right.

They were married six months later. Within a year and a half they'd had their first child, a son. He realized that in order for them to keep intact both what he had saved and the small dowry and still live in the manner in which he wanted them to—well, but of course not lavishly—he would need more money. So he took another job, part time, helping out in the Douglass' main bar in the evenings after the food had been prepared and his assistants—for by then he had acquired three of them—could take over in the kitchen. Filomena, his bride, was not happy about his staying away so much, especially at first, but in the end she understood the necessity and acquiesced in silence.

The bar of the Douglass, like the hotel itself, accommodated only the finest. Light sparkled on crystal chandeliers, the rug was a tapestry of deep, burnt orange, shipped from New York as were the rest of the fixtures, and the brass rails and spittoons were polished like gold. The mahogany bar shone, too, carved and waxed by the finest craftsmen in the city. The clientele matched the surroundings. The wages for the bartenders were nothing to speak of, but the gratuities were dependable and generous, and the harder Andrea worked, always faster, always more efficient, the better they got. For a while at first, nonetheless, he wasn't making enough to justify the extra time, so he worked harder yet, reminding himself to smile even as he fought the fatigue that crept up his legs and hung along them like weights. It got so that by Sunday night, the last before his single day off, he would find himself rooted to the wooden slats of the back bar floor, his eyes down, one hand fast on the bar's edge and the other on a glass or a coin, asleep on his feet, but before anyone would notice, he would be fully awake again, putting the glass away or dropping the money in the register without seeming to miss a beat. Yet even with the increased tips, he still was not bringing home what he felt was enough.

This went on for several months. Finally, after considering the bar's operation and watching his fellow workers, with whom—especially the female ones—he always tried to be as friendly as possible, Andrea decided to do what he was learning to do now in such situations: rather than looking around for another game, he upped the ante. Before long he was bringing home six or seven times what he had been. Filomena was delighted. At that rate, she said with an expression of anticipation that he could actually feel as well as see, they would be able to have a house of their own in no time—because by then she and the baby had practically outgrown their three small, drafty rooms. And it would have to be quick, too, he would reply—giving her a smile full of satisfaction and something else she didn't quite recognize yet—because things couldn't last as they had. Of that, at least, they could both be sure.

It was at about that time that a new group of customers began to make their appearance in the Douglass' bar. They were well dressed, clean-shaven, and neat, but, somehow, standing in groups of twos and threes, or more often alone, spread out along the bar, they seemed a bit too serious, too businesslike, to fit in with the rest of the customers, who, even though, or perhaps because, they had money, knew how to use it to have a good time. These men would come in at various hours in the course of an evening, order a drink—just one, never a double—and sip it most of the night. Regardless of when they arrived, they always spent more time watching the bar and the people around it than drinking or talking, and they remained without fail until closing time. They were there for one reason. The hotel had noticed that the bar's business was off by roughly a fifth of its normal take. The drop had come despite the fact that the holidays were nearing and the crowds, if anything, were up. At first the manager, a clever though notably self-conscious young Irishman named John MacShane, whose father had a share in the hotel's business, was confident that the discrepancy was due to a clerical error or something of the sort. When the problem not only refused to go away but indeed got worse, he had his own people watch and, quietly but methodically, begin to question the bartenders, the girls, the bookkeeper, and eventually just about everyone else who would have occasion to touch liquor and/or cash in the course of a day's or evening's work. MacShane found nothing. That was in early November. By the middle of the month he had decided to hire spotters—though he did this without mentioning it to anyone, so as not to stir things up any more than his campaign of questions already had. He told the new employees what to do and warned them not to cause any trouble, even if they did see something. Instead, they were to wait and then report to him the next day. Everything was to seem exactly the same as usual, without exception. The Douglass, after all, was still the Douglass, and he was still running it his way.

    The girls could tell the difference right off, so not even one night had passed before all five of the bartenders knew about it, too. The inspectors watched as the money was taken and found its way into the registers, they watched as tabs were established and grew; they watched as the liquor was served, as it moved back and forth across the room, and as the empty glasses came back, and, all the time they watched, the bartenders and girls watched them watching: MacShane hadn't taken into account that that was part of *their* job, too. But the spotters found absolutely nothing. The entire operation ran smoothly and openly, and the six registers all rang and filled exactly as they were supposed to. The investigators made that report every day for three or four weeks running before, on a bright Monday morning in mid-December, MacShane thought he saw what was wrong in the picture.

"Six?" he blinked, trying to conceal his dismay. "Six registers? "

"Yes, sir," the tall, red-moustached spotter replied. "Same as always."

"Not five. Six. You sure?"

"Yes, sir, just like I told you," the spotter replied confidently. "Just like I've told you all along, every day, day in and day out all these weeks now."

"Fine," MacShane said curtly and tossed his pen on the desk in front of him. "Keep doing exactly what you're doing and come report to me tomorrow, same time."

For the moment he knew he couldn't say any more. No one could know yet—after all the trouble he'd had, he couldn't take a chance. The report to the owners was going to be tricky enough as it was. So he'd have to make sure himself, as usual. Instead of upbraiding the spotter, he stopped on his way out to yell at the girl in the office who, unbeknownst to him, and fortunately or unfortunately, depending on whether the point of view in question was MacShane's or Andrea's, spent every Monday at lunch with her best friend, Mary—Marie, actually, but Mary had always sounded better to her in English—one of the girls who worked in the bar.

That night MacShane himself went to check. He smiled nervously at the bartender and fumbled with his glasses, trying to gain time to find out what he had to find out. He ordered a drink on the excuse of his brother's upcoming wedding, despite that he had never been in the bar alone before and didn't have an unmarried brother—but he hadn't thought of any of that, the need for excuses or anything of the kind, since it should have been so easy, just a smile and a glance and a quick count. Except that there were only five registers, just as there should have been and just as, in his heart, he had known there would be. He stood watching for a while longer, finished his drink while cursing the inspectors under his breath, and left—not happy with them for having raised his fears and wasted his time, but nonetheless relieved that he had been right. That couldn't have been it. No one was that stupid—and certainly not a whole goddamn cadre of them.

By midmorning Tuesday, Andrea had almost finished packing their belongings into the last of the trunks, and by noon everything was prepared for the journey to Milwaukee, where he and Filomena would be taking their son as they had planned. It was actually two weeks earlier than planned, but he told his neighbors that it was to beat the snow, since, by all lights, they'd been lucky up to then. And besides, he added, at least at the start they would be staying with her relatives, who had invited them in the first place, so a few days early or late wouldn't make any difference. It would be easier for her earlier, anyway, in her condition.

After they'd said their goodbys and were ready to leave definitively, Andrea made one last trip to the hotel, just, he explained, to say goodby, which he did, and to leave an address, which, of course, he didn't. He took the rear entrance, passed behind the bar, and entered the room off the kitchen, where he removed the few personal belongings he kept beneath the cupboard in the corner, his small Tuscan cigar case and the book of phrases, and then he flung the cloth off of his brainchild—his pride and joy, purchased for *quattro soldi* in a North Clark pawn shop, lacquered and polished and buffed by hand to match the others exactly. He lowered it into the crate to carry it out and lifted it gently into the back of the wagon he'd borrowed from his former employer, the carter, for an hour or two. As he climbed up and made ready to drive off, he nodded once and tipped his hat to the hotel in memory of his friend Marie, then flicked the horse's behind to start them off down the street.

Before departing he had also taken care to reset the clean towels and the bright glasses on the back bar, and he couldn't help but smile when he stuck some extra sawdust into the screw holes, just as he had done every night except on Mondays for the past two months, so that they wouldn't find them at least till the next time they cleaned, and maybe not then, either. While he drove down the street, already feeling, somehow, nostalgic, it didn't even occur to him that he was also removing any need for the young Irish manager to report anything other than the result that the accountant's error, wherever it had occurred, had been righted and that business was once again as good as ever—indeed even better, since, despite the fact that they had unexpectedly lost one of the best men they had ever had, they had taken on a new bartender, German, it seemed from the name, who appeared to be attracting a regular clientele of his own, because in the past few weeks, happily enough, profits had not just returned to normal but actually increased.

In all, Andrea had managed to take home nearly one-sixth of the bar's income for those last months, in addition to his tips and his two regular salaries. When they were settled on their own in Milwaukee, after three months or so of wintering with his wife's relatives, he invested his savings—which, given the times and his circumstances, were considerable—in the purchase of a tavern with living quarters above it for his wife and their boy and the child on the way. The tavern had a small comfortable bar with a kitchen in back, set off the street on a corner in a quiet neighborhood. He was tired now of moving from one place to the next, and he had chosen that spot to put down roots and to raise his family. Milwaukee was a growing town then with a good number of opportunities for anyone willing to take advantage of them, all of which attracted him at first and which continued to please him to the very end, despite the way things worked out. After Andrea's travels and his now well-known, if somewhat mysterious, success, he felt himself, in the words of the saying that he never got right—because of the interference of the other saying, which he could not quite recall, almost the same but with another meaning—for the first if not the only time, "a big fish in a small pond." And he liked the feeling.

The tavern was his, the only possession of substance that he had ever owned, and he threw himself into the venture with a will that showed his newly acquired sense of pride *and* security. During the twenty years or so that he owned the tavern (handling the lone cash register himself and keeping track of all the records, too, each and every night), he presided with dignity and unfailing perspicacity over the dealings, aspirations, and disputes of his clientele, which included just about everyone in the neighborhood except for the youngest children and the women. He listened to his customers' stories of failure or, more often, their tales of success as they played cards or dominoes, or as they worked their way through the huge bowls of steaming pasta—spaghetti and fettuccine mostly, but ravioli with cheese and raisins, too, on the special days when Filomena had the children's help, for by then there were five of them, two sons, first and last, and three daughters in between. At every story's conclusion he would wave his hand magisterially, and, in a voice whose quiet accent only heightened its authority, he would render his opinion. Whether or not his suggestions were followed— or, on the rare occasions when he would offer his influence, personal, or more likely, financial, whether or not his help was actually accepted—within the tavern and neighborhood around it his word went undisputed. Because he was always right. In the course of his dealings he had discovered the secret for success, and he followed its rule religiously. Whenever he didn't know the answer to a question or didn't want to become involved, he simply said so, put down the small black cigar with which he fidgeted but which he had probably not even lit, and went back to polishing the bar and pouring out the wine and beer. His silence wasn't so much golden as enigmatic; but it worked. That was the point as far as he was concerned: it worked. So that if and when he spoke, his word was law. He finally had what he had wanted, the security of the owner and arbiter, the respect of the *padron.* Or so he thought. Because he still hadn't recalled the other saying.

His family, in the meantime, was getting on in the world, too. The girls were quickly becoming old enough so that he had to begin thinking about finding them suitable husbands, and the boys were beginning to make their own way, the older one even working a real job, and a fancy one at that, as a clerk for the city court. It is true that Andrea's influence had helped Michael get the position downtown in the first place. His father's word and reputation had gone before him, before his tall dark forehead and strapping shoulders, and had perhaps opened the door for him, at least a crack if nothing more. But that wasn't all that was necessary. Milwaukee still was not Chicago, later run on influence, bravado, and little else by Torrio and his apprentice Capone and by "Big Bill" Thompson, who got the job of mayor of Chicago by threatening to punch the King of England in the nose and kept it by being, if anything, even less scrupulous than the other two. In fact, in the ambiance of Milwaukee it never occurred to Andrea's son that he might not have to work hard and do well, which he did, since he had never known anything different and since it was clear from the start that merely showing up on time every morning was not enough. In fact, he did better than just well. Despite his youth, his work was extraordinary, and within a year he had been promoted twice. By Michael's twenty-second birthday he was making enough money to be looking for a wife to go along with the importance of his new position and prospects. All of which is why he was so angry the day that Andrea told him what he had no choice but to tell him— never mind his misgivings, and even his doubts—since, until the very moment, two days later, when Michael actually nodded yes, Andrea was still not completely sure that his son would consent to go along with his scheme.

What had transpired was simple, at least in its broad outlines, so simple that it seemed almost innocent, with the logic and inevitability of innocence, even when it was in fact convoluted and confused. Early the month before, at the beginning of the summer, someone had come to Andrea for a contribution. In and of itself there was little significant or novel in this. By then he was approached on almost a monthly basis for all sorts of contributions— some political, some for charities, even once for a local dance club, and he had always given at least something in order to keep up appearances, as well as to insure his friendships should the time come, God forbid, when he might need a little something in return. He actually enjoyed doing this, since he felt, rightly, that the mere fact that they came to him demonstrated his reputation and confirmed his importance in the neighborhood. This time he didn't recognize the man—short, broad-shouldered but not stocky, close-shaven except for the thin moustache, and noticeably well dressed, almost too well for the usual cadger—so, naturally, he asked.

"What's it for?"

The man with the thin moustache smiled and put his hand in the pocket of his wool suit—nice, but too hot for the season, really, Andrea thought—jingling his coins then pulling at the silver key chain on his belt loop, turning it over and over in his hand as he spoke. "It's for insurance," he said. "You know, for your health."

Andrea smiled, but he shook his head. "I've already got insurance."

"This is a new kind," the man said. "There's even a special clause that protects your bar from damage, too."

"But I don't need it," Andrea replied gruffly, because he still hadn't remembered the other saying.

"We think you do," the well-dressed man smiled. "Why don't you think about it? Just take your time and think about it."

"No, I don't need it, and I don't want it," Andrea began to get mad. It was his neighborhood, after all, and he didn't need anyone to tell him how to go about managing his affairs.

"Think about it, that's all," the other counseled with an amicable shrug of the broad shoulders. He let the silver chain drop and slipped his hand in his pocket. "Just *think* about it. *E poi ci rivediamo.*" As he left, Andrea could hear his whistling down the street.

So Andrea thought about it. The answer was still no, but he kept on thinking. When the man with the smile and the silver chain came back, in the cool hour of the evening this time, the man going inside the bar rather than waiting for Andrea on the street, Andrea told him again. The other suggested to forget the money for this year—a special dinner, with the ravioli they had heard so much about, would be more than enough as a sign of his goodwill. So the chance was there for the taking, and Andrea took it. For who? he asked. Special dinner for who? He heard the name, but it meant nothing to him, Italian, probably Neapolitan or Sicilian, but nobody he'd heard of. So he figured he'd try a feint of his own, and he mentioned the name of a politician, an important one downtown, who would not like to hear what was going on. It was just a bluff, but even if it hadn't been, that, it turned out, would have made no difference.

"Who do you think suggested to sell the insurance policies in the first place?" the other laughed, standing back on his heels, the silver chain in his hand, then he leaned over the bar towards him. "And by the way," the man added, as though it were just an afterthought, "we've decided to improve the coverage. Now you get protection from fire, too. It's highly recommended. No extra charge." He turned to go, receding through the room, which at that hour, before the arrival of the real crowd, was still almost empty, and would be for a while longer. When he got to the door, he turned back, smiling, fingering the silver key chain in the dimness. "Think about it," he said. "That's all we ask." And then, except for the whistling, he was gone.

For a while after that Andrea did not have time to think about it any more. Filomena had been sick with a cold, nothing it seemed, a few sniffles, except that it wouldn't go away. Then the coughing started, constant, ever deeper, and by the time they could talk her into going to the hospital, as the doctor had suggested over a week earlier, it was too late. She died the same night, of double pneumonia. Andrea was crushed and incredulous—for weeks he went around mumbling to himself, over and over, blaming himself. From a little cold, who could believe it? How was it possible? Now he and his children were really alone. They would have to fend for themselves without her and everything she did for them.

So when the man with the silver chain came again, Andrea was taken by surprise. The whole matter hadn't even crossed his mind for weeks. The man had come back once in the interim, it is true, but had missed him. This time the man talked without listening to objections, and when he left, turning on his heel, the smile was gone. By then, Andrea had learned the identity of the man's boss—by chance, really, but gradually he had put the pieces of the puzzle together. It was as he had feared. He was an important man, new in town but strong, with money and friends and an entire crew of "salesmen" to dispense his services. What could Andrea do? Every day now he was going about, here, there, and everywhere, asking his friends for advice: he, Andrea Mariagrazia, who had always given *his* opinion rather than the other way around. Now he was reduced to going literally from door to door to ask for help. Even the business at the tavern had fallen off drastically, since, after Filomena's death, his hours were so irregular that no one could tell when it might be open or closed, and no matter what anyone said, he would not let the girls or his young son take over for him.

The suggestions he got were varied. Most of the younger men urged him to stand up for himself, to use his influence if necessary, but at all costs to refuse to be pushed this way and that like a cork in the water. The older men counseled caution, but with less conviction and no offers of assistance. He had to do something, he knew that. Still, he would not pay, of that he was sure. His stubbornness was not a result of faith in the law or lack of money. Nor was his predicament any different from that of many others. In the course of his one-man canvass, he had heard of any number of owners and businessmen in the neighborhood and elsewhere who had been asked to pay, some, it was said, a great deal more than he. It was just the idea of it. He had always been his own man, the only one to decide his fate, and he would not pay fealty to anyone. The tavern was his, and Filomena's, no one else's. Why should he buy protection he didn't need? It was all a sham. He considered for a moment, not without bitterness, that perhaps this was now part and parcel of owning a tavern, or maybe of owning anything, so that they should put it in the bill of sale. But the thought repelled him. Besides, people like that had never bothered him before, so why should they start now?

In the end he took the suggestion of one of his friends, and purchased two dogs, the first, half collie and half shepherd, to protect the house, and the second, a lovely little dalmatian that won his heart despite its uneven disposition and finicky tastes, to protect the bar, since, according to the seller, it couldn't fail to warn them at the first smell of smoke. With the dogs on the watch, he began to feel all right again, almost as though the old days were back and his troubles were over. Three weeks later, when he came to open the tavern in the afternoon, Andrea noticed that the door was unlocked, even though he had closed it himself the afternoon before. There was no sign of anyone breaking in. Inside, everything was exactly as he had left it, except for the dogs' bodies visible in the half-light from behind the bar, one piled across the other, with a set of match sticks tied on a string around the dalmatian's neck.

Close to panic, he rushed to one of his oldest and most trusted friends, Giovanni Ranallo, a man schooled in the old ways, whose family he had known since even before coming to America, and who already knew something of his predicament. After asking for his promise of secrecy, Andrea told him what had happened. Giovanni listened, considered—as in better days Andrea himself had done—and at last told him that there was nothing he could do, not a thing. It didn't seem as if these people were going to go away. If Andrea wanted to stay, he would probably have to pay them or others like them sooner or later, whether he liked it or not. Perhaps it would be better to pay sooner. But all in all, he couldn't say, nor, really, could he help. But, he added, there was someone who could—perhaps. Giovanni leaned back in his chair and produced a pair of cigars, holding one out to Andrea. The two of them were by no means, Giovanni reminded him, the only ones in America from Castel del Sangre. Did he remember Nicola DeMartino from his childhood? Andrea nodded, though he had to admit that he had not kept up the ties as he should have. Giovanni lit his cigar and paused to reflect. Nicola would be coming for one of his visits to the city in a few days. He had a family now, too. Giovanni leaned forward with a glint in his eye: three boys and a girl, if he remembered correctly.

But what could Nicola DeMartino—who did not even live in Milwaukee but in some small town hundreds of miles to the north—possibly do to help him now? That's what Andrea wanted to know. And when he saw him two days later, in the back room of Gianni's house on Myrtle Street, that was the first thing he asked.

At the start, Andrea was skeptical. It is true, he could leave Milwaukee without difficulty—indeed the thought had already occurred to him, with Filomena gone, and his family nearly grown, and his position in the community no longer the same. If he did, he would not go back to Chicago or to New York, that was certain. Those places were part of his past now, and he knew it, not of his future. Moreover, he knew that there was no guarantee—probably just the opposite—that what was happening to him now would not happen again, only worse, in Chicago or New York or perhaps in any place like them. Because at last—too late—he had remembered the other saying: "The big fish is the big fish and the little fish is the little fish, and the big fish eats the little fish." And it has nothing to do with the size of the pond.

"But why?" Michael asked too, later that evening. "What's it called? New what? Why *there*?"

"Because that's where the family is. It's as simple as that," Andrea answered with a show of bluster that would perhaps have proved convincing under different circumstances. "There are others, too, of course," he went on. "From Italy and New York and Chicago, even some from right here, the Granellos, for example, your old friends, you'll see. And now they'll all be your relatives..."

"Our—"

"It's perfect for all of you," Andrea continued. "Except for Jackie. There are three boys, just right. But only one girl, so Jackie can come and work until he's old enough to—"

"To what?" Michael interrupted, trying to contain himself until he had heard the rest. "Old enough to what?"

"Why, to marry, of course," Andrea replied. "What else have we been talking about?"

After all, it had been an even trade, and a good one. Nicola got three more than respectable dowries, and in exchange they got the land. So all they had to do was to sell the tavern, a deal that Giovanni could take care of for them, and move.

"But who in hell is this Nicola?" Michael started to lose his patience .

"Now you listen to me," Andrea yelled back. "Where is your respect, talking to me like that? When we're talking, you listen—I talk. Understand? You might be a big man downtown in that fancy office. But as far as the family is concerned, you're still a kid with milk in his mouth and shit in his ass—don't forget it—and especially when you're talking about your father-in-law."

Andrea sat back with a sigh, exasperated but relieved, too, now that it was all out and Michael had not actually said no. At least now Andrea had told him, even if he didn't like it. The girls would be less trouble. He smiled at Michael in apology, but his son just stared back at him, the incredulity and outrage still on his face. "It's a nice name," Andrea tried. "New Providence. I think we're going to like it."

"New for who?" Michael said bitterly, as he headed out the door and down the stairs to the street of the only town he had ever known, or, until then, had ever planned on knowing. What a fine reward for his work, he thought, with the resentment welling up inside him, a fine result.

But in the end he had no choice, he knew that, too, so when they left Milwaukee behind and headed north, he went with them. He couldn't take the activity of the city with him, but he took the drive and the desire to work at something and succeed that now was ingrained in him, part of him, and maybe always had been. The arena had changed, and about that he *was* bitter, but the game wasn't over, and couldn't be, even if he wished it so. Which, anyway, he didn't. At first the new town seemed strange to him, but eventually he got used to it, used to seeing nothing but relatives every time he went in to buy seed or nails or fencewire, and even to having new ones he'd never heard of before popping up at every turn, so that the clerks at the bank or those who sold him whatever it was he needed at the general store would end up giving him their—and his—family lineage before he could walk back to the wagon and escape to the safety of his own fields and home— his, not theirs.   Or at least so he hoped.

In point of fact, even though the situation was disconcerting at first, it was really not so different from the town his father had known in his childhood. Before leaving Milwaukee, Andrea had agreed with Nicola DeMartino that Michael's three sisters would take Nicola's three boys as husbands, and that Michael would marry Nicola's only daughter, Maria. Nicola got the three dowries (in cash, from the sale of Andrea's tavern), to be split among the boys. Michael got his dowry in land, given to him in faith but with the title in Andrea's name, just in case, since Andrea still didn't trust other people's methods of accounting. The entire set of exchanges worked out perfectly well on paper, as Andrea had insisted, and in practice, with the exception of the discomfort that Michael began to experience somewhere about the seventh or eighth time, still in the first week, that a teller or a farmer or even the friendly but loquacious clerk in the little local post office would introduce himself as his cousin and began with great enthusiasm—after taking a deep breath—to retrace the entire family tree.

The money left over from the sale of the tavern—once the expenses had been paid for the move and for three fourths of the cost of the weddings and the huge party afterwards, with the cakes and wine and flowers and the clothes and accessories right down to the sugared almonds to throw—went to purchase the wood and tools to build the house for Andrea and Michael and his bride, and to begin to farm the land. All of which was fine, except for one detail. Neither Michael, as was to be expected from a city boy, nor Andrea, as no one would have thought, knew a thing about farming. Andrea had simply been too young when he left Italy to have learned anything other than the most rudimentary procedures for using a scythe and herding goats, only one of which was of much use on a dairy farm in New Providence. When Michael realized what this meant, he lost not just his composure but also his voice, as was to be expected after several hours of shouting at the fields and the rocks and even the trees. As soon as the tempest had passed and Andrea saw his chance, he began to explain, but his words were useless. Once more Michael felt betrayed, and this time he swore it would be the last. But that still didn't do him any good. He had a house and a farm and a family now, but he knew he couldn't keep any of them unless he could learn the occupation which had been forced on him, and to which he had submitted only out of filial obedience. In the end, after the explosion, he had no alternative but to deal with the situation as it was, not as he had hoped it might be. He had already learned that much. So he swallowed his pride and taught himself: or, more accurately, he let Maria teach him.

She saved him then, really, at least that once. Whatever happened afterwards could not tarnish that. Of course, the people in town or his neighbors on the little dairy farms scattered all around them *could* have told him how to set up his fields and rotate them, what wheat grew best on flatland and how to plan the corn rows so that they would take right on the hillsides, how to decide which trees should be cut from the clump of hardwood at the back of his land to help the growth of the others, how to set up the fences for the cow run to herd them into the barn, which kind of manure made the best fertilizer, how many horses, cows, and hogs to buy at first and how much and what variety of seed, and what the cost of chickens was at the current market (though no one could have told him what the smell was like—some things he had to learn for himself, and did). They could have told him, but they didn't, for the simple reason that he wouldn't ask. This whole venture had not been his idea, but he decided that if he was going to go through with it—which he was—he was going to be the best at it, the best there was, absolutely and bar none. Which meant he had to know everything already. Which, of course, he didn't, but which, fortunately for him and for Andrea, too, she did. Some of her people had been there since the local timber industry had given over to farming in the 1880's—picking tiny sites for their farms, like the ones they knew from Italy and weren't afraid of—Nicola being only the latest in a long line of immigrants, which meant that they knew what to do and how to do it, and so did she.

So she told him, raising her hand to cover the smile that indicated not so much that she wanted to be coaxed as that it was his role now to coax her, in order for her to be able to tell him. Whatever she could not put easily in words, she showed him. The few things that she had never seen, or just plain didn't remember, she asked her relatives about, but quietly, indirectly, with the smile that remained faint despite the dark eyes shining, while she asked her questions with an interest that she kept oblique at best, so as not to expose Michael to their growing—though, thank God, still silent—doubts. In the course of the first two or three years of their lives together, working side by side every day except Sunday, unlike the Swedes and Germans to the south of them, who didn't need their women in the fields, or the Calabrians to the west, who wouldn't let them out of the house to be seen by anyone, she managed to teach him everything he had to know to start up the farm—and so his new life—and to make it go. But more than that, the most extraordinary part of it, really, even beyond maintaining the house and cooking and keeping the old man happy, too, to the extent that she could, was that she managed to do all of it without ever having to acknowledge to anyone what she was doing, even to herself, since that would have meant making him acknowledge it, too, that she was doing something other than what wives normally do for their men in the everyday course of events, and that she was doing it without any expectation of praise or gratitude or even of recognition. Because that would have ruined it, sunk the entire project like a stone, both for him and for her, not to mention the family that was soon on the way. Even though she never permitted herself to say or actually to think that such was the case, she knew it, instinctively, and in fact had known it all along, ever since she'd first seen him, the darkly handsome man of medium height, though he looked taller, with the ramrod-proud back and the glint in his eyes of something that was not quite anger or sorrow but that was close to both, with enough defiance added into the bargain that people would know, if they were close to him and clever enough to see it, not to cross him if they could avoid it and not to betray him at any price. Only Andrea had managed to do that and escape unscathed, and even he had now had his last chance at it. Never again, Michael had sworn to himself, after the cold journey north to God-knows-where, followed by the shock of his father's ignorance not only of the land itself but even of what to do with it once they had it. All right, he had thought to himself, they were there and that was that. But never again.

On the other hand, the fact that he didn't mention it to her, his need, his debt, or she to him meant that he really had acknowledged it. He knew, and she knew that he knew. He could tell it in her smile and in the music of her voice, the notes of which came to him across the broad green fields in the rhythm that never seemed to tire, neither in the scorching heat of midday nor in the cool of the darkened barn in the early evening, nor even at the day's end, in the warm, bright kitchen. For the moment, at least, and actually for a long time after that, it was a bond between them, their knowledge, that was protected and nurtured in the silence of their accord.

The result of his work, after three years, was the best small herd of dairy cows in the county. Everything they worked for now, from the field corn for silage, to the green pasture land, to the single bull (but no chickens, at least not after the first year), was geared to one end: getting the cows to produce the milk that went to the dairy to be tested and credited and shipped. Things went so well for him that when his brother Jackie and his young wife both died in the pneumonia epidemic that swept the county in the early 1930's, Michael could afford, at Maria's suggestion, to take in their only son, Joseph, eventually Gianni and O.B.'s father, to live and work with them as their own. On Maria's advice—in part out of her knowledge of him and his habits and in part out of a shrewd guess—he had bought the small, fawn-colored guernseys and jerseys rather than the big, docile black and white holsteins, with the result that even though their operation was smaller and their product less voluminous than normal, the butterfat content was the highest anywhere around. And it was the butterfat that the dairy measured and paid for. He got more money for his milk than anyone else, and soon after the other farmers were talking about him no longer as an ignorant city boy but now with respect and even a trace of jealousy. Nevertheless, he did not convert completely to the accepted ways of his new life. He retained enough of the old habits and interests that the others commented on his success despite his oddities, since he was the only one in that part of the county who managed to run and work a farm himself and still never get down to care for the cows until well after 9:00 a.m. in the morning. What they didn't know—and what probably would have surprised them even more—was the cause for what seemed to everyone else such strange hours. It wasn't so much that he got up late (which he did) but that he turned in late—at least by their standards. After supper and the evening chores, with everyone else asleep in the quiet house, he would go through the newspapers—one from the Twin Cities, as many others did, too, and a pair from Milwaukee, as only he did—searching eagerly for news of the world he had left. Later still—as he sat enthroned on the huge old rocker that he had set next to the first thing he had bought when he could keep a dollar or two from the profits on his account at the dairy, the deeply polished radio, which was now tuned to the voice of the world coming to him in the stillness of the night—he would rock and nod off and awaken and rock some more, listening all the while to the sounds of the life he had been forced to leave and to which someday, not soon he knew, but, he swore, someday, he would return. So on into the night he listened and rocked and slept and listened, because when the chance came, he wanted to be ready.

Andrea, on the other hand, didn't even bother with the Milwaukee newspapers. Why should he? At last he had everything he had ever wanted: a comfortable home and family, a place to spend his afternoons (Sino's, the local tavern, which was just like his old place had been in Milwaukee, except that since he didn't own it but only presided over it he no longer had to worry about the cash register and the records). He still had an audience for his pronouncements on any and all subjects, because everyone in the Italian community in town knew he was the one to ask. He had come from the world of the city, yet if he wanted to he could speak to them in their own language, and so every afternoon he would sit in the warmth of the back room, its dimness traversed by the glowing tips of the Tuscan cigars, as he played dominoes or cards with the bright Neapolitan decks and dispensed his advice: just like the old days, only better.

Whenever he tired of his role as village patriarch, which happened occasionally, he would return home to indulge himself in his most recent delight, the game that, like *bocce*, required patience and skill but that, as he quickly discovered, could be pursued and enjoyed just as well by a sole player, independently of anyone else, enjoyed even better, really, because when you play alone you never lose. He would stand at one end of the pit along the side barn they had built to keep the horses and their feed, dressed in the neatly pressed shirt and the dark felt hat, the black stogy protruding from his mouth as he turned the shoe in his hand, with half of his attention on the spike at the far end and the other half on whatever else came to mind: Italy, the new Ford, his supper, whatever. Then he would pitch the shoes and listen for the clank! clank! and walk to the other end to gather them up and repeat the process, back and forth the entire afternoon, all by himself. That is, until one evening eight years later, when the youngest of his grandsons, Joseph, Jackie's boy, in the midst of bringing the cows in, saw the old man pitching the shoes and heard the clank! clank! coming toward him across the pasture as they hit the post, and couldn't help but think: why *just* him? Because he knew he could learn, too. And what's more, he knew that when he did, he could beat him.

So he did: learn, that is. For the rest, Joseph would wait. He practiced in what little free time he had between school, slopping the hogs, cutting beans, and whatever else they had him do as the youngest and weakest, not to mention the closest to the ground. He didn't really have spare time as such, since at the suggestion of the schoolteacher, who had noticed how quick he was, he had already started sending away for and receiving the fliers and pamphlets that would tell him how to: how to be a door-to-door salesman in his spare time, how to be a part-time librarian, how to be an inventor, or an actor, or even a fortune hunter. Every evening—except for Saturdays, when he and his brothers would sit on the living room floor listening to the radio which they were certain had been bought specifically for the purpose of getting the Barn Dance from Chicago every Saturday night—when he was supposed to be doing homework he had in fact prepared in a few minutes on the sly during class, he passed his time pouring over the pamphlet's slick pages, not because he actually intended to be any of those things, now or ever, but just because he had a passion to know about the world beyond his everyday circuit around the paths of the farm and the road to the brick schoolhouse and back.

The effects of all the books and pamphlets were not, he realized too late, entirely good. Among other things, they earned him the reputation as a sissy. In order to counter it, one of his older brothers, Dominic, got him to pick fights with his adversaries instead of listening to their taunts, and then, once the fights were over and he had won, Dominic would go around to the older boys standing about watching to collect the change he had bet on the outcome, yelling and threatening on his own and even using his fists if need be to help collect. Just from looking at Joseph, no one could guess his strength and especially his speed, but Dom knew from his own experience, and so he pocketed all the money every time, as long as their game lasted, which, in the small community, wasn't long. When it was over, in part as a normal recompense and in part at Joseph's insistence, Dom showed him how to hold the shoes and toss them, with the three-quarter turn in the air so that they would stick and not be deflected when they hit the post, and Joseph began to practice, with the idea of beating the old man instead of just his classmates.

Every Sunday, after they had dressed and paraded off to the church in the countryside between the farms where all their relatives went with their families to hear mass and to show off their clothes and children while they exchanged comments on the week's weather and events, he would return home and put his clothes away, changing back into his dungarees and making sure he got the shirt—Dominic's, to tell the truth—that had the arms that were too loose, but that, just so, were perfect for tossing the shoes with the smooth, rhythmic motion and the full sweep that Dom had shown him, and Joseph would pit himself against the old man, with his old man's smile and clever eyes, and naturally, Joseph would lose.

That occurred each and every Sunday in good weather for two years. Then one day in late autumn, with the wind up and the dark clouds racing, Andrea felt the tightness in his legs, but not from the cold, and even the horseshoes themselves seemed heavy and hard, deflecting like rocks as they hit the post and bounced away, and when they went to add up the score Joseph had won.

After that, to his amazement—though not to Andrea's—Joseph kept winning, every Sunday, week after week. Andrea was more than willing to shift from champion to mentor, which he did immediately and without reservation. "Here," he would tell the boy, yanking his arm up higher and showing him how to put the strength of his legs into the motion exactly the same way each time. "Like this. That way we both do well." Already the look in the old man's eyes had changed. He was getting old, he couldn't deny it. But somehow, the energy in the boy made his own aging more of a necessity to be accepted than a failing, part of a long, gradual process rather than a precipitous decline, and he respected the boy for it, because at last Andrea felt that he knew what time was—that the boy had taught him what no one else had been able to, what he had never been able to see in Michael even though, or perhaps since, the example was right under his nose, or perhaps it was because the boy's drive was a natural grace, given rather than something he had had to work at. It was the same energy that made the boy declare a few years later, irrevocably, once and for all, his desire to be a lawyer (after seeing the respect in the eyes of the men and women standing in the churchyard as they looked at the newcomer and whispered "avvocato: uomo di sostanza"), and then began studying to that end, after taking care to fail Latin and thus silence all talk of him fulfilling the expected role of the youngest son by becoming a priest. And it was the same drive that led him eventually to the university in the state capital, though first to the state college in White Rock, where he worked in the dormitory kitchen cleaning pots and pans at night and filled all of his remaining hours with study, except for his occasional attendance at the Saturday night parties at Mrs. Hillroy's Young Ladies' Home and Boarding House, where he met one of Mrs. Hillroy's girls who waited table in exchange for a room to share with three others, and talked with her exactly four times before asking her to marry him. A proposal which she refused, of course; but in regard to which, after a respectable time, she at last reversed herself—despite the fact that he was Italian and she was not, and, more to the point, that he was Catholic and she was Lutheran. She consented only on certain specific yet convoluted conditions, which he in his turn accepted at once, since he didn't really care one way or the other but only wanted to love her, in every sense of the word, and to start in at it as soon as possible.

Her family was certainly more understanding of and enthusiastic about the odd marriage conditions than his was. They had come to that part of the state from Pennsylvania, where they had been for over three generations, so when they came to Wisconsin, they were already Americans, not Germans or immigrants at all, but Americans, period, with American ways and customs and language, due to the fact that they had never known anything else. They were Lutherans and deeply religious, but they were also experienced enough to know that there were other religions with different beliefs and rituals of their own and with followers just as devout, with whom they had no choice but to coexist, even though all the others were wrong.

Johann Britzen had settled in that part of Wisconsin because he was a farmer—a dairy farmer and a good one, but a gentleman, too. He wanted to make sure his sons knew how to read as well as farm, so he took upon himself the task of reading aloud to them each evening from his "two authors," Shakespeare and God. He was surprisingly impartial. Every once in a while on a Friday he would pause to place his finger on a page of *Macbeth* or *A Midsummer Night's Dream* or, if it were a Sunday, on II Corinthians or Revelations, and, with a smile and the comment that he was reminded of a certain passage from the other, he would begin quoting as confidently and as accurately as though he were indeed still reading rather than reciting from memory. During these sessions, as always, he insisted that they listen but not that they take to emulating either his manner or his interests. Indeed, when William, the eldest son, decided to become a lumberman—a venture that took him north to Duluth and then back to the Hines camps, where the work taught him to estimate the number of board feet in a tree at sight, to love the timber itself, and to hate the backbreaking work of cutting it, while paying and feeding him well and costing him exactly one and one half inches of the first finger on his left hand—the old man nodded and did not object. Not just, it must be said, because he was willing to be reasonable but also because he knew his son—knew that he wasn't a quitter but that, even if he did have a headful of odd ideas, he wasn't a fool, either—and knew he would be back before the year was out and ready to settle down on his own place, for which the old man had already picked the spot, next to his, below the rim of maples, so he'd always have the memory there to see, if he wanted it, green in the summer and scarlet in the fall, then stark, massive brown, as though actually standing in wait through the winter and preparing for the sap to run in the spring.

When William returned to the rolling pasture lands from Duluth he brought something else with him besides his wounded hand and a wallet full of cash. He brought her up to the house, smiling proudly like an explorer in a new land, and introduced her to his father: "Meet your new daughter," he said and pushed her forward. And in fact, the old man did treat her and her baby girl more like blood kin than in-laws.

She had come from Duluth, where William had met first her brother then her and her child by a deceased husband, a cardsharp—and a good one—her brother had once said, and a dead shot with his smooth, bone-handled German pistol. But the one time William broached the subject with her, she caught her breath and looked so strange that he resolved to himself never to ask again, and never did. Her family was Swedish, but they had been in America long enough to have lost all memory of Lund, whence her Grandfather had come in flight from the military conscription in the early years of the century. He had taken the boat across the North Atlantic to New York, then around the Great Lakes past Cleveland and Detroit before docking in Duluth. There he heard of fabulous open lands free for the taking, and he headed west. Sometime in the late fall, he made it to Minot, North Dakota, where, with his hands stiff in his pockets and his shoes frozen to the floor of the drafty train station—they told him it would be cold, but not that cold—he saw a poster made up by the Canadian government offering a fare of a penny a mile to anyone going west on the Canadian Pacific. With the eleven dollars and fifty cents he had left in his pocket he could go a thousand miles and still have enough for a good meal and a bottle of whiskey. Or, he thought, he could give up, turn back, head home. After half of the bottle of whiskey, feeling warm and surprisingly cheerful, he decided to take the Canadians up on their offer: better a landowner than a soldier, and better alive and moving than whatever the alternative might be.

He arrived in Saskatchewan the next evening, still warmed by the heat of the train and the liquor, but suddenly cold again as he hauled his suitcase onto the empty platform. From then on, he knew, he would have to work to keep warm. He took a job as a clerk for the winter—cutting bolts of dry goods and lifting sacks of flour while listening and talking to the storekeeper's children to learn English—and then as a field hand with the first arrival of good weather. He staked his claim on the land he'd picked, black loam above red clay, with the prairie grass knee-high and rolling, near a spring. He filed on it in the late summer, as soon as he had money for supplies, in plenty of time, he thought, though even before he'd finished digging the cabin's foundation the cold weather was coming on, so that at night he had to pull the boards over the hole in order to keep the snow off of him while he slept. In the morning he would remove the boards and brush himself off, thanking the Lord that he hadn't either frozen or burned to death from the little stove he kept in the corner, and then continued sawing and nailing. He had the cabin up in four days even though the studdings had been wrong, and the roof turned out to be so low at one end that he had to stoop whenever he moved about. For food he had his flour and sugar and all the rabbits he could hit—if he didn't tear them apart with the heavy Swedish army rifle he'd inherited from his dead brother—and once, out of the blue, when he wasn't prepared, a young antelope, the last of the herd, which he killed in desperation by flinging himself at it and finding the artery with his jackknife. Exhausted, but exhilarated by his luck, he dragged it back and flung it up on the roof to keep the carcass from the wolves that howled outside the whole night through.

By the next fall he had a crop—not much of one, to be sure, but enough to harvest—and he even managed to start a little garden, so he'd have fresh vegetables to keep up his health, just like they'd had in Lund before the military conscription (and the subsequent consumption) that had taken his brother. Inside of five years he'd made enough of a profit off his wheat to sell the land—the flat prairie he'd worked and harvested but never cared about one way or another, since even though it was generous, it was just too flat—and returned to Duluth, where he stayed long enough to find a woman and court and marry her, then headed downriver till he got to Bay City and saw the bluffs, exactly like Lund in miniature, and stopped.

He built the house by himself on the one he called Törson bluff, for his dead brother, a full three-story frame house with six fireplaces and a widow's walk on top, just like in Sweden, and retired on his earnings to watch his wife raise his family while he sat before the great stone hearth, looking out over the bay, blue-green and grey in summer, white in winter, and drinking his whiskey. He let his eldest daughter help his wife take care of the other children—twelve in all—and kept to himself, with only the incessantly bright light in the icy gaze to let on that the fire was still in him. It still seemed alive years later even after they'd found him keeled over in a drift at the bottom of the bluff, having managed to get considerably drunker than Noah had ever dreamed of, the eyes still bright with that strange incandescent glow and the smile yet on his face, though by then it might have been rigor mortis rather than drunkenness that had put the smile there since it had been two days before the snow stopped and they could really look for him at all, finding him only because the same wind that had covered him over yielded the body from its temporary white grave. After that the family began to split up. By two years later, lightning had taken the frame house at the top of the bluff, leaving only the stone hearth. The older sisters and a brother had gone to Minneapolis and St. Paul, and the middle two to Duluth, where William met them, making a friend of the brother, and, of the sister, with the clear blue eyes and quick smile, his wife.

From the beginning there were distinctions between the Swedes and the Germans, but one thing was unquestionable: they were all Americans—so much so that none of them ever felt any other way. Life in Crooked Falls was simply not like that in New Providence, where the Italian part of the community felt the constant, undeniable difference between them and everyone else—a difference that, to be sure, was further subdivided as Abruzzese, Calabrian, and Sicilian, but that, no matter what minor internal refinements were made, would not disappear. William Britzen built up his and his father's farm just outside of Crooked Falls and never suspected any distrust or bitterness from the rest of the community or anything other than approval and acceptance, for the simple reason that that was all he had ever experienced.

Not that life was easy. In point of fact, he was required to do the work of two, since his father, in response to his return from the lumber camps, had decided to retire—happily, but retire nonetheless—to his cabin amid the maples, so as to spend his days walking and checking the trees and his evenings reading, in his north-woods version of the gentleman farmer. In time there was a second child, another girl—his this time—and so more work to do. As the years went on and the old gentleman got older and weaker, William had to do not only the farming but also the work with the maples, sugaring off every March inside the hut as chill as death where he could see his breath rising and little else while he sat beside the huge dog with the sweet tooth, part setter and part lab, boiling the sap down to syrup, some to be distributed as gifts and repayment and some to be sold. By then he had built up a tidy, self-sufficient operation, so that the profits from the syrup and the cows' milk and his wife's sewing fed back into the purchase of seed and equipment to make the fields produce food for sale and fodder and winter silage. With the help of his neighbors, who shared their equipment and labor at harvest time in exchange for his, and who helped him pass the winter with their stories and jokes in return for his, the entire farming unit, within the larger unit of the farming community, was self-sufficient and self-perpetuating, like a wheel spinning happily within a larger wheel that, in turn, was spun by it.

Even as the times changed and his type of farming became rarer and rarer—until most of the old neighbors had died off or moved away, after selling out to larger holders or to cooperatives, so that almost no one actually lived on the land anymore—he kept to the old ways on the little farm below the hill topped by the strip of maples, branded bright red each and every fall, without fail. He could watch the others leave or change, could even feel the changes all around him, but he would not submit. He would still go north with the old man and their remaining neighbors to get his deer every fall, toward the end even positioning the old gentleman—with enough rye and snuff to keep him occupied at least for a time—near the edge of a clearing and, along with Jake Arndt to pick the spot, and one or two others, driving the game with his thirty-two Remington through the deep woods toward the road and into the sights of the old man's rifle. During the rest of the year, William would check on him every morning, taking the path bordering the fields to the hill and then, with a kick to get the leaves and brush out of the way, up to the cabin, where most likely the reading light from the night before would still be lit. He would check to see that the old man was in the chair with the book folded on his lap, or up and about, or, less likely, in bed (where, if that were the case, the special light he'd affixed to the headboard would still be on and one of his four or five authors—since by then, to the concern of the feverishly devout community, he had added not only Milton but also Melville and even Dickens—propped on the otherwise empty pillow beside him). This, regularly, until one morning in April, when the sugaring was done and the work in the fields lay waiting for his return after the winter's absence.

William walked the path along the pasture that lay silvered in the morning dew, colored momentarily now like the blanket of the bed he'd left too early, and entered the woods. The going was harder there, uphill, and he stopped for a moment to get his breath amidst the morning stillness. Through the trees he heard a partridge begin drumming, and he thought, regretfully, no, no time for that now. A bird twittered in the branches high up toward the sun and flew off; William started up again, whistling. He let himself into the dark cabin as usual and entered the main room, where beneath the rack of guns the fireplace stood empty, without even an ember despite the April chill, and everything was still once again, but not like the woods had been: this was too still, he knew that. And, contrary to what he was accustomed to, there was no light anywhere. Through the window he saw the bird again, twittering, and then watched as it flew between the trees, upward, and vanished. He found him twenty minutes later, his back propped against the base of the oak where he'd been quietly surprised, the book on his lap open to Genesis, his thumb marking the verse where he was to pick up again, though he could have recited the passage in his mind as easily as read it. He had no gun with him. Even his face looked peaceful, as though poised in the instant of reflection and at the same time extending that instant, in the way that in time had become characteristically his, so that thought, in the peaceful arc of its fulfillment, could become understanding.

They buried him in the clearing beside the cabin, next to the grave that had been awaiting him. William carved the cross to match the other, thinking of everything, all the while, in just the reverse of what was actually true and happening, by imagining his father still alive and then dwelling on his own death. Of course, he got it all wrong, as was probably just as inevitable. He couldn't know that unlike the old man, he would not go suddenly but gradually, by steps—even though he would try, and to a surprising extent actually succeed—to keep the signs of those steps concealed by furtively administering to his own care, pilfering his wife's nitroglycerin pills from the medicine cabinet (which she, ironically, did not really need) and making sure that Drew was never further than arm's reach once the pains in his chest had become so frequent and obvious that he even had to let Drew or Jake Arndt drive, though still not admitting it was anything other than an occasional missed step on account of his glasses, and certainly not fainting, since men didn't do that, and that's all there was to it. In the last two years, when he really did fear the worst, he would abruptly ask to see his grandchildren for the oddest reasons and at the strangest times, regardless of season, since each time he was sure there would be no other, and the fear seized him that he would never see them again. On the other hand, he didn't alter any of his activities, from casting for trout in the Rush River and for bass and northerns on Green Lake to hunting partridge and pheasant with Jake Arndt to chasing after jackrabbits in the snow with his .22. And above all, thinking to save them from the knowledge and pain of his condition, he never told them about it, with the result, although he couldn't have realized it then, that what was in fact gradual and inevitable appeared to them, when it came, as not just unexpected but also inexplicable. Nor could he have known that the coincidence, in another county, of a traffic accident and the death of a big black dog chasing down a dusty road with the apparent desire to protect a group of boys from a machine that had posed no threat to them in the first place would combine, in his grandchild's imagination, with the shock of his own seemingly sudden passing as the image and then the prolonged obsession of crime, reason and reflection to the contrary notwithstanding, so that, despite his own personal kindness—indeed his total and singular inability to create or deal with evil in any form, or even with the day-to-day, worldly mutations of chance and time, or old Sol, as he called it—he would live on indestructibly in his grandson's mind, somewhere behind the figure of magic and benevolence, as the grey, shadowy and finally unintelligible body of guilt and fear. But all that, as he put the finishing touches on his carving, was years away; and so he reflected on his own death, on its peace and serenity and what he took to be, in his mind, its promise of absolute finality.

After the service and the hymns, he and his wife and the two little girls walked back together down to the house below, silent, reflective. William continued to work the farm as a unit among the adjacent ones of their neighbors, all working together at the crucial times of the year, in the spring with the sugaring and planting and in the fall with the harvesting and butchering. In the winter evenings and on weekends, they played cards and listened to the radio. While the others listened to the talk and the music, the two girls, Helen and Jane, listened not for news of the world but for the romance of the voice from another world, a world far away and unalterably different from theirs, yet which mirrored theirs in their minds, so that Prince Edward and his bride were at once uncannily heroic and tragic yet, in the same instant, in the announcers' words and voices, just like them, in love just as they would be too, they knew, because that was what love and the world were like and because no one, not their mother or friends and certainly not their father, would ever have thought to tell them anything different.

Helen went away to the state college in White Rock with one of the neighbor girls, patiently expecting love like that, and in the meantime reading the assigned books and attending classes, and waiting table at Mrs. Hillroy's. At first she had been afraid that college would be too hard and White Rock too big for her, but soon she had overcome her fears and settled into the rhythms of the college's life. She had been there for six months, managing to keep her dreams and most of her ideas about the world intact, when she met Joseph. The first thing that struck her was how different he was. These differences and his deep, demanding impulsiveness attracted her, but they scared her, too. Still, once they had met and talked, the distance between them seemed less each day, the distinctions almost trivial in comparison with the strong, close friendship they built with each other, so close and strong in fact that it began to consume all their thoughts and conversations. Gradually it shut out their other friends and even their families and relatives, since they agreed on so many things together and on so few things, now, with anyone else. They even agreed on the foods they liked, though *that*, at the beginning, was not so easy, especially for her. Years later, she could still remember the first taste she'd ever had of the Italian sausage seasoned and cured on the back porch of the Mariagrazia's farmhouse, as she bit into it and tasted the sweet heavy meat, with everyone around the table watching as she tried to chew and smile at the same time, her dark blue eyes suddenly watery and her blond hair trembling with the shock that must have shown on her face as she hit the first of the red pepper and the old man looked up from his ravioli and the full plate of scrap-ends, beside his personal jar of the dried and grated firecrackers, and smiled too, nodding his head in approval. "Well now, that's all right."

    And it was, too, since after the first surprise—and the realization that the inside of her mouth might never be the same again—she got to the point that she not only tolerated but actually liked them, at least now and then, and provided there was plenty of water within her grasp. In the few instances that they didn't see eye to eye, he always ceded, if only temporarily, waiting and letting her take her time, much as had her father, who had demonstrated in so many ways, despite his attempts at concealment, that she was his favorite, from taking her with him on the wagon and later the tractor, to bringing her the strong young lambs, to choosing her as his partner in all the picking contests—which in point of fact wasn't just favoritism, since her hands were quicker and, despite their slender, even delicate appearance, stronger than any of the others. It broke her father's heart, naturally, to see her go. But he had no choice when he saw that, once the delay of the war was over and his future son-in-law was back, ready to begin the years of study for the bar he'd only just been contemplating when the army had called him—taking him from White Rock to Madison to New York and then Sicily, London, Paris and at last back home—they still seemed, despite everyone's predictions of doom, to agree on everything. Everything, that is, but the staging of the wedding itself.

"Two weddings," he protested in amazement. "Why two?"

"One for me—us—and one for you," she answered simply. "For your side."

"I don't get it," he said. "We don't have sides."

"One Lutheran and one, uh, Roman. You see," she said rather than asked, knowing he had to see, in fact, had seen, probably from the start, because they really had been that close.

At first, he went along without a fight. What was the use, he thought, when she would most likely change her mind anyway or maybe forget all about it. But then he hadn't figured on the intransigency of his own Church or on the strength of her will. In New Providence, Father McCormick, a kindly old priest, but unfortunately a stickler for ceremony, insisted not only on giving them the formal rites of instruction but also on having her sign the pages pledging to raise their children in the Church. Even worse, he had her read the document aloud with him to make sure she understood it all, which she did, to her frustration and humiliation and, in the end, to the priest's regret as well. Because the placid old man could not stand to see women cry, much less while they were shaking their head and yelling at him through their tears. For her this was serious business, and she wasn't going to give in without mounting a protest. In the end, of course, she did consent, her signature firm, if somewhat stained from the renewed gush of tears, but only after a wait of three weeks, and only after having been assured by her Lutheran relatives that, no, she wasn't being extreme in her reaction to what the Antichrist in Rome and his personal representative in New Providence were trying to do to her and her children—who weren't born or even conceived yet—and that, yes, they would certainly help her arrange a Lutheran ceremony in Crooked Falls that would show those Romans how to have a real Christian wedding, in the spirit of Christ and not just of an hysterical version of Mary, and that would probably be enough to get even with all of them, Aunt Hilda going so far as to suggest (undoubtedly at Uncle Erwin's not entirely guileless prompting) that it might even help tweak the Pope's nose, though only indirectly, it was understood.

In New Providence, all this fuss was viewed at first with total incomprehension and later with dismay and suspicion. What was so strange about making an agreement before the priest, they wondered. There was nothing out of the ordinary about it and no real cause for alarm. If in the future certain things happened, or didn't happen, depending on the couple and on chance and on God, of course, and there was more or less of a family, no one was expected to follow such agreements to the letter anyway. True, they must be made—but like *any* agreement must be made, *in theory*, so that *in practice*...well, one must wait and see. After all, if there had been no plan in the first place, what would be left to wait and see *for*? If they followed her way, there wouldn't be any game left at all. Of all his relatives, only Andrea, who came to respect the value and protection of principle and formality all the more as he grew older, would have sided with her; but in actuality he had passed on long before anyone could have asked his opinion.

So in the end, to keep her and everyone else happy, they had the two weddings, the first in New Providence in the morning, the second that afternoon in Crooked Falls. For her, both of them were, of course, special. But the one in New Providence, at the little Italian Church set in the countryside, hilly and steep, like a miniature version of the Abruzzi, was, in spite of her reservations and all the uproar that she had caused on both sides of the family, the most memorable, what with the candy-covered almonds tossed in the place of rice (but not too hard, thank God, as she had feared at first), the musical exchanges of the groups speaking animatedly to one another in threes and fours and fives, and the quick dark-eyed children scurrying about afterwards, yelling out their challenges to each other and chattering like squirrels, laughing as they chased back and forth among their parents and their relatives and crouched beneath the tables loaded with cakes and fruits and the special green liqueur made with the hundred herbs, any one of which, as far as she could tell from the aroma, would have been sufficient by itself to knock a normal person to the ground. So in the end, despite her misgivings—and her pride in the quietly reserved afternoon ceremony at the church in Crooked Falls—that one, the first one, with all the warmth of the clustered groups, was the one she remembered.

Part of the reason for the lasting impression was, undoubtedly, that the first of the ceremonies not only represented but also confirmed the change in her—their—life, confirmed it for everyone to see and feel, all together and, at the same time, each of them individually. Which is what she wondered about—how strange, she thought, that on *her* wedding night, back in New Providence again (this time at *his* insistence), thinking over all the events of the day, she found herself wondering not about herself or even about him but about someone else—as she lay beside her husband of a little less than twelve hours, in the soft warm bed where, for the moment at least, she did not even desire sleep, listening to the night wind above them and the sounds of his breathing, after the excitement and the driving passion, steady and rhythmic now, while, far below, she heard the swing and thud on the floorboards as the rocker went back and forth, then stopped momentarily, only to pick up again, back and forth, louder and stronger deep into the night, while she lay there alone with him, but not really alone, listening and wondering: Why?

Years later, in the same country churchyard beside the same church in which the couple had been wedded the first time, there was another celebration. This one, too, included rites of passage and coming of age, but less directly or less ostensibly so. The event in question was the yearly festival celebrating the harvesting of the crops, held in that community at the beginning rather than at the end of the harvest, in order to make sure it would correspond with the Church's celebration of the Assumption of the Virgin on August 15th, as though the purity of the one would somehow sanctify—or at any rate make acceptable—the fruition and even license of the other. To the priest and to some of the parishioners (in particular the older women, widows most of them, all of them grandmothers, heavy-set and quiet, curved like black stones over their rosaries) this consideration was of some significance, though not necessarily of a positive sort. To the children, however, it meant little, and to their older brothers and sisters, the town's youth, nothing at all. Because as far as they were concerned, the town's festival and the party at the church afterward were not so much in honor of anything—the Church or the harvest or even the weather—but instead were opportunities in their own right: to be enjoyed and exploited for themselves, as adolescents in all climes and in all periods have always been ready to do. They most likely did not know the word "fruition," but they needed no one to teach them its meaning: *they* were it.

That was the year in which Gianni and O.B. really separated. Gianni was now on his own, to find his own friends, and O.B. had told him so, outright, face to face. The reason was simple. O.B., since they were there only for the summer, visiting from Chicago, was a special attraction for New Providence's youthful population, and especially for the girls. They all knew him, since he and his brother and their family had been returning to visit for years, so he was hardly a stranger; but at the same time, he simply wasn't around all year, to talk and chide and gossip, so in certain ways they were freer with him than they might have been with the boys from the town itself. This was true enough downtown, on the town's main street, where a few of them were even old enough that summer to drive their parents' cars up and down through the dust, windows open and radios blaring, past New Providence's one movie theater where there were always two shows on the marquee, whether or not they were in fact playing; but it was especially true first at the festival in town and then at the celebration at St. Anthony's on that summer afternoon.

When he and O.B. had arrived at the crowded churchyard that was already sticky with the August heat, O.B. had quickly said goodby to Gianni, or, more accurately, told him to get lost, thus leaving Gianni to his own resources amidst the groups that had gathered between the tables filled with bowls of punch and platters of cookies, and that were waiting more or less patiently at the booths set up for raffling chances and toys and even kisses. After a while Gianni found two boys his own age, George McCallum and Tom Castells, and drifted off with them toward the waterslide. They took turns there and at the other games, and Gianni tried to enjoy himself, but after what had seemed an interminably long period (actually just under an hour) he set off to find his brother again, despite the fact that not just O.B. but by then even their parents had told him that he was to find new friends and leave O.B. alone, since O.B. was growing up and had his own friends now, too old and too big for him.

Later, Gianni wished he had done as he had been told. But he was bored by himself, and he missed O.B., and he couldn't help it. He checked the booth where the men and older boys were shooting the BB guns, and where he knew he should have found him under normal circumstances, nodding and flashing his smile to challenge all comers, but he wasn't there. Nor was he at any of the tables or other booths, or among the new group gathered now at the waterslide, where Gianni had circled back to check once more before giving up. By then he was tired and discouraged enough to head home. Before he did, however, he let himself into the dark church basement to find the bathroom, trying all the doors to see which was which since everything was freshly painted, with an odd yellowy paint that looked from the color as though it were left over from one of the local auctions, and whatever signs there had been once had been removed while the paint was drying. He tried door after door and discovered nothing but closets and then had finally found the handle he thought would be right and heard a noise inside and reached out to turn it when, to his astonishment, he heard first a curse and then, amidst the sounds of zippers and snaps and material swishing, he heard his name, not just said but screamed as O.B. appeared from around a coat rack—followed by someone else, with a shriek that was definitely female, although just whose he couldn't tell for sure, as the skirt swished and the blond hair flew by him and up the stairs. The big door to the churchyard hung open a moment, empty, with the light streaming in, then banged shut as O.B. turned with his hands gathered at his waist and glowered at him.

"Well, all right, then, come on!" O.B. yelled, flushed with anger and still struggling to stuff his shirt-tails into the front of his pants, while Gianni stared in shock. "Aren't you satisfied yet?" And then, when Gianni still didn't move, "Well, come on, dammit! We might as well go home. What are you waiting for? Don't worry, you won't miss anything now." O.B. started off. "There isn't going to be any second show."

All the way home, over the dusty road and the broad, hot fields with the clouds up and the wind going, O.B. wouldn't say a word to him or even slow sufficiently to allow him to catch up. But once they'd passed the last fencerow covered with chokecherries and thorn apples and reached the farmhouse, something else was going on, something darker and deeper than Gianni's confusion and regret or even O.B.'s anger. Charlie, the elderly neighbor who was not family, but who Grandpa said was just as good as family since he was their godfather, sat quietly at the big table in the bright kitchen with the others, but they weren't laughing or talking about Charlie's vegetarian diets (which he followed religiously, their father said, except when he came to their house and Grandma was cooking) or about the free social state, which was another of his favorite topics because he believed in it. Instead they were all talking in low voices about Aunt Min, who sat alone in the corner, huddled with her head in her hands, and about something else, just what was unclear, except that it had to do with Aunt Min and her husband, Uncle Josh, who wasn't there, and their cousin, Richie, who was, sitting with them now, looking woeful, at the head of the table beneath the overhead lamp, turned on even though it was still light out, with the steam rising up from the milk-white bowl and the towels before him, which, every now and then, Aunt Rachel or one of the other women would dip into the bowl of water and place against the gash on his forehead or the big purple bruise between his cheekbone and his eye.

"Yes, well," they could hear their father clear his throat as they listened with their cousins from their place on the stairs in the other room, straining to peek around into the kitchen. "That's what happens when children get mixed up in these things."

"But it's not his fault," Uncle Dominic said even more quietly, almost whispering, "at least not this time. I don't believe your boy's perfect either."

Gianni, from his perch on the stairs, felt O.B.'s weight shifting beside him, but Gianni did not move or even turn to look at him. Then they heard someone else say something, and then Charlie said, "Well let's hope there's not another time, not like this anyway. Now, if we had a *true* society, why—"

"That's neither here nor there, you know that," Uncle Dominic cut in, his voice angry and cold now. "And as for another time—don't worry, there won't be one. I'll see to that myself and make sure of it. This will be the end, now that we know, believe me. Don't you worry about that." Uncle Dominic's voice rose and then stopped suddenly.

"Please, Dom—" someone else began, but the voice trailed off.

"You'd better keep him in for awhile anyway," their father said. "I'm not suggesting anything, but you better keep an eye on him now, for your own good as well as his."

Someone said something that sounded like a question and then Grandpa spoke for the first time that they'd heard, answering with a finality to his voice. "Yes," he said, "It's time for it now." Then they could hear the scraping of chairs and the sounds of the boots on the wooden floor as the men got up and began to go outside, all except for Charlie, and their aunts came out of nowhere, bustling in to where they were huddled on the stairs to marshal them all off to bed.

"But what—" they began to ask. Aunt Rachel and Aunt Fil held up their hands, and then Grandma came and gathered them close to her so they could feel her soft chest and the warmth of her breath. "Don't ask," she whispered. "It's not for you, not yet," she gave a long sigh that felt to Gianni as sad as anything he could imagine. "Just don't ask." And then their aunts ordered them off to bed. "And go right to sleep now!" So he and O.B. and the others all went up, all except Richie, who remained at the table where Gianni could still see him over his shoulder, sitting with his eye gone completely shut, his head over the bowl of water, reddish now, like a sign or a mark, and then Gianni felt his grandmother's hand, pushing him away from the downstairs and the bright, incomprehensible world of boots and voices and lights and back up to their own darkened room, in which even O.B. seemed a stranger now, since O.B. appeared to know already whatever it was that was to be known, while he, Gianni, now more than ever, felt doomed to remain in permanent residence, stranded and alone in his ignorance, left behind once and for all.

Gianni and O.B. eventually found out—Gianni years later, O.B. considerably before him—just what had been the cause of the uproar. It turned out that Aunt Min's husband had proven, over the course of more than a decade without offspring, to be a less than interested companion. Richie, on the other hand, had by then already acquired no mean repute for nocturnal exercises (though from all accounts he wasn't actually too particular about either the time or the place, or too smart about it either), despite the fact that he wasn't out of or even really well into his teens. He was a tall boy, long-armed but somewhat gangly, with full waves of dark hair and a handsome smile, and by the summer of his fifteenth year his reputation preceded him in the county wherever he went. But even though he was willing and, by all testimony, more than competent—what little public testimony there actually was, that is—he was a boy and not a man. So even though Uncle Josh, who each time they heard the story retold would be changed from English to German to Swedish to God-knows-what, whatever, but not Italian, was justified probably in his anger, maybe in his suspicions, and certainly in his frustration at seeing Richie in his house practically every day, on that hot Saturday afternoon when he returned from town with the new fencewire in the back of his truck and found the two of them there alone in his home, thus making the boy an intruder—in the kitchen, it is true, but alone nevertheless—had a right to be angered, he still should have kept his temper like a man and done things the way they ought to be done. He should have gone to talk to Dominic first instead of letting himself explode, cursing the boy as he chased him outside into the yard and taking out that pent-up anger of his with his fists and his belt strap before running back inside to get the 12-gauge—which, fortunately for both of them, wasn't any good, since by then the boy had at least had the sense to use the legs God gave him and had scampered off out of range of Josh's gun (which was the one thing he knew how to shoot) if not of his wrath.

Later that night the men went to talk to Josh, in committee, and took care of the matter (extending only so far as it had to do with Aunt Min and the boy and no further, since the rest was no longer family business). No one heard another word about it until years later, when enough time had elapsed for the details to have been forgotten and the story to start. That was just the way they handled things in that community. When there was trouble, it was ignored as long as possible, and if in the end something happened that wouldn't go away, they dealt with it among themselves, the men deciding and acting as a group, silently and surely, without any options either offered or expected. Michael had learned this—finding out as much from Andrea's earlier mistakes as from his successes—and acted accordingly, knowing that when the time came it was better to lead than to follow, but that it was always better to wait and choose the *right* time than to move too fast or too slow.

Of such things, the recognition of evil, be it treachery or deceit, and the necessity of dealing with it in some way or other, Johann Britzen, his son William, and even their farmhand Drew, knew next to nothing. Of the three of them, surprisingly enough, Drew, albeit endowed with the least foresight and ambition, probably had the sharpest eye for the quirks and ironies of human behavior, nearly as sharp as Jake Arndt himself. One of Drew's favorite stories concerned an incident that had occurred when he had first arrived in Crooked Falls, more than thirty years before, and the Britzens' neighbors, Jack and Clare Connolly, had just put in the community's inaugural berry patch, to which they pointed with unconcealed pride. Jack had planted and, at the start, worked the land, but the patch was really his present to his wife, since she'd always wanted to be able to make fresh pies from her own berries and put up the jams and jellies herself. Once it began to produce, she took to tending it on her own. At first it was nice for her to get away for a while, since the patch was far enough off to the side of their property, below the trees, so that she couldn't even see the house as she weeded the ground, pruned the bushes, and picked the berries. When she got too busy and couldn't make time for it, she enlisted the aid of her children, which was probably her first mistake, although Drew, when telling the story during a game of cards in the parlor or while sitting on the front porch on a Sunday afternoon talking to more recently arrived neighbors, would never stop to point that out, because he was invariably in a hurry to get to the good part.

The system worked fine for a while, he would explain, until one year—because of too much rain or too little, or because of the cold, or the heat, or something, he was never sure which so he usually tried to mention all of them, more or less in one breath, and hurry on—there just wasn't much of a crop. At that point, Drew would stop and wait for Helen's mother, if she were there listening and not lying down on account of one of her headaches, or, in later years, Helen herself, to ask what happened then, so that he could go on again, which at last he would.

"Well, by then all the Connollys—and not just the little ones, but Jack himself—were so used to having the homemade pies and cobblers and such that she just hadn't any choice but to go out and get the berries somehow, so that she could keep on making them happy." Then Drew would stop again in his recitation and shift uncomfortably in his chair, fingering his pipe, expectant but silent as a stone.

"Well, all right then," someone would pipe up. "Where'd she get 'em?" So Drew would nod in acknowledgement, leaning forward.

"It wasn't really *where* that was important," he would say, "since she didn't actually have to go out like I said: they brought them to her. It was *who*, that was what was the important part."

Here Drew would stop again and ask, "Well, aren't you going to ask who? And how they got them in a bad year? And how they knew the Connollys would be needing and willing to buy them in the first place?" He would sit and light his pipe till someone did ask, and then he would hurry on, because now he was getting to the good part.

"Well, those Connolly kids," he continued with his smile growing, "hadn't been picking berries for more than a season or two before the fun got wore out of it. So they looked around and saw what everyone naturally does, their Poppa included, when there's work that we can't or don't want to do"—unless Helen's father were there, in which case he would skip the explanation—"so the older boys decided to set up in business themselves and hire the job done out of the pocket money that was given them for store candy and such, and that they shouldn't have used anyway for that purpose, just as though they were grown-ups themselves. At first they simply paid the younger ones to do the job, while they went off fishing or swimming, retrieving the buckets from where they'd been placed under the bushes on their way back home and taking the berries in to their Momma, until the young ones staged a revolt and refused to spend their time picking instead of swimming and playing with the others, and naturally threatened to tell. So they put their heads together and came up with a solution. Instead of doing any of the work themselves, they asked the new kids, the Catlins, to do the picking for them. They noticed it right off, of course, how the berries waiting for them when they returned from the river seemed fewer and fewer, though at first they didn't think too much of it. They were just kids, after all, and the weather was hot and the swimming good, and maybe the crop *was* as bad as all that. Till one afternoon they got back and they couldn't help but do something, because there weren't hardly any berries at all, but just a note left there, scrawled by those Catlins, with the words, 'Berries all done.' Which was in fact the case. Because even their Momma couldn't find anything but bare bushes and green ones left when she finally did get down to see for herself—although they'd just told her, they hadn't showed her the note or explained anything, of course. So when she didn't yell but just shook her head and went back up to the house, they felt bad, sure, but they thought, too, with relief, that then it was over."

    Here Drew would stop again, but just to catch his breath and ready himself for the last stretch, and he would continue without waiting for anyone's urging. "But, of course, it wasn't over, because when the kids got back to the house that evening for supper they could see that instead of being upset their mother seemed pleased and happy, just as though everything were all right again. And sure enough, the next day at dinner, when their father and the men came in from the fields, they could smell the sweetness of those pies all through the house. Jack Connolly saw 'em there, cooling on the ledge near the window and smiled like an old crocodile, just like always. After dinner, between mouthfuls, he asked her where she'd got them and what she had to pay anyway. So she told him that he better just be satisfied and not ask, because she'd got the only berries in those parts—though the exact amount was none of his business anyway, since the household accounts were all hers—and even if they had cost a little more than usual, that wasn't so strange in a bad year. All of which, in fact, was truer than she knew. But Jack was a curious man, although it sure wasn't doing him much good, so he said that even if she wouldn't tell him the price at least she should tell him where she managed to get such good berries. So she told him. Those new kids, she answered, the ones who always seem to be running about now, the ones with the smiles like little angels, Kaplan, or something. 'No!' She heard her own brood calling back to her as they headed for the door like Indians, having finished, she noted, surprisingly fast, and, even more astonishingly, not waiting for seconds. 'Catlin, Ma, the Catlin kids,' they called out. Then the oldest one stopped. 'But don't worry,' he said, 'they're gone now,' at least making an attempt before letting the door slam behind him and rushing off among the others. It was probably that parting 'Don't worry' that didn't fit right and finally made her begin to see what she should have seen all along. Because, despite the Catlins' smiles, they weren't angels. Those really had been the only berries around and they knew it, too, since they'd been given a chance to have first-hand experience from the very best bushes, as she found out shortly thereafter, the only ones that would still produce even if the weather were bad and the berry-pickers less than reliable. So, the berries, those fine berries she'd paid so much for when she had no other choice and still hadn't regretted doing it, yet, that is, the ones that had made such a fine pair of pies and so had come to her rescue" (here Drew would begin to sputter with laughter) "those really *were* good berries: because they were hers." Then, when he managed to stop laughing and get control of himself again, he would take care to explain the good part to everyone until he was sure that they understood, despite the fact that they had all heard him tell it at least once a year and would most likely continue to hear it until either they would stop listening or Drew would stop telling, neither of which seemed in the offing any time soon.

So Drew, at least, had an eye for life's ironies, even if he remained utterly dumbfounded when it came to dealing with them. For the man that hired and maintained him, the question was different. Rather than being incapable of dealing with, as his wife called it, the devil, or even the run-of-the-mill duplicities of everyday experience, William Britzen simply refused to see any of them in the first place. Just two years after his eldest daughter had been married, in the building next to the church of her second wedding—which was the county courthouse in Crooked Falls, so old and decrepit that anyone could see it was a scandal for the community, even if it was the county seat; but they still couldn't get the vote to build a new one as long as the countryside had more votes than the town, and that didn't seem any too likely to change in the foreseeable future—William Britzen sat in silence as the clerk read out his name and the name of the man who had accused him of trespassing, on property posted in plain view, where the river bends inward, just as that sneak Jonathan Snipes had claimed and, as Snipes had claimed, too, the best spot for a duck blind in the country: because why else would they, William and Jake Arndt, who had discovered the site, just as he had always picked out the best spots for every type of game by some inexplicable intuition, and who, as was equally normal and inexplicable, had got off scot-free, certain that as always no one could have seen him and that William Britzen would never mention what everyone already knew anyway—why else would they have been waiting out there in the freezing cold of a late October morning for those birds to come across in the first place? He stood formally accused of bringing down the ducks that were, by law, not his but Jack Snipes's. William sat silent because that was the point. Maybe Jack Snipes had understood the law correctly and maybe he hadn't, but whether the accusation was legally correct or not (about which William was more than willing, indeed pleased, to admit his ignorance), it was simply not right, of that he was certain. It was not right to stop good hunting on nature's land, whether Jack Snipes happened to be the technical, and temporary, guardian of that particular stretch or not. It had never been right before, and it never would be. That's all there was to it. That's how William lived. Things didn't change that way, and on that, at least, he would stake whatever they asked.

He remained as silent and steely-eyed as all the saints through the entire procedure of the clerk's pronouncements, the two-bit lawyer's badgering—who was only there because he was one of Snipes' relatives—the judge's cajoling (and just that, nothing more, since he and His Honor, Bill Wilson, had been hunting partners on more than one occasion in territory that was not altogether different from that in question), and right up through the final bang of the gavel, brought down in frustration as much as anything, since by the end the judge had begun to plead with him, "At least nod if you can, William, to let me know you can still hear. Or if that's too much for you, how about just raising your eyebrows to show that you understand that the complainant, that is, that Jack Snipes has agreed, has offered, after consultation with the court, that is, uhh, with me, to let the 'use' matter drop, if you will just admit to what everyone already knows to be the case, that is, that you were in fact trespassing on posted property. Now William, couldn't you raise your eyebrows just a little?"

When it was over, William stripped the nineteen one-dollar bills off the soiled roll and laid them down one by one before the clerk, who sat counting them out; then he put in the hundred pennies, dropping them, too, one by one as the clerk's complexion went from baby pink to nearly rose red, to make up the rest of the fine that even Drew had known his boss would have to pay in order to get out of that courthouse (since the body, or bodies, of the crime had naturally been disposed of long before, so there was no other possibility except for monetary restitution). Now, at last, William seemed about to say something, as he stood shaking his head, though not at the judge or indeed at anyone in particular. But he put his hat back on as though he'd thought better of it, as though just mentioning Jack Snipes's name or even responding to his accusations or those of his cohorts in any shape or form would have tainted him forever. He headed down the aisle looking straight ahead, still without uttering a word, since if they couldn't see on their own that the spots for duck and pheasant and the crossings for deer were always open for everybody's use and belonged to no one—which is to say, to everyone, as they always had, unless of course someone else got there first—no matter what a group of overly clever lawyers and politicians, who had possibly never been in the woods in their lives except to relieve themselves in an emergency, had written down for their particular ends, he sure wasn't going to bother to try to explain it to them. So he walked out into the bright May afternoon, momentarily oblivious to the noise and the bustle of his neighbors in the town square, his head held high and his bearing somber, even victorious by his standards, if exactly nineteen dollars and one hundred cents lighter.

"Fine afternoon, isn't it?" he nodded, fingering the edge of his grey homburg as Mrs. Whittaker and her sister, the local postmistress, passed by beneath the birds twittering high up in the swaying shade trees. He turned almost automatically toward the sawmill but after a few steps stopped and reversed himself.

"Let's go home, Drew," he smiled at last. "The day's too good to waste it altogether."

Michael Mariagrazia was certainly a different man, perhaps in a different world. Despite his initial inexperience with farming and his stubbornly odd ways, he had built up the neatest, most efficient dairy operation in the county, and he had no intention of letting some Sicilian bumpkin ruin it, especially one with a taste and even, it seems, a nose for, of all things, turkeys. At first, of course, he hadn't known any of the details. But he had learned long before that when a Sicilian gives a quick smile—too quick, in fact, since that was the point—and even starts talking about being a part of the family, something is in the wind, and whatever it turns out to be, it's certainly not going to be anything good. Because that's what he did the spring morning that he first showed up, bringing the big milk truck up the rutted drive past the house to the barn and climbing down to greet Michael like a long-lost friend, with that smile tossed backward over his shoulder before he even hit the ground and then the hand out to introduce himself, a short, wiry fellow with a name to match, Alberto Beddu.

"But call me Berto," he said, shaking hands as though he were going to pass out a card. "Everybody does. Besides, I like to think of all the folks on my route as part of one big family. Maybe not everybody feels that way, but I do, one big family. Even if they are all adults and no kids." He smiled at his joke and then went about the work of collecting the cans of milk from the storeroom at the front of the barn.

Still, it wasn't the introduction that bothered Michael. What really bothered him came after the spidery little Sicilian had finished storing the milk cans along the sides of the truck and scurrying to secure them before he climbed back into the cab and crawled across the seat behind the wheel, and started off. It was just as the truck began to slide forward, when he turned to wave good-by through the big window, the expression gone from his face, that Michael could see the slit of the mouth where the grin had been. It was the dark slit beneath the beady eyes, the detritus of the earlier warning, that told him that his first reaction had been right.

By then, it was true, Michael had a lot to look out for. By rotating his fields in the order Maria had suggested and adding a field of clover to the one of alfalfa, and by setting the planting times for his peas and beans so he would get two crops of each, different kinds and in an order different from everyone else so as to get the highest price on the seasonal market from the canning factory, he had managed to increase the number of cows to forty without raising his costs or reducing what everything went to support, the herd's rich milk. His friend, Dick Howard, the manager of the dairy in Cameron, knew just like everybody else that the Mariagrazia farm produced the highest butterfat content with the least apparent effort of any of the farms around, and that even the labor of the women and the children in the barn and the fields was factored into the formula to ensure that the equation would keep coming out exactly right, as it had been then for over three decades. So no one was more surprised than Howard when the driver brought in the load from his new route and the total number of cans was off.

At first Howard said nothing, since he didn't want to make a mistake. After all, what if the error had been theirs? So he waited another week. When the number didn't change, however, he checked once more to make sure nothing was amiss at their end and then called Michael.

Michael hadn't known what to think. He always tried to be at least as aboveboard as necessary—though he knew and used the trick with the salt licks before he shipped what little stock he sold to South St. Paul, since just because the signs plastered up everywhere said to "Ship 'em all," that didn't mean they couldn't send a little extra juice along with them, or more accurately, in them, so they'd arrive happy and heavy and ready for the slaughterhouse, if a bit waterlogged—and he was usually willing to expect the same from anyone else, at least until he had good reason to believe otherwise. It was the second call, two weeks later, when Howard told him that not only the amount but also the butterfat measure was down, that gave him just that reason.

What annoyed him was not so much that his product was in danger but that, he felt, his reputation was too. His operation was the best, bar none, despite the fact that he had not asked for that life in the first place, nor would he have accepted it if he had been consulted. But now that his operation was his and therefore the best, he was going to keep it that way. Period. Michael checked the cows one by one, and he rechecked the meager records he kept (this more out of an allegiance to the memory of his brief life as a clerk than anything else). But he found nothing amiss. So he decided to do what he hated to do but what, given the circumstances, seemed his only recourse, and he picked up the phone.

"You're being what?" asked Robin Elroy, the county sheriff, whose little twenty-acre postage stamp was actually near enough to the Mariagrazia's that Michael could have just about as easily gone outside and shouted as pick up the phone, though a call did seem, somehow, more proper and official rather than just neighborly. "Well which is it then?" Elroy asked half in amazement and half in disbelief as Michael responded. "Cheated or robbed?" Elroy insisted, breaking into the stream of Michael's complaints. "First off, you've gotta tell me, cheated or robbed, not both. And even if you do, I'm not sure I handle cow cases—outside of rustling, that is, which we haven't had here for over ten years if I remember right. Have you tried Jack Evinson yet?"

Jack Evinson was the local veterinarian. At this suggestion Michael knew he'd made a mistake, so he asked to be remembered to the sheriff's wife, as Elroy did in turn to Maria, and abruptly rung off.

He had taken the wrong tack, he could see that: what would Robin Elroy, with his broken-down shack of a house, his straggling chickens and scrawny cows, and those fancy but worthless horses, care about a plot to ruin him? Still, he didn't regret having made the complaint, because Robin did mention it—probably more out of disbelief or amusement than duty—to other dairymen in more or less similar conditions, and it turned out that several of them had in fact been having the same problem, though not as acute a one. So Michael knew he'd been right the first time and hadn't really wasted his time. And besides, there were other ways to handle problems of this kind.

"I couldn't figure out if some of my cows were off or if I just wasn't reckoning right or what," Gene Castells told him between coughs while they stood on his back porch a few weeks later and watched Charlie's lantern swimming up to them through the darkness as he walked the drive and mounted the porch.

"You better watch that cough." Charlie squinted into the light of the porch.

"Ain't nothing to worry about." Castells pulled his handkerchief from his pocket and coughed again. "Let's go shoot awhile."

When they got down to the silo with the .22's Michael set the lanterns where he thought best, then changed two of them at Castells' instructions.

"Jesus." Castells raised his rifle, apparently not bothered by the stench of the barnyard. "Look at 'em scatter." Then Castells and Charlie began shooting at the pairs of bright beads that shone momentarily and vanished back into the blackness, picking them off as they would in the booths at the fair.

"I want to thank you both for helping me out again like this," Michael said. "They were running wild—god I hate rats—and I sure don't want to wait until summer to do something about them."

"Well." Castells turned and put his rifle up, pulling out his handkerchief again. "There's no way we can get all of 'em with popguns." Charlie kept shooting, paying no heed to the others.

"You don't have to." Michael shook his head and spat. "That's one of the reasons I asked you down here. Look, I want to know more about that other way, that stuff you were talking about over at Sings. That new stuff."

"But it's awful powerful, you know, bound to get anything in sight, and it works fast as the plague, with no quarter for whatever it gets into and no relief for mistakes. Really, for anything less than—"

"I know." The lantern's reflection caught Michael's smile. "But suppose you just tell me how to set it out now, and I'll worry about the rest."

Castells shrugged and turned to go but then turned back. "Now that we're here anyhow," he said to Charlie, who at last had put his rifle up, too. "Let's go out and get some in the stubble. It should be almost as good out there, hell, maybe better." They each grabbed two lanterns and headed out as Michael motioned them forward, then watched the flashes as they shot.

"Listen," he told them when the evening's sport was finished. "I think you ought to wait a while before telling anyone else about this stuff with the dairy, or even complaining any more."

Michael took a pull from the jug and passed it. "It looks like Elroy doesn't care for cow's milk anyway, and from what you tell me Dick Howard has decided to claim there wasn't a thing wrong at their end of it in the first place, so let's just wait a while and see what happens."

"But what about *our* milk?" Castells and Charlie protested almost in unison.

"Don't worry," Michael smiled again and took the jug. "I won't let it go on too long. Why would I? After all, who's getting hurt the worst?" He handed the jug back to Castells, who took one last swallow and said goodnight. Amidst the sounds of their boots in the dark on the wooden steps Michael's voice called after them. "Just keep quiet. It'll work out, and soon. You can take my word for it."

Two days later Michael was at George Olson's store—which Olson had inherited from his father, the first person in the non-Italian part of town whom Andrea had met, and who had inherited it from his—picking up the poison that Castells had told him about. While Michael was waiting, he saw one of Maria's relatives who lived out near the eastern county line. They greeted one another between the bolts of dry goods and the dusty barrels of coffee, and shook hands.

"It's been quite a while, Franky," Michael said loudly. "Anything new out your way?"

The other man shook his head. "Nothing except for that turkey farm." Michael cleared his throat and looked away, and the other lowered his voice. "The one I told Maria about, with the darn smell so bad now that every time I pass by coming into town I have to roll up the window. But nothing else to speak of. You got that problem of yours taken care of yet?" Michael's smile passed quickly enough so that if one hadn't known to watch for it, it would have been impossible to say whether or not it had been there at all, much less if it had been malicious: because, after all, he was one of *her* relatives.

"No, not yet. But don't let it bother you," Michael assured him as Jimmy Granello came up to say hello. "It's nothing I can't tend to."

When Olson came out from the back and saw Michael between Frank and Granello and heard what Michael wanted, Michael could tell from the way Olson fingered his wire storekeepers glasses, pretending to adjust the wire rim, that he was uneasy.

"Look," said Olson, a man humorless by nature, almost bookish, except that he hadn't read a book since he'd been a child. "I hate to sell this stuff, especially to a dairy farmer. If only a little were to get into the milk, you could end up with a batch of corpses. And it will probably kill all your cats, too," he added, fidgeting at the thought of it in the crisp white shirt. One of the sleek storecats rose from its spot on the counter and scurried off as though it had understood, and Olson winced accordingly. Michael stood waiting for his relative's question about turkeys and prepared to head it off, but contrary to form the other said nothing. He could see that the storekeeper's concern was genuine, however, so he told him that Castells had warned them and that, anyway, they'd already tried everything else, short of setting up a stand and a Gatling gun.

"Well all right," Olson deferred. "I do make a tidy profit on it. But you be careful, Michael, is that agreed?"

"Sure," Michael smiled, examining the box with the red letters and black design on its cover. "Of course, I will—you know me, George."

In order to be sure, Michael actually put down some of it, just to see if it really worked as well as everyone said, which it did, although having to dispose of the carcasses afterwards, what with the filth and the stench, Michael reflected, was probably worse than living with the damn things in the first place. So at last he was ready for the crucial step in the project that had begun almost two weeks earlier, just after Dick Howard's first call. He thought it through again while he seeded the corn in the warm spring sun, riding the drill behind the horses that knew the field better than he did, so he could give them their heads and let his mind wander, unless he intended to finish a job late, in which case he'd have to jerk them the other way every time they reached the end row and they started to head in the direction of the barn, following their absolutely accurate and unfailing and therefore treacherous clocks of hunger and habit instead of his whimsy. From up on the drill, he could see the rolling pasture filling out and turning green again, now that the patches of snow had gone, and along the field's edge the fence that had been mended by Paulie, the latest in a succession of boys he'd hired beginning years earlier, after the last of his sons had left for different occupations and he'd decided against trying to conscript his grandchildren as helpers. Even the seeding was ahead of schedule now, so it would be a good year, as long as nothing unforeseen happened to ruin it, which it wouldn't since that was his job, not just to sweat, but also to plan. Around the same time that he had had the news from the dairy, he had heard talk, in bits and pieces as usual, about the new arrival in town, the Sicilian, who apparently had some money, or at least enough cash to give the impression of money since he was buying land and supplies and equipment for an operation that turned out, to everyone's surprise and to his new neighbors' consternation—at least those down wind—to be the county's first turkey farm. So everyone wondered: Why, with any money at all, would anyone want to start up one of *those*?

George Olson, true to his nature, had an answer. "There's money in it, if you set it up right. Doesn't make any difference what the smell's like—it'll pay for itself in a year or two, and then all the rest is profit." He would tell this to anyone willing to listen in the dusty front room of his store, as he stood beside the pot-bellied stove, which went full-blast to ward off the damp chill of early spring.

"Besides, he would say, as he opened the stove door and stooped to show his refinement by spitting inside rather than on the floor, "if you work it right now, the government will give you all the money you need to start it up and get it going, except for the feed. I seen by the newspaper that it's part of their new program. That's what my cousin in St. Paul told me, too. All the money you need," he would say with the far away look that he got whenever money and profit were at issue. "Hell, I don't care what you say, I think this fellow's pretty smart. And everything that I've heard about him only tells me that I'm right."

But it wasn't until the new resident turned out to be not just the county's latest proprietor but also the dairy's new driver that Michael took an interest in turkeys, a subject that had never concerned him before one way or the other; and it wasn't until Maria's relative out near the county line, who hated the stench of turkeys almost as much as Michael hated that of chickens, had pressed the point, by luck, really, if not entirely by chance, that Michael had finally begun to put the puzzle's pieces together.

"Well, come on!" he could hear Frank shouting excitedly through the receiver even before Maria had passed him the phone, "Michael? Come on, now! You know what they eat, even if Maria doesn't, don't you?"

"They slop 'em, I suppose," Michael profferred, "like chickens."

"Yeah, yeah, but with what? That's the point."

But Michael didn't answer. He didn't have to. He'd known since he'd first heard the tone of the other's voice crackling out of the receiver, urgent, very nearly hilarious, even triumphant, because he was one of *her* relatives. And by then he had undoubtedly heard not only about the Sicilian's turkey farm, but also about some of his other doings.

"They slop 'em with milk, if they can get it, Michael," the voice came crackling over the line. "The richer the better."

From where he stood on the drill he could see Castells waiting for him below the trees at the field's end. Castells watched as the horses crossed the field, seeding it, with the man behind them seeming taller against the blue sky, the figure outlined in the sun but the face lost in shadow, dark and for the moment shapeless, as though that of a total stranger. When the horses reached the end row Michael got down and called for Paulie to take them in.

"I'm sorry." Castells waved his hat in apology as the boy led the horses off. "I didn't mean to interrupt." He would not normally have bothered to mention it, but there was something in Michael's gaze that surprised and frightened him, something he had not seen before in all the years he'd known him.

"Don't matter," Michael said simply and the look vanished, though Castells could perceive its trace hovering behind Michael's sudden smile. "It was about time anyway."

They walked past the line of trees and scrub into the clearing, away from the road, where Michael motioned to a stump. While Castells sat, Michael knelt to scoop the leaves off the top of the spring then took the dipper from the peg on the tree and lowered it into the water. Before he drank he looked up, holding out the dipper. "Good and cold, now." But Castells shook his head. "So, what's new?" Michael asked once his thirst was quenched.

"I just wanted to let you know that our troubles might be over," Castells smiled.

"Well, now. I thought you weren't going to talk about it anymore?"

"I ain't been," Castells replied. "Folks talk to me. Jack Evinson told me this morning—and he'd heard it from Dick Howard three days ago—that the sheriff is going to look into this milk stuff after all. Elroy got a call from the Cities, some government fellow, so it's a big deal now. The milk's just a small part of it, naturally. Only thing is, no one's supposed to say anything about it, at least for a couple more days, on account of it being a secret."

"But you're here telling me!" Michael watched him closely.

For a moment Castells looked confused. "That's not what I mean. I mean—well, I knew you'd want to hear, Michael," he began to apologize. "What good has all this secrecy been anyway?"

Michael caught himself and did not curse. "For the moment, you just let me worry about that. All right now? But I do thank you for the news." He motioned again. "You sure you don't want a drink?"

"No thanks," Castells shook his head with an embarrassed smile, maybe just confused, or maybe like someone who knows more than he wants to say. "I'm not thirsty."

"Now listen, Gene," Michael said with his voice as calm as he could keep it. "If there's something else you've heard—anything, even if I might not like it—now's the time to tell me. Now, not tomorrow, not later, now. Understand?"

But the confusion on Castell's face and his silence only confirmed what Michael had suspected. Castells knew nothing more for certain. Or if he did, unlike Maria's relative, he would never admit to it. He had no reason to. Michael would have to trust him.

"Come to think of it, I guess I do have a few things of my own to do," Michael went on, rising as he spoke. "You're sure about that water now?"

At last Castells took his meaning, and the two men started off toward the barn. Before heading for his car, Castells turned back toward Michael. "I guess I should mention one other thing as long as I'm here," he said quietly but firmly, as though he had prepared his words beforehand and had finally decided that this was the time to say what he had to. "It's about that milk truck. I've seen it coming and going here at the weirdest hours, in the afternoon and once in the evening, when it couldn't possibly have been time for a pick-up. The boy wasn't around to notice it, from what I could tell. I don't want to stick my nose into—"

"I know," Michael cut him off. "I know all about it," he repeated even though he didn't, not for sure. But he knew what was sufficient, all he wanted to, anyway. His burden was heavy enough as it was. "Don't worry about it further, I'm taking care of it." Then with finality: "But I thank you anyway."

As Castells started off, Michael set about his plans with a surprisingly ginger step, plans which now would have to move along exactly right, because there might be only one or two more chances, and he didn't want to miss them, not after coming to this point. "And don't you worry!" Michael called after Castells' old blue Plymouth as he eased down the drive. "I'll talk to you again later, you can be sure of it. But until then I won't tell a soul—and you'd best keep quiet, too." Otherwise, he thought as he watched the car lurch away, everyone within twenty miles will be barking to warn the fox off.

He walked to the machine shed cursing Elroy under his breath. When you need them and want them, he thought in exasperation, the fools with their shiny badges won't do a thing; but just as soon as they see they might be able to put their foot in it and ruin everything they're the first to jump your way. He entered the dark shed, amidst the heavy fumes of the axle grease, knowing he would have to work fast, but not so fast that he would make a mistake. He pulled his gloves on and reached up behind the post to retrieve the box with the figure stamped on its face which, despite his own consciousness of the irony, he still couldn't help but think of as the Jolly Roger. Too bad, he thought, that he couldn't use it directly on the fellow himself. But he knew the ways of the world well enough to know that indirect action, or at least the appearance of indirection, was always best. Even if what was at stake was both his livelihood and, in the world he had made and lived in, his face.

Now, timing was everything. He brought the cows in at the regular hour, walking behind them with the stick in his hand as always and urging them forward, "Gwon! Gwon!" An hour earlier than usual he touched the boy's shoulder, more solid now than he had realized beneath the sweatshirt and smock, and told him to be careful, which he felt he had to do, and sent him home. He locked up as usual and walked the drive to the house, stopping to relieve himself in the stubble behind the pumphouse—which, happily, held the deepest well in that part of the county—just as he always did before going in for the night. He could see the stars, the Great and Little Bear together with their friendly glow and the easy whiteness of the Milky Way in the deep spring sky, so he knew the radio's voice would be clear as a bell, with that seemingly unnatural clarity it had on such nights, as though the announcers and musicians were just next door, or even in the yard, or he were with them wherever they were; and as he stood there his mind wandered to the places far away, Chicago, Nashville, Milwaukee, and then, as though by the metonymy of the natural act, to that other business, and he felt himself shiver. He buttoned himself and mounted the porch, his step lighter now that things were moving, his mind in motion, not at rest, but nevertheless peaceful.

The next morning at 9:00, when the milk truck came up the drive toward the barn, Michael, contrary to his habit, had already been up for hours, having shocked Gene Castells with the first phone call he'd ever made in his life before 8:00 a.m.

"Ain't seen you for a while," the Sicilian driver brought the truck to a stop and greeted him, adjusting the stained kerchief at his throat and brushing an imaginary fleck of dust from the front of his filthy overalls.

"Oh, I've been here, all right, don't worry about that." Michael touched his moustache. "It's just that I've been in the fields when you've come before—or fixing that damn back fence that keeps falling down every time I turn away."

"Where's the boy today?" The driver began hauling the containers of milk to the truck between his big gloved hands, looking around nervously with the dark gaze.

"He's here, don't worry," Michael smiled. "I've got him working on a job in the other barn."

The driver scurried to secure the containers, as Michael stood watching, the slight, quizzical smile spreading on his face. "I heard your route's growing," Michael said from where he watched. "I figure that's why you're always in such a hurry."

"It is in fact," the Sicilian looked up from his work, his unshaven face beaming. "They've given me two new stops just this past week."

"They must like you at the dairy."

"Oh, I have to ask for the work, you know. But yes—we get along all right, you could say."

"It must be tough fitting extra calls into your route without running late," Michael offered. "Don't they care when you get your load in?"

"At the dairy? Sure they care. Damn right they care—I keep a perfect schedule, always have," the driver said proudly, seeming pleased with the chance for conversation, so Michael could hear the pride in his voice and see it in the way he held his head, and he knew he had him where he wanted him. "I'm in with my first load by twelve and with the second by four exactly, no mistakes," the driver said matter of factly. Then with a wink and a conspiratorial nod he added, "I could do even more, of course, but there are other things in life besides driving a milk truck."

Michael bristled but did not let it show. "That's right," he went along. "I guess I did hear somewhere you were single." The Sicilian gave a strange smile over his shoulder, suspicious, Michael thought, but then it was gone, and he had finished with the load. He scampered behind the wheel again, and all Michael could see was the little dark head with the slit and the shiny eyes looking down from the tall window as the grotesquely large glove waved and the truck started off.

"See you the next time," the driver called back. Michael stood watching the truck depart through the dust and gain speed, with the morning sun winking brightly on the cab as it turned the corner of the drive, not slowing, and headed onto the road. When it was gone, he turned and spat once.

So, to make sure, he would have to wait until one o'clock, a few minutes past, perhaps, but no later. He figured that the schedule would permit just enough time for a man in a hurry to drive out to the eastern county line two times, if he arranged his pick-ups right and if he didn't linger to talk or have any trouble on the way, one time between the first and second circuits and once at the end of the day, after four o'clock. In his mind now, Michael could see the little fellow, scurrying about, trying to keep everything on schedule.

He went into the barn to set out the poison, enough to make it appear authentic—not that anyone would check, since not even Elroy seemed interested, but just to make himself feel better about it, like when he arranged the papers just so on top of the stool after he'd read them or when he downed the last of the beer in the glass even though he didn't want it, just to make it look and feel right. After finishing in the barn, he walked the rise at the edge of the pasture, from where he could see the boy working on the fence as he'd instructed him to, even though for once it didn't need it. In order to fill up the time, he got the tractor and began to turn over Maria's garden, as he'd done each spring since they'd been married so that she could have everything—including the tomatoes and the sweet corn, which was for humans, not animals, unlike the field corn that Maria swore people in the Cities ate in their ignorance—and so that she would not have to depend on Olson's store to order anything special for them except for the olive oil and vinegar, the wine coming from the huge casks Andrea had installed in the cellar, according to Michael the one piece of knowledge the old man had brought with him from Italy that had ever done any of them any good.

He walked up the drive a little before one, went through the house into the back porch, shifted the papers about aimlessly for a few minutes just to be certain, and to be sure Maria was far enough away that she wouldn't hear, then returned to the dining room and picked up the phone.

"Dick? That you?" he asked when he had finally convinced the boy who had answered that he had to talk directly to Howard. "Has my load been brought in yet?" He knew it had and didn't wait, talking over the other's response. "Listen, you better set mine aside. Is there still time for you to check it? That's right. I think there might be something that's got in it. That kid of mine just told me."

"What?" the other asked sharply. "What's got in it?"

"We've been putting out some of that new rat poison Olson's selling, and I think some of it might have got into the milk. I just noticed the open box now—your driver's come in hasn't he? That new one?"

"Yeah," the other responded. "Been and gone." So Michael knew his timing was right.

"Did he drop all of it off?" Michael asked. "Maybe you should try to reach his next—"

"No, no use bothering with that," Howard said. "The load's all here. I'll put it aside. Don't worry, you're in time. I'll have our people here check it."

"You need me around for anything?" Michael offered.

"No, of course not—not for the moment anyway. There's no rush. If I need you, I'll let you know." After a pause the other continued. "Oh, Michael, by the way, has Robin Elroy talked to you yet?"

"Not today."

"Well, he said he was going right over. Gene Castells seems to have told him about something he feels he ought to look into—you know, the big sheriff. He'll probably be there soon."

"All right," he said. "I'll be waiting for him," and he rang off, smiling at Castells' precision, or at least his predictability.

Less than an hour later, Robin Elroy was out front knocking. "I've solved your problem," he announced, looking as satisfied as the cat that had just introduced himself to the canary. "Gene Castells called me yesterday and gave me the last information I need. I even checked at the dairy, with that snooty Dick Howard. It's been the new driver of theirs all along—though I didn't want to tell them too much just yet and let them take the credit. Anyway, now that I'm sure of it, I'll take care of everything and you won't have to worry."

"What would I do without you?" Michael smiled.

"The only part I'm not sure of is how to find him without letting anyone know that I'm looking. I don't want him hearing what I've already heard and getting it into his head to bolt."

"I know where he'll be," Michael said.

"Well then, if you'll just tell me, I—"

"We."

"I can...Huh?"

"We can. I'm going with you."

"That might not be such a good idea," Elroy protested. "This is official. Why would—"

"Don't get upset," Michael slapped his shoulder. "I don't want to steal any of your credit. It's just that, well, you might say I'm curious."

"All right," Elroy yielded. "Where is it then?"

"I said I knew where he'd be, and I do," Michael smiled again, "but not until after four o'clock. There's plenty of time yet." Michael motioned his guest in. "Why don't you have some tea, or a glass or beer. Maria! Maria!" he called out. Then he turned to Elroy again. "Go on ahead to the porch, the Milwaukee papers are on the stool, if you want to look at them. In the meantime I've got to make some calls." And then again, "Maria! Maria!"

What Elroy had found out was what Michael had wanted him to find out. The Sicilian had started his turkey farm with a government loan—for which, as collateral, he had put up a house in Minneapolis that he did not own, although no one knew that yet—but once he got under way, the amount of the loan and the cost of the operation simply would not tally, nor was his salary from the dairy adequate to make up the difference, no matter how many hours he worked or how many stops he took on for his route. In fact, the more he worked the less time and energy he had to give to the turkeys (about which Dick Howard and the others at the dairy had cared nothing, at least prior to Elroy's call), with the result that even though he kept working harder and harder—tired all the time now, always on the move, moving too fast even to think— he ended up actually accomplishing less and less. What made things so bad was that he had contracted for the turkeys from the start, so that notwithstanding the fact that he was already too busy for any one man, his operation was continually expanding. Therefore, in order to make all the figures come out right (without paying for the feed that he could not afford anyway) he had to skim more and more milk to satisfy the regularly—and to his mind almost diabolically—increasing population of birds. Since he constantly needed more milk, and since, as everyone knew, Michael's milk was the best available anywhere around, he kept taking more and more of it. In the end he had no choice. He could not return the money or sell the operation until he had gotten it to where he could make a profit on his note for the house, and he could not do any more for the dairy than he was already doing. To his chagrin, he couldn't even give up and default on the loan since the house he'd put up for collateral belonged not to him but to his girlfriend, who wouldn't be especially grateful at finding herself out on the street when she'd been led all along to hope for so much good to come out of it all. The government clerks, first in Minneapolis and then in

White Rock, had assured him that the entire program was set up to help folks like him get started, but they never told him that, without at least some capital, starting from scratch was risky at best and, at worst, just plain foolish. No matter how hard he struggled—and he did—the point at which he would turn the corner and suddenly find himself rolling in green seemed to keep getting further and further out of reach. The odd thing, really, was that except for Michael no one had been suspicious earlier, given that he seemed forever in a state of nervous exhaustion, with the frantic manner and too quick smile of a character in a silent film rather than a driver for a local dairy.

As far as Michael was concerned, on the other hand, the Sicilian's problems were his own and therefore of no import to anyone else except, perhaps, for his family. If he couldn't manage his affairs and pay his debts, then he was liable for whatever might happen, period. And as for that other business, he would take care of it at the same time and in the same way, adding it into the bargain. After all, no one had ever given *him* something for nothing. But in point of fact none of that was why Michael was so angry. If the Sicilian would have stolen his possessions and flaunted it, or even insulted him out in the open, in town, say, at Olson's, or at the dairy, he would have reacted quickly and surely and then forgotten the whole affair. But by covertly taking what Michael valued most, the one thing which, despite himself, he had worked so hard to organize and produce and for which he was justly known and respected, and then by using it for a bunch of reeking turkeys, the Sicilian driver had committed a crime that in Michael's eyes was unpardonable. And since he had broken not only the law but also the tacit rules of custom and exchange by which they all lived, Michael was free to do whatever he chose, not only to retaliate and right the wrong done him, but also to teach the son of a bitch a lesson.

Which is just what he expected to do that afternoon as he and Elroy pulled up under the stand of oaks beside Castells' old blue Plymouth a little after four o'clock.

"Where's your driver?" Elroy asked Howard.

"He hasn't showed up yet."

"You sure he's coming?" Castells asked Michael.

"He'll be here," Michael told them both. "Just like I told you over the phone. Be patient for a few minutes, and you'll see for yourselves."

"You looked at his set-up yet?" Elroy asked, strolling off toward the yard and the metal bins where the turkeys would be.

"I wouldn't be in too much of a hurry to go over there if I were you," Howard said, while Castells pulled out his handkerchief.

"Why not?" Elroy asked.

"I just wouldn't, unless your stomach is a helluva lot stronger than mine is."

"There now, what did I tell you," Michael pointed across the grass toward the road where the big milk truck was just turning off, raising the blackbirds from their perches on the roadside fence. "Here he comes," Michael said triumphantly.

A moment later the driver stepped down from the cab in his filthy clothes, surprised at seeing them there waiting for him, and nervous, with the fatigue showing in his face even more so than usual, and without the smile. After all, maybe his operation wasn't a secret, but it wasn't supposed to be the site for a town meeting, either. For a moment he stood speechless, glaring from one to the other of them, as though searching for a hint at what move to choose next, except that there were no more moves; and, as he realized that, his features took on an aspect of composure, even passivity, that seemed, from where Michael stood, almost relief, like the feeling when the game's nearly finished and, even though you know you're going to lose, you haven't lost yet, so all you have to do is to sit back and watch as life becomes affirmation all on its own.

"Been waiting for you to get here," Elroy said in that flat, noncommittal tone that proclaimed him sheriff at the same time as it made Michael and Howard so annoyed.

"Well, that's my route you see," the Sicilian started, smiling now. But then he saw the look on Howard's face and gave up on it. "Look, what do you want," he tried to brush them off. "I've got work to do."

In spite of himself Castells broke into laughter, which trailed off into a cough as Elroy began to explain patiently, methodically, why they had come. They knew about his skimming the milk to feed his turkeys, and the agriculture office in the Cities knew that in order to get the loan in the first place he'd put up collateral that wasn't his in any sense, to put up or not. They knew he had two extra stops on his route, both right where they stood, and both for feeding, one just after his first delivery at noon and then another after his last pick-up at 4:00. They even knew why he'd selected Michael's product to skim the most from.

"That was your mistake," Howard interrupted. "Taking too much from just one source."

"The only thing we don't know is why you'd go to all this trouble in the first place," Elroy said. "If it just seemed so easy or if—"

"Look," the Sicilian said. "Ain't none of you said nothing that shows anyone has a problem except you." For a moment he looked strangely at Michael but then persisted. "You ain't shown me *nothing*, understand? Now unless you've got something to say, I'd appreciate it if you'd let me alone. In case you ain't had time to notice, I'm busy." He showed his teeth, not smiling, and turned away.

Elroy moved to grab him but Howard held him back. "Let him go ahead," he said to Elroy. "It won't take long." And then to the Sicilian as he headed off, "I wouldn't be in any rush to start now. But you'll see what I mean."

When Elroy made a motion to follow him, Howard held him back again. "Let him go," Howard said.

"But it's my job," Elroy protested.

"Haven't you understood yet?" Howard asked in disgust as the Sicilian crossed the grass and neared the bins. "Can't you see that Michael has already done your job for you?"

And in fact he had, as the rest of them were to see, too, a moment later, after they had moved toward the bins from where the Sicilian's shouts were coming, his language strange and fully as opaque as though he were speaking in tongues. The spectacle that greeted them when they turned the corner was so odd—even Michael was struck by the sight of the result of his labors, as he stood watching the man hunched over, his face purple in the midst of all those small whitish bodies, tinged with purple too, strewn across the yard wherever they had fallen as though some wild unheard-of beast had savaged them and then gone to the trouble of heaping them one on top of another in the yard and the bins like piles of rag dolls—that if the scene hadn't been so grotesque it would almost have been comical.

"Come on, let's go," Castells pulled at Michael's arm as Elroy took over. "Let's get out of here. Jesus, the damn things smell even worse dead than they do alive."

"You ought to stay awhile," Howard said to Michael, "You want to get your credit right."

"What do I care about that," Michael said to Howard and Elroy, not alluding to that other business, since even to mention it now would have ruined everything. "I never gave a damn about the milk, the *amount*," he said as Castells started toward the cars. "All I wanted was the turkeys that he made with it—and I got them.

You take care of the rest, and see that it doesn't happen again. Now *that's* your job."

So it seemed the only one who did care about the animals—not the feed or the credit or even the law—was the one who went crying across the bleak, littered yard now that he had seen what had happened to them. The Sicilian's reaction was understandable, to Howard and Elroy and maybe even to the others who heard about it, when they found out what had been at stake. When the Sicilian talked, once he got a hold of himself so that he could talk again, it turned out that his girlfriend in Minneapolis had expected such great things from his ventures that she had gone out and borrowed against her house on her own, apart from him, to the tune of four or five thousand dollars worth of clothes, furniture, and the like, with a silver chain and a diamond pendant tossed in for good measure. According to him, she was just sitting home waiting with her hands outstretched, amidst five kids (at least one of them, it seemed, his), for the debts to be paid off and the money to start pouring in. Nor was that the worst of his problems, since she, at least, had property of her own and a trade to ply, whence had come the other children, although he swore she had quit "working" after she had taken up with him, at least while he was still in Minneapolis. His other liability came in the form of a real family—wife and children, all legal and proper—stashed away in Duluth, more frugal than the girlfriend but if anything more pressing in their demands, since the contributions they required were for such necessities as food and clothing and shelter. So he was being squeezed from both ends, which explained why what Michael had seen in his eyes that first day had been less than fear but more than just worry, the sort of preoccupation that will drive a man along even though there is no special direction to its movement, with the result that he *does* a lot but without much to show for it except the action itself and, eventually, the bitter, disorderly residue of fright.

None of which, of course, was news to Michael since he had heard it all, and more, when he had checked on things himself through his cousins in Minneapolis and his relatives closer to home, and none of which, in the long run, changed much of anything. Neither the Sicilian's problems nor his women concerned him in the least. At any rate, that's what Michael thought as he sat in his rocking chair on the cold spring nights, alone, following the voices coming over the radio. True, the fellow had had his reasons. But on the other hand, who had ever told him to go ahead and do as he pleased and to break all the rules in the process? What had ever made him think, ever, that he could show up out of the blue on one day and on the next set out not only to steal but actually to soil his property, his family, and his reputation—everything Michael wanted and knew that he should want—and then get off without so much as a scratch? The Sicilian driver had trespassed on his life and on the lives of others, and when all was said and done, he'd got just what he deserved. What proved that Michael was right was that no one, not Elroy or Howard or Castells, not even Charlie, no one, had blamed him for what he had done, nor had anyone said that any of what had happened had been his fault. In fact, Michael's plan had worked so well, and so thoroughly, that he had become a hero of sorts, at least locally, with reports circulating out of New Providence and then reaching back to greet him every time, for whatever reason, he would travel to another town, so much so that, years afterwards, Gianni and O.B. still heard about it—even though they never did get the last name quite as it should be.

In the nights that followed, after the discoveries and the clean-up and the talk around the stove at Olson's store, as Michael rocked into the early mornings, drifting off and coming to in the darkness, still rocking, his feet hitting hard against the planks of the floor in the house that he had built, he listened to the voices coming from far away, from Milwaukee and Chicago and even further, reassuring in the unwavering constancy of their companionship, in their distance and anonymity; and he would rock and nod off and reawaken, recalling the sight of all those white and purple bodies clotted together, and then remembering Maria and that other business, thinking, so the Sicilian had had his reasons after all, the weaselly little son of a bitch, so what? He'd had his, too, goddamnit, and his were right.

III.   Hunt

Their truck rattles between the pines and lurches into the clearing hacked out of the forest in front of the cabin, the trees' outlines just now coming clear through the greys and browns of first dawn, as the big metal doors open and slam shut. Once O.B. has the cabin unlocked, they begin hauling things from the pickup into the dusty front room, keeping up a sort of half-run because of the cold, first the bags and the boxes of flour and soup and coffee and then the guns, going back and forth again and again over the frozen leaf-covered ground. Before Gianni has been able to get all of his own things in, O.B. already has a fire going in the fieldstone fireplace that Jake had built into the wall and that runs almost the entire far end of the cabin. As Gianni stands watching the flames leap above the hearth across the vapor of his breath, his feet numb on the hollow planks of the floor, he is amazed for the thousandth time at how fast O.B. has managed to get everything straight. But by then he is too tired even to indulge himself in the quickly growing warmth of the fire. They have traveled all night so as not to lose the first day, and in the truck Gianni had stayed awake even at the end, long after his usefulness as navigator, such as it had been, was over, so he could follow the spectacle of the stars in the blackness above them as the dipper spilled and Orion tracked his prey across the night sky. Now, despite the excitement and his anticipation of all that they would find—no matter what Kaseras and company had claimed—Gianni's exhaustion has grown deep enough that he has no choice but to sleep.

"Back room or side?" he asks O.B.

O.B. nods in the direction of the side-room, looking almost disappointed, as though he doesn't want to be bothered with that yet, entranced as he is by the orange flames of his handiwork dancing to life on the hearth. "Jake and the others will be here by noon," he says perfunctorily. "We can take the bunk-beds in there next to Jake's. There are more beds in the back room, anyway, never mind that it's colder in there, too. We might as well have our pick, unless Jake objects."

Gianni gets out the sheets and locates Jake's spot for the blankets in the heavy chest in the corner. After yanking the curtain across the window and finding himself suddenly in darkness again, he strips down to his underwear—the union suit he had begun to use even before seeing Jake Arndt again—and crawls between the sheets, at first smooth and cold as ice, to make him shiver, but warming quickly to his body. Later, Gianni will remember saying something to the effect of offering to help O.B. with the guns after a while, then stretching himself out, with the noise—oddly comforting regardless of its strangeness—of O.B. clanging around at the stove to start the coffee. Then, despite himself, he is drifting on the deep sea of sleep.

This is early on a Monday morning the first week in November, in the forest along the furthest edge of Washburn County in northern Wisconsin, where Jake Arndt has sworn there are more deer than you can shake a stick at, if you just know where and how to find them, or better yet—if you want to save yourself the trouble—how to get them to find you.

* * *

Then he is chasing through the trees at breakneck speed, following his prize as if in a dream, in the perfect purity of action and pursuit.

* * *

Of course, nothing of the kind ever happened around here before—never—at least nothing to top it, not that I've heard of. And the bartender would be the one to know if it had, take my word for it. Not that I'd spread it around, naturally: no need to worry about that. Complete confidentiality, that's my motto—and why everyone opens up, I guess, like a river—hell, more like Niagara Falls some of them. But this time it's really too much to hush up. They all know already anyway, since for days it's been run up and down by everybody who ever knew them, and by some who didn't and still don't and now maybe never will. Ever since that afternoon when the cops came, or whatever they were in those funny outfits. They sure didn't look like any cops I ever saw, no matter what Uncle Martin says, though I guess he ought to know after all those years tramping around on the state payroll himself. And they did have badges—little tinny ones with a funny title stamped on them, inspector of this-or-that, or some such. I tried, but I couldn't see that well to make it out. One thing was plain though, they were from Illinois and not Wisconsin, anyone could tell that. So maybe they were special officers like Martin said they were. Anyway, I figured it must have been all right to talk, at least as things stood then. Even the cops never suggested I had to clam up or play deaf if people asked. Besides, I probably know more than anybody—they were right to come to me. And besides that, well, it's good to get it all out in the open. Read 'em and weep, or bleed, as the case may be. Take your pick. That's what I told them, too, with those squirrelly little eyes of theirs and their mouths full of questions. It's good to talk straight about things, plain and simple, because what does it hurt? That's what I say: the truth never hurts.

As for that stuff about honor and pride and respect, well, as far as I'm concerned it's worth exactly what it costs, which is not one red cent. In point of fact, you could say that that's where all the trouble began around here in the first place, if you just look at it right. Quick tongues and hot air. Hell, I bet even the brothers didn't know what all the fuss in here was about, much less that big-spending Ben Kaseras and 'Five' Bronson and those brayingass friends of theirs. Funny thing is, when they talk to you now, they all tap their fingers on the bar so cocksure, as if they really know what happened, and not only what but why, too, swaying back and forth with their bright chests puffed out, like they'd discovered the golden brick of truth way back and had been perched right on top ever since, cheery as you please. Well, bullshit, that's what I call it, even though I might not say so out loud—you learn pretty quick in this line of work that a couple of swipes with a bar-cloth at a spot or a fly will go a long way toward changing the subject—'cause they'd probably stop coming in to tell me their life stories if they knew what I was really thinking. And who'd want that? A bar full of deaf-mutes? Who'd ever come back? Jesus, we'd go broke in a week—not that that makes any difference anymore, I guess—or maybe it will anyway, I don't know. So as it is, they tell me everything just so, every petty little detail from their bird's-eye view. Slide down to Riley's and tell Johnny Bubbles all your troubles, that's what they say. And I'll be goddamned if a lot of them don't do just that.

So, yes, I did talk to the nice men with the badges, answered their every question, A to Z. But, of course, I didn't tell them everything and certainly not about the bets and the brothers' guns, especially the deer rifle with the lead weight in the middle and the aim as true as a twenty-dollar gold piece, or so they said, despite the fact that it was near twice as old as either of them. So why tell all and get myself in up to the armpits? Why should I? Hell no, not me. I just followed their questions and let them lead, nothing more. If they didn't know what to ask, I didn't tell 'em. And besides, they wouldn't even take a drink. Not after I thought of it and offered them one on the house, like O.B. always said I should with official types, or if we were being held up or something. Can you imagine that? A Sunday drink at Riley's and they turned it down. Flat. Just like cops, come to think of it. You can never tell what they're going to do next. Hell, I think I would rather be stuck up. So, no, I didn't spread it to the breeze and tell them every little thing. Of course I'm honest—maybe to a fault, even to the point of being proud of it—but show me where it's written that I've got to be stupid, too.

At the start of it, even before all the bets, or what I thought was the start, since I'd never noticed anything related before (though it did occur to me later that I might not know the brothers as well as I'd thought, in spite of the fact that I've worked for them for over three years now, which is as long as they've had the place, and which means that I'm the only real bartender they've ever had—all those kids don't count—trusting me to open up and, before they did well enough to have a day-man, namely me, so I wouldn't have to stay up all hours anymore and walk home with my head turning every which way to look out for the punks and the goddamn junkies moaning in the gutter, to close out, too, counting up and then putting the evening's take under the third row of bottles laying on their side in the beer cooler in back). Anyway, at the start there was that odd conversation between Gianni and O.B., just last spring, hardly nine months ago, though it seems like ages now. They were sitting at the bar exactly as they had on a hundred other slow afternoons, the jukebox off, Gianni sipping his draught and O.B. leaning over to toy with the swizzlesticks and clinking the ice in the J.T.S. Brown he had me special order for him every month. They'd been talking quietly, not intense, not like the arguments over sports or the lickety-split riddle games the two of them would play like kids, but quiet and nice, hunched together, going over old times from the little bit I'd pick up now and then, like usual when they were in after the early crowd has cleared out but before the boiler-makers come in through all the doors calling out for their beer. That's a funny time in here in that season of the year, between say, four-thirty and five o'clock, because even though the lights aren't on yet, the daylight has started to fade and it's hard to see much, like looking across a park in the early evening, or just before dawn. But in spite of the dimness I could see the change in Gianni's expression, the way he paled with surprise, shock even, and I remembered it later because it was so strange for him, he was usually so placid, completely out of character, at least as far as I could tell, which I have to admit wasn't much, since in the end Gianni was always a closed book to me, even if we did have the same name, more or less.

They'd been talking about their Grandpa, I was pretty sure of that, since—along with the few comments I'd picked up while I was washing the glasses and restacking them on the back bar—that had always been one of their favorite topics. In fact, it was just because it was such a regular subject that I hadn't really been listening too close. So for all I know they may have already been at it for a while when Gianni lurched forward, white as a ghost, and I started paying attention. Lucky enough, it wasn't too late, either, 'cause they started to go back over it again, I suppose just so they could get it straight—or so Gianni could, 'cause by then O.B. seemed to have gotten Gianni calmed down, and he was doing most all the talking, going about it in that make-no-mistake way of his, using his fine, big hands for emphasis like a conductor, so that it sure looked like O.B. knew precisely what he was talking about and that he wanted Gianni to know he did, too.

"He'd had it for years," O.B. said nice and clear, waving his hand. "He just let everybody know not to talk about it, and especially not in front of us. That was the way he wanted it. That stuff he gave out about losing his balance was his way of keeping it from us, nothing less, nothing more."

"But Grandma was the one who had the pains and took those pills," Gianni protested, still upset, as he had every right to be, from what I could tell. "*She* was the one—"

"Yes, she was—but it was pure hypochondria, exactly the opposite of him. She got the doctor to prescribe the nitroglycerin for her because she was a nut, and a vocal one—and with the money and all, she could afford it—and he snuck the pills out of the medicine chest because he actually needed them even though he wouldn't admit it." O.B. swirled his ice and placed the glass gingerly on the bar. "And as for the pains, what about the times we'd go wading in the Rush or the Trimbell—you remember, you were old enough then—and he'd get in halfway and suddenly remember that he'd left his favorite fly in the tackle box on the bank, and he'd have to turn and go back? What did you think was in those little containers he guarded so carefully in there? Or even the time you just brought up—but do you remember why we were there at all? Why all at once we were supposed to go up north for a 'vacation' in the middle of winter? Hell, he came to the station special to meet us and then couldn't even make it to the train."

"But I remember him tripping," Gianni insisted, still pale though, while O.B. just kept right on, barely noticing.

"'Cause—right—he 'tripped' on the platform, with all the people gathering around to help him, but he wouldn't even let himself be helped, except to have Drew do the driving on the way home to the farm after they'd picked us up. Or the time by the Snower's woods with the twenty-two's..."

O.B. went on but by then Gianni had stopped listening. From the way he looked it seemed he was concentrating on something else, which he was, because as if out of the blue he shook his hair from his forehead and started talking about the dogs they'd had when they were kids, the big labs that they always loved to talk about, the kind strung tight as a fiddle, with a coat black as pitch.

"You remember that Nero was hit the same day?"

"That's right," O.B. nodded, still sure, crisp, because he hadn't noticed the change yet.

"Funny," Gianni hesitated. "It always seemed to me—I mean I always felt—that somehow the two things were, well, connected."

"No," O.B. said simply and shook his head. "Except for you, if that's the way you wanted it."

A minute or two passed, then all at once Gianni turned and, again totally out of character, asked with a voice so full of bitterness you could feel it oozing out of him. "Well, why didn't you tell me then? Why didn't any of you tell me that his heart had been bad all along, that it wasn't anybody's fault? That it wasn't any truer than one of those dreams I used to have? Goddamnit!" Gianni started to rise, his face suffused, menacing, the first I'd ever seen anything of the sort out of him. "Well," he shouted. "I'm asking you. Why not?"

You really have to hand it to O.B. He managed to keep hold of himself even then, sitting on his stool looking even more surprised that I was, to tell you the truth, and a touch defensive, too, because you could see the hurt in his brow and in the slope of his shoulder, like he'd been hit, the way it is when he's telling you something that's none too pleasant for either of you but that has to be said like it or not—and when you can trust what he says to be the truth.

"Gianni," he said, "I thought you knew. Otherwise I would have told you. How was I to know you'd feel that way about something like that? Hell, I felt as bad as you did about Nero. They made all of us feel bad enough about that. But not that way. I just figured you must have known." Then he did one of those other things he does, he lifted his arm out to grab Gianni's shoulder. I still remember them there like that, as the lights outside began to come on and brighten the bar, Gianni looking down now, quiet again, and O.B. reaching out to him, the two of them standing there as if in relief. "Honest, Gianni," O.B. repeated, his voice firm again, certain, consoling. "I thought for sure you knew."

So, I figured, it sure must have been something that Gianni should have known, because at least he didn't shout anymore—which was just as well anyway, since by then the boilermakers had started coming in. Instead, he nodded and said that he'd have to rethink some things. Which he did, I guess, because after that afternoon he and O.B. talked more often, so intensely that Gianni wouldn't even get up to shoot the balls off the pool table like usual, going over things that O.B. either knew himself or had heard from his cousins or had guessed—and guessed right, it appears, from the evidence, or at least that's what Gianni seemed to think, judging from the way he listened, asking his questions and nodding and falling silent again evening after evening as the darkness gathered outside and the lights began to come on. Of course, I'd try not to butt in when they were huddled together like that, so even if there was a problem—if one of the salesmen was in and, as usual, had got the order wrong, which they all had such a knack for, except cousin Jamie the redhead, who was too honest to stay in that business anyway, with the quick, innocent smile that really was, and who ended up where he should have been all along, as the beverage man at one of the Church schools hereabouts, or if Billy-Club the flat-foot, with the cigar butt squashed in his mouth and the rotting suspenders slung across his shoulders, sauntered in to clean the keg lines (in his spare time, according to him, which must have been whenever his feet got sore from carrying that big gut of his around his beat), though I wasn't supposed to say anything, since O.B. said that this was Chicago, not Never-Never Land, like it or not, and it was better to have the corner cop cleaning out your beer lines than your till, not that O.B. couldn't have seen to it downtown if he'd had to, but this way he didn't have to—I'd take care of it myself and let them talk, which they were sure doing a hell of a lot of. Gianni must have been doing a good bit of recollecting on his own, too, because as the weeks went by and O.B. kept showing up after going downtown to his office and Gianni just kept showing up period, hours before he'd take over behind the bar, since there's not much for an ex-railroad fireman turned newspaper reporter—for a week—turned social worker—for all of six months—turned bartender to do during the day anyway, Gianni seemed to have more and more questions to ask, until he was interrupting O.B. with comments and versions of his own almost every other sentence.

Some of it, I must admit, sounded pretty interesting—not all of it, of course, and then I didn't know all of the background, either. Not that I'd ever eavesdrop on the brothers to find out, mind you. But some of it sounded all right. Like the stuff about O.B. and their cousin Richie, for instance. Now, I'd known about O.B.'s exploits with Sherrie and girls like her for a long time—known probably more than O.B. knew I knew and certainly more than Gianni knew, most likely more than he does even to this very day or at least I hope so, given the way he got to feeling about Sherrie himself—but I had no idea that O.B. had had such a variety of practical experience with the fair sex going back so far. From the way O.B. talked, it was mostly their cousin Richie's doing. But the aunt must have pitched in to help out quite a bit, too, as a sort of participant-observer, so to speak, since it seems that Richie and the aunt—whose husband had apparently only been able to get it in shape for service once in ten years of marriage, discounting his interest in farm animals and, it seems, potential young farm hands—had already been greasing each other's wheels for quite a little while by the time that O.B. was getting old enough to know what curves were for, outside of baseball.

I can't remember all of it, but it's not often that a thirteen or fourteen-year-old kid like O.B. had been—his brother and all, and Gianni hadn't even had an inkling—learns firsthand the real excitements of the hayloft, and it sure didn't sound anything like those games of tag that he and Gianni used to talk about, including every which way, from what I could tell, over, under, around, and through, not that the position is the important thing, of course, especially at first, with their taut young breasts and eager tongues, or the way that a girl's soft, full lips are good for kissing and a whole lot more, too, if you whisper right and show them till they move them up and down in the heat of the loft just so, with their fine hair falling down and tickling across your tummy—with the scar over O.B.'s brow probably bouncing like an acrobat—as if a nice smooth stick was even more fun than a lollipop. Not that Sherrie was at all like that, of course. Hell, if anything she knew too much to need any teaching, which is probably why O.B. got to like her in the first place, and why she was able to get Gianni into the state she did. Oh, she was eager too, all right and—I heard—the very best around at what she did. But that's another story.

Anyway, it sounded like O.B. was able, thanks to the thoroughness of their tutelage, to turn right around and teach the girls in town how much fun those lessons could be, which I guess he and Richie eventually took up giving together—and which must have been Richie's undoing with the aunt, but that's a different matter—first to the older girls and then to the younger candidates, all of whom wanted to do the best they could, like being the first on their block, even if properly speaking they didn't have blocks. And I guess Gianni must have been pretty surprised about it all, too, from the way his mouth hung open as O.B. got to the details of who, what, where, and how.

I must say that the rest of what they were going back and forth over held much less interest, at least for me. After all, who cares if they spent all those summers together or if Gianni was stupid enough to get himself up on a horse—and a big one, from the way they talked about it—without even knowing that when you're holding on for dear life you do it with your arms and knees, and not with your heels, which will only make the damn thing go faster. I mean, it's the human that's supposed to have the brains, isn't it, not the animal. Or the question-answer games with the aunt whose name made you think of Philadelphia, or the jokes about the Green Lake that really was, and the Ricci brothers who weren't—I mean, so what? Actually, their one grandpa, the city-boy turned farmer, sounded O.K., the one with the old non-stop rocker, the way he took care of all the necessary business, and especially that two-bit thief who stole his milk to slop the chickens and roosters with and who seemed to have stolen something else, too, that only O.B. knew about. But the other one, the ex-lumberman with the bad heart, seemed like a complete zero. Or maybe it wasn't so much his fault as the way they talked about him. All that Snow White fairy-tale stuff just never set right with me. Hell, it's childish—something you'd never expect from the brothers that way, and in particular not from O.B. So what if the old fellow was a saintly sort? Jesus, everybody shits now and then, don't they, like it or not. That's just the way things are. There's no sense in mulling it over, and even less in pretending it ain't so. As for that twenty-two, well, if you want my opinion, Gianni was probably too young for guns anyway, even though he did have a point, at least about being let down. Maybe if the old man had spoken to him like Gianni wanted—"just once, one word"—it would have made all the difference, who knows. But hell, what was everybody supposed to do? Make believe that no one has birthdays except for him?

If there was one member of that whole crew that sounded at least bearable, it was the old hunter, Jake, the one that their German grandpa used to be so tight with. I guess he really wasn't a hunter in any official sense, but that he just didn't have much else to do with himself after having been gassed in the war (the first one, with the mustard gas that, even if you only got a whiff of it, stained your lungs for good, or so they say), and then getting a nice army pension so that all he had to do was to farm the little forty-acre plot beside his stream and walk the ridge into the woods, looking for something to occupy his time by shooting at it, or thinking up practical jokes to play on folks in town like fixing up that stump in the woods to look like a bear or putting the geese in the old woman's pantry. The brothers must have liked him too, from the way they talked about him—completely different from how they were when they mentioned the old fellow, like the difference between whispering about the King and chuckling with the Court Jester. Hell, it had apparently been him who kept everybody from coming apart at the old man's funeral. And that sounded pretty good, too, his taking them all into the old man's den and presiding with the head of the twenty-six point buck glaring down, and telling them joke after joke, till even the old fellow himself would have sat up and cracked a smile.

Of course, there was a serious side there, too. But it seemed sort of hidden away amidst the laughter, so it wasn't so hard to take. I guess the hunter and the old man had been friends for a good long time, long enough for him to know the brothers' mother as a kid, before she had married their father or even met him. So that when she did meet him and take up seriously, old Jake was right there to look on and applaud. When their father had come back from the war, after flying the paratroopers into Italy and then into France, he had brought some of that silky white material from the chutes back with him, as a souvenir more than anything, and following the wedding the hunter's wife, Beatrice I think, started making the material into little baby suits, since that was one of her specialties, having been a seamstress in St. Paul before meeting the old gassed-up ex-soldier and hooking up with him for good. Anyway, that's another thing that Gianni had never known about—or hadn't known all he should have, anyway. Since he remembered seeing the suits that he and O.B. had worn, and hearing about how they were made and all, Aunt Bea sewing away to her heart's content, but he'd never thought to ask: why suits? Why more than one, since he and O.B. had always shared everything else, one after the other as O.B. grew out of things and handed them down and he grew in. You see the second one, the one Gianni had got, hadn't been meant for him at all; nor had he thought or known to ask why Aunt Bea had been so kind, protective almost, even when he'd been playing with the chickens she kept or fooling with the eggs she'd sell to have a little pocket money of her own tucked away, and he would manage to break one, as he apparently did with regularity, since instead of slapping him as she should have the very first time, if you ask me, she'd grabbed his arm slick as a dream and held it tight—that, he remembered, the sudden almost man-like strength in those fingers and her face coming down close, the long dark hair and milky complexion—her eyes studying him more out of bafflement than anger, and then, when the reflection in their deep pools had vanished as quickly as it had come, she would let him go to find O.B. or her husband or both. Because there had been another child, too, but it was late, a change-of-life baby they used to call them, and in the end it was just too late. So maybe it was right that it should have been the hunter who told the stories and roared the way he did at the old man's funeral, since it was sure better than breaking down like their grandma had done or just moping in the corner, and since he was probably feeling worse than any of the rest of them anyway. Gianni found that out, too, some from O.B. and some on his own, like everything else those days, even though by the look of things it seemed he still hadn't found out all that he wanted to once he'd got started, not all. But he kept at it, taking it in, something like the trickle of water that first fills a glass and will a whole sink, too, if you just let it go on long enough.

    Exactly how that old guy Jake got to know all that he knew about hunting and the woods—that I never found out. But no matter how it was, he was sure a lot more entertaining to hear about than those two grandpas of theirs, even the sensible one. Hell, if you ask me there wasn't anything concerned with either of them you could make out straightaway. Every time it seemed you had them in your grasp they'd slip away again. The only good thing about the one, the one who couldn't stand talking about money and who couldn't have dealt with trouble even when he could see it coiled at his boots—so how, I felt like asking O.B. more than once, how could he ever have done any better with the rest of them, all those years after he was dead and gone, if he couldn't have handled them when he was alive and kicking—the only good thing, anyway, was that you knew you couldn't figure him out. But there was something else about the way O.B. would mention the other one, too, the one who got robbed but took care of it—or maybe it was just the way O.B. would watch Gianni every now and then for his reaction when he thought nobody was looking, forgetting about me washing the glasses in front of the big mirror, and the other old man came up—that made me think that maybe O.B. knew or suspected more than he was letting on, or maybe even more, in the end, than he had wanted to know himself.

At a certain point, though, you could tell that Gianni was so stocked with information, with things to think about, that he was ready to burst. People get that way. I see it every day in here. I could see he'd reached his limit the day he stormed in here like a bull entering the ring. Or maybe that wasn't it at all, maybe it was just springtime, or too long for him to go without any activity besides sitting on a stool bending his elbow and thinking, or, hell, maybe it wasn't Gianni in the first place but just that damn pool table. I always say, where there's a pool table in a bar, there's trouble. Got trouble? Get rid of the pool table and the trouble will go with it, sure as you please. It wasn't my fault that Gianni was so good at it. Actually, on account of the action and the betting and the fights that usually went along with it, you would have thought that it should have been O.B.'s game, not Gianni's. But there was something else to it that set just right with Gianni—and not only that odd mixture of motion and intensity that the game was made up of. There was something so natural and fluid about it, too, though in a strange sort of way, that made it right for Gianni, not for O.B. It sure didn't take much imagination to see that what happened when Gianni moved around the table with the cue in his hand, shifting in and out of the light from the triple lamp, was that his mind moved down from his head to his hands—as if they were trading places for a while and were mighty relieved to do so—and then from there to the stick itself, so that what seemed all motion and precision and speed, with the balls clicking together and thumping into the pockets one after another as though half by force and half by themselves, wasn't anything other than a continuous but punctuated dance with a flow and logic all its own, in which Gianni, apart from the stick and the light and the table and the chalk and the motion of the game, was completely lost. Afterwards, he'd seem utterly drained, but peaceful, too, like an Indian at the end of a smoke.

But, anyway, I could tell right off that Saturday afternoon, from the way he stormed in and slapped his newspaper down—

judging from the neat crease in it, most likely unread—and went straight to the back of the bar and started tossing the balls across the soft green felt and into the banks, that something was in the air. It's funny, Gianni is usually so quiet and inward, but once he's going, he's like a jukebox—get him plugged in and drop in the quarter and no matter what button you push you're going to get a tune. And from the way he was acting, I figured we might get more than just one or two. Later on I found out what had caused it, in a manner of speaking. Gianni had been out to his folks' place for dinner, I guess with other people, too, some of their high-toned friends O.B. used to chuckle about, and had started checking up on some of what O.B. had been telling him, just what I don't know, but I'm sure that whatever it was, the answers didn't tally. I guess Gianni didn't take it too well, because it still hadn't worn off the next day, which is when he came in here and stalked to the pool table, chalking his cue and leaning over so the folds of his blue shirt hung open and smooth, and started knocking the balls into the pockets like they were coming out of a cannon. After a while O.B. came in, and went over to see him. Before O.B. had even had a chance to say hello, Gianni was glaring at him and asking, "So the old man was the one who had all that money—is that right?"

O.B. smiled and tried to evade the question, so he led Gianni off to one side, with his hand on his shoulder, and talked to him quietly for ten minutes or so. After that, O.B. took Gianni's state for what it was and left him alone. In fact, now that I think about it, even though that was certainly the thing to do under the circumstances, leaving Gianni at the table to work off steam by himself, in that instance it might have been better if O.B. had talked to him a while longer. Because it didn't work off but just increased as the feeling locked in. But what was odd, in fact—and where all the problems with Ben Kaseras and them really started—was what happened after that.

In the past, ever since the brothers had set up shop at Riley's, there had been any number of games with Gianni and O.B. teamed against Kaseras (who shot good pool too, despite his belly that draped out over the table) and his loudmouthed friends (who didn't shoot so well, but acted like they did), with the coin-box disconnected so they could play straight fourteen-and-one instead of eight-ball or last pocket like the rummies or nine-ball like the kids. They'd bet on those pool games almost every week—just like the bets on the weekend games of touch football or on the pros on TV—with bets mounting on bets and splitting every which way and doubling and turning into side bets on banks and kisses and combinations. None of that would have been anything out of the ordinary. But there was something different that afternoon, and at least in that sense Kaseras had a reason to take it as he did. Oh, it wasn't the money that mattered, or at least not just the money. Kaseras was a sheet-metal worker turned contractor then builder himself, so he didn't have to worry about counting his pennies. But in his agitation, Gianni neglected to jam the pockets so it would seem he'd missed or to hold back and take only the tough shots instead of running through the balls one by one like shooting fish in a barrel. I guess Gianni just forgot, since I can't think of any other explanation. From behind the bar, through the smoke toward the back of the room, I could see that what happened when he practiced, which he always did alone, was happening then, too, maybe even without him realizing it.

    Kaseras hated to lose, but he hated to lose bad even more. He had broken, looking like a caricature of himself with his little brown cap to cover the bald spot, and after O.B. had missed and Big Jimmy White, Kaseras's partner, had scratched, it was Gianni's turn. By the time, somewhere in the third rack, that Kaseras—having gone from his usual pasty white to splotches of pink—scraped one of the bar stools over the wood floor or pounded his cue or did whatever it was he finally did to break Gianni's concentration and bring him back to the world of the living, it was already too late. Besides, even though Kaseras had got Gianni's attention, he'd also made him mad, like waking someone out of a dream—not just upset, which he'd been before, like I said, and which had probably supplied the fuel for the game—but really mad, since, having run well over thirty balls already and being far enough along to make going back impossible, Gianni chalked, took a deep breath, winked at O.B., put his head back down, and kept shooting, putting a kiss in the corner and making a cross-side to finish the third rack. And he would have run out the fourth, too, except that by then he and O.B. (who was as dumbfounded as the rest, because usually, if all else failed, Gianni made provisions to miss at one point or another before things got embarrassing and/or the customers got angry) had already reached fifty, thus finishing both the game and, in the same instant, what turned out to have been a very precarious friendship. Not that that in itself made much difference, since being friends with Kaseras was nothing to brag about anyway if you ask me. In point of fact, Kaseras was obnoxious enough that the game actually ended at forty-nine rather than fifty. At the last shot he reached out and grabbed up the ball with that hand of his that looked like three-day old pork, and he most likely would have grabbed up the whole table if he could have, his now uniformly pink jowl shaking with rage.

Later, it occurred to me that that was the first time, during the yelling afterwards about cheating and respect, with Kaseras waving his cue so I thought he was going to bust it for sure, that all this stuff about "pride" and "honor" really came up. By a week or so after that, those had become regular customers around here, stopping in damn near every day. But if you took the trouble to think it through—like I did that afternoon, once the doors had closed behind those self-styled cops, or whatever they were—that had been the first of it, that day that Gianni was so worked up about something else that by the time he looked up and realized what he'd done, and that Ben Kaseras, for whom Gianni had even less regard than O.B. or I did, had been the unwittingly innocent recipient of such good fortune, he decided to take the opportunity for what it was and not just beat him, which would have been too easy anyway, but rub his nose in it, too.

Oh, Kaseras was mad as a hornet all right, take it from me. Actually, thinking about it now, I guess that if O.B. hadn't been there watching, there would have been a fight. And as much as I hate to clean up after those sorts of things, it might have been for the best too (even though by himself Gianni never would have had a prayer), something to clear the atmosphere, so to speak. As it was, all Kaseras and his friends could do, with Gianni smiling like a schoolboy and O.B. perfectly cordial, seeming genuinely to want to patch things up, but holding his stick in front of him, leaning on it and flashing that what-do-you-think-I-might-do-with-this look of his, was to let the whole matter drop after a good lively discussion, like I said. But whatever anyone did, the trouble wasn't going to go away, Kaseras being what he was and with his friends always around to remind him. So instead of disappearing, it began to fester.

"All right," Kaseras had finally put down his cue, glaring at Big Jimmy White now, too, and lifting up what was left of his beer as though to drink it in peace, because there were other people looking on now. "All right," he looked straight at O.B. "But next time it'll cost you more, and we'll see to it that it won't be so easy," he said, meaning God knows what. Kaseras put down his stein and turned to go and then turned back again, dropping the ball so that it rolled over the felt toward Gianni. "For you, either, little brother." And with that he stalked off, past the bar and the noise and out the door, shoving his ex-partner out of his way as he went.

Gregory Lucente

Now, to see why that first scene and the others it eventually led to were so important, you have to understand what the bar meant to the brothers and just what Kaseras and his group meant to the bar. The funny thing is, *that* was the part the cops, or whatever they were, didn't even want to hear about. "Just the stuff about the two brothers," they kept saying, "you can skip the rest." But trust me when I tell you that unless you understand Kaseras and them, none of the rest of it is going to make any sense at all.

From the outset, the bar had been a joint venture, between O.B. and Gianni. O.B. had heard about the place from the real-estate dealings at his office downtown, a nice old place about to be put up for sale in a fair-to-middlin' neighborhood on the north side, one that had gone from Irish to German to middle-class (and respectable) Spanish, a little rough-and-tumble but not bad. So when it came up for sale the brothers were ready and they got it from old man Riley for a song. They added the pool table and rebuilt the back bar, in addition to putting in the little kitchen for sandwiches and such to make the beer go down easier. But they kept the name, since somehow "Mariagrazia's" didn't seem quite right for a bar, even if the neighborhood wasn't Irish anymore. From the very first Gianni made all the plans—what sort of liquor to order and how much, what kind of beer to have on tap, how many stools at the bar, how big the kitchen should be, and what sort of lighting they wanted (including the rack of lights for the pool table, which he insisted be one of the old nine-foot Brunswicks with the slate bed rather than those seven or eight foot lightweight bar tables that you see everywhere else nowadays), and what sort of customers, over the long haul, he was aiming to get. Once Gianni had decided and the two of them had talked, O.B. took care of all the arrangements. And there was a lot to be done, too. O.B. made the contracts for the work and for the regular orders, talked with the salesmen (including their poor mixed-up red-headed relative), and went downtown to handle the details with the City.

It was fun to watch him do it, because O.B. always showed a lot of class. One day a fellow from the Building Department came in to poke his cocky nose around the back rooms, and even though we'd never had any electrical problems to speak of (and I sure would have been the first to complain if we had, since I prefer not to get fried), the creep claimed he'd found all sorts of things wrong with the wiring and the fixtures, although of course he'd missed the real danger spot, the triple-headed extension behind the jukebox. He left word for the brothers that he'd be back the following Wednesday, so when I told O.B., he just asked who it had been and shrugged his shoulders, putting two twenties in an envelope and telling me to give it to the fellow first thing, with a big smile, which is what I did. Usually that was enough, but this fellow got his feathers all ruffled, and turned the envelope aside with his shiny pinky, saying now he'd found even more things and that he would have to come back at the end of the week. Most likely he'd just seen the name "Riley's" outside and nothing more. So when I told O.B., he shook his head, with a look of genuine displeasure on his face, almost disappointment. "Greedy bastard," he said. "Now he won't even get the twenties."

So the next evening when O.B. came from downtown he brought in a fellow with him, a big, ruddy-looking guy in a white shirt but with grit around his nails dark enough that I could see it as he reached for the glass of beer I had set in front of him on O.B.'s orders.

"Meet Black Jack McClure," O.B. grinned and patted the meaty shoulder in the white shirt as I reached out my hand. "Don't hold back on the beer, now. I want you two to get to know each other. Jim here is our new building inspector." Whatever route they gave the other one, God only knows. But that was sure the last I ever heard or saw of him. Because by then, even though O.B. wasn't the sort to brag about it, he was getting to be pretty well known around City Hall.

At first the kind of people that came in didn't make much difference, even to Gianni, but as time went on, of course, both of the brothers, and especially Gianni, wanted to build up a regular group. It was all right to keep the holdovers from when Riley had the place (except for the heavies, whose fights I could do without: to tell the truth, even the billy clubs placed strategically every five feet along the back bar were more of a worry for me than a comfort), like the two old fellows who would hobble around the corner with their canes every morning, predictable as clockwork, just as I was mopping the floor after I'd started working days—at first they wanted to know why we hadn't been opening till late, and although they seemed a little indignant, you could see they were relieved, too, with the light shining through their glasses of beer, since they'd been worried that they were going to have to find another place to stop for their refreshment during their morning constitutional; or the neatly dressed, dark-haired fellow, balding, who would always ask for port (at first I had to give him wine, but Gianni took care of that) and who seemed perfectly normal until he got the glass in front of him and started talking, mostly about losing his son, which he made sound as though it had happened a week or a month before, though I found out later it had been during World War II, and about other topics, too, equally cheery, and he would keep going in the same tone of voice hours on end, whether anyone was within earshot or not, looking at his port, talking to it but not drinking it, till it occurred to him that he was supposed to drink something to keep the house going (which Riley or someone must have told him) and he would tip the glass back and down its contents in one gulp, then cough to get my attention, pausing just long enough to order another one, and resume talking, not addressing anyone in particular, not even me, but depending on me being there nonetheless, rambling on in the monotone that by then had stopped being simple monotony and had turned into a calm, steady delirium, because, I guess, he had no one, and nothing else; or the Irish firefighters who would come in with their big rubber suits and hats reeking of smoke if they had been on duty, or in their street clothes if they had been off, and who in either case always ended up the same way—after an hour or two of shouting and laughing and first ordering me then threatening me then pleading with me not to admit to their wives calling on the phone that they were there—asleep with their foreheads resting dead-square on the bar and their snores rattling the rows of glasses that were piled up in front of the mirror, providing what seemed endless entertainment for the other customers, until it went on too long and I would have to wake them up and get them headed home. All of those, and the others like Uncle Martin or the boilermakers, or the kid who for one beer would give a recital of Shakespeare—Macbeth's soliloquy, he claimed—and for two would burst forth into what seemed to me like pretty much all of *Moby Dick*, were fine as far as they went. But it didn't take much to see that they weren't ever going to make up into a real, bona fide group of regular customers. So that was where Ben Kaseras came in—or was supposed to, except that he'd been following a different track—him and his loud-mouthed, whiskey-and-beer-drinking crowd of rugby players.

Besides being pretty heavy drinkers, Kaseras and his cohorts also got the new Riley's a reputation—and not a bad one at that—as a "sociable" bar with an impressively rowdy local crew, but in a good sense, not at all like the old blood-and-guts heavies in Riley's day had been. Most of them, including Kaseras, lived in the neighborhood or at least within walking distance (crawling distance on late Friday or Saturday night), so the group really was a little like the home team. And they did make up into a team eventually, Riley's Rebels (Gianni used to call them Riley's Rummies, but he never had liked rugby anyway). On alternate Saturday evenings, the bar would host the players from both teams, ours and whoever the opponents had been that week on the local circuit. At least at first, rugby seemed to draw a tonier crowd than the softball or touch football teams sponsored by other bars around town, and both Gianni and O.B. were happy enough with the group of folks they were starting to get, since now they were selling gin and scotch as well as bar whiskey and beer. Even Kaseras was able to see that rugby was a classier sort of game, upscale, so you'd say.

"It's a gent's game—gent as in gentleman," Kaseras explained to one of the recruits when he and O.B. were first enlisting enthusiasts, because at first, you see, O.B. and Kaseras were best buddies. "It's not like football or softball or any of that. In rugby, when the other guy makes a good play, you pick yourself up and shake his hand and congratulate him—'well done, old chap'—instead of slugging him. Then you get him later, in the confusion, when he's forgotten about it and you can fix him good."

"But how do you play it?" the prospects all would ask.

"Boy, you've got me there, pal, you sure have," Kaseras would smile through his broken teeth and give his wheezy laugh. "But we'll worry about that as soon as we get the team set up. I tell you, though, if you really want to know, go on over to the field in Rockland Park on Saturday afternoon and watch the team from Whatney's. They've been playing for a couple of months now, so they should have figured out what they're supposed to do. I don't know who they'll be matched against, but it should be somebody good. You know, this rugby stuff is a big deal now around town. Except for the South Side, naturally." Kaseras gave his wheezy laugh all over again, "'Cause this is a white man's game."

He was right, of course. There were a lot of teams starting up (though not even one of our Spanish clientele joined in), and Riley's Rebels—after an early period of uncertainty and some shock that any game requiring so much quickness could also include such brute force, and without any protective padding—turned out to be one of the best teams around, beating Whatney's What-Nots and after a season or so even Tiny Miller's Milwaukee Avenue Maulers, before losing to O'Banion's by only a few points and one broken jaw, which Danny O'Banion swore happened (to Tim Shaunessy, one of our holdovers from the old Riley's) as the result of a fall, and not a punch, but, hell, Tim couldn't even remember when the lights went out, so who can say?

Anyway, the whole thing—the kidding and the games and the competition itself, not to mention the extra business—was good for the bar and for the brothers, and for O.B. especially, since once he got started playing he became pretty good at it, maybe, all in all, too good. So maybe that's what happened—it was just too damn much of a good thing. And besides, O.B. never had been one to let well enough alone.

The problem was that once the competition spread to betting on the games with players from other teams, bets grew on bets. Oh, there wasn't any question of underhandedness—the guys bet because they wanted to win, no holds barred. And it wasn't just rugby, either. Pretty soon they were betting on everything—from rugby and pool to the baseball and fights on TV to the local elections. Once it started, it seemed there was no stopping it. It was as though the competition was alive in the air they breathed. It got so that O.B. and Kaseras and Kaseras's buddies would have bet on who'd have to get up next to go to the little room, or whether the next fellow through the door would be tall or short, blond or redhaired, with a side bet on whether or not he'd be by himself, and a fifty-to-one kicker on whether he'd be cross-eyed or using crutches.

O.B. or Kaseras or one of the others would be in drinking a beer and chewing pretzels, looking up at the TV now and then, and all at once someone would say, "I'll take Los Angeles by two." And if the other fellows held off he'd say, "All right, by three—everyone knows their pitching—you can't get a better deal than that!" Or whoever it was would say, "Daley can't win again, no matter what. He's nothing like his old man was. He doesn't even have the whole organization behind him. Hell, haven't you read about all the fights they're having? Here's twenty that says he won't get out of the primary. Hell, all right, here's ten more that says he won't even finish second." Or if it was someone who really was watching the TV: "Here's five dollars that the Dow Jones will be down on the evening news. You want odds? Hell, here's five more that says you can't even tell me who Dow Jones is! Let our favorite bartender judge. Hey, Johnny!" At which point I would look for something else to do, or something to swat at with the bar-cloth, because I didn't want any part of that action.

O.B. loved every minute of it, though, that was easy to see, never mind that it was all small-time. But Gianni didn't care for the way things were going, not one bit. Funny, Gianni was single and free whereas O.B. had his business downtown and a wife, Denise, and two kids, a little boy five and a little girl three, each of them cute as a button when he'd bring them in Saturday mornings and sit them up on the bar, pink and bright and both of them smart as tacks with their ever-fresh haircuts, accompanied by a big black dog, Corey they called her, that looked just about ready to eat the bar, or at least most of the stools, but friendly, too, in the rambunctious sort of way that labs have. Yet for all that, Gianni was more serious about things and, really, more responsible. It was as though after all his moving around—Chicago to Minneapolis to New Orleans to Seattle and back again—and after all his different lives, what he really wanted was to settle down in peace and quiet for a while. Not that Gianni wasn't interested in the betting and the action. Don't get me wrong. Every time O.B. or even Kaseras would take a bet, Gianni would be right on top of it, watching what was going on like the hawk waiting for the prey to start across the road. But he never made his move, never joined in directly on his own, at least not until the very end. And by that time he couldn't help it, because the way O.B. had arranged things Gianni didn't have a choice anymore. But generally speaking, even around the pool table, where he could have cleaned up no matter what the odds were, Gianni preferred to hold back and watch rather than to bet. And besides, he always used to say, skidding the balls across the felt like he would to amuse himself when no one else was around to play, if you really had the touch, you didn't need to convince anyone by taking their money at it.

With all the betting, there was bound to be fights, and so there were, more and more of them, enough that some of the regulars started betting on them, too. That was really the part I didn't like. "Jesus," I'd tell O.B. as some poor bastard was getting turned around and shoved out the door, "the place is getting to be like the old Riley's." But at first he'd just laugh and shrug it off like a joke, as though I were only kidding or, even if I wasn't, as though I should have been, since it was none of my business anyway. He reacted that way right up to the day things got personal and Kaseras and his buddies landed Charley Swenson in the hospital.

That afternoon, about three weeks after the pool game with Gianni, was really when the split came between Kaseras and O.B. They never felt or even talked the same about one another after that. The whole thing started, like so many things in here, over absolutely nothing. At first, O.B. hadn't been involved at all. Come to think of it, he hadn't even been here, which is too bad, because if he had been I'd be willing to wager that things wouldn't have gone so far, at least not in the direction they did, and that none of what happened in the end would have happened at all. Or maybe I'm wrong about that, maybe the whole thing was destined to happen sooner or later, one way or another. Charley Swenson had been another of the holdovers from the old Riley's, but after a while he'd gotten in pretty tight with O.B., too, even if he was the quiet sort. One afternoon last spring, around four thirty, he was drinking a beer and minding his own business, watching TV like usual, when Kaseras came in and sat down next to him. I remember because Charley had been alone at the front of the bar, and practically alone period, except for some on-strike types shooting pool in the back, and because that's about the time I get my second wind, while I'm getting the bar set up for the brothers in the evening and waiting for the boilermakers to come bouncing through the doors. I remember thinking that if I felt tired from what I'd been doing, trying to sweep up and drawing beer all day, it wasn't hard to see why Charley looked so exhausted and didn't have much to say, since he'd been up since five, like every morning, to get his truck ready and his deliveries set for his route.

But he did seem even more tired and a lot more sullen than usual, quiet but nervous, too. Or maybe it was the beer, which he'd never been so good with anyway, or maybe things at home weren't going well or something. Because when Kaseras started kidding him about delivering soda pop for kids instead of holding down a man's job, Charley didn't take it like a joke, and that just spurred Kaseras on to rib him even more. Still, I'd never seen any trouble between him and Kaseras before, so I wasn't paying much attention. It did strike me as strange though to hear the bitterness in Charley's voice when he blurted out, after all of Kaseras's big mouth, "O.K. I know what you're up to. You want to make a bet on something. Well all right, let's bet and be done with it! I'm more of a man than you are, period—more than you were yesterday, are today, or will be tomorrow—or any day you like."

With that, Charley got a funny look in those deep Norwegian eyes of his, blue like ice frozen in pools, with a clarity that almost makes you feel like you might fall straight into them and never get out again, and he lurched himself round to face Kaseras. "So I've got five bucks here that says..."

Kaseras looks at him, waiting like he was supposed to for Charley to finish the line, and then, after nothing but silence, finally asks, "Says what? You big dumb jackfish? Five bucks that says what?"

Kaseras hasn't even got all the words out when Charley shifts on the stool again—but just a little this time, because he already has Kaseras to his left, like he's wanted all along. Then he shouts, "Says you won't get up after this!" And he follows through with that right hand that hits like a mule, and Kaseras drops straight down, dead weight. Not very original, I have to admit, but effective.

I got to say that I wasn't sure what to do—whether I should reach for one of the billy clubs or jump up and down and applaud. So I just stood watching while the fellows from the back started coming over to see what all the commotion was about. Charley was close to right about one thing. It did take Kaseras a good, long time—considerably longer than I've seen him take before—to get up. But Charley was wrong, too. Because when Kaseras did get up, he was mad, and when Kaseras gets mad, he gets mean.

What was worse, Charley hadn't looked too carefully before he'd picked his spot, or maybe he hadn't wanted to, because the guys coming over from the pool table in the back were all members in good standing of Kaseras's personal fan club. Charley was just getting down off his stool when one of Kaseras's buddies shoved into him good from behind. As he was lurching forward, Kaseras slapped him with a left then caught him in the side of the head with a beer stein, something like clubbing a marlin. Charley was stunned but not finished, and he and Kaseras, who was swearing to beat the band, tussled for awhile before Kaseras's buddies started joining in and popping Charley on the head with whatever came to hand.

That was the way things stood when O.B. and Gianni came in. You have to hand it to O.B., it never took him long to size up a situation. He waded in between the two principal participants and grabbed a hold of Charley, who by then was showing signs of being on his last legs, thanks mostly to Kaseras's little helpers, and finally succeeded in getting them apart, all the while yelling at both of them. Gianni was following right behind, as usual, and he grabbed the big Norwegian by the arm and started to lead him away. But Kaseras's friends kept taking shots, and when one missed the Norwegian altogether and got Gianni instead—right on his temple—it was the last straw for O.B. He started in on them, too, one by one, while Gianni was getting some ice to put to his wound.

O.B. was really marvelous to watch. He had the cleanest, most efficient style you could want in a boxer, just like John L. Sullivan must have had in the bare-knuckle days. I don't know for sure where he got it from, but Gianni said one of their Italian uncles had spent a lot of time working with him when he was a kid. He'd wade in and pick one of them out and feint once or twice and then tag them good with a straight right or his left hook, and down they'd go, neat as you please, practically like swatting flies. The trouble was, while O.B. was cleaning out that half of the bar, sort of like mopping up on Sunday morning, and Gianni was nursing his headache, and Kaseras was stuck in the corner licking his wounds and calling encouragement to his pals, the rest of Kaseras's buddies, the ones who didn't want to risk going up against O.B., were measuring the length of their pool cues alongside Charley Swenson's head and shoulders. I finally got O.B.'s attention to let him know what was happening in the back of the bar behind the pool table, but by then the damage was done, and all that was left was to get Charley out of there.

O.B. was fit to be tied, as could be expected. Once they'd loaded Charley into the back of a station wagon that belonged to Jimmy O'Toole, who was just coming in from a four-alarm fire and, fortunately enough, had left his car parked across the street at the end of the alley, O.B. didn't hesitate to start in on Kaseras. He dressed him down good, with the Italian curses that were O.B.'s specialty and that sounded bad enough to make their mark no matter what the words actually meant. When Kaseras gave that wheezy laugh of his, O.B. reached out and slapped him twice, hard, so you could almost hear the report, with the skin white for a split second before it flushed bright crimson, and then O.B. put up his fists. One of the leftovers in the back of the bar started to laugh in anticipation, but Kaseras didn't want any more, not one-on-one with O.B. anyway, and he stepped back.

"Why did you have to pick *him* to bait?" O.B. shouted, half scolding and half in exasperation. "You know he's got troubles: suddenly out of work and a wife on wheels. Don't you know what I'm talking about?"

"That's not my problem," Kaseras said, looking like he wished he'd never seen or even heard of Charley Swenson and his domestic problems. "Anyway, I didn't start it," and he gave that nervous laugh of his again, swearing it hadn't been his fault but backpedaling, too, this time so as to keep his distance.

"Listen now and remember this," O.B. told him, apparently having given up on educating Kaseras about Charley's particular situation and turning to more general questions of etiquette. "I don't want that kind of fighting in here, period. I don't care how it started or what it was about. And as for your big, tough pals with the sticks, you can tell them to go beat up on their sisters and to stay out of here. We don't need that kind of business. At all. You got me?"

Well, maybe Kaseras did and maybe he didn't, but by then one thing was certain, he was through listening, since he'd backed up about as far as he could go and his only choices were either to start forward again, which to tell the truth, it didn't look like it was even under consideration, or grab the doorknob; and a second later he was out the door and onto the street. At any rate, he must have got a little of what O.B. said, because his friends, at least those who had showed their fancy moves with the pool cues, never came back in here again.

Or maybe they were just worried about what would happen if Charley wanted to have them identified. Which, of course, was unlikely, first because it's tough to recall the distinguishing features of the tattooer when you're the one getting tattooed; second because O.B. didn't want any cops coming around here under any circumstances, for obvious reasons; and third because even if the Norwegian could have recognized them, he would have had to find a way to get Kaseras' friends to come to him, since he wasn't going anywhere soon with a fractured skull and two cracked vertebrae. From what I heard, even the lawyer O.B. finally got to talk to him advised him not to take it any further than it had already gone. I figured that, if he was lucky, it wouldn't take the whole six months that the doctors were talking about. But it was plain to see that he wasn't going to be up and out of the pretty white hospital room with the plastic flowers (so maybe he really did have trouble at home, how do I know, he was always so tired and quiet) anytime soon.

Anyway, that was the watershed for Kaseras and O.B. Kaseras had beat up on the Norwegian, sure, and his friends had put their seal on it, too. But O.B. had beaten up on Kaseras, and he had done it in a way that neither of them were too pleased with. Because Kaseras hadn't been so much beaten as humiliated. He'd been made to back down. In the long run, it might even have been better if O.B. had danced Kaseras around the bar a couple of times and finished his fighting days for good. And O.B. could have done it; even if he's not huge, he's big enough, and fast and beautifully efficient, like I said. As it was, on the other hand, Kaseras wasn't so much canceled out as given a rain check. Now it was even worse than it had been after the pool game. So I waited and watched for the next event, uneasy as could be, and not knowing for sure what might happen. But that was all I could do, since it's built into the job: wait.

Those were not, it's true, the very best of times in Riley's. Maybe O.B. was just bored now that all the betting had tapered off. Even the rugby players seemed to have lost their edge and tamed down. Looking back now, I can see that the whole episode of Charley Swenson cast a pall over the place, although by unspoken agreement no one ever mentioned the fight itself. Oh, Charley's name would come up occasionally, someone would wonder how he was doing and who had been to see him last and whatnot, but discussing the fight, either its first or its second round, was strictly taboo. Even the firemen seemed better behaved than usual, as though someone had announced a rule that they couldn't pass out until they'd made polite conversation for at least an hour and that, in any case, they couldn't threaten the bartender with dismemberment just for letting their families know where they were and suggesting that maybe somebody should come down and pick them up, or at least send over a pillow and a pair of pajamas (hold the toothbrush). But whatever it was, boredom or something else I don't know about, that's when O.B. started coming in all the time with Sherrie decked out in the three-and-a-half-inch heels and her big smile, chatting and laughing and hanging on his arm.

After a while, it even got to where she was coming in when he wasn't here, as though she were waiting for him. So I got to talk to her quite a bit, like it or not. Actually, she wasn't so bad when she was alone. That was the difference: whether she was with a man she was trying to impress or not. I guess she must have given up on me from the start. Too bad she didn't give up on Gianni, too. But it's his fault if he was stupid enough to let himself get led round and round like a cocker spaniel on a leash. There's no question but that she was pretty, I'll give her that, with those big dark eyes and the chestnut hair piled just so on top of her head, the little curls on the side and the streams falling down her neck. She could have looked a lot better, too, if she hadn't worn so much makeup—especially the eye-shadow—and if she hadn't been trying to keep the chewing-gum business afloat all by herself. Or maybe she was nervous underneath that brassy exterior, and that's why she always had something in her mouth. She was lucky it wasn't all food, either, because you could see from the fullness of her hips that, even though she was tall, it wouldn't take much before she'd start putting on weight. Still, I bet she would have looked more than just all right in a pair of those tight jeans some of the girls who come in here now wear. Not that she would be caught dead dressed like that. No, sir, not Sherrie. Nothing but the fanciest for her. So maybe that's why O.B. liked her, to have someone to show off to folks. God knows Denise never left the house and the kids. Or at least not that I ever heard of, and she sure never came in here. But that still doesn't do a thing to explain Gianni.

Maybe Gianni was reacting to what had happened with Jean and the one before that (the one I never met, Sandie, I think). Maybe losing two good chances inside a year and a half would be enough to make anybody pick a sure loser the third time around, so he wouldn't even have to bother with trying to come up winners. Not that Gianni had sworn off, or anything like that. He just seemed to have froze for awhile. As for Sherrie, it's not hard to see that if O.B. sends her down here to sit around all afternoon until he decides to tear himself away from his real-estate business and show up, well, she's sure going to get bored, isn't she? It's only natural, if you ask me. And a lot of that time, Gianni was the only one around to talk to, except for me of course. So it stands to reason they're going to get to know each other. There's nothing wrong with that.

Still, it was funny at first to see the two of them together. They were such different types—and not just that she was taller than he was and talked twice as fast, between her gum and her cigarettes; but they had really different characters, too. Gianni was dark and reflective and reserved, and she was, well, none of the above. He liked pool and shooting by himself, while she liked going to clubs or to the track or even just being out on the street as long as she could feel that she was in the midst of, and, I guess, being watched by, everybody else in the world. Even when they talked, it seemed like neither was really talking to the other. He would weigh every word deliberately as always, quiet and careful to say things just as he meant them, while she would talk lickety-split, as though she'd taken up the scatter-shot theory of conversation and if she just hurled out enough words sooner or later some of them were bound to hit the bull's eye—or at least get inside the target—and end up making sense (although just what sense, God only knows).

One thing that you couldn't help but notice, though, was the way Gianni watched when she talked, his eyes fastened on hers, dark and expressive, as though just the experience of looking at her was worth having to pretend to follow all the noise she made. And when he wasn't watching her eyes he was looking at the lines of her body or at her clothes or her hair, the way it framed her features and fell down her neck. So, yeah, I got to admit, in the end it did him some good, too. Because he'd been locked in that deep-freeze for a long time, too long if you ask me. Even if Sherrie wasn't just what he needed, or exactly what I would have recommended, at least she brought him out of it and got the engine started thawing. Believe me, life feels a lot better if all your parts aren't frozen stuck inside a block of ice.

I think, though, that for all the fascination and the fawning and the heat, nothing ever really happened. I'll probably never know for sure, and I know I'll never know exactly why. But that's my guess: that despite the flame that leapt up between them, and everything that Gianni had seemed to want so bad, nothing ever came of it, at least nothing you could put your finger on, so to speak. I never even found out for sure what put an end to all the carrying on either, whether O.B. got wind of it or what. But after it was finished, when she had stopped coming into the bar so much, and never without O.B., and she and Gianni had gone back to being just nodding or at best handshaking acquaintances, it didn't seem to make much difference what the reason was, not as far as Gianni was concerned. Because by then the thaw had turned into a flood; and he'd found Diana, too.

In fact she turned out to be exactly what he'd needed—and, in all but that one crucial respect, just the opposite of Sherrie. Among other things, she was the nicest girl, with the sweetest way about her and the kindest disposition, who'd ever come into Riley's as long as I'd been there, bar none. Not that I'm fool enough to think that Riley's is the acid test. Oh, it's better than the clubs on the south side or the joints out in the county, or, say, the downtown lock-up, but nobody's claiming that it's Ding-Dong School. I just mean that I thought she was a damn nice person, and that I'll live a good long time before I'll meet a better one (despite what all came out later, when it didn't even count anymore, really). Gianni thought so too, you could see it right off.

The first time I saw her they'd just ducked in out of the rain. She didn't have a hat, and Gianni's umbrella, as usual, probably wouldn't have worked right even if he could have gotten it open, so when they came in they were all huddled over together looking like nothing so much as a pair of drowned rats. As soon as she took off her coat and shook out her hair, though, I could see how pretty she was, with those green eyes and that quick Italian smile, just like O.B.'s. She had a lot of style, too, the kind that shows up even in little things, like her rings, two small purple stones, something akin to the color of the amethyst that Gianni said he and O.B. used to look for in the fields when they were kids. But that day she would have had a tough time looking stylish with all that water running off her; so she didn't try, just tossed her hair and came right up to the bar with Gianni and smiled as he introduced her as a friend. I could tell from the way he said it and looked at her, and from the way they both glowed, despite having gotten caught in the downpour, that she was a lot more than that. How much I didn't realize until later, of course, but you could tell it was a lot right from the start. Even O.B. could tell that—and O.B. took to her about as quick as Gianni had, you could see that too.

Gianni asked me to draw two beers, and when I looked to check she nodded, and she drank it all, too, though she let Gianni have his shot all to himself, even while he kidded her about it.

"I only drink whiskey when I'm out with the boys," she smiled. That she gave as good as she got was, I soon found out, part of her character.

"All right, next beer she has to pay for herself," Gianni said to me, for which she gave him an elbow in the ribs, and a good one judging from the way Gianni winced. We talked a lot that day, waiting for the rain to stop so they could get back to Gianni's without a boat and fix something for dinner. She told me about her people in Italy and her family in Chicago, not far from my old neighborhood, it turned out, on the near south side, but all changed now from the bungalows and the little shops that lined the streets when I was growing up. I liked her right off, I can't deny it, and I liked her more every time she came back; and I especially liked the effect she had on Gianni. What Sherrie had started Diana took as far as it would, or could, go. Odd how that works sometimes, two girls as different as night and day and yet the results were one continuous change for the better, more like a tag team, or like pass-the-baton, rather than hide-and-seek. Diana even got him to thinking in a different way about his own past, and the summers on the two farms with O.B., until he was looking at things less and less like the bitter little boy who never got the candy. Diana was particularly interested in the Italian side, of course. She would ask Gianni and occasionally O.B. for details about the family and the way they did things and where they had come from; but it was easy to see that she wanted to hear about the other side, too, whatever they would tell her. At times she would talk about her own people and where they had come from in Italy and how her grandmother took her once to show her off to her aunts and uncles who still lived there, in a village up in the mountains outside of Naples, I think. Then Gianni would get going about the guns again, the .22 and the old man's rifles. But even that didn't appear so bad to him anymore, it seemed, at least not the way he told her what he remembered, going on and on about how great O.B. was and all.

While Gianni was talking, you could almost feel the spark, and as far as I was concerned it was nice to see, with one thing leading to another like a train just easing out of the station and then picking up steam, going faster and faster with the whistle blowing and more and more power, until—well, that was it: until. I guess it was just too nice to be true, and, in the end, Gianni's same old luck, because the 'until' turned out to be that son of a bitch Ben Kaseras.

Not right away, of course. Gianni and Diana had their share of afternoons together in here before that came, and I swear I got as much out of those times as they did, watching their expressions and feeling the excitement as if I was with them or even was them. It was one of the better parts of the job, and one of the few really good things about that glum period in here after Charley Swenson's "mishap." I don't know firsthand what their lives were like outside the bar, of course, but they must have got on together pretty good in a lot of different ways judging both from how Gianni was acting and from the way that she looked. Even O.B. said he'd never seen so many dimples on just two faces. Not that Gianni would ever talk to me about that—not to me and not to anyone, maybe not even O.B. He was too reserved for that. So things were good then. And even when the trouble started again you couldn't really see it at first. I defy anyone to say that they could have predicted what was to come, even after all the trouble between the two groups, O.B. and Gianni on the one side and Kaseras and them on the other. Of course, that pool game hadn't helped, the one in which Gianni forgot to think to be nice and cordial, then after the to-do with Charley Swenson things were still worse. But it wasn't just because of Charley, either, since by then the fights and hard feelings had spread so far that they had got into the rugby players, too, and had split them down the middle just like everything else around here. After that Kaseras wanted to get both Gianni and O.B. So when one of the onlookers in here heard Gianni extolling O.B.'s virtues with a rifle one afternoon, I wasn't too surprised that he picked out that new note of pride in Gianni's voice and saw it more as another challenge than merely as a simple statement of fact.

"Really, now? How good?" The voice was loud, especially since it was only four o'clock on what up to then had been a slow afternoon and there was almost no one else in the place, and it was tinged with the same feelings you could notice now when the boys were so busy making bets. It belonged to a fellow named William J. Bronson. That's what was printed on his calling card, but everyone called him "Five," short for "Five Fingers," because he was always slapping people on the back and shaking hands, just like the huckster, or as he put it, the salesman, he was. To my mind, the moniker came from the fact that after you shook hands with him you always had to hold up your hand and wiggle your fingers to make sure you still had all five left and that he hadn't made off with one or two of them under cover of all the gibberish. O.B. never really disliked 'Five,' but he didn't seem to take to 'Five''s cohorts all that well. Just a few days before—I remember it because O.B. usually didn't bother himself about the daily clientele, that being Gianni's bailiwick and all—O.B. had wanted to know who the new fellow coming in with Bronson had been, the one asking about him, and when I told him that I didn't have the faintest, but that he carried quite a roll on him, and openly, too, not disguised, O.B. said to let him know if he came back, not Bronson, that is, but the one with the black suit and fancy tie, or anyone like him with Bronson: Black Sammy White was O.K., but if it was anyone else, I was to let O.B. know.

Anyway, Gianni wasn't very pleased about 'Five' butting in just then, since Diana was there and they were talking between themselves at one of the tables along the back wall, even though it was true that Gianni had been getting carried away again and gesturing and talking louder than usual. He must have hoped that if he didn't respond, Bronson would go away and leave them be. O.B. had had to go straight from his office to check on the kids and some trouble at school, I heard later, so for the time being Gianni could only sit and hope for the best. But no such luck.

"Good as that rifleman fellow on TV?" Bronson chuckled. "Good as those sharpshooters? Huh? How good?" And this time the voice was loud enough so the folks out on the street could have heard it, had they cared to.

"What does he want, Gianni?" I could hear Diana ask. You could see she didn't know what to make of Bronson, with his sweater hanging like a big black bag at the side of the pool table. From behind, in the mirror, I saw her look away and at the same time reach out and touch Gianni's arm—which she never did in public—as though she wanted him to answer and get it over with. But then she didn't have to worry, because when Bronson turned away only to turn back, swinging his beer like he was getting ready for another round of questioning even though he hadn't got an answer to the first one yet, Gianni cut him off before he really had a chance to get started.

"Well, 'Five,' if you want to know so bad, why don't you ask him?"

"'Cause I'm talking to you now."

"Yeah, yeah, I know," Gianni smiled. "But like I said, you should really ask O.B. yourself."

"But —"

"After all," Gianni pointed, "he's right there at your shoulder."

Bronson swiveled—lost for words, though of course, only momentarily—since in fact O.B. had just come in, his coat on one arm and Sherrie, all perfume and chewing-gum, on the other.

"Me and your brother here were just talking about you," Bronson slapped O.B. on the shoulder with one hand and grabbed O.B.'s arm with the other.

"Is that so," O.B. smiled, showing the bright teeth. "What on earth could a busy man like you be doing wasting your time on a subject as dull as me? I can guarantee you won't make any money off it."

"Well, you never know, do you," Bronson smiled, "until you make up your mind to try."

"What's up?" O.B. turned to Gianni.

"Well, I was telling Diana some of the things we used to do when we were kids, and 'Five' came over to help the conversation along."

"Hey," Bronson protested. "All I did was ask."

"Nice, polite, and considerate, like always, right 'Five'?" O.B. slapped him on the back.

"Well, how was I to know we've had Roy Rogers and William Tell all wrapped up in one right here in front of us all this time? You should have told us."

The give-and-take between them went on for a while before Kaseras came in, and then the talk about guns and shooting got more and more animated until O.B. seemed to be fed up and looked at Gianni and said, in a voice still steady and jocular but a good bit louder than necessary, "So how about a game of pool, brother? I hear you've been shooting pretty good lately."

"Just one question," Gianni asked as he turned away to leave Diana and began tossing the balls onto the felt one by one. "Who's buying the beer?"

"Don't worry about it," O.B. winked. "It's on the house."

When O.B.'s like that—offhanded but serious, loud but more firm than pushy or high-strung—it's hard to know what he's really thinking. I couldn't tell if he was just taunting Kaseras, if he was actually interested in challenging him to something or other, or if it was a little of both. Both, I suppose, looking back now. But like I said, O.B.'s not always so easy to figure. Anyway, two days later, the plans for the trip and the bets that went along with it were set. It was on a rainy Saturday afternoon when more or less the same group was in the bar, trying their darnedest to match the Old Man's rain with their beer drop for drop.

The bet itself was simple. The funny thing was, this time it was pretty clear, to me at least, that not only wasn't it for the money, it wasn't even for the competition. This time the important thing seemed to be that action—energy, really—between O.B. and Kaseras, and between Gianni and Kaseras and all the rest of them, that had been increasing ever since the afternoon when Charley Swenson got himself run around the block. Or maybe ever since Sherrie started showing up here and teasing everything in pants while she was supposed to be waiting for O.B. Anyway, it couldn't have been the money, not from Kaseras and Bronson's side, because this time the bet wasn't for money. It was, of all things, for that old man's gun, a big Remington, if I got it right when O.B. was describing it, the one that he had used and then had left to O.B. in his will—or maybe not, maybe there wasn't a will, or if there was that wasn't in it, because Gianni seemed to think the gun belonged to him, too, at least in part. So maybe O.B. owned the trigger and barrel and Gianni the stock. I guess I don't know exactly. But anyway, one thing was clear: if the brothers didn't get a deer, Ben Kaseras got the entire gun all to himself, though God knows what he was going to do with it other than blowing his foot off.

There was more to it, too, I think, between Kaseras and the brothers, but that's the part I was on to. I still remember how it happened. O.B. and Gianni were talking louder than usual again, as though they didn't mind at all being overheard, and when they said they were going to go north, hunting, 'Five' Bronson butted in right on cue to say that he bet they wouldn't even get out of the city. O.B. laughed in his face and told him everything had already been set, so he'd as good as lost that one before the words were out of his mouth.

"All right," Kaseras piped up. "You might go. Damn, anybody can go running through the woods with a pop-gun. You could even take your pal Charley out and give him some fresh air, since he probably needs it more than either of you do. But I'll bet you don't come back with anything, I bet that you get totally skunked, except for what you may be able to collect on the roadside. And I mean it." Kaseras stood there and glared, like a bull with his herd around him watching from the pasture, big and set and stupid, and less than friendly, so you couldn't really ignore him even if you wanted to.

"Well, how much would you like to put on it?" O.B. said with a spark in his eye that I could see reflected in the mirror along the back bar as I ran the cloth around the rows of glasses, though for the life of me I didn't know what that spark meant.

"Don't ask me 'how much,'" Kaseras said in that huffy way of his, as though all of a sudden money wasn't good enough for him, mad and insulting, but hurt, too, in that way he gets sometimes, like after that pool game. "Ask me 'what.' You get me? Let's think of something more appropriate."

"Well, I'm open to suggestions...."

"How about that gun you've been talking about, the one you've kept in 'mint condition.' Thirty-thirty, isn't it?"

"Thirty-two Remington," O.B. corrected with a smile. "The finest rifle for deer ever made. I didn't know you fancied yourself a collector."

"I don't," Kaseras countered. "Well, how about it?"

It was at this point that Gianni stepped in. "I'm not sure that's really the best idea now," he began, speaking, I guess, as a part owner of the gun. But O.B. waved him off and then put a hand on his shoulder to keep him quiet. You could see Kaseras thought he had them now, because, like I said, it wasn't the money or even the gun. It was the feeling behind it.

"That'll be fine," O.B. smiled. "Now what can we arrange for your side of it? It shouldn't be too hard to think of an adequate sum. Unlike some folks, my brother and I are not adverse to plain cold cash. Johnny Bubbles here could even hold the stakes, should he be so inclined."

So I could see from the flash in his eyes that I had been right and O.B. had something in mind—it was just like him, that's for sure—but I still didn't know what.

Behind the bar, later on, after the terms had been proposed and agreed to, I heard O.B. talking to Gianni again, quietly now, in his don't-worry-about-a-thing voice, because Gianni still didn't seem any too pleased. Although I've got to admit that, except for him, everybody seemed happier than they had in Riley's for a good long time, really since the first of the troubles started. I poured a lot of whiskey that afternoon and evening and drew a good measure of beer, too, but it wasn't like it had been in the months before that, during the late summer and early fall, when as soon as I'd sold a decent amount of liquor I'd have to start worrying about turning my back to the crowd, and I'd have to keep an eye out pretty much all the time, using the mirror to see the fights getting ready to start, because more and more, once they had started up it was too late to do anything except to give the boys a wide berth and let them beat their brains out in peace; and the later it would get, the nastier the results would be. But by that night, the old feeling was back, with the jokes and the laughter under the smoky lights, and everybody was happy—drunk, maybe, but happy drunk.

Everybody, that is, except Gianni, who wasn't either.

"How could you let Bronson and Kaseras talk you into a deal like that?" Gianni asked, or rather blamed, O.B. "And especially with *him*? We don't even know for sure that Kaseras can cover it."

O.B. looked at him strangely. "They didn't talk me into it," he smiled. "Kaseras just thinks they did."

"But the gun—"

"Look, kid, it adds interest, which is the spice of life. Oh, sure, Bronson is an S.O.B. you're right about that—and I couldn't give two shits about him. But Kaseras is another matter altogether, and don't make a mistake about it in any way. The opportunity's just too good to pass up."

"All the same, I still don't see how you could have done it."

"That's simple— because we're going to win," O.B. said, still smiling, confident.

"How in hell can you stand there so goddamn sure of yourself?" Gianni leaned over to get a glass and tried to whisper so his voice wouldn't carry past the back bar.

"We have a secret weapon," O.B. leaned over too, now, conspiratorially. "A mystery guest."

"O.K. What have you got up your sleeve this time?"

"Jake Arndt."

"You're not serious."

"I am. It's a perfect idea. If Jake'll help, we'll end up with enough deer for each of us and enough left over so we can bring Kaseras back his very own carcass."

"But you don't even know Jake'll be willing to go along with it," Gianni continued to protest.

"Yes, I do."

"How?"

"That's where you come in."

"Oh, for Christ's—"

"Because you're going to talk to him."

"How can I talk him into it?" Gianni pleaded. But I could tell from his voice that he was already giving in, and so could O.B.

"Because I know how convincing you can be once you get going, a little slow at getting started, maybe, but thoroughly irresistible in the stretch."

"Well, for our sake, I hope you're right—not that I think you are, but I just hope you are."

"And anyway," O.B. sighed, finished now, content, but something else, too, I wasn't sure just what. "Anyway, Jake was nice to me because of Grandpa. But as I remember, it wasn't hard to see that Jake always had a soft spot for you." And then, cheerful again, that and nothing more. "Don't worry. You can do it—I know you can. Besides, Jake will love the idea—it'll give him a chance to get going again. So just don't worry about it," O.B. reached to draw himself a beer and then turned to give me one of his patented winks before sauntering off across the barroom, with a stein of beer in one hand and a cigarette in the other, toward his friends who, by that time, both were and were not his friends.

*   *   *

It wouldn't have been hard. If the old man had just once taken us both and kept the promise, let us both hold it and shoot, and say I'd done it right. And meant it, because by then I could tell, and so could O.B. It's a funny thing—even if I'd missed completely, left the can sitting untouched on the post or the bird unscathed, wheeling away into the blue sky, or even if I'd hit into the backside of some unsuspecting cow getting her supper across the fence—then I could have walked off and felt good for awhile, if he'd said so and meant it, and forgot and probably never have thought about it again, at least not that way. But he never did, not once. Who could say why? It could easily have been so; it just hadn't. Or even if he'd never mentioned it at all in the first place, or never acted the way he did, as though it was already a certainty, set and almost done, as though he could promise that time would last forever. But that's the way he'd been: so that no matter what I couldn't forget.

Of course, I never told Jake Arndt any of that. I never fooled myself that I could tell him everything. Anyway, he'd been around enough when we'd been there to see for himself and draw his own conclusions without having me to help him along. Not that telling Jake what to think would have been easy. He had pretty definite opinions, and even if Beatrice did favor me, like O.B. had said, on account of the baby they'd lost after the war, well, managing to tell Jake what was what seemed about as likely as managing to tell the horses and mules that they shouldn't be hungry at feeding time. And the result was likely to be the same, too: a good kick when you weren't looking, in one of those places where you wouldn't forget and make the same mistake again any too soon.

I said that Jake had been around when we were with the old man, which was true to an extent, but not completely so. He really wasn't with us but with Grandpa, most often at the sawmill or out hunting together. That's why Jake had got the cabin in Washburn County, so he and Grandpa and the others, but mostly those two, could go deer hunting or tracking or wading for trout in the stream running alongside without worrying about getting hauled into court for trespassing every time they turned around. Despite the trout, it wasn't so much for the fishing that Jake had chosen the spot near the river. For Jake, the trout were a sideline. He'd picked the spot because it was near the trails that the deer would follow in the fall when they were foraging for food and would want to stop for a drink. Grandpa had always said that if someone knew more about the woods and about hunting in them than anyone else, that someone was Jake Arndt. So I guess he knew even more than Grandpa, or at least Grandpa sure thought he did; but Dad and O.B. thought the same, too, for that matter.

I'm not sure how much our father would have known or cared about it, really, but I did know that Grandpa and O.B. were right. When it came to the big woods, Jake was a past master. I hadn't seen all that much of it when I was little, but I remembered him giving us the honey from the hollow tree near the sawmill and taking us out after partridges in the woods near Grandpa's, with the birds flying like shooting stars through the streams of light, and him and Grandpa and later O.B. shouting back and forth across the clearings and having their contests to see who could down one of them first. So when I went to see Jake in Redwing that October, after leaving O.B. to run Riley's on his own, with Johnny Bubbles to keep an eye on him and to talk his ear off with those tall tales of his, I figured I'd at least have something to reminisce with Jake about. As it turned out, and as I probably should have known anyway, it didn't make much difference what I had to say, since no one was ever going to accuse Jake Arndt of being at a loss for words.

The trip to Redwing isn't short, but on a clear day in October it makes a good drive, if you know the roads. There are two ways to get there: the interstate's flat, white slab or the local roads running through the valleys and around the hills of the dusky green countryside just beginning, in that season, to change to bright orange and to the hazy purple that reminds you of pipesmoke. It takes longer to go by the local roads, but those are the ones that I knew and remembered, so time didn't seem to make any difference one way or the other. Anyway, I was pretty sure that Jake wouldn't have so much to do that waiting for me was going to bust him—or that if it would have, he just wouldn't have waited. Over the years I'd learned at least that about him: he was as good a friend as you could want, but he was also pretty damn close to being the most independent man God had ever put together and stuck on this earth.

On the way up, I got lost just once—well, not really lost—I simply missed a turn. I figured that I was still an hour away from Redwing, so in order to save a stop, I pulled into a gas station, if you could call it that. It wasn't much more than two old pumps and a bucket of water on a little patch of dust alongside the road, with an apron off it where a boy was working on what looked like at one time must have been a Harley similar to O.B.'s, but now wasn't much more than a patchwork of rebuilt parts under what appeared to be at least a score of successive paint jobs. The owner came out right away, I'll say that for him, a springy old fellow with a tanned, weathered face and the usual gritty fingers.

"Where you headed for?" he asked as he started the pump.

"Redwing."

"Well, unless they moved it and decided to keep it a secret," he smiled, "you'd better swing around, cause it's back the other way. Or at least it always has been." I must have looked a little sheepish, because he added right away: "It happens all the time—the road's not marked too well back there. I think the county wanted the business to come this way, even if it's by mistake."

"I sort of thought I might have taken a wrong turn."

"I see by your plates you're from Illinois. Chicago?" When I nodded he added, "Up for the fair?"

"The what?"

"The fair at Redwing—they have it every fall, for their pottery and for the shoe factory, too, I think, but it's really just an excuse for everyone hereabouts to take a day off and drink some beer and play horseshoes." He set the pump up and reached into the bucket for a rag to start on the windshield. "Then what you up for, if you don't mind my asking?"

"To see a friend. And to get some information—on deer among other things."

"Well, if that's what you want," he said over his shoulder, "and if you're going toward Redwing anyway, I have just the fellow for you. A friend of mine, in a manner of speaking. An old guy, older than me, with a bum leg and a wheeze, which he claims came from being gassed in the war—the first one, which shows you how old he really is. But the best hand at deer hunting in this country.

A fellow named Jake Arndt." Before he saw the look I gave him he added: "Just a little over half an hour's drive up the road toward Redwing, not far at all. Tell him I sent you, if you want. Name's Billy Hodge. But you just tell him the fellow at the service station in Mill Creek. He'll know."

"But Jake is the one I'm going to see." We both looked at each other, half in astonishment, and then the old man started to shake with laughter. He seemed to think it was more funny than weird, though I guess maybe that's just the way things seemed to happen in those parts.

"Goddamn now if that ain't the way! So Jake's become a regular institution—even out of state!"

"Hold on now. I've known Jake Arndt since I was one year old—known him personally, I mean. His reputation, whatever it may be, doesn't have a thing to do with it."

When he calmed down enough to light his pipe, he told me how he'd got to know Jake, which wasn't at all the way I'd suspected. It turned out he was new there and had gone to one of the fairs at Redwing and had asked casually about the fishing and hunting in that part of the country. He had been directed to Jake purely by chance. So he hadn't known Grandpa or Drew or the Connollys or any of the others, either, which I guess was just as well, since one coincidence like that per day is just about all my system can take.

Back on the road I thought about what the fellow had said and about Jake, how much I wanted to see him again and, at the same time, how uncertain I was about what I might find. It had been a long time since I'd been around him, that was for sure. And the more I thought about it, the more anxious I got, until I started to think about Diana to get me calmed down, the amethyst blue eyes and quick smile, how she felt next to me, and all the rest; but the feeling of remembering her and missing her, too, had the effect of making me want to go ahead and see Jake and get back home, as though thinking about her gave everything else a different perspective, because not only did I miss her, feel that sweet, physical longing, but at the same time she gave my life a central point and an order, too. Of course, realizing that made me miss her all the more, watching the trees fly by, so I went back to concentrating on the road and on where I was going and why; and in under an hour I was pulling into the long winding lane that ended at Jake's farm.

I saw him in the yard, working with the scythe in the bright sun, the blade gleaming each time he raised it with the big hands and the strong, short arms that always made him look like there was too much of him for the scrawny chest (from the gas, I suppose) to hold together. When he saw me getting out, the scythe stopped and he hurried toward the lane through the long grass, his overalls flapping down the hill. It was still warm in the afternoon sun, and I could feel the breeze on the sweat at the back of my neck. Jake took off his striped engineer's cap, revealing the white line of his forehead, and slapped my shoulder, his broad tobacco-stained smile showing the same ragged teeth, so I knew that nothing had changed and that I needn't have worried, that time really had stopped, or passed quietly on its way elsewhere, leaving him untouched and unchanged. What had done the old man in once and for all didn't seem to have affected Jake in the least, even though his sudden hand, as I took it in mine, felt rough as dried leather.

"Well I'll be damned." Jake's face beamed with the tobaccoed smile. "Just have a look at you now. You've gotten big enough to bait your own hook, by God."

"Always was."

"Like hell you were!" he laughed and slapped me again, this time in reproach. "Come on up and see Beatrice," he extended his arm. "She's been waiting for you."

I held back for a minute. "Just one thing. I'm here for tonight, and then I've got to get back. So please don't either of you take offense if I can't stay on longer. It's not my choice. You see?"

"Gianni—just as you want," Jake replied, surprised, it seemed, but not offended, at least I didn't think so from his look. "Stay as long as you like. Or whatever. But come on up now and say hello. She was baking all morning," he smiled. "All afternoon, too."

Sure enough, we found her in the kitchen, amidst her bowls and flour and just-cleared countertops. She looked older than I remembered or even imagined, her black hair all but solid grey now, silvered, but maybe that was to be expected. I could see the shadows deep in her eyes, despite her smile. I guess we can't all be immune like Jake. I reached out to take her hand but she grabbed me and pulled me close, so for a moment I remembered the aroma of the farm women, strong and clean but not cloying. They wanted to hear about O.B. and about Mom and Dad, so we talked about them as I ate the hot biscuits and drank the coffee she'd made with the egg in it, just like years before. I told Jake about the fellow at the filling station, but he didn't seem at all surprised. After a while I took my bag up to the room at the end of the hall which they had always kept empty, at least as long as I could remember, and set my things down on top of the big feather bed. When I came down Jake had gone out to the porch, and the whiskey bottle was waiting on the table beside him, so it was time to tell him the reason I had come and why it was Jake's help, and his advice, that we needed more than anything else. Over the bottle he told me what I wanted to know—and then some, as usual. I interrupted from time to time to ask a question or make a comment, or, as the shadows lengthened and the air grew crisp, to pour again from the bottle. But once Jake got going, the show was never anybody's but his. Maybe that was why he had been so close to the old man, as though Grandpa did the thinking and then could relax and not worry about the other part, since Jake did enough talking and moving about for any number of people. Grandpa used to say that Jake was the only man he knew who could dance up and down while still seated, and I guess that part hadn't changed.

"It was with your Grandpa, rest his soul, that I used to do the kind of hunting I liked best. But I don't suppose that will surprise you, if you remember him. We met first in 1920, I think, just a short while after the war. I had gone to have my lungs checked by one of the state doctors, who happened to be on a call then in the Hines camps outside Duluth. When I walked in they were working on another fellow, who'd lost part of the index finger of his left hand to one of the company's specially honed saws. That was your Grandpa. What struck me about him, as I remember, wasn't so much his physical strength but his composure, as though he could have lost a lot more than half a finger and still not have gotten upset, because he was barely off the table, the hand wrapped in the huge bandage, when he looked at me, a total stranger, and said, 'Well, it could've been the other hand, and then I'd have to learn to hold a pen and a rifle all over again. So I suppose it could've been worse.'

"After that I didn't see him again until almost five years later, when he was back in Crooked Falls and I had taken up on this place. In those years he was always busy with Drew and the farm, so I didn't really see that much of him until—well, I guess it was about the time that your mother had met your father, and then right away your Aunt Jane left to get married, too, and he was alone more. That was when I really got to know him, hunting mostly, and of course that goddamn trout fishing of his—you haven't really experienced life until you've spent at least one full morning soaking wet inside a pair of rubber hip boots, having stepped into the deepest hole in the Rush River—but mostly, thank God, hunting. There wasn't much about the woods itself that I could tell him, but there was plenty about what lived in the woods that he hadn't known, or maybe just hadn't cared to. Probably that, knowing him. Because the woods aren't always sunny and nice, and what they hold can be unpleasant, too, dark to say the least if you don't know how to deal with it—that is, how to handle what you have to handle and how to avoid what you don't. Of course, the trickiest part of going after deer isn't the woods or the deer or anything else but the other hunters. We didn't care for that much, either. And what was even worse than having all those other folks sashaying every which way toting rifles was not being able to *see* them, so that almost every fall there'd be some fellow—sometimes even cold sober, believe it or not—who'd get his deer, sure, and one of his neighbors along with it. Besides wearing a patch of red, the best way to avoid the two-legged animals, and to get a deer too while you're at it, is to find a spot along their trails and set up a stand. In order to do that, of course, you have to know where the trails are and which ones they'll be moving along at that time in the fall. So that was where I came in.

"It's a funny thing, though, but the best stag we ever got wasn't shot from a stand. Oh, it started that way, with your Grandpa, restless as usual, waiting for something to come close enough to see. It was the first morning out, as I remember, that he heard the leaves rustle and the birds whistling in surprise and the tree-frogs suddenly silent, but he wasn't sure just what it had been— a deer or something else or the wind—or if it might not even have been just his imagination, except for the birds. The next morning he heard the same sound, coming from pretty much the same direction, but he still couldn't see anything. As a matter of fact I think he had more or less given up on it. He almost seemed resigned to getting skunked for once. But then the morning of the last day he saw it again, and not just fleetingly, as you'd expect, but head-on, the clearing suddenly quiet as a church, with the thick neck and the head high and belligerent, and the rack of antlers at least twenty points, the big buck looking down at him as though the deer was more curious about your Grandpa and what the hell he thought he was doing in his woods than vice-versa. Your Grandpa, who was at times too honest, told me later what had happened, and that he had been so startled that he'd actually forgot to take aim, much less shoot. So then he was sure he'd lost his chance, since by the time he'd thought to raise his rifle the stag had vanished back into the trees again, just as suddenly as it had appeared.

"But he hadn't lost him, because in the early afternoon he heard that same sound, coming from the same place, with the birds going strong. Only this time, he didn't wait for the deer to come any closer. He took out after it like lightning, following the sound for the first couple hundred yards, as the noise grew and faded, but then losing it altogether. Pretty soon he got the trail and followed that, the tracks in the dirt and the marks and broken twigs where the chest and shoulders had moved through, making their way. But then all at once he'd lost that, too; it had just disappeared. He stood at the edge of a broad clearing—with the swamp grass still and the dark water in the center glossy as a picture in the crisp fall light, and even the breeze gone calm—tired now, listening to the forest and caught up in its silence, resting to get his breath, without a trace of the big buck or a hint of where to look next. And then the birds started up again at the far side of the clearing. The stag appeared unfazed, calm as you please, walking through the jack pine out into the clearing like visiting royalty, as though it had come back to see and even to meet whatever it was that was following, though your Grandpa wouldn't have said that. He got a clean chest shot, so that the head was untouched. That stag's antlers had twenty-six points, and by God its meat was still tender. That was the head that was in your Grandpa's den above his old oak desk, and I'm convinced he looked up at it, from figuring the bills and payments on the money he'd lent out, in surprise and admiration and maybe even a touch of pride every day until the day he died, even though he wouldn't have admitted that, either."

Jake talked for a while longer, then we got up and he took me down the porch and across the field, into the little woods. In the sun of late afternoon that cut down through the branches to the bed of leaves beneath the oak and birch and popple, he told me what he would look for if he were the one doing the looking, and he tried to show me. "You have to understand," he said, resting on a stump and getting his tobacco out. "For what you want to know, it's not quite the same in a little patch of trees like this. But you'd look for the same sorts of things, the tracks and twigs, and the spaces between the trees for paths that might lead to food for foraging and to springs and streams for water. You have to remember where high ground is, and where the sun will hit at different times of the day. And you have to watch for snakes." When I noticed the light in his eye I turned so fast that he started to laugh, because it was only a pine snake slithering off the other way as fast as it could. "But watch out," he cautioned, putting his snuff away. "There are rattlers sunning on the high rocks at midday into fall. So be sure to keep an eye out where you step even if you're taking a shortcut and moving fast. I'll never forget your mother and her sister racing in wild-eyed with their hair flying in the wind whenever they thought they'd seen one. But there *are* some—so be careful," he smiled like the devil. I knew he was concerned, but he wanted to have his fun about it, too.

That evening Beatrice served the kind of meal that I remembered from Grandma Britzen's, and I felt just as good afterwards as I had when I had been little and the others would come up and tap my belly and joke about it when it had gone tight as a drum.

"Does your Mother still cook ham and biscuits for you?" Beatrice asked. "I remember she used to make the best biscuits in the county—after your Grandma." The only difference now was that along with the ham and string beans and biscuits and yams there was beer, too, so that by sundown I was more than full. After the apple pie and coffee, Jake got the bottle down again, complaining that he only had company once in a while and he might as well take advantage of the few occasions when it turned up. Beatrice smiled and started to clear, and we went out to the porch again to sit in the dusk, as the cool wind played with the embers from his pipe and stirred the leaves of the big oaks, so that I had to listen closely to what he said in order not to lose every fourth or fifth word, because he was talking quietly now, especially for Jake.

"He was the best man I ever knew, your Grandpa, if also the toughest to figure out. He even took the blame for me the time that Jack Snipes hauled him into court for trespassing, after I'd set up the sweetest damn duck blind anywhere from here to Lake Superior, just because the spot happened to be on that son-of-a-bitch's property—and Jack not really thinking of using it for that matter. I don't think he even got angry at Jack Snipes for it, not personally anyway. It was like the time one of the Connollys took the motorcycle he used to love to race around on." I gave a start and Jake smiled. "Yes, but I don't suppose you knew about that, the old 'Indian' your Grandpa had for two or three years, I believe, before the Connolly boy took it on a lark and wrecked it good, your Grandpa mad not at the boy but at what the fates had left him, the pile of metal that had been so sleek and swift and then in the blink of an eye was nothing but broken pipes and twisted steel. Anyway, as for the Jack Snipes deal, your Grandpa just took the whole thing for what it was worth—which wasn't much, as I remember. Not that he couldn't get mad, mind you."

Jake paused to work at his pipe a while before going on. "I've never seen anybody more worked up than he used to get with Gent (I'm not at all sure now if your Grandpa named him or I did), that prize weimaraner that he'd gone to the Cities to get and paid an arm and a leg for—nothing at all like Billy or any of the mutts I used to keep for coon hunting around here, and nothing like that real dog you folks had, nothing like Nero, but never mind that. Gent was a refined sort of animal, overbred probably, and so skittish that goddamn if he wasn't just scared to death of loud noises, so that with the first shot old Gent would take off over the rows of cornstalks with his tail between his legs—going the wrong way, of course. And then when he came back he'd *follow* the hunters the rest of the afternoon instead of working the fields out in front. I'll never forget the first time it happened. As the birds flew off, William turned in disbelief and started yelling at the dog, and the madder William got the louder he yelled, his voice echoing above the stalks, and so the more scared the dog got. With every word the dog just kept going faster. It was quite a sight, William stock still, booming away, and Gent scampering further and further, scared as hell by that time, until William got hoarse, thank God, or Gent would have ended up in the next county or maybe all the way across the line into Minnesota itself and home again. I used to worry that he was afraid of rain, too, since every time it would start to sprinkle he'd run in and hide under the bed. But it turned out it was the thunder that might go with it that he was scared of. Finally, William decided that the dog's mother must have been caught in a storm while Gent was still inside of her and there was nothing to do but accept the fact and leave the poor animal be. Hell, he not only forgave him but didn't even sell him. For awhile, though, it was a helluva lot of fun to see old ironsides Britzen fit to be tied every time he wanted to get a bird for his dinner.

"Yes, your Grandpa was quite a fellow." Jake leaned back and I could see the embers in the pipe bowl start to glow again. "And one of the best shots with a rifle I've ever seen, the only real competition being Drew and your brother, and now that I think about it, I'm not so sure anymore about Drew. His eye stayed just as sharp, too, right up to the day he was gone—or damn near it, anyway. The deer that we got, some of them, were nothing short of magnificent, like I told you. Still, it wasn't really the size so much that counted, but the style—something like that, almost as though they were more like humans than animals. One of the finest of all of them was the last one your Greatgrandpa got—or I should say, that we helped him get, since he was really too old to move much on his own anymore. But he wasn't willing to give up getting his deer any more than he'd have given up church on Sunday, neither of which you could blame him for, I guess, or any more than he'd have given up his spirits either—he wasn't at all like your Grandpa. We had left him on the road, more of a wagon path, really, but good enough to get the car down it. We were always a little anxious about leaving him alone, since the bucks are all sexed up and tough in November and likely as not will charge a lone man, thinking he's more like competition than death. But that never bothered your Greatgrandpa at all—in fact, I think he kind of liked the challenge at his age. So the old gentleman sat and waited, chewing his tobacco, with the door open and his Winchester resting out through the window, just so he'd be ready. Meanwhile your Grandpa and Drew and I had gotten around behind a quick young buck that hadn't noticed us. The wind was right, and besides he was too interested in foraging to worry about the likes of us. The wind came up higher, and I was afraid it would shift and that that would be the end of it, that he'd get the scent for sure. Then the wind did shift, and I thought we'd lost him for good 'cause he took off like a bat out of hell. But he didn't get far before he saw Drew running through the trees and waving his black hat like a madman, just opposite the side of the woods from where I'd told him to go—which actually wasn't surprising since Drew didn't have much of a knack for doing what you asked, unless it was your Grandpa doing the asking, of course. But this time, I have to say, it worked out all right. That buck must have thought he was heading home to Galilee, too, 'cause he just swerved forty-five degrees and kept on going, fast as a blinded mule. A moment later we heard the shot—just one—and when we got back to the clearing by the roadside, there was the old gentleman standing under a tree with a full eight-point smile under his yellow moustache. We butchered it for camp meat, but we kept the head and your Grandpa had it mounted for him, because the head and antlers were small but still nice. In fact, I think that your brother still has it somewhere, if those ravens you call cousins didn't snatch it up first. As I remember the old man sat in camp for the next day or two, playing solitaire and nodding off from time to time, sipping his schnapps and smiling between naps. But that was the last one he got. We were lucky that way, because he died the next spring, if I recall."

Jake took a sip of his whiskey and went on, remembering the afternoon's bird hunting across the open fields, and as the wind calmed and the stars began to show, I knew that I had been right, that time had stopped and nothing had changed, that he still felt the same, and was the same, just as he had always been. "Have another drink," Jake offered, pensive, as though, I thought later, there might have been something else he wanted to say, that he wanted me to know. "I've seen pheasants with their strong wings cutting across the wind, and I've heard their sizzle on the stove, smelled the flesh roasting, tasted its richness and felt its burden: and I've lived to trace the birds' image all over again, drifting away, still in flight. I've lived that way." He stopped and set his pipe again. "And your Grandpa did, too." Then, before lighting it, he took another sip from his glass and added: "Despite his failings." But it already seemed too late then, past the point to ask what he meant by that, even if he could have or would have said, and my head was already filled with the talk, and the memories of the hunt—Jake's memories—and the whiskey. So, in spite of myself, I let it go. Maybe I shouldn't have, maybe if I'd asked I would have saved myself a lot of trouble in the end. But it doesn't make much difference, really, because the moment had passed, and it was gone.

That night, as almost always now, as in my childhood when it would happen each night and almost every day, too, I dreamed.

It started with Diana, which was usual now, with her smile and her smooth white skin, as she drew me up and down like the river's current, steadily, sweetly, all at once breathtakingly. Sometime later O.B. and Kaseras were fighting, hitting each other in the chest and face as the blood streamed down Kaseras's cheeks and nose and smeared over O.B., too, so that, watching, and at the same time watching myself watch, since I'd had the dream before and knew that it was true now, I couldn't tell in the midst of the confusion who was bleeding and who wasn't. Then I was all by myself in the big woods, feeling glad to be on my own, alone and moving fast. O.B. was gone, but I could still feel his presence, and the old man's, too, inside the woods.

But this time I had the rifle. There was somewhere that I had to reach: I didn't know where, but I knew that I would recognize the place and what it was when I saw it, so I kept moving, knocking the branches away from in front of me as I headed for high ground, climbing now, with the river gorge off to my side and the rocks coming into view where they lined the dark bank. The air was grey, tinged with fall's chill, but in my exertion I had begun to sweat, so I threw off the hunter's cap and kept moving. Before long I found the trail at the top of the ridge and began to follow it, careful to keep my balance along its twists and turns so that I would not fall into the dark cover of leaves or, beyond them, into the deep, rock-filled gorge.

The path straightened out and started downhill. A snake slithered in the leaves alongside, but I raised a stone to kill it. Then all at once the path turned through the pines into a big clearing and I saw what I had been heading for, the biggest buck I had ever seen, standing tall and majestic between the trees, lifting its antlers, waiting.

I stopped short, wondering what to do and trying to understand the counsel of the birds, but I couldn't, and before I could decide, the buck had vanished. Breathlessly I gave chase. The going was hard, but gradually I settled into my stride and felt my breath coming regularly, full and steady inside my lungs. After a while I could hear the sounds of the buck out in front through the trees, and as the sound came louder, I picked up my pace, moving fast again on level ground, so fast that I had forgotten my fatigue and had become melded with the action of pursuit, absorbed into the action, and as I worked harder and harder the pursuit became not so much easier as smoother, fast but effortless, too, so that with every step I felt stronger and stronger, and just as I rounded the last curve before the black stone face of the gorge, there it was, across the river, watching me closely but distant, too, huge in its magnificence. It was the most wonderful sight I had ever seen, and I knew that it was just for me alone. Then when I looked again it wasn't a deer anymore but rather a mixture of man and animal, half man and half beast, with the body of the stag and a human face, and as I got close I could suddenly see the body gone and the face that of my greatgrandfather. I could feel O.B. close now, too, and I heard the old man's voice coming, so it sounded, from nearby, echoing, and the gun booming, so that I knew with utter certainty what it was, and then O.B. was gone and the old man had faded back into the trees, too, because it was the moment of my triumph and yet the moment was not part of time, no past or future only now forever.... *And I was riding the horse....*

I came awake with a start to find myself in the dark room, with the sound of an owl screeching outside the window and my nightshirt clinging to my chest, so that I could smell the whiskey in the sweat, as the memory of the images receded, leaving their residue of power and fear.

Early the next morning, after coffee and biscuits in the big kitchen—with the recollection of the night before already fading—I started back toward Chicago and O.B. and Riley's, harboring a feeling of expectation and optimism. I was chastened, perhaps, but I was also certain that for once, at least, I had found out what it was that I had needed to know. It is true that I could not have said exactly where that feeling and its totality came from—from Jake, O.B., or from somewhere else—but for the time being that seemed to make no difference, indeed to be utterly insignificant, as I headed through the serene countryside into the brilliant gleam of the midday sun.

*   *   *

So, I figured, what the hell, if Kaseras wants to be an asshole, let him. Who am I to tell him how to run his life? And anyway, he was a good mark. He always had been. The point was to keep the game going. And he was grateful for it, all in all: ever since that mess blew up after the fight with Charley Swenson and he'd been so thrilled that I'd talked Charley's lawyer—Charley's lawyer in a manner of speaking, understand, since Jack Benton was one of my best friends downtown, not to mention what he owed Zeke Wood—into convincing the old Swede to forget about suing Kaseras's undergarments off, along with what was under the undergarments, which is what Charley would have done had he had his way at first. I met Kaseras in my office special and told the big jerk there was only one stipulation, that he couldn't tell a soul about it, including Gianni. And Kaseras went along—just goes to show what a deuce he was deep down inside, despite all his money, about which almost no one knew, I suppose he didn't even think I knew all of it, but what else are friends downtown for if they can't keep you up on who's worth what on the latest balance sheet—since if he hadn't agreed, and everybody had found out what I'd done for him, all the leverage would have been gone, kaput, and I would have been just one more joe who had helped that oaf out of a scrape. And then we got the next deal going quick, the one for the apartment building on South Water Street. But as it was, I'd had the pleasure of knocking him around—which had practically been worth it all by itself—and of having him in my debt, too, at least in a figurative sense. It was sort of like the fellow with the donkey: initially, you had to get its attention, and then you had to keep it interested.

And as for Charley Swenson, well, first of all, you can't help everybody—I'm not the goddamn Goodwill—and second, Charley should have stayed around for the next lesson—the one about the left hook—before he suddenly found himself with Kaseras getting up and his right hand already spent. I mean, shit, if you've only got one punch to your name, you might as well stay at home or keep everybody to your left side all the time if you do go out, or better yet stick to lemonade, since one's plenty enough to get you into trouble but almost never enough to get you out of it, at least not in the grown-up leagues. So maybe Charley was just so blue that he had wanted to go down all along after all, like Gianni said. I don't know—that's not my business. Anyway, he gave me a chance to get another hook into Kaseras, two-pronged, too, and for that I'll be eternally grateful, bless the big Swede's heart. I have to admit, I was to the point where I needed it, or something like it, pretty bad. As for the seven and one-half months in the hospital, I can't be responsible for everything. That's what we have insurance for.

And as for Gianni, well, hell, he's been goddamn dreamy since he was a kid. If he wasn't busy daydreaming about one thing he was busy with another. And I can't always be worrying about taking care of him, either. I sure could never bring him down to earth, not even Diana had succeeded totally in that, despite her truly—to say the least—extraordinary capacities. Anyway, as far as that's concerned, why should I have cared about his so-called girlfriends, or about explaining things to Denise. O.K., it worked out just dandy that he felt the old man's rifle was part his, too, but that's not my fault either. Too bad those creeps had ransacked the old man's cache before we got there—Christ, they even beat the mortician by a full day—and cleared out the shotguns, or we might have been able to turn a pretty penny on them, too. Anyway, as long as Gianni kept thinking it was just the rifle, everything was fine—'cause after he'd once accepted the idea, he sort of warmed up to it, and in the end he actually took it over for his own, as was typical of him, too. Oh, I know him all too well. It was a dream come true—so why would he need or even want to turn a profit? No, the less I tell him about that or anything else the better, just like always. It's best to keep things the same they've been. After all, who knows who he'll be picking to confide in next? He might even start talking to Johnny Bubbles for all I can guess. And hell, he just doesn't need to know what he doesn't need to know. Like the fellow says, ask me no questions, and I'll tell you no lies.

* * *

"Why don't you get the brandy while I work at this."

Even though it was already past mid-April the evening was still cold—more than just chilly, Gianni thought as he stood rubbing his arms and waiting, after dinner, for his father to get the fire roaring on the raised hearth—downright cold. And he found himself looking forward to the warmth of the fire and the brandy as much as to the chance, at long last, to have a talk with him.

"French or home-grown?" Gianni asked, sure of the answer, but posing the question out of deference. Without waiting for a reply he reached behind the crystal decanter and got the frosted green bottle. He poured two snifters, and, as the two of them sat in front of the quickly growing flame, warming the brandy in their hands, they listened to Gianni's mother clearing the last of the dishes to the kitchen. When he'd arrived she'd been happy to see him, commenting that it had been a long while between visits. She had taken his coat, just as in times past, then brought him his drink. But now she had left the two of them alone because she knew that Gianni wanted to talk. As Gianni watched the brandy rolling down the side of his glass, he gathered his courage and broached the subject.

"When he left us, you mean, at the end?" his father responded. When Gianni nodded his father shook his head, the hair still thick and black despite the streaks of white. Even in the dim light of the study, Gianni could see the smile as the firelight flickered across it.

"It's not just what a man turns in when he's done that counts, but the whole way he uses it—including the ups and downs—while he's here. You—all of you, and especially your mother and O.B.—concentrated on what your Uncle Henry and your cousin did about the inheritance when Jane died—or, really, before she died, like I guess you know. And there's no doubt that it *was* disgusting, playing around with other people's money just so they could have it to themselves in the end, as though they really could have hid it from the rest of the world—a classic mixture of stupidity, avarice, and pride all at the same time, with more than a little resentment tossed in for good measure, I have to admit, though I never could figure out exactly what the resentment was about. And the way they trooped in and raked through the stuff that was left in the house on Juniper Street before anybody else could get there was pretty awful, too, especially since Drew still lived there, even if only technically because by then the nuthouse had been his real home for more than a few years, almost, if I recall, since Grandpa Britzen had passed away. Your mother especially took that part of it hard, though frankly I guess it was just because nobody likes to think of their sister as having been in cahoots with what turned out to be graverobbers. It certainly couldn't have been for what they got—I don't think your mother would know which end of a shotgun to put on her shoulder in the first place, much less how to handle an old set of Colts. But all of that, when you get down to it, was really just a matter of fine points. The things that counted—

the chances he had to help or hurt, to make his mark on the rest—had come much earlier. And not only in the way you and O.B. think, either. Oh, sure, he helped with some things—you boys mostly, in the woods and on the river, but that's not the whole story, Gianni, no matter who's telling it."

He turned the brandy in his large, dark hands, his brow furrowed. Gianni glanced out the window past his own reflection, over the back porch and into the trees, the flames of the fire flickering in the pane. When his father spoke again, his voice had the authority of the lawyer and businessman that he was, unquestionably successful, self-assured, and something else, too, that Gianni recognized only fleetingly, though he could not have said what it was or where, exactly, it came from.

"It's not my favorite topic, but since you ask, I'll tell you. There wasn't a year during the entire time you boys were growing up that we weren't in hock to your Grandfather—and not just a nickel here and a dime there, but up to our necks. Oh, I suppose it wasn't all that strange for the period—the G.I. Bill simply wasn't enough to get along on and get a university degree and raise a family, so lots of people needed help, and they would get it from relatives and friends nearly as often as from banks. The part that was different about the old man was that most folks, if they had all they needed and really couldn't have wanted more, like his situation after he had to sell the farm because of his allergies and had moved into town, most people, anyhow, didn't get to acting like bank collectors every time a payment came due. It's true that by then the old man had been making loans and collecting principal and interest for a good long time, and habits are hard to change. But it always seemed to me that family matters should be different. Of course, that's just one perspective. Anyway, it doesn't help relations much when every time you go on vacation—up north, for us, which, then, was the only kind of vacation we could afford—you end up getting a needle jabbed in your side. I know that for you and O.B. it was also the best kind of summer, the only kind you would or could have wanted, but for your mother and me, it was also, and in some years only, a question of finances. Ah, we were broke all right, flat broke. But frankly, so many other people with young families around here were in the same position that, while we were at home, at least, it never seemed so bad. Until, that is, we'd show up every summer in Crooked Falls and, when you boys would go whooping out into the fields, your mother and I would follow the old man into the den—which in those days he called his 'office'—and he'd close the door under the deer head and sit down behind the big oak desk to figure out what five percent per annum—or whatever percent he was using on that part of the loan, because there had been more than one crisis and more than one "arrangement" to resolve it—would come to that year, and what the payment on the principal would add up to, as the fine line of india ink traced the figures so that, upside down, I could see the maze of them grow and grow until he'd worked his eyebrows and rechecked to make sure, a little surprised himself, it always seemed, before he'd turn the balance sheet around atop the desk and move it toward me, to show us the result of all that figuring: every year, without respite except once, after you were born, and your mother broke down in tears when she'd gone up to go through the procedure alone, since she handled our accounts, such as they were—most often in those days, ten or fifteen minutes a month would have sufficed—and she knew that no matter what the final figure turned out to be, we couldn't pay it, because there was simply nothing left. By that time, even for your mother, the old man's money had become more of a yoke than a help. You could see it in her eyes. So instead of paying or not paying—because, you see, I still hadn't learned not to hope for that, hadn't learned once and for all that Pennsylvania Dutch isn't just a kind of food or custom, that for him, and them, not paying was simply not within the realm of possibility—we took another loan, on the spot, to pay for what we couldn't pay, and, I guess, to keep the cycle going and the minute design of the figures intact. Those weren't easy times, Gianni. You boys never knew anything about it—though if you hadn't been so young, it would have been plain as the nose on your face—but every time we needed something new, no matter how big or how small, we had to have his help and his approval. And the figures had to tally, no matter what, at least until the balance sheet was locked away in the desk for the next year, and the cash or check had been doled out."

    He shook his head and looked away for a moment, toward the back porch, sheathed in darkness, as though thinking of something he'd left out. "Bitter times, now that I remember them, probably better forgotten. I'm not saying that he was Simon Legree, mind you—and, in a way, I have to admit, I don't know to this day what we ever would have done without him—but as the good Lord is my witness, he sure wasn't St. Nick, either. No matter what you and O.D., and even Mabel and your mother, despite her tears that one time, might have thought."

*   *   *

Of course, I had to say yes, since it was William's boys who were asking me—or, if not exactly his sons, his grandsons, which is the next best thing and not even the next in this case, because he never had boys of his own, just the two girls, that is, after a fashion, and he treated and thought of those boys as his own—however luckily—no matter how young they were then. Funny, when they were with him running through the woods or along the river, they seemed older than their years could have been, especially the eldest, O.B., and they made William seem a good spit younger, with all the energy he'd had when I'd first met him, before the illness that had moved him off the farm and into the little one and one-half story house on Juniper Street, with just the half-set of stairs so that, supposedly, Mabel wouldn't have to climb.

The problem—why, it's just natural—was that I didn't know anymore what they knew or what they were like or what they could do by themselves. But, still, I did it—for William and, I guess, deep down in part for myself, too. Because after a time your memories, especially of someone like that, become a part inside of you and aren't just something outside anymore. Besides, as things are now, I've lived too long anyway. I'm better off if I can help somebody else now. Gianni was the one that told me what they needed, and, to tell the truth, it seemed simple enough. Some help and a little advice, a few supplies, a couple of days at the cabin in deer season, and not much else. I was pretty sure that O.B. would be able to handle his part of it on his own, since he had been a crack shot even when he was a little fellow; and he'd always helped Gianni out, too, brother to brother, just like the good book says.

Not that I didn't have my doubts, especially about Gianni and that little-boy nature of his—nervous but not really energetic or productive—that he never seemed to get over, and that you could still see cropping up from time to time, and even about Stevey—though less, I've got to say—and you can just forget about that darn Tom. But except for that one, they were all good boys, and I was happy they'd come to me and that I could help. Beatrice seemed pleased too, when you got down to it, though of course she wouldn't ever have said much about it one way or the other, she's always so quiet about things like that, not like those women who jump up and down and get their panties all stained every time the men go off for a few days on their own. And I knew that, if he'd still been around to give it any thought, Drew would have been pleased, too. But none of that, really, none of it, was why I did it.

I did it for William.

* * *

Gianni awakes to the sounds of O.B. tinkering with the rifles. While he has been asleep the weather has changed, covering over, but now the sun has returned and the patches of snow that dot the clearing have already begun to melt off. "The guns have to be cleaned," O.B. explains, sitting in the sunlight of the kitchen with the shiny parts spread all around his feet and on the handcarved chairs and table. "Now is as good a time as any."

An hour later Jake Arndt and his nephews have arrived, the one, Stevey, from Duluth, Beatrice's sister's boy, the other, Tom, older, from the Cities, Jake's step-child from an earlier marriage. Gianni had first heard about him the night that he and Jake had talked. "Yes, I was married before," Jake had admitted. "But anybody can make a mistake. It just takes a man to be able to see it and then do something about it. In my case, I saw it, and right away I lit out. 'Course the war came soon enough after that and split everybody up anyway, so all told, the result would have been the same."

O.B. greets them at the door and shakes hands with everyone, except for Jake, who slaps O.B. on the back and then Gianni, as he spits tobacco juice over his shoulder into the clearing for luck. Inside, Jake unwraps the cloth in which Beatrice has placed the butter and biscuits, and O.B. brings the metal coffee pot from the stove while they draw the chairs around the big table. Gianni is glad that Jake is finally there, and he likes Stevey, whom they've known since they were young; but even though he tries not to let it show, there is something about Tom that simply doesn't strike him right.

Not even Gianni is sure just what, whether it is his offhanded way of looking about the cabin and the woods, as though perhaps it might have been best had he stayed where he'd been, or his surprise that the biscuits and fried ham and eggs are all that there is for breakfast, or the way he grins when he asks about the number of deer they are allowed to take by law, or maybe his urgency, so that when Jake starts to tell him patiently, he cuts in, "No—not all together. How many each, that's what I want to know," his teeth large and bright against swollen gums. Jake looks askance at him, that much is obvious, but the old man answers despite his scorn for greed and the thirst for blood.

On balance, Jake seems happy, happier than Gianni has seen him since the old man had died, as Jake's gnarled hands chase an imaginary fly from his face, his cheeks flushed with excitement. Jake is certain that they will get something, the only question being just what, which, as he says with a wink to let them know it isn't as though he hasn't tried, is the part that even the good Lord himself won't answer, not yet anyway. As Jake pushes his plate away, he reaches up to rip a page off the calendar, which reads March, 1955, a good long time out of date, and then uses a blunt pencil to begin a map. He divides the woods around the cabin into sections and indicates the high points and the trails running through each of them, and the streams and the pathways that the deer will take to the farmers' fields at the edge of the trees where they go to forage. Then they draw cards from the cabin's deck to choose their ground, at least for starters. O.B. gets the King straight off and goes first. When Jake nods, O.B. takes the ridge above the river. Gianni gets the forest floor below, where Jake has drawn the crossing of three trails, two of them leading to the river and the third up the ridge toward the highlands.

"Milt Johnson got a twelve-point buck along that riverbank four or five years ago," Jake comments. "There's a spring in there, too, just off the trail, where they come in to nuzzle through the leaves. I've seen the white patches on the bark where the bucks have been getting ready for their fights there. I'll set up a stand near the rubs—if you want," he smiles, "with some of Joe Barnes's patented doe scent."

Jake marks the place with an "X," and the others choose their spots, with Jake's pencil adding new marks after each turn. As Jake puts more and more about the woods onto the paper, the map begins to take on a life of its own, with signs for springs, clearings, changes in timber, and streams, all within what would have been roughly a morning's hike from the cabin's clearing, the center of the map's world. Jake marks the rapids with hatches where the water roars like a train and makes a cross at the little falls at the end where the old man used to cast for trout while Jake hunted along the bank and into the trees. As the chart becomes a maze, Jake puts the energy of his memory into its design, recreating the woods in the circles and shadings and the crisscross of the thick grey lines amidst the smells of the coffee and the tobacco. He tries to tell them again, as his hand moves the pencil back and forth over the yellowed paper, what to look for and how to place their shots if they can; but in the end he draws a circle around his design and sets the pencil down. Having closed off his realm, he contents himself with reminding them abruptly to be careful and wishing them luck.

That afternoon, after watching Jake and O.B. trudge up the slope toward the ridge side by side, O.B. with the red cap swinging in his hand and the old man's Remington under his arm, Gianni makes himself at home in the stand that Jake has set for him near the spring. Through the snarl of young poplars, he watches the last leaves fluttering on the oaks high above and takes a pull now and then on the flask that O.B. has left with him to keep warm: "It's a helluva lot better than those little hand-warmers," O.B. smiled. "The ones designed to warm you in one minute and burn you to death in two. But don't get overly wrapped up in it, if you know what I mean."

Three hours later Gianni still hasn't seen a thing other than a few birds high in the branches. But with the bourbon in him he doesn't feel too bad, either. He takes another pull on O.B.'s flask and sets the rifle beside him, letting his thoughts wander until they settle on the old man as he remembers him from all those years ago. To tell the truth, some of the more distant relatives, hangers-on and free-loaders more than aunts, uncles, or cousins, didn't actually believe that Gianni *could* remember the old man, he had been so young. On more than one occasion when he had been talking, they seemed to think that he had somehow dreamed up what he knew rather than remembered it. He recollects their reactions from the funeral, and he is offended all over again, since in life the old man had seemed to belong more to them (and they to him) than to anybody else, as though his life and theirs had been intertwined; and even now the thought of him having a life apart from theirs seems unthinkable, although in fact it is true that they only saw him during the summers, until that once, just before the end.

As Gianni thinks of the old man in the woods with the Remington, he remembers the story of the stag that Jake had told him. He imagines how big the deer had been, his head high and his shoulders strong like a boxer's are strong, the huge antlers tossing up and down and then, moving with the speed of light, vanishing into the trees. Then he thinks of the bet with Kaseras, the son of a bitch, and considers who is going to beat whom. It seems to him, at that moment, that there is no doubt any longer; and he settles down to wait, sipping and watching. Before the flask is empty, he has fallen asleep.

He comes awake with the realization that he has heard a sound, off through the trees, but he is not sure whether he has heard it only in his imagination or whether it has been real. He wakes up slowly, still dozing, as he often does after a deep sleep, no matter how brief; but now when he hears the rattle of the branches again he is certain that something is there, something real, and not just one of his dreams. He listens intently, but it is too dark to see anything—too dark for that time of day, really, but that doesn't matter to him then—and he hears nothing more.

At first when he mentions it at supper, skirting certain details, Jake laughs, taking it as a joke. But later he lets Gianni know in unconcealed disappointment that he has understood more than Gianni has actually said and that if Gianni is unable to stay awake, much less alert, he has no business in a stand with a gun. Gianni is stung, feeling more betrayed than embarrassed, even though Jake has waited to talk to him alone, and he resolves to himself to do better. In a strange way, it pleases him deeply that the others haven't got anything either, in fact haven't even caught sight of anything, not O.B. nor anyone else.

Gianni continues to feel the same after the next day's hunt, again with no luck. Initially, none of the others will admit to being disturbed by their lack of success, though later on, while they are playing poker the second evening, Gianni can see, despite the others' raucous laughter and Jake's more or less constant patter, that O.B. in particular is preoccupied, since he doesn't try even one bluff and hardly takes more than a hand or two regardless of opportunities that he normally would have sprung upon without a second thought. When Stevey suggests obliquely the possibility of giving up and heading home, O.B. shoves the deck of cards across the table and onto the floor with a vehemence that surprises even Gianni, though for the time being he doesn't make anything more of it. Only Tom seems intent on the card game, watching each hand closely and arguing whenever he loses, which he does with regularity, flinging his cards down in dismay as though O.B.'s anxiety were contagious and finally ending the evening with a curse for his losses and a vow to make up for them with a kill the next day. It is the day after that when Jake, who in reality is no more satisfied than O.B., decides to stalk the deer so as to move them toward the rifles rather than vice-versa. Still, all that morning nothing happens.

Then, just after noon, Stevey finally gets a twelve-point buck. Gianni hears the shot, and when he reaches the clearing where he has seen the red caps through the trees, Jake and Tom are already waiting with Stevey just beyond it, beneath a large oak. It is easy to see how proud Jake is, his smile beaming from ear to ear. The old hunter kneels down and turns the head upward to look at it. "Not a mark," he says to Stevey. "Just like I would have done—when I was your age." Jake takes his knife to the deer's chest, and when he has cut it open, he grabs Stevey's hand, still trembling with the excitement of the shot, and shoves it inside the red gash, staring intently at the boy while Gianni watches in fascination.

A while after that Jake butchers the deer for camp meat. As he works at it, some of the blood splatters into his tobacco pouch, which he gives to Stevey so that he can draw in the life of the animal through the smoke of the pipe's bowl. Later that day O.B. gets a pair of partridges to go with the venison. "I'd cleaned the shotgun and they just sort of wandered into my sights on their own account," O.B. explains. "Besides, I figured I should make sure I could still aim and shoot just in case I did come across a deer by chance."

But despite his banter, O.B. remains visibly displeased, and he reminds Gianni that, in the terms of their bet, Stevey's deer does not count. "We have to do this on our own," O.B. insists as he cleans the Remington for what seems the hundredth time. "There's no way around it. The bet, and the responsibility for it, are ours, not theirs. Don't let yourself forget it. We can't put our feet up and get comfortable just because of Stevey's good luck. So for chrissake, Gianni, keep trying—or start trying—whichever it may be."

The following morning Gianni waits in the stand, alone as before. Although the previous evening he felt discouraged, now he is anxious and intensely hopeful. In the night it has snowed again, and the ground near the stand is powdered white. There is an edge, a crispness to the woods in the early morning that he had never really gotten to know, in large part because of his sleeping habits, which were so long-standing that even as a child he could remember waking up alone and waiting for O.B. and Grandpa to return from their morning outings to the woods or the river, where they'd gone just after dawn, hours before, without disturbing him from his sleep. But now he discovers to his astonishment that he likes this time of day in the forest. When he descends to the river for a drink, he startles two beavers working where the banks narrow before opening into a pond; and on his way back he watches the birds feeding and hopping back and forth between the pines and oaks, scolding an occasional squirrel that gets in their way and preparing for the cold. His eye catches a bunting flit like a butterfly in the sun, and he remembers standing alone as a boy, with the net Grandpa had made for him, watching the butterflies on a summer's afternoon deep in the forest.

By that time the others are all too far away to see or hear him. O.B. and Jake have gone up to the ridge again, and Stevey and Tom have taken their separate paths from the cabin, pursuing the routes that Jake had drawn for each of them. As Gianni turns around in the stand, he feels the flask in his inside pocket knock against his ribs. But he decides that it is still too early and that he will wait an hour before he permits himself his first pull. He busies himself moving his feet and rubbing his arms in the rough wool coat to stay warm, then feels with gratitude and almost surprise the relief of the whiskey sweet and searing in his throat. Once, he thinks for sure that he has heard something move in the trees beyond, off where he cannot see, or where he has been too slow to turn his gaze: and a second time, half an hour or so later, he is certain of it. But when noon passes and still nothing has come beyond the sounds of the birds singing in the ghostly twists of the branches high above, he begins to work on the flask more attentively. Before long his head is heavy and his thoughts are all mixed together, with images of Diana, Kaseras, O.B., and the old man spilling over from one to the other, and he is lost in the haze between waking and sleep. Soon he is sleeping deeply, but even in his sleep the chorus of noises in the woods around him penetrates into his mind. In the midst of his darkness, Gianni can feel the presence more than see it, as he catches the odor of musk, its dark pungent smell: and from a great distance, far away on the other side of the river, he can see the antlers rising. As the smell grows stronger and threatens to overwhelm his senses, there comes a crash in the bushes nearby. It is the same sort of noise as before, but considerably louder.

  He wakes with a start to the sight of the animal so close that, had he been quick enough, he could have reached out his hand and touched it where it stood above him, its antlers twenty points or more, at once utterly pure and supremely indifferent to him. So the buck is not a dream, Gianni knows that much. But he is also paralyzed by its sudden presence, and in a flash, before he can make himself move an inch, the stag has disappeared. Gianni snatches the rifle and starts out, the challenge of its scent still reeking in his nostrils as he follows his prey through the tangled trees.

  He moves along the worn path then cuts into the brush where the buck has bolted up the ridge along the river. He fends off the branches and brushes the spider webs from his face as he goes. It all seems exactly as he has dreamed it, with his breath coming hard at first then easing off as he gets his pace and his stride steadies out. The light of the November afternoon is already growing dim, and the colors of the woods fade quickly, blending together. He cannot see the stag, but as he mounts the ridge, he traces its hooves and the damage it has done to the bushes in its path and continues to feel the scent in his nostrils, so he knows he is on its track.

When he reaches the top of the ridge, the trail is less twisted and he moves forward swiftly without effort. Before long he comes to a clearing with three paths leading out of it and no clear sign showing which to choose. While he stands in dismay trying to decide on the one to take, with the birds twittering again amidst the chorus of tree-frogs, something worse than having to choose suddenly occurs to him: he smells the scent of the pines and the snow and nothing more. The musk is gone. He turns quickly, retracing his steps then beginning to circle in hopes of recrossing the trail in the snow. After a while he finds himself at the top of the ridge again looking over the scoop of the river far below, with the deadfalls jutting out beyond the rounded shelf of snow to divert the current, the pieces of ice floating by, and the boulders strewn all along the banks. Then the smell hits him again, but it seems different now, distant, almost taunting, borne on the wind, no longer intimate. As he gazes down at the curve of the river, he sees the antlers lifting, near the water but just around the bend on the other side, not out of range but perfectly blocked from any shot by the thick stand of trees.

"Damn!" he shakes the rifle at his side, useless now.

He watches the antlers nod as though in acknowledgment and then begin to move off lightly between the trees, with a grace that is almost offensive. A moment after he hears a voice come booming through the woods behind the stag, distant but clear, recognizable, stronger with each moment, until Gianni catches sight of the red splotch floating among the sticks of pine and the mass of birch. The voice is Jake Arndt's, and it is coming toward him. So the buck hasn't won after all, not yet.

Now again Gianni has to choose—the path back the way he has come or the one before him, the straight descent to the river. He hesitates only a moment, though later, thinking back, he will realize that it had seemed much longer. Oddly enough, no matter how much he will dwell on the events of that afternoon, just why he makes the choice he does he never really knows. But once he has decided, he sets out with only one purpose, backtracking, resolved to beat the stag if it—or better, as it—recrosses the river on the surge of Jake's drive. He has never moved more swiftly, though now he is unaware of the mechanics of his flight, his mind white in its intensity and his feet sure and steady beneath him. He hears Jake's voice boom once more and that is all; the struggle of branches fly by as he rushes headlong with the awful smell in his nostrils again, rich, potent, and pure, the odor of his challenge and, he feels deep in his heart, of his victory—like O.B. but better than him, like the old man but better than him, too. Gianni feels his presence everywhere in the woods now, almost an apparition, pervasive yet invisible.

Then he hears the crack of the rifle, crisp, definitive.

"Damn!" he explodes, yelling it this time, as he holds his chest and shoulders rigid to keep control of himself. But he stops a moment only, so great is his longing. He heads on, confused, his heart full and his eyes all at once cloudy.

Then he hears another shot, and again more voices, urgent now. So perhaps, he thinks, it is not over yet, as he races forward, his breath coming fast again and his heart sounding in his head, the branches scraping his face and rushing past, the colors all in a haze, the sudden red splotch. He pulls up with the stench growing strong once more, mixed now with that of his own sweat, then he continues along the trail until he comes to an opening in the trees and, suddenly sensing the old man's presence all over again, sees it emerge opposite, beneath a broad white pine, the antlers rising in their shining invitation, stately, majestic, too majestic, and seeming ready to charge, as Jake had told him it might. So Gianni lifts the rifle, and he hears the thunderclap of his shot echo in his ears and sees the red center blossoming as, dazed now, with a sigh he can hear but not feel, he lowers the rifle down until its stock comes to rest on the soft mat of the pine needles at his feet.

That is the last he can remember—not the sight beneath the pines across from him, nor Jake and Stevey coming up, not even the view of the real deer as it stumbles into the clearing that is still green and brown yet flecked with white and falls in a red pool, going down first on its forelegs and then, struggling but failing, finally letting its head drop to one side with its magnificent rack of antlers—but instead the feel of the rifle butt nestling into the wet needles, that and thinking: there, now I've showed them, now, at last, thank God, I'm done.

* * *

So that's the way I heard it, and that's the way I told it to the duo of Keystone Cops. It wasn't Gianni that first realized what had happened, which was what they'd been told, or what they'd figured by themselves, as would have been perfectly natural—I never knew which—but instead Jake and the boy, running on the heels of the deer, which they had driven across the river and into O.B.'s sights, and which O.B. had hit, but not just right, not in the head but too high in the chest for the heart, at least too high for the bullet to take immediately, and which had turned then to head frantically back toward Jake and Stevey until, seeing them, it had turned once more, taking a second shot from Stevey before, already dying, it made its run, the last, this time ending up at the edge of the clearing but no further, its strength seeping from its wound and from its mouth into the same mat of needles that Gianni stood on and that supported the butt of his rifle. So it was Jake and the boys that saw not only the deer where it lay along the trees with its beautiful, unblemished rack of two dozen points but also Gianni, with his rifle propped at his side, and, across the clearing, O.B., with the serene look on his face.

I couldn't tell them much more, but at least I could show them the head and antlers mounted behind the bar: after all, as Gianni had insisted despite everything, it was still O.B.'s prize. And anyway, like I said before and I'll say again, there was really no reason for me to tell those two clowns any more, even if I'd known more to tell—which, of course, I did, since I haven't been a bartender all these years for nothing. But these guys were just stand-ins—even if you took them (and Uncle Martin, too, though he was a bum) at their word—not real cops at all but some sort of sheriff's police, filling in as a favor for their compadres in the north woods, who apparently hadn't done their job like they should have the first time around. Because they're supposed to investigate each and every "incident," as they say, no matter how minor, bar none, even if it's just a formality. Of course, like I said, this stuff's serious business up there. I don't imagine they want every son of a bitch that can hold a popgun running through the woods killing off his fellow man as easy as you please. So how could you figure it, that they'd let them all take off in a flurry, without so much as a so-long, at least from what those two ersatz boys-in-blue had been told. Oh, they knew who O.B. was all right, that's for sure, but as for the rest, they didn't know anything. The funny part of it was, they didn't seem to want to find out much either: just tell us about the two brothers, they kept saying—for a courtesy call, nothing more—and skip the rest, whatever it was. Which in fact was all right with me, since I never thought the bet was all that important by itself anyway, just an excuse and no more, at least at first, a wager and that's all, a stake, or a spur, a way of getting the ball rolling and keeping it going, unimportant by itself except, of course, for what it led to.

So I told them exactly what they wanted to hear: next to nothing. They didn't want all that b.s. about fighting and betting, and certainly nothing about pride and honor—all the stuff that got O.B. and Gianni into that mess in the first place—which to tell you the truth was just fine since, like I said, I'd never believed in any of that anyway. I told them about the hunting trip and whatever details I knew, which didn't really amount to much and most of which they'd already found out about anyway all on their own, like the good little weasels I guess they were. And I didn't say one word concerning all the tomfoolery about money that O.B. had got himself caught up in: because they never asked.

They stood in the dim light of mid-afternoon, when there aren't many people around here anyway, and, like I said, not acting all that interested, fidgeting with their change and lighters and such and glancing around the empty bar like they couldn't wait to get out of there and back to their office, or whatever, so they could make out their report and get the job over with—exactly like Uncle Martin described it, just filling up space in the wide world and marking time, which, apparently is what it means to be on the government payroll these days, or maybe always has for all I know, or care, quite frankly. So anyway, I really couldn't get too excited about playing to an audience like that. And if they'd already talked to Gianni like they'd said, what could I say that was new? Pretty soon, I got to admit, I found myself rattling off the answers as mechanically as possible and slapping the specks of dust with the bar-cloth from time to time just to keep myself entertained. Then to top it all off they even turned down the drink I offered them on the house, which I swear has never happened to me before, here at Riley's or anywhere else, with the excuse that they had to get back to whatever and finish up their work. Which I guess they did, since, with that, they turned on their heels and marched out the door onto the street, and I never saw or heard from them again. Thanks be to God, might I add.

So I didn't tell them what I thought about Gianni's "mistake," as they'd all taken to calling it by then, or about the things I'd heard between the two of them that—if you ask me (but of course, they didn't, at least, not that)—seemed to explain part of it, if not all of it, the things about the old man and about his hunter pal and the odd—or maybe just nutty, I don't know—ideas that Gianni seemed to have about them when he talked with O.B., not to mention those dreams. And I didn't say much about Kaseras and the rest of them, either, since the dime-store cops didn't want to hear about it, or about O.B.'s part of the bet—and that particular little detail of the side bets he'd spun off of it—since I was pretty sure not even Gianni knew about them, and since the two nice officials, in spite of their know-it-all airs, didn't know enough to ask. Things like that happen all the time, what do they care? So I told them what they did want to hear, about O.B. leaning—or really, I guess they said, resting back—against the trunk of a white pine, with the big chunk of his right shoulder that just wasn't there anymore, and his gaze tilted upward beneath the hat, his face quiet, the scar above his eyebrow still, serene, it seemed, despite the blood, and looking for all the world like he'd breathed his last.

  So yeah, like I say, I was happy to see them go—relieved more than anything. Because it had given me a chance to get it all out in the fresh air and what they didn't find out was their fault, not mine. And now I've told it all, everything I know, more or less, which, like I said, is the way it should be, nice and plain and open. It's the best way. Because—and I know from experience—even though it might sting a little at first, in the end the truth is really the best policy all in all, take it from me. The truth never hurts.

IV.   Fugitive

> Death will come only when the web of destiny is spun.
> — Kallinos

"It would have been easier," Gianni went on, "if he had just died. At least in some ways. I wouldn't have found out what I did, or, better, I guess, I would have found out in a completely different way, at a time when things were over and done instead of all a mess like they are now. And I wouldn't have had to deal with him, only with his memory. But then—when you think of it—in the long run that's not so easy either. After all, the old man—the other one—had taught us that, and taught us well. Because people come to an end, and hard as it is to accept, life ends; but memory and its wounds go on no matter what happens. So maybe neither one, alive or dead, is so much better or worse as just a different kind of pain."

As they sat on the porch, glassed in now in December, he couldn't help but notice, as he looked out, that the brown matted grass of the little lawn running down to the street looked more like cured tobacco than grass as it waited for the snow to come and cover its bleak reminder of death with the north's dizzying white. In between the sips of the lemonade that she had gone to no little trouble to make fresh for him, and that she still insisted on calling *limonata*, she would ask, waving her delicate hands in the air, and he would answer, as in the old days, on the porch of the farm house, except that now she was not probing a child's seemingly boundless imagination and he was not responding purely from fancy, or so, at least to him, it seemed, given the seriousness of the circumstance, his feelings of awkwardness, and the fatigue that had crept up his spine while they talked.

Aunt Fil had wanted to know, as it was her right to. But for Gianni it was more than that, at least as far as it concerned her— as distinguished from the rest of the seemingly endless parade of friends and relatives, all with their morbid curiosities. She had always been special to him, since his earliest memories of the wonders of the summers in New Providence, and he to her. Maybe because she had been the youngest, too, he had come to think later—and besides, of all the sisters, she had always been the most beautiful, with her ivory skin and dark hair, and her almond eyes, Grandma Mariagrazia's eyes. So he had driven willingly the some two hundred miles to the white clapboard house in the small town where she lived now, just half-way between Chicago and the two farms in the north, in the middle part of Wisconsin where the terrain is still flat instead of rolling or, nearer the western border, hilly with the fells and crags where the river has been busy eating away at the land since well before Blackhawk and his braves put that country on the map.

It was warm on the porch, almost hot in those places where the afternoon sun came through the windows and cast its mark across the wood floor and up the wall, and as they talked Gianni could feel the heat on his arms and his forehead, despite the cool draughts of lemonade.

"The worst thing," he began, hesitant and quiet but no longer awkward, searching for the right words now but sure of himself and his thoughts at the same time, "wasn't so much knowing what had happened as knowing what everyone else was saying about it. There were days, especially at first, when Johnny Bubbles—the bartender—claimed that by rights he should be getting paid twice, once for tending bar and once for running a news agency. But, of course, almost none of what the customers thought was "information" was at all accurate. Johnny Bubbles would try to set people straight, but even he didn't know half of what there was to know. And everybody—but everybody—seemed to have an opinion, enlightened or not."

"At first, the cops' visit had at least had the one good result," he continued with only a note of sarcasm, "that everybody hushed up. There's nothing like the boys-in-blue showing up to make a crowd catch its breath. But of course they didn't do any good at all beyond that, not a single iota. And once they'd gone off to make what they called their 'report'—about which none of us ever heard another syllable—the talk started up again, worse than ever, too, since the 'police' were involved, although from what I could tell the difference between forest rangers on a courtesy call and real cops is only slightly less than that between Alabama and Alaska. Fortunately, their little tête-à-tête with Johnny Bubbles didn't affect O.B. one way or another, not his spirits and not his condition, which is, like I said, guarded but, officially, 'good.' Which means that as long as the infection doesn't get worse and he doesn't do anything rash, he should recover all right, though he'll never be able to use his right arm again—that, at least, seems pretty sure. But except for that, he should be like new within a few months' time, as things stand now."

"As things stand now?"

"That is, if the drugs keep the infection down and if the physical therapist—eventually—is able to help him. Then there's the mental part—morale, I guess—but the doctors don't seem to be too worried about that."

"And do you have trust in the doctors?" She must have recognized the response on Gianni's face because she hurried to add, "I mean that as a question—I'm not doubting you, or them. I just remember Father and the way they managed to get everything wrong until it was too late to help, or to matter, so that in the end all they could do was to blame—"

"No," he shook his head, "this isn't like that, from what I understand and remember about Grandpa. With Grandpa, there was never a correct diagnosis until—you're right about that—until it was over and done. But this isn't a question of diagnosis. Determining just what it is that's gone wrong isn't so much the problem as knowing how to deal with it. And in that sense, at any rate, the doctors who are treating O.B. seem pretty good, to me at least. I'm no expert, that's for sure, but I have to admit that I'm more than satisfied with what I've seen and with what's been done so far."

Through the open door, he could hear the whir of the kitchen fan, and it was only after listening to it for a moment that he became aware of the silence that had fallen between them. He looked back at her, at the smooth creases in the face that was aged but still handsome, once so vivacious, and now, if anything, too quiet and patient. He hurried to speak, to start again, since the emptiness brought the doubts he was trying so desperately to escape.

"It's still hard to see him there like that," Gianni continued, no longer certain of what to say, with an edge to his voice now that he could not control or dissimulate no matter how odd he found it. "It doesn't seem right that he's stuck in that bed without even being able to get up and walk around on his own, tied down by that maze of wires and tubes. I always thought of him as the embodiment of activity and strength—almost like raw energy itself. Both of them the same—that is, him and Grandpa Mariagrazia."

He stopped all at once, surprised by the discovery: "I guess I always thought of them both that way, him and Grandpa. Completely unlike our other Grandpa."

"Your great uncle, really—but I guess you know that."

"Yes, I remember being told—along with O.B. But it never seemed to make any difference or even be comprehensible. Anyway," he went on, grateful for the change of subject, "what I remember most clearly about Grandpa Mariagrazia is more his separateness and his strength than his relation to us—as far as that goes, he never had that much to do with us—or with any of the grandchildren until toward the end, and then only on occasion, and only out of what seemed a sort of *noblesse oblige*."

Aunt Fil smiled at the expression, then took a sip from her glass. Gianni could see the light returning to her eyes as she spoke. "He wasn't always like that, you know. Not really. I mean, things are never so simple as they seem, especially with those you only see from a distance. Which is, of course, why he went to the trouble of creating that distance in the first place and then kept it up. When we were younger, he hadn't been that way, or not so markedly so. Even I can remember, in the darkness of the winter evenings, when he would have time—in that season—to sit and rest and rock us in the warmth of those big arms, and the smile, through the light of the fire that warmed the room against the howl of the wind outside, that came down the chimney and carried the odor of the burning logs into that of the garlic and tomatoes and onions and bread. He would hold us and rock us in that chair of his when we'd been upset, and rock and rock, all the while keeping those big, warm arms tight around us, like being inside the oven, so tight and warm it would take your breath away.

"But there were other times, too, in that same room and the same darkness, when they'd been playing that awful game of theirs—him and Paoli DeMartino and the Ricci brothers and their friends—what they called the 'passatèll.'" She shuddered as she said the word. "I can still see them raising their glasses at the bidding of the king and his helper, who would lurch out of the shadows into the light to shout the sorts of things that shouldn't ever be said aloud, much less yelled out. Although I suppose that, after all, that part, the public part, was finally less important than it may have seemed to an innocent ten-year-old girl watching in secret from the cold landing above them, fascinated and horrified into silence. Then, as I watched, the mere idea that they would yell those things at each other—haranguing, cajoling, boasting, as though they not only knew all the details of the private affairs of their companions but were in fact the only ones to know, making a virtue of their vicious knowledge—seemed unbelievable to me. I don't know another word for it. And it *would* turn them into beasts, great grey and white locks of hair tumbling down their faces flushed deep with the heat of the wine as whoever the leader was would take his stance, setting back on his heels in the worn pants and flowing shirtsleeves, to raise the purple glass into the light, shouting. And *what* they would shout to the others was every bit as awful as the animals they turned into.

"One winter's night was worse than anything that I had seen before. The game had often been terrible, once they'd got going, but after this they never played it again, at least not in our house. First, as usual, they began with the cards to determine the leaders. One of the Ricci brothers started it—now that I remember, I realize how drunk he must have been already—but at the time looking down from my secret place into the glow of the light below, it seemed to me that he must have been possessed by a demon to be acting like he was, frantic yet serious, and oh so urgent. And it wasn't just him, either. They were all that way, excited and loud, going at each other with the avidity of bulls challenging one another for the prize. From the first of the Ricci brothers the order went to the second, who, in the course of his shouting, pretended to pour the wine for Paoli DeMartino but then wouldn't let him raise it to drink, and he said something about Paoli—or about his family, I couldn't tell which—that made Paoli's face go so dark you could see the color creeping beneath his hair. Then Father spoke, but unlike his usual manner he didn't change the subject—I don't know why, whether it was the drink or the heat of the moment or some other reason, something else between them. He continued to address Paoli, who at first shook his beard and refused to respond. But that only made the others yell more, so Paoli drew himself up to his full height—since he was a tall man—and looked first at the Riccis then straight at Father, because, you see, he felt he'd been betrayed by the one closest to him, by one of his own.

"'Some of us know when to let go and when to hold back,' he began, and I'll never forgot the way the look on his face deepened and set. 'Some of us know the old rules and know not to break them.' His voice had been low up to then, but he raised it now as he held out his empty glass and pretended to drink from it. 'I drink to each of you, and particularly to you, Michael, Andrea's son, whose father knew who his friends and his family were and knew not to confuse the two—and who also knew where his wife was in the afternoons when he was busy with his work.'

"This last he spat word by word at Father, although he barely got it all out before the others erupted in shouting and pushing and insults and threats. Oh, I don't even remember all the rest, it was all so violent and so horribly mixed up. But that was the last time I heard that awful game, and the last time that Paoli DeMartino, or any of Mother's brothers, ever set foot in our house. Because—and you should know, even if you don't—that by then Mother's doings were pretty much old news. So there was no reason for Paoli to throw it up in Father's face like that, in front of everyone, even if Father had gotten carried away just the moment before. It wasn't right, that's all there is to it, and then he wasn't used to the wine anyway. But you see, that's how we found out—I found out—that things weren't always right between them, though I could scarcely have guessed then either the nature or the extent of their troubles—which, we found out later, went all the way to the Church. Good heavens," she smiled secretly at the thought of being misunderstood in this regard, "as judges and referees, you see, not as active participants. But I guess, all told, it didn't stop *then*, either, since the dealings with the 'authorities'—ecclesiastical and otherwise—went right up through that time that Father caught the Sicilian driver stealing his milk and who knows what else, despite their age. Because that never stops," and here she smiled again at Gianni's reaction, "no matter what the age: believe me, I know. So you see, he had every reason to maintain a certain distance from the rest of the world, including all of us, and all of you."

Gianni sat speechless, letting his gaze follow the shadows of the branches outside as they rose and fell in reflection against the porch's back wall. When at last he achieved the concentration necessary to say what he wanted to, and found the energy, his voice was steady, serious, so that it was not immediately apparent that he was trying his utmost not to appear overwhelmed—except that she knew him too well to be fooled, any more than, despite his cleverness, the little boy had really been able to fool his attentive interlocutor all those years before. "They all have to fall eventually, I guess, one by one. It must be part and parcel of the process." He thought for a second of O.B. but did not say anything. Instead, he let his mind wander to the other, Grandpa Britzen, the one he still thought of as the old man of stone, and he mentioned the name again. "At least he was always definite and clear, if not in his own mind and body at least in his relation to us, to me and O.B., as precise and dependable as the stars in the winter sky."

"Was he?" she demurred.

*   *   *

It was almost a month later, in that uncertain period between Christmas and the New Year, when Gianni found out the point of his aunt's question, if not its answer. Normally an invitation from his mother and father to come to dinner in that season would not have been the occasion for any anxiety whatever, but now as he pulled in the drive and walked to the house through the twilight, with the extent and the prospects of O.B.'s recovery still in doubt, he was unable to summon any enthusiasm for the obligatory semiannual visit (the other being his birthday in mid-April). Except, that is, for the fact of that question that Aunt Fil had let slip just as he was reacting to the news about Grandpa Mariagrazia, and that had kept buzzing in his ear all the way back to Chicago.

"Oh, yes, I knew about it, of course," his mother said. "We all knew, sooner or later. There's no way in the world that you can keep anything like that a secret for very long in a small town like New Providence, and naturally the relatives—even the newly admitted ones—would hear about it, if not from members of the family, from neighbors in town, or even at the bank or the market. You can't hide things when there are so few people around that you keep bumping into the same ones day in and day out. So we all knew, were all bound to, somehow or other. Still, that's not to say that *what* we knew was simple or even uniform."

She left him for a moment with a delicate wave of her hand, no longer strong as he remembered, and went to check the roast in the oven, then came back smiling, since everything was done as he liked, with the light gravy and carrots and celery and mushrooms, no peas. She leaned to smooth his hair back before taking up her chair again across from him, while they waited for his father's return to start their supper. Her eyes, from where he sat, seemed to shine deep grey, almost blue, though in that light it was hard to tell what color they really were, since they took on the hues of their surroundings like chameleons. But the nature of her enthusiasm as she recalled the old man could not be mistaken.

"He was quite something, your Grandpa Mariagrazia. You know, despite all the trouble (and the sort of stand-off between the families, your Grandpa's and your Grandma's, before the monsignor finally settled things to everyone's agreement, if not exactly to their satisfaction), following that run-in with the Sicilian milkdriver, your grandfather was regarded as somewhat of a hero across four counties. I'm surprised Fil didn't tell you, though maybe she never really knew, she was so much younger than the others. Oh, they were dairy counties, it's true, hardly Chicago or New York City, filled with people whose primary livelihood came from producing milk and selling their product to the local dairies—but a hero nonetheless. They'd even heard about it in Crooked Falls, and weren't at all hesitant to tell their neighbors, either. We can thank God that even then they didn't know the half of it, that that was just one more episode in a long series of decidedly less than heroic adventures. But that's often the case. One shot is enough, Jake Arndt used to say, if it's aimed right.

"And then you have to keep in mind that there are two sides to every quarrel. Grandma Mariagrazia didn't have it so easy, either, all things considered. She had to do the work of five people with the skill of ten—cook, barber, seamstress, farmer and even what you might call agricultural advisor, among others, all the while having to put up with your greatgrandfather, too. Thirty years of being told that you just can't get anything quite right—and to have to listen to it in silence, in your own house—well, she had her own side of things, too, even if at first it was just a longing to get away for awhile that sort of got out of hand. Not that she had the most to complain about, not by a long shot. The one that was by far the worst off, if they'd asked me—though of course none of them did, or ever would have thought of it, inquiring after the opinion of a blonde blue-eyed Swede and a Protestant to boot—the one who really *did* have a right to complain was your Aunt Min."

Gianni remembered the quiet, retiring woman in the black dress, black as though suited to mourning for the husband and the life that would never come, was never to be, and so were forever lost, with the pallid features and downcast eyes, that, when they finally turned up to smile,startled you with their intensity.

"Do you remember how sweet she was to you boys when you were little? She was like that with everyone, too, not just the children. Though she was especially good with children, so that everyone felt what a shame it was that she seemed to be one of those people who never managed to have a boyfriend, too plain, I guess—though that wasn't the case at all once you got to know her—so that the boys never tried, but flew right past toward the flashier ones, with the quick chatter and open arms. Until Josh, that is. I remember still how happy everyone was for her, and me, too. None of us knew the hell that lay ahead for her. And it was some time before anyone found out, either. Oh, I guess we all had ideas, you know how it is. All those years and no children—especially then, and on the farm—who else was going to help them with the work? I even remember that your father had been worried about

Richie always staying out there so much, practically like it was his own house, and then that summer when it boiled over and Richie came back like a battered pup all bruised and cut. Lucky that Josh wasn't a better shot, or a quicker one. But you see, there you have it, right there, that's another time when your Grandpa was exactly right, in the way he dealt with Josh after the run-in with Richie. And Josh deserved it all, too, *everything* he got from the group that went to call on him, for ruining Min's life that way. It was fortunate for him that no one had heard the other things yet, the stories from the young boys around town that Josh had made 'friends' with, or those men would have been a good bit rougher on him than they were. Anyway, that's when your father and Dominic split, which was too bad, when you think of it and of all that they had been through together since the times when they were schoolboys and Dominic would set up the fights for your father—goading his schoolmates into trying to best him—and then would bet on him and share the profits on ice cream or at the local movie house. And I suppose Dominic had a right to be touchy, he was so embarrassed by everything, even if he wouldn't admit it. But your father simply couldn't countenance Richie's behavior, even though he was Dominic's boy. And then, later, when O.B. got so in thrall to his older cousin, we naturally had to stop that, too—for which, I'm sure, not just Dominic but also O.B. has always felt betrayed—it's always those closest to you, that's by definition—since he and Richie *were* good friends. But we couldn't have O.B. gallivanting around New Providence all summer with Richie and the local girls, it just wasn't correct, or even sensible, although by then, thank God, at least Min wasn't involved anymore, since I guess she'd decided it wasn't going to work out so well trying to recoup her entire emotional life through the good offices of a fifteen-year-old boy. Or maybe it was jealousy after all, when she heard about his other exploits. Because like I said before, people talk. Anyway in the end the result for her, after a period of utter ecstasy, which no one in their right mind would have begrudged her, and quite a few bitter memories, was the same complete isolation, just as before. Not abuse, mind you, but total disuse, which is a good deal worse."

    He knew that he had to bring her up, to make her stop, or he would lose the opportunity to ask what he had come to ask, while she went on and on about the other side, Aunt Min and Richie and Uncle Dominic and all the rest, most of which he had already heard time and again, though in different ways from different people, and he still liked her version best: but he had come to inquire about something else, not the safe, distant, easy things but something closer, the old man, and as he sat listening to her voice going on and on, he thought *yes, I know all that, yes, yes, but that's not what I want to know, so tell me what I want, tell me about the old man, yes, yes, I know...the old man*, and when she finally paused to reflect, searching her memory for a name or a date, he leaned forward and seized his chance.

"Aunt Fil said that...when I told her that I'd always felt Grandpa Britzen was...was as solid as the rock of Gibraltar...in his relation to us, anyway...she said that...she asked me...*as he thought, no, not like this, this is the chance but you're losing it, say what you want to, ask what you want to know...but what do you want?*: "Who was he?"

Of the two of them, it would have been hard to tell who was more surprised. Gianni sat listening in his mind to the words that he had said, hearing his voice like an echo while her deep blue eyes studied him, quizzical at first and then thoroughly astonished as she realized the full meaning of the question. When she understood—from his tone, its edge of urgency even more than from its persistence—that this time there was probably going to be no escape, she sighed and, apparently, resigned herself to telling him everything that he wanted to know, or at least everything about which he already knew enough to form definite questions. On and off, the conversation, or monologue, really, since once she started up again there was little hope of—or purpose in—stopping her, ran through drinks and the arrival of Gianni's father, who listened, too, as though hearing the story for the first time, enraptured and, Gianni thought, oddly quiet, and then, in its final stage, through coffee and brandy, back on the porch again, as the chill air of the late December night vied for dominion with the spirits and his mother's voice, constant, certain, and earnest in a way that he could not recall hearing it before.

By then he was no longer surprised—though his father seemed disconcerted enough at hearing her discuss it openly that he spilled the lion's share of a double Manhattan, before retiring for the night and leaving the two of them back on the porch again— that the old man was in fact not the old man, or at least not in the way that they had always felt him to be. Because he and O.B. had never been told the one detail that just about everyone else in the family had always known, that their mother had gone with her mother when she had consented to marry William Britzen, who, according to all accounts including this one, could not have cared less whether or not his wife had had another husband, nor what that husband's end had been, though to hear the other relatives tell it—Grandma Britzen's, that is—the other's end had been certainly less than felicitous, and perhaps a good deal less at that.

But none of that was what, for the moment, really bothered him. As she talked, with the light from her glass reflected in the dancing blue eyes, he could not help but wonder, and after a time finally ask, not so much who the old man wasn't, which he knew, or even who he was, of which he at least had an idea, but who "he"—the blank, mysterious absence—had been.

"But of course that's the one question I can't answer. You might have guessed that much, anyway." She watched his gaze closely, waiting for his reaction. "But don't think that I haven't tried. For a time, a very long time, while we were still children, old enough to know the right questions by instinct, but not how to ask them intelligently, we simply accepted that it was one of the things we weren't supposed to mention. And even if we had, I doubt very much that your Grandma would have told us. That's just the way she was. Later, of course, when we began to wonder in earnest, the power of fantasy took over and we managed to invent marvelous scenarios in which he would suddenly return from his hideously prolonged journeys to save us from whatever dragons seemed the most frightening at the moment. After that, when our interests took on a more studious bent, we started to think of him as a real historical personage—which, of course, he had been, though not in the sense we gave him—and to speculate on his origins and his ways, who his people had been and what his life had been like. For the longest time, your Aunt Jane saw him as a Polish sea captain with an eye for the ladies whenever he found himself in port; whereas I tended to fancy him a trader from the east, who had worked his way across country selling stylish clothing and other finery, though for the life of me I couldn't have said just what. Then after that, quite naturally, we began to look around and consider the possibilities closer to home, not understanding all of the implications, of course—the Connollys and the Whittakers and the like—which eventually put a stop to the whole process, because it had become so obviously absurd, even to us."

"But not Drew?" he asked, caught up in what he regarded momentarily as a sort of game, one in which it had been his turn to ask the question. He felt himself shiver as he finished and waited, aware now that, by asking what he had asked, he had also accepted the fact, once and for all, that the old man was not who he always had been. The model vanished with the bond, smoke after fire, spent now with only the memory left, quiet, deceitful. So at long last, he was certain, assured that it really was not his fault, and that even if it had been, he had not been flesh and blood, blood of his blood, but only a figure, like someone in the history books or the newspapers, but not his—not his and O.B.'s. And all at once, the old man seemed to be gone.

His mother's voice brought him back again, lilting now, almost humorous at the suggestion.

"Oh heavens no, not Drew," she smiled. "Well, I have to admit that we did have our curiosity about him, too, your aunt and I. After all, once that sort of thing gets started up, there's no stopping it, especially with adolescents. And we did make some marvelous discoveries once we were going, though not in that vein, you understand. Because Drew, for all his weaknesses and deficiencies—all of which, of course, only made him that much dearer—had had a very interesting time of it before he'd showed up in town and your grandpa had taken him in and gave him a chance to earn his way. We learned all sorts of things from listening to him, even if we had to ask Grandma to help us sort them out afterwards, since Drew tended to get things a bit muddled, especially the more exciting parts and those in which he'd been involved directly. Oh Drew was something all right. Once he'd start telling things it was like rolling a snowball down a hill—you couldn't ever tell where it would end up at the last, or what size it was likely to be. I think that he was so pleased that someone wanted to know about him that he would have kept talking day and night if we hadn't tired of listening, or if Father hadn't found us and cut him off with a reminder of the chores to be done. The winter time was best, the three of us sitting beside the fire in the sitting room, since there was less to attend to then. We would listen together, your aunt and I, two young girls avid for adventure and romance; we would listen and dream.

"He told us of his earliest memories, before he'd come to America even, as a child in Romania, hiding under the big bed in his parents' room in the little house on the Danube when the soldiers would come through looking for deserters, the children seeing the captain's jackboots glisten in the light from the fire on the shiny floor and holding their breath so as not to be noticed. And then, when the spring came and there was a halt in the fighting, he told us of the wonderful, spacious dances along the river, with the men dressed in rigid finery and the women in their long, flowing gowns, all reflected in the lights on the river, shimmering and swaying to and fro with the music of the band. And then of the hard times, after they'd immigrated to the coast of New Jersey, and of the life among all the other immigrants."

She took a sip from her cup before going on, her thoughts seemingly entwined in memories, her own and Drew's as he'd reported them at their urging and as they had subsequently pieced them together. "After a few years their father had had to go back. He'd been caught in one of the immigration checks in the crackdown during the 'red scare,' and they had deported him as quickly as you could say 'Jack Robinson.' So quickly, in fact, that they hadn't bothered to follow up on his assertion that he was alone, single, and without family, so Drew and his mother and brothers stayed on in New Jersey, with an aunt and uncle who'd entered legally, and waited for him to return. Drew remembered his mother going to the dock whenever the big boats would come in, waiting for her man's arrival. Which never came, of course. He had been arrested by the army as a deserter the moment he'd set foot back in Romania, and the next morning, along with twenty of his fellow villagers, he had been summarily shot. In New Jersey they couldn't do anything but wait at first, then after the news came, brought by townsmen fleeing on a boat just like the one they'd taken themselves, their mother continued to wait, going every day to check the docks and the shipyard, asking for news. She simply couldn't accept what had happened, or what she had been told had happened, and she seemed to believe that if she persisted and kept on trying, eventually the story would turn out differently. That's when Drew began to assume more responsibility, as though, for all his weaknesses, he really were the man of the family."

He sensed her drifting again and made an effort to bring her back. "So it wasn't Drew," he said crisply.

"No," she went on, reflective, unhurried. "Not him, I'm quite sure now. Sometimes—sometimes I had an inkling, something strange, a shiver, once or twice a strong one, but no, not Drew. It wasn't your Grandpa—that is, your Grandpa wasn't your Grandpa. I know how you boys worshipped him, as though he were the model for both of you, paired together like the Dioscuri in the constellation, the ones we read to you about when you were children. I hated to think of telling you then, when you were little. I was sure it would either confuse you or break your hearts, or both. So I didn't say anything. Please don't hold it against me now—I thought it was best that way, and I suppose I would do the same all over again, if I had to. O.B. was so serious about his hunting and fishing, and you were so dreamy, but intense in your own way, too. I couldn't see that anything would have been gained had I told you then what I'm telling you now. And I don't think *he* would have taken it well, either, especially after all he did to help us out when you children were first born." Her face clouded momentarily before she continued. "I remember how embarrassed we all were, all of us in our different ways, when your father and I had to borrow more from him the second time, after you arrived and we were so broke that we had even considered trying to attract pigeons to capture and eat like some of our neighbors did," she smiled at the memory, "who caught them and called them 'squabs.' Your Grandpa was so generous—everybody knew it in that little town, too, and they all admired him for it. I don't know what we would have done without his help. I remember riding back on the train from Redwing with you all wrapped up in a blanket in my arms and a thousand dollars in cash—not a check, because we couldn't even wait that long, but actual cash—sewn inside the lining of my prim cloth coat. But, no," she finished, "I know how much he meant to you, but it wasn't him, and it wasn't Drew either, of that much, I am sure. At least this way," she smiled, "you needn't feel constrained any longer by the model."

Gianni watched her in the silence, the light reflected from the room inside showing on her face and making it seem more austere than he knew it to be, resigned yet, in her own way, spirited, not defeated in spite of the dirty tricks that life had played on her. It wasn't easy to accept what he had learned, but then he had no choice. The old man was gone—if you didn't count the fact that more than twenty years after his death Gianni still sensed his presence, within him, every time he'd pass a lumberyard or even a single freshly downed tree and catch the full scent of the timber on the breeze—Gianni knew that now and that there was no means by which to bring him back to ask him, or to have him change the story so that it would turn out right and sensible as it should.

And he knew that she didn't know. He thought about what she had said, thinking of what he had lost, but the emptiness was too great, abysmal. Just thinking of it made him shiver. He would have liked to have taken the discoveries more philosophically, to be able to sit back and accept what he simply did not know and, for a minute, to let the notion, the feeling, beguile him. So what if she didn't know. Anyway, he thought, it wasn't just that fact that he wanted to know, or at least not just that *one* fact, but everything, the whole texture and design right down to the finest, frailest thread of all. And then the next moment, he knew that he never would know that, knew none of them would or ever could know that, and that if they did they might just as well freeze up and topple over and never move again. Because that, it stood to reason, would be the end for sure.

No, he—better, they—were bound to keep looking, sometimes searching not so much for anything in particular as for more things to look for. He knew, or felt then, as he watched her sitting there before him, confused and only a little bitter, but rigid, unbroken, he felt the thrill and pulse not of the fact but of all the facts known and unknown and just coming to be known, of the maze and the challenge of the search itself. But still, as he sat there, he couldn't keep himself from wondering, with a force so sudden and strong that he almost spoke aloud: *who?* and *why?* Then all at once he imagined himself watching a hawk sweep through a seine of trees and cut away into the dusk, and he held the image until he heard his mother's voice come to him, bringing him back.

"You let me—us—know how he is now, Gianni, when you go and see him. We'll keep checking too, of course, but you let me know right away. Promise?"

* * *

Gianni did go to see O.B. again shortly after that, but for the time being there was nothing to tell: his condition unchanged, stable, the wound healing slowly but healing nonetheless, the same sterile impersonality of the hospital, antiseptically bleak, overly warm, oppressive. By now the nurses recognized him, at least. He knew that this was not really a point in his favor, since their awareness of him derived from his behavior on the second or the third of his visits, when he'd made a point of complaining about not having been notified when they had moved O.B. to a new room. He still felt his reaction had been justified, if perhaps a bit excessive. He'd gone to the room in intensive care—where they had put O.B. when he'd first arrived, already imprisoned in swathes of bandages with tubes and wires going everywhere—but at Gianni's entrance he had found the room totally empty. He panicked at the sight, not so much thinking or fearing the worst as *feeling* it, and the feeling that O.B. was gone forever overwhelmed him. Rather than returning to the nurses' station, he began rushing into rooms along the corridor, checking the occupants of each one and causing quite a scare in many of them, until finally the head nurse on the floor, Mrs. Brandt, got hold of him and explained what had happened (which was simply that O.B.'s condition had stabilized and that, since he no longer needed twenty-four hour attention, he had been moved to another room two floors up). Before ascertaining that much, however, Gianni had raised enough of a racket—more with accusations than with anything so refined as questions—to make a name for himself among the staff, and the young nurse who accompanied him now eyed him from as much distance as she could get as they walked down the ghostly neon-lit hall toward the room where O.B. lay waiting.

His chest and shoulder were wrapped so tight that it almost seemed as if he were an exhibit of some sort rather than merely a patient, and there were bandages around his head now, too, where he'd fallen back against the pine; but all in all he seemed unchanged from the time before. Gianni said hello and as O.B. responded his eyes flashed in the old way, confident, serene, with the little white scar over his brow dancing to life. They conversed for a while—Gianni doing most of the talking and O.B. responding primarily with his eyes or an occasional smile, since his breath was still too short for him to speak more than a phrase or two at a time—and the visit seemed pretty much ho-hum, at least as far as Gianni was concerned. O.B. wanted to know about his wife and children, how they were getting along and such, and he asked about the bar and if the take were steady in his absence, which it was. Up until a few minutes before Gianni had to go, about 1:00 p.m., everything seemed perfectly regular, predictable. Then O.B. got a glance at Gianni's watch and all at once he seemed anxious, nervous about something, his eyes wandering and his answers becoming even briefer than before; but he didn't say what it was and Gianni did not feel that he could press him. Gianni knew him well enough, he felt—even under those conditions—to tell that O.B. was trying to get rid of him, but he could not for the life of him imagine why.

At one on the dot Zeke Wood, O.B.'s 'friend' from City Hall, walked through the door with his twenty-dollar cigar, unlit, of course, and his fifty-dollar handshake (for Gianni: O.B. had to settle for an elaborate wave). For a moment O.B. brightened and seemed happy to see him. But Wood had little to say other than the usual pleasantries and the gestures of sympathy and commiseration that are commonplace at such times. Wood was competent at that sort of behavior, but no better. He was what Gianni thought of as a 'private' politician, a mayor's aide who worked behind the scenes on behalf of the elected officials who by contrast have to answer to the public and who therefore have to be both patient and, at least in appearance, fair-minded. Wood was neither. But Gianni was surprised and not just a little offended when after only a few minutes Wood said goodby to O.B. and prepared to leave. When Wood heard that Gianni had to go, too, Wood asked if he could drop him someplace, which seemed to upset O.B. all the more.

* * *

So maybe it's not so bad that he's seen Wood after all. Sure, they'll talk now, that's unavoidable. But so what? Wood hasn't got a big mouth—that's precisely his business, or part of it anyway—just the opposite of Johnny Bubbles, thank God. At least Gianni hasn't heard about that other thing yet, beyond the mess downtown, I could tell that. And he won't, either. I'll make sure of that with Sherrie when she comes to visit, like I know she will. I'm sure she will.

No, it's the mess downtown with those other fellows that I've got to concentrate on now. All right, so I'm not Goody Two-Shoes. Still, who could have foreseen anything like it? God, in the end even Black Sammy White called in his markers on me. Apparently being tapped out is a bigger deal than I'd figured. So the South Side folks won't help this time around. Damn them. I guess they weren't quite so far out of the way as I'd thought. Of course, bad news travels like wildfire in these circles, everybody knows that. But that's what I've got to do now: concentrate. Just forget about Gianni and even Wood and that other stuff and concentrate. It would also help to get out of here—and to get a chance to see the sun again and walk around in the fresh air if nothing else—but for the moment I'm not too worried about that. Just concentrate, damnit, that's all for now at least, concentrate.

* * *

Gianni and Zeke Wood left the hospital together, but only after Gianni had taken care to spend some extra time at O.B.'s side, assuring him about things that he, Gianni, really did not know and trying to keep his spirits up. Gianni reached Wood at the entrance, and as they walked out of the building and into the bright sunlight Gianni was still less than pleased with the brevity of Wood's visit—after all, he was supposed to be not only one of O.B.'s business associates but also a close friend who had known O.B. since they were kids together in school—and Gianni did not hesitate to tell him so, sharkskin suit or not.

"Oh, it wasn't really a social call, not this time, anyway," Wood said matter of factly as he stopped to put his sunglasses on and light his cigar. "All business. We'd heard rumors downtown—you know how it is—so I just stopped by to make sure he was still whistling above ground, as they say. One look was enough for that."

Wood's response did little to improve Gianni's spirits, or to relieve his doubts. Why had O.B. become so nervous all of a sudden? Had he not wanted them to see the other? And if so, what reason could he have possibly had? True, Wood was an important figure for both of them—he had been instrumental in getting the liquor license for Riley's when the two of them had taken over, and in getting it quick, without the usual year and a half wait, and in smoothing out various problems with city inspectors thereafter, not to mention in countless other matters many of which were known only to O.B. But what could Gianni possibly have to say to him that would bother O.B.? When Wood not only made good on his offer of a ride but also invited Gianni to lunch—at a French place on the north side, rather than at the usual politician's haunts in the Loop—Gianni was surprised but pleased, too, in a way, and he accepted in the hope that he would find out the answers to at least some of his questions, which he did, and which turned out to be exactly contrary to what he had expected.

They parked on a side street and walked to the restaurant through the noon-hour bustle of shopkeepers and housewives, considerably more pleasant than the curt crowd of businessmen and secretaries downtown. The maitre d' greeted Wood and showed them to a table near the back, amidst the warm glow of mahogany and chandeliers. As the waitress took their order, Gianni reflected to himself, though also to a certain extent out loud, that he had never really known very much about (or, as he kept to himself, thought very much of) Zeke Wood, primarily because of Wood's association with, first, 'Five' Bronson and, second, Ben Kaseras. Wood had a gold tooth that gave his smile a sinister appearance, but Gianni did not feel that this was anything other than surface, and he had no fear of him.

"Just the reverse, if you want to know," Wood smiled, and this provided one of Gianni's initial surprises. "'Five' Bronson is an asshole—but Ben Kaseras, despite his neanderthal demeanor and less than even disposition, is something else again."

"How do you mean?"

"Bronson is a salesman, a middleman, nothing more and nothing less. On his own, a zero. But Kaseras has money he hasn't even counted yet—probably couldn't, even if he wanted to, which he doesn't—and what's more, he's smart enough to know what to do with it. I'm surprised you didn't know." At this point Gianni looked up and found Wood studying him. "O.B. knew without a doubt—you can be sure of that."

"And just how do *you* know?" Gianni attempted to regain what he considered a lost advantage in a match that he knew to be in progress but about which he felt he knew very little else. By then the waitress had brought a pair of steaks and a bottle of French wine—Wood knew how to use an expense account, Gianni observed—and as they began to eat Wood replied, mild, confident, if just a bit tense.

"Knowing is my business," Wood smiled his best private politician's smile. "The day I don't know who's bankrolling what in this town is the day that I'm out of a job. The mayor's office doesn't run on sugar and spice, you know, like the good ship lollipop. We run on cash, which comes from capital, which resides with—and occasionally comes from—donors. The press calls them investors, which is fine by us, as long as the money keeps coming in. This is all beyond taxes and city bonds and all that official stuff, you understand. Every new plant and high rise—especially the ones for which the zoning has to be approved, or, better yet, fudged—means money for the government, which is us, and which eventually helps the people, naturally, just like the system is supposed to. If some of the rest of us benefit a bit extra in the meantime, well, who does it hurt?"

"But Kaseras isn't in that league. He couldn't fund a campaign or finance an apartment building if his life depended on it."

"It doesn't," Wood said quickly, in a remark that Gianni did not understand immediately, "and that's one of Kaseras' great skills. But anyway, you may be right, Kaseras isn't King Midas; but I wouldn't underestimate him, either, if I were you. Remember that building on South Jackson that caused such a stir because it was going to eclipse the old Union League Club until an agreement was worked out? Well, Kaseras had a piece of that. And the construction of the new aquarium? He had a piece of that action, too. And as for not being in the limelight, in fact that's one of his advantages, that he's not so big that he draws publicity like the real heavyweights around town. It makes him a lot easier for us to deal with, too, not that I do it directly, you understand: that's O.B.'s job. Because we never wanted him involved, see, just his money. Sort of like the old coot with the money in a shoebox under the bed, if you know what I mean, just waiting for somebody to come along and show him what to do with it."

Wood went on about City Hall and high finance, but the drift of the discussion did not change. So far Gianni was mildly surprised by what he had heard and at the same time somewhat disturbed, since he had begun to feel that Wood was sparring with him to no purpose. But what came next caught him completely off guard. Simply put, Wood accused him of being a liar and a cheat. Not in such plain terms, of course. Wood was too well schooled in the ways and means of intimidation and vituperation to be so blunt, but the general meaning was there and Gianni had little trouble discerning it, no matter how fancy the phrasing. The meal, which was excellent, had been over for a while and the waitress was serving coffee when Wood suggested they have a brandy to finish it off properly.

"You have the time for it, I assume," Wood asked.

"Nothing but," Gianni replied, looking around the room at the pictures on the wall, all of which portrayed motion but which, at the same time, created an aura of comfort that conveyed the message: stay, take your time, do not hurry. "Seeing O.B. was my sole responsibility of the day. Now all I have left to do is to get back to Riley's—and I'd rather deal with liquor from the drinking man's side of the table any time."

The brandy came and Wood swirled it reflectively in his glass. When he looked at Gianni his gaze had changed, more relaxed now but more assertive, too, with a glint in his eye that Gianni had not noticed before. "Look," Wood began, "I like you, and you know how much I think about O.B., what we've been through, and what we've been for each other in the past. So why don't you and I quit playing ring-around-the-rosy—or is it cat-and-mouse—and start being honest with each other. Just for a while," he smiled, so that the gold tooth shone suddenly. "It won't hurt all that much."

Gianni was taken aback, and he took a healthy sip from his glass before responding. The waitress reappeared to make certain Wood was pleased with everything, which gave Gianni more time to think. What could Wood possibly be talking about, he wondered. What had his visit to O.B. and his odd description of his intent meant in the first place? And why the invitation to lunch at a posh out-of-the-way restaurant if this was how he felt? In the end, Gianni concluded that directness was the best and, at least in the midst of utter confusion, perhaps the only policy.

"I don't have any idea what you mean," he said. "Not a clue. I'd like to know, believe me, but I don't. And that's all there is to it."

Despite its veracity, Wood appeared to take Gianni's statement not as an admission of ignorance but as a further challenge, and his response, that of the expert player who in this case was playing well below his level without realizing it, was as quick as it was severe.

"Hey, champ," Wood said, placing his brandy carefully to one side on the white cloth. "I'm not sure who you're trying to fool or why, but let's just cut the crap. I know that you know about your brother and Kaseras, and I know that you know about your brother and me. I know that you know because I could tell from O.B.'s reaction today when he saw me walk in and all he could do was watch you and worry that you'd let me know just how much you knew. I could see it as plain as the nose on your face, or his, for that matter. What do you take me for anyway? A jumble-brained idiot? And now I'm going to tell you what I'm going to do to O.B. and to you, too, if you don't hurry up and—"

Wood must have finally understood the look on Gianni's face, something between protest and amazement, because he stopped all at once, sighed deeply, and sat back. He reached for his glass and took a sip of the brandy before going on, his voice calm now, its tone changed.

"So he had you fooled, too, huh kid? I'm sure you don't mind if I ask: How does it feel?"

Gianni shook his head, as confused as before. "I still don't know what you're talking about."

"You mean that you *still* haven't found out, that you still think that you took that trip as part of a bet on a worn-out rifle and nothing else, without knowing that Kaseras represented your brother's bankroll and that I, well I, or we.... Wait a minute. You mean you really don't know anything?"

"Isn't that what I've just been trying to tell you?" Gianni asked, beginning to smile from embarrassment.

If Gianni had not been so stubbornly naive in the matter, he understood later, he probably never would have learned very much more from Wood. But Wood had enough of the politician's arrogance—and in this the 'private' ones are no better, or maybe actually worse, than the others—so that his pride was wounded by Gianni's ignorance. Wasn't it obvious that Wood was an important factor in his friends' business affairs, as in everything else, and that his relation with O.B. was not, could not have been, merely that of old school-boy chums? Well, it was obvious to Wood, and he felt that it should have been obvious to Gianni, too, even if he did have to explain it, which, between puffs on his cigar and sips of his drink, he proceeded to do.

In point of fact it was not news to Gianni that Wood's help had gone well past the 'official' business like that first license, which, it turned out, had been merely a question of fooling a pair of over-worked liquor commissioners and then bribing a third. But Gianni was astounded at just how far, according to Wood, it went, as though every financial deal that O.B. made from his office downtown benefitted from Wood's inside advice and only went forward with Wood's seal of approval. After all, Wood was in a position to know everything going on throughout the city, political, financial, or otherwise, and why shouldn't he help out an old friend who was bent on making it big? The figure of O.B. that Wood described struck Gianni as a caricature—a mixture of exaggerated greed, boundless ambition, and, worst of all, total disdain for anyone with whom he found himself to be in competition. But, like any caricature, it incorporated enough basic elements of O.B.'s character to work, at least in part. And what did Wood get out of all his good-natured assistance? On this point Wood was silent, but it was not hard for Gianni to imagine it to be a fair percentage of the resultant financial turnover. And how did Kaseras fit in? Easy. Kaseras had money, and not O.B.'s kind of money, paper written on, and chasing after, other paper, but real money: capital, solid and unquestionable, built up over three decades of smart, sound acquisitions. And capital was precisely what O.B. needed in order to keep his deals going, and especially on the riskier ventures that he, Wood, knew to be sure things but that O.B. couldn't get a bank to finance because he couldn't explain how he knew they would work. Nobody could, see? Because half the time nobody was supposed to know. So that's how Kaseras's money came in, to permit O.B. to use the information that was supplied to him by none other than the finest listening post in City Hall.

"All O.B. had to do was to follow my advice and to keep Kaseras active, and it didn't much matter how, as long as a constant interest—O.B. would say spark, but I prefer my term for it—was there. Oh, believe me, I know it wasn't always all that easy. After the shellacking Kaseras took in that fist fight when O.B. let himself go, we had one helluva tough time for a while. Delicate work, if you know what I mean. Massaging a fellow's feelings rather than his pocketbook just isn't up my alley at all. And it took one very nicely trumped up deal, with as fast and sweet a return as you'll ever see, to get Kaseras to glimpse the light again and return to our way of thinking. Ruffled feathers last for a time, sure, but profits are there forever—if you work it right. So that stuff about the rifle was just a minor part of the real action: hell, even the side bets that O.B. spun off of it weren't all that important, really, just sauce to keep the turkey floating, if you'll excuse the expression. We were in a very tight situation, in the middle of a deal that was slow but far from going sour, unless Kaseras backed out. Because, like I say, Kaseras is not dumb—he just needs a little something to keep his interest up, that's all. And O.B. sure knew how to do it, I'll give him that, a master if there ever was one. But then I'm sure you know all about that, lots better than me. The whole idea about the hunt and the bets was a beautiful touch, a little out of the ordinary, I have to admit, but just the right ingredient. No one but O.B. could have come up with an idea like that."

Wood noticed the look in Gianni's eyes again, because he rushed to add, "Oh, I don't mean to offend, believe me. And what's more, I wouldn't worry if I were you. So we were both suckers, so what? It happens to the best of them, sooner or later. At least this time it's no big deal. I guess things are easier for me—that's what I was checking on, like I told you—because I can work out any payment schedule in the world, with one possible exception—what I call the court of last resort—as long as the fish is still on the line. You'll have to forgive me again for the expression, but a corpse doesn't handle its debts too well, at least not in my line of work. Anyway, like I say, I wouldn't worry. I'm sure that stuff about the pop-gun, or whatever it was—not to mention O.B.'s condition—will all work out for the best in the end. Even Kaseras will feel the same way and come up smiling, you can take my word for it."

"I don't—I can't," Gianni said quietly but resolutely. "I don't believe a single word that you've said about O.B. or even about Kaseras."

"Well that's an easy one, pal," Wood smiled again, once more the cock of the walk as he reached for the check. "Just ask 'em."

After that, Gianni began to realize not only how little he knew about Wood but also, despite the regular proximity, how little he really knew about Kaseras. Gianni spent the rest of the afternoon at Riley's thinking over what Wood had told him, weighing Wood's information against his own, and when that failed to produce conclusions, indulging in the sort of speculation that Johnny Bubbles' patter and a bottle of scotch tended to inspire. So O.B. had wanted to get rid of him at the hospital so he wouldn't see Wood and find out—just the opposite of what Wood had believed. Shows you how clever Wood was, Gianni thought. But at any rate, Wood was absolutely right about one thing, as much as Gianni hated to admit it even if only to himself: it was well past time that he and Ben Kaseras had a little tête-à-tête.

Gianni had a further lesson when he saw how receptive—friendly, really—Kaseras was and how willing to talk. At Gianni's request, they met the following day at Riley's, where they occupied a table in the back of the bar for most of the afternoon, sharing the better part of a bottle of Jameson's (chosen out of deference to Kaseras's taste) while Johnny Bubbles flicked the specks off the mirror and the customers drifted in and out. Just because Kaseras was considerably milder than Gianni had expected did not, however, mean that he had completely lost his edge. After a few drinks he was open and relaxed, but he retained that assertive confidence that made him a difficult opponent. Among other things, he did not fail to remind Gianni of his own dependence on O.B. and, somewhat to Gianni's discomfort, to point out the loss of esteem that he had suffered because of it.

"Oh, I know you may not have realized it yourself," Kaseras smiled. "It was clear how much you were wrapped up in O.B. and his image. After all, he is your big brother. But, yeah, we all felt that way. Look, kid, there's no way in the world that people are going to respect a copy as much as the original. You have to admit it, you did tend to stay in O.B.'s shadow, especially when things got rough. And you were pretty obnoxious about it, frankly, always using your brother as a shield. It must have grated on him, too, from time to time." Gianni felt Kaseras was watching for his response, and he tried not to give any. Kaseras shrugged and went on. "But that's just a guess. Anyway, maybe the whole thing's not so strange when you think about it." Kaseras took a sip of whiskey and seemed to think of something else that he wanted to say, because he had a strange look in his eye and went on quickly. "One thing's for sure—and I'm telling you this straight, kid, so don't take it the wrong way, because no matter what you may have heard, I try my best never to hold a grudge. When you shoot pool, or whatever, you ought to play on your own, not as part of a team. You're just too good for that, and the way things are, you're guaranteed to have problems if you double up—the pool part of it is your specialty, so leave the odds-making and the betting and all that crap to someone else and concentrate on your game—alone, if you know what I mean. That's your natural style, from what I've seen, or at least it ought to be. Sharing's O.K. up to a point, but too much of it—in any sense—isn't good for body or soul, if you get what I mean."

Gianni nodded, even though he had the feeling he was not getting all of what Kaseras meant. Kaseras continued, inquisitive now, probing. "So what's it going to be like now that O.B.'s not around to take your heat? I guess you'll have to take care of things on your own, including this." Kaseras waved his hand to indicate the bar, but Gianni had understood without the gesture and he seized on Kaseras's comment as an invitation to discuss what really interested him.

"Handling financial matters isn't my strong suit, but I'll manage. Just what was the relation between you and O.B., anyway? The financial part of it, I mean."

It was as if he had turned on the spigot. Once asked outright, Kaseras was nothing but information. In fact, as Gianni listened over the course of the afternoon, it became clear that Kaseras actually enjoyed talking about his business affairs, and that his enjoyment in relating them was intimately tied up in the delight he experienced in playing out the deals themselves. This was a side of Kaseras that Gianni had never seen, or even guessed at, enthusiastic, good-natured, and shrewd, showing the very mixture of energy and intelligence that, to Gianni's surprise, reminded him of O.B. Not that Kaseras actually worked the deals first-hand. No, that, according to Kaseras—who more or less reaffirmed what Wood had told Gianni before—was where O.B. came in.

"And, believe me, he was wonderful at it, a miracle-worker, really," Kaseras grinned. "Funny, I was sure you knew all about it, the two of you had always been so close. O.B. never seemed that secretive to me, and I don't see what he would have had to keep quiet about, at least until the end. Anyway, the way we did things was simple enough. O.B. would let me know when something looked good—usually something one of his friends downtown had tipped him about—and I would arrange for a transfer of funds—very discreet, you understand, handled by the best of banks, and almost always with extraordinary results. In fact, in all the time we did business together I never suffered a setback, not one. Oh, the last deal was going slowly all right, there's no doubt about that, and I know that O.B. was getting worried. But, really, there was never any chance that I would pull out, and, if you ask me, he should have known it himself. He'd just been too good in the past for me to do anything like that. We'd had our rough spots before, you know all about that, but this wasn't one of them. Sure, I would say a few things now and then, but just to put some pepper up his ass, if you know what I mean. Nothing more."

Gianni could see that Kaseras's imagination was moving now and that the Jameson's wasn't hurting. "You know what it was," Kaseras asked conspiratorially, "that last deal? It was the sale of the old Marshall Field's building on State Street, which was a big deal because it involved both a hefty piece of real estate—one of the busiest blocks this side of Times Square—and a landmark of sorts. The idea—and it was all O.B.'s—was to keep the street part as a store and turn the rest into condominiums, strictly topdrawer, of course, and just what downtown needed. Oh, it wasn't an official landmark, not yet—not a Historic City Landmark, declared by the Commission that makes those decisions—but a landmark anyway, informally, for everybody from Saturday shoppers to taxi-drivers to hookers (and believe me, the business district's not nearly so sluggish on that score as you might think). Of course, that was the problem and, for us, the added advantage. O.B. had found out from Wood both that the building was for sale and that the owners were putting it on the block for a very special reason, which was that the Commission had in fact decided to consider making it an official landmark, which, simply put would mean one thing: no sale, then or ever. So the company wanted to hurry, which logically would keep the price down, and I—or, better, O.B.—wanted to hurry, and the only thing that was holding us back was the goddamn bankers, who always seem to prefer sitting with their thumbs up their ass to doing any business at all. It wasn't that they were overly scrupulous or anything like that—putting one over on a mickey-mouse city commission wouldn't have bothered them in the least, especially since City Hall needed them equally as much as they needed City Hall. No, the banks were just being slow and stupid, period. Sure, there were other partners—a deal like that doesn't go through over coffee and doughnuts, one to one. But all of the others wanted to move too. So it wasn't really the financing itself that was causing the trouble, but the banks and their usual mix of endless paperwork and cold feet. O.B. knew we were all in agreement and wanted to beat the City to the punch, and he knew that the delay was hurting the deal's prospects, but it was pretty clear to me, and I suppose to everyone else, that for the life of him he just didn't know what to do about it. The banks were insistent on plodding along. And that, unfortunately, was where 'Five' Bronson came into the picture."

At the mention of Bronson's name, Gianni touched Kaseras' arm, motioning for him to keep his voice down since Johnny Bubbles was moving closer and closer behind the bar, with his ears pricked up as usual. By then Gianni was tired enough of his listening in so that he didn't mind waving him away unceremoniously. Kaseras went on, his voice lowered but his enthusiasm for the story undiminished.

"'Five' added that extra touch without which everything probably would have gone just fine, sort of like the piece of string hidden in the cat's dinner. Oh, I know we were supposed to be friends—that's certainly the way he wanted it to look, and I didn't object. But I had never really been able to stand him, no matter what he or anyone else thought—though I suppose he knew, actually, because he may be obnoxious, but he's not stupid."

Gianni took another sip of his whiskey, not knowing how to react to what Kaseras was saying.

"There's something about 'Five'—I'm sure you've noticed—so that he always manages to show up just when someone least needs him—or, better, when the situation least requires him, because he doesn't deal in *people* but in *circumstances*. And O.B. had got himself into the sort of circumstance where 'Five' would undoubtedly have seemed useful. It's too bad O.B. didn't just come directly to me, but I guess that was the point, the very thing he was trying to avoid. Maybe like he avoided telling you things, I don't know. Anyway, like I said, I wouldn't have been scared off no matter how much time or money O.B. needed, but I suppose he didn't realize that. Too bad, really. Because 'Five' and his friends were a lousy second choice—and believe me, that's a nice way of putting it. You probably know about O.B.'s gambling debts around town, almost everybody does, with the exception of some of his more straitlaced creditors, who wouldn't have been pleased to know exactly what O.B. was doing with their money. I guess in the end, that was one of the things that soured his life at home, too, though I'm sure you knew more about that than I did. The funny thing was, he really didn't do that bad, it seemed to me. Oh, he would lose from time to time, and on occasion he would lose big, but he would always make it back, either on football or basketball or at cards, because, honestly, he was just so good at it. It was part of his nature, I guess, the risk-taking—like that old motorcycle he used to fly around on at a hundred miles an hour when he had nothing better to do with himself." Kaseras looked quizzically at Gianni but then went on. "So what if he bet more than most people, and considerably more than he could easily afford? If it gave him that much of a rush, maybe it was worth it. It wouldn't have been a problem except that he had a bad streak—horrid, really—just as our deal on the building, the one that he had been tipped on, was shaping up. So his credit was nil exactly when he needed funds to keep things going. And, if he couldn't go to the banks and he wasn't going to come to me, who else but 'Five'? Zeke Wood, your brother's friend downtown, told me the score, but only much later, after it didn't hurt anymore to let things out. Not that Wood was my friend—forget it—but just because his pride was hurt. Yet at first he was quiet as a churchmouse. I think it might have had a little something to do with the fact that the deal was still in the works, although most likely it was plain old-fashioned discretion more than anything else. Because Wood could be discreet, at least when City Hall was involved. And in this instance, they were involved twice, so to speak, once at the beginning, through Wood, who had started things off with his special information, and once at the end, through Bronson's pals in the First Ward, who were so generous as to help O.B. out with a bag full of extra cash when he needed it most."

Despite himself, Gianni cringed: Kaseras noticed it and hesitated. Even Gianni was aware of who it was that ran the First Ward, though Kaseras knew considerably more about the finances of the operation than he did—not, however, from first-hand experience but only from what he'd been given to understand by Wood and others, since Kaseras had never had anything to do with that sort of financial arrangement.

"Wood has an expression for it," Kaseras smiled. "Maybe you've heard him use it: 'the court of last resort.' Once O.B. had gone to them, there was nothing Wood, or anyone else, for that matter, could do for him. Technically, I suppose the First Ward and the Mayor's Office are affiliated, though not in a competitive way, since the two operations don't overlap. But still, Wood has to respect his 'colleagues,' even if their interest in politics as such is secondary at best, and it was considerate of him to warn me. It's always amazed me that the ward that contains not only the city's biggest stores and banks but also City Hall itself is the one that they gave over to the outfit. But that's history, I guess. And anyway, it's their business, not mine. So Wood was discreet in his way, he only told me about it later, but that still didn't help O.B. And once things had got going, 'Five' Bronson, despite his inflated sense of his own importance, couldn't help much either. After all, it's tough to tell the folks in finance to have a warm glass of milk and get some rest when the loan in question is a quarter of a million tallied at upwards of a hundred per cent per month. And their collectors aren't especially gracious either, if you know what I mean, nor do they ever have problems with memory loss."

Gianni recalled the tall quiet man in the black suit—at the time, he'd actually thought he looked more like a maitre d'—who had come around in the fall looking for O.B., with 'Five' Bronson tagging at his heels, and now he understood what the point of the visit had been. As Kaseras had gotten to the part about O.B.'s last creditors, he had hunched over in his chair, his voice becoming quieter and quieter until he was speaking in little more than a whisper, like a man leaning over to speak to a small child—indeed so quiet that even Johnny Bubbles had given up and gone off to draw beers for the boilermakers who had begun to populate the open end of the bar. But now, unburdened, Kaseras leaned back and spoke up, his hands gesturing confidently, as Gianni's friend now, and he returned to the subject of the hunt. "So, all in all, I guess O.B. was just trying to keep things going between us—not that even the side bets added up to that much—just hustling for the joint, as it were, to keep things moving. The hunt itself, ironic as it might sound, was inconsequential, just a ruse. I think Wood was right about that, if that's what you want to know. Because, like I've told you, once O.B. had done what he'd done, he was desperate, like finding yourself in for a dip at lunchtime with a tankful of barracuda. I think by then he would have tried anything to keep at least one source of cash on the line—hell, who wouldn't have?—including that crazy bet of his, or yours, about the old man's popgun."

At seeing Gianni's expression Kaseras hurried to add, "Well then, what more can I tell you? That I'm certain O.B. would have told you everything himself sooner or later, and that you're not to blame anyway, for any of it? Well, O.K., kid, don't worry about it. Believe you me," Kaseras took the last of his whiskey, "it's just not worth it."

* * *

So, what the devil was I supposed to think? All I could tell was that nothing that I could tell before had been right. Or almost nothing. I still thought more or less the same about Johnny Bubbles as I had always thought, so I guess there was still hope. But, like I said, not much, because all of a sudden everything else, and I mean everything, seemed upside down. Or maybe it wasn't so sudden after all, maybe I should have seen what had been going on from the start, like Wood and even Kaseras seemed to have thought that I had. Maybe it wasn't O.B. or anyone else that had changed but me. Sometimes, a lot more often than I would have liked to admit, in the early afternoon when I was sitting in the back of Riley's watching the flies dance along the bar, or alone at night, I hated even thinking about it. And I would do everything I could to avoid it. The less I knew the better, period. But no matter what I tried, it only worked for a while, and there you were again, with the exact same problem all over. Whatever I did, I just couldn't seem to escape it.

Mildly put, it was simple: how could O.B. have done what he did? And how could he have done it to me? But nothing's ever that simple, so I didn't want to get ahead of things. First of all, just what had he done? True, he hadn't lied to me outright, but he sure hadn't come clean with me either, and on more than just one or two accounts. The financial business was important, and not only because it would have been nice to know what he'd been up to downtown in that office of his. After all, Kaseras and even Wood, in his way, were acquaintances of mine, too, and it wasn't exactly a pleasure having them take me for an innocent klutz, or, worse, an ignoramus. And besides that, I own a part of Riley's, too, and it would have been nice to know that my partner, be he brother or no, was bartering at least a portion of his share on the black market. I sure wouldn't have wanted Al Capone, or whoever it had been with Bronson that day, showing up at my door. But worse than anything, worse than the money and the deceit and the half-truths, worse than all of that was the gun.

That was the part, on my own, that I couldn't make myself believe: because it was more than just a gun, it was much, much more. It was part of the old man and the reminder of everything that he had been to us, through all those summers, all those years. By treating the old Remington as though it were just another object to trade or bargain for, no better or more valuable than, no different from, anything else that could be pegged at the same price, O.B. spat on our past, his and mine, and everything that it meant. Now the old man really was gone, dead and buried more surely than he had ever been when he'd merely had the misfortune to die, because putting a corpse in the ground is nothing compared to destroying the image that endures past it. With what he'd done, O.B. had put us in the same category as our thieving, chicken-shit relatives who had cheated the old man's estate out of his money and robbed his belongings right out from under poor old Grandma Britzen's nose—not that *that* was so hard, since she seemed to have trusted them to the very end, almost akin to the way that I had trusted O.B., I guess. So O.B. had taken one dream, a dream that, for us, had been real and true, and traded it in on another, a cheap, tawdry question of dollars and profit, without either a heart or a soul.

But, when I really got to thinking about it, the worst wasn't the part about the gun itself or even about the old man. The worst was the part about O.B. and me. Betrayal is not my idea of fun. And if I couldn't trust him, who could I trust? Even that feeling, though, brought strange effects with it, since, hard as it was to lose my belief in O.B. and his ties to me, extending, like everyone knows, from mutual admiration and quiet friendship to out and out protection, at the same time that very loss succeeded in setting me free. But free from what? A protector I'd maybe never really had, and, as for the old man, an image—whether ancestor or begetter seemed then to make little difference—that had not been sturdy enough to weather what, by the other old man's standards, would have seemed the puniest of storms? No matter what anyone says, it had been nice to have a definite past and a secure present, a point of origin and a place to hang my hat, and I wasn't too happy about O.B. wiping them away with one stroke, even if he did clean the slate for me at the very same moment.

At times, especially in the beginning, if O.B. had just been honest with me, come right out and told me what the score was, which is to say, what was going on in his life and why, everything would have been at least tolerable, if not easy. Still, I knew O.B. had had his reasons for what he had done; and he *had* been clever about it, after a fashion. In fact, the more I thought about it, the more I realized that being honest with me wouldn't have solved any of O.B.'s problems, and might actually have made them worse, since he would have just had one more set of worries. No, honesty itself wouldn't have been nearly enough, any more than it would have been for either of the old men. But still, it would have helped. And then I wouldn't have had such difficulty believing that O.B. had done what he seemed to have done, a difficulty that, like I said, wouldn't go away, no matter how hard I worked at it, worrying things over backwards and forwards, and no matter how long I waited. So I finally got tired of mulling things over to no end and decided to do what, by then, I'd known for a long time that I would eventually have to do in any event, like it or not: I went to see O.B. again.

I have to admit there wasn't a great deal that O.B. could do, outside of nodding his head and looking uncomfortable, since pretty much everything Wood and Kaseras had told me turned out to be true. Oh, sure, some fine points of interpretation had to be cleared up here and there, but all in all his activities, business and otherwise, had been pretty much what the two of them said they had been. He lay sitting up, with the bouquet of red and yellow flowers Denise and the kids had left supplying the only bright spot in the room, his pallor if anything even gloomier than the dull, offwhite walls. He was still enlaced in a tangle of tubes and bottles, but the bandages had finally been removed from his head and at last I could watch his full face as he talked, the small white scar dancing up and down over his eye each time I mentioned the things they had said about him. It was sad, really. What else can I say.

"Well," he asked after a time, "is there anything I can do to help?" Because, I suppose, he still felt his role was that of the protector, since he'd been so used to it. "The financial part—the various payments—have all been taken care of to date, so you needn't worry about that. But if you could use any help with Kaseras or Wood or with—"

"The fellows with the deep voices and the winning ways?"

"—Or anybody—"

"Just tell me, is that all of it then?"

"—I would certainly do whatever I could to.... Oh, hell, don't worry. Whatever it is, I'll take care of it."

"Like you did before?"

"I said I'll take care of it, everything. I said it, and I meant it."

"Is that *all*?"

"Yes, everything of any importance." But now the scar was going again. "Everything. That's all."

His face showed a weak smile once more—the fourth or fifth time I'd seen it that afternoon, so that by then I was almost used to it, though that afternoon had been the first of it, the weakness, I'd ever seen on him—and a moment later I was gone.

As I left the heat of the hospital behind and walked onto the sidewalk, the air outside seemed suddenly fresh, better than anything I had felt in ages. I stopped to look up at the fleece of clouds overhead and to take a few deep breaths before going on. When all was said and done, after all, things could easily have been worse. O.B. had confirmed what I feared, but, by doing that he'd also presented me, whether he knew it or not, with a nice, neat package, putrid, maybe, but manageable nevertheless, something stable and fixed and, best of all, somehow external to me, as though I were no longer involved as a participant in any of the things that I'd been mulling over but instead could retire to watch from the sidelines, or, better, from a last-row seat, like a distant observer in a darkened hall. The problem was still there, but, since I had already thought it through and O.B. had confirmed what I had thought, that seemed, in one sense anyway, the end of it, as though my worries were over and I could let it rest in peace. No wonder I was breathing easier—not that I felt like jumping for joy, you understand, but at least the storm seemed to have passed, and I had come through.

It was while I was crossing the parking lot that I saw Sherrie hurrying toward the hospital, her chestnut curls shaking in the breeze, and her chewing gum going full steam. She was, of course, going to see O.B.—she had no other reason to be there—but somehow she acted as though she hadn't wanted me to know about it, as though she'd been caught doing something that she didn't want to be seen doing; and she tried her best to brush me off and get away as quickly as she could. Funny, if she hadn't acted so strangely, I probably would have thought no more about it and gone on my way. Because she had every right to go and see O.B., that was plain. And he would undoubtedly be happy to see her, that was clear, too. But as it turned out, the nervousness wasn't about herself or even O.B. alone, but, surprise of surprises, about someone quite different.

* * *

So what the hell can I do from this bed? God, get me out of here. I told him not to pay so much attention to those damn heroes of his—the old man or Jake or anyone else—I told him. Gianni, what good are they? They don't help you to do anything, unless knocking them over counts for something, which it doesn't, good lord, me included. You're supposed to destroy the copy, not the original. But from here I can't take care of any of that, much less of the things that really matter. For chrissake, help me. Oh my God, find a way to get me out. That's all I ask. Get me out of here.

* * *

After Gianni had a chance to consider it, he would at last be able to say what he thought. Because it is always better to wait and get some distance on things before you form a definite idea about them. Anyway, that was his opinion. Yet, this time, regardless of how long he waited, things did not seem to get better, but only worse. Since Sherrie had acted so strangely Gianni made a point of going to see her, because, naturally, he was still worried about O.B. even if he was angry with him, too; and he figured that if Sherrie knew something that he did not she should tell him. But it was obvious from the outset that she was less than delighted with the visit.

"What the hell do you care?" she yelled at him. "When have you ever really cared about him as a person rather than as your idol, as a sort of cheerful Superman? You—none of you—have any idea of the way he suffered when things started to go wrong. It amazes me how little sympathy he got from any of you. So the hell with all of you, you and Denise and all of those so-called buddies downtown, who from what I can tell want him to stay alive only so that they can keep sucking the blood out of him. What a disgusting group you are, all of you."

He tried to calm her, and to explain that she had her company a little mixed up, but she was running too hot to cool down right away. He had seen her worked up before, in lots of ways, but never anything like this. "Well, just tell me," she went on, her face flushed and her eyes bright, "and then I'll shut up. When have you *ever* done one thing for him without thinking of yourself first and what he could do for you? When, in the last two years, did Denise ever bother to listen to his troubles without first yelling at him about losing a few dollars or coming home late or something equally silly? Did you ever have the slightest idea of how restless he was when he went on that stupid hunting trip with you, that he was anxious as a colt just to do *something*. and that he was dying to talk with you but still didn't feel that he could. Or that he probably would have been happier if he'd never come back at all? *You* should have been the one to know, or at least to sense it, if anyone could. But Christ, I guess they could write a book about what you've never been able to figure out. And what about now? What are any of you doing for him now besides sending flowers and hovering around looking out for your own benefit, like vultures waiting for a corpse. Goddamn you and all of your friends! Damn your souls to hell!"

She went on for quite a while, flinging those looks filled with equal measures of anger at the world and adoration for O.B. And Gianni had to admit that some of the things she said did hit home. Gianni had never been as generous to O.B. as he had been to him, for instance, and not too many other people had, either. It was just that O.B. had always had an awful lot to give. But, overall, Gianni really couldn't figure out what the point of all the screaming was, except to exculpate O.B. and belittle everyone else, so, more as a last resort than anything else, he went, innocently enough, to see what Denise might know about it.

It was Denise who finally drew him back inside things, inside so deep that even Gianni, for all his hopes, gave up the idea of ever extricating himself again. They had never talked very much, but when they had it was always crucial to him, even if usually too late. She sent the kids off upstairs with a swish of her housecoat and stood looking at him, her hands on her hips, her face broad and handsome, and the skin still taut, but lined with wrinkles, many of which, he knew now, O.B. had most likely put there.

"Yeah," she nodded, "O.B. seemed plenty restless, but not because of inactivity. If anything, it seemed just the reverse to me—he had too many irons in the fire, and he seemed pretty sure that at least one of them was going to end up burning him. Not that he confides in me much anymore," she shrugged. "After little

Mary came along, our relations changed, since I didn't want any more of them. But I'm sure he told you about that. Anyway, that's what it seemed like to me—overwork, if anything, and lots of evenings away on what he called 'business.'"

Gianni glanced anxiously around the room at the dark wood floors leading to the bright kitchen on one side and the living room on the other, filled with Denise's beloved orientals strewn about regardless of any threat that three young children must have posed to them more or less constantly.

"Oh, I know that he wasn't always occupied with business, at least not of any financial sort. I'm not blind or foolish, you know. But I wasn't always sure who he was seeing, or if I even wanted to know who. And I'd heard all about this Sherrie—'Five' Bronson told me, delicate and friendly in his own inimitable fashion. Anyway, she wasn't the only one, of that I'm certain, any more than Goldilocks only had one bear."

Gianni could not keep his smile from showing, but she went on, seemingly oblivious. "But I thought I understood that Sherrie was *your* girlfriend, and that you were going around as a foursome. At least, I thought that's what 'Five' was getting at."

"No," Gianni said quickly. "That's not the case at all. Please understand—I wouldn't have done that—especially not to you. Believe me, Denise, not to you."

"Well, all right," Denise said at last, obviously displeased but not as upset as Gianni had feared she might be. "All right, so that's who Sherrie is. Now will you please tell me who this other woman is that I've been hearing so much about."

"Who?" Gianni asked, puzzled.

"The one he'd been seeing so much of lately," Denise answered, her voice strong and clear, "before that trip of yours. Don't pretend you don't know. 'Five' Bronson told me he'd been seeing her for months at least—that girl named Diana."

With that, at last, Gianni had discovered what Kaseras had meant about playing alone, and what that sickly smile on O.B.'s face was all about. The image of Diana flashed through his mind, pristinely for the last time, and he felt the blade turn twice.

* * *

So Gianni had been used, too. Not just betrayed, but used. It wasn't fair, he knew that; but so what? Maybe there were no limits anymore, or maybe it was just that O.B. didn't have any. Gianni hadn't been with Diana for a while, but until he saw Denise he'd at least had the luxury of memory. Now that was gone, too. What more could O.B. possibly want? Gianni simply could not say. From then on, he felt himself drawn into the maze with no exit in sight and no hope of one, caught in the same web as O.B. Perhaps it was true that he had thought too much of both of them, felt too much for both of them, and the result had been inevitable from the start. Maybe Sherrie had been right after all: Goddamn all of them.

He saw O.B. once more soon after that. Gianni was not looking so much for a confirmation this time, since now he no longer had any doubt but only a dull ringing bitterness. O.B.'s bandage had not changed significantly; his eyes were cloudy. The impressions that, for Gianni, were to remain clearest, so that, years later, after everything else in that room had become blurred and faded, were two: first, the terrific strength of the grip in which O.B. took his hand as he left, as though all of the force left in that otherwise weakened body had suddenly descended to the hand taking his in parting; and, second, the small white scar above O.B.'s eye, which, for the first time that Gianni could remember since they had been children, had gone utterly still. One thing more that he remembered, although less vividly, was that through the knowledge and the sorrow of O.B.'s eyes, deep behind the surface of his gaze, from time to time the flicker of that smile would come alive again: so he recognized, finally, that there was still going to be something else.

* * *

That's what Kaseras had thought, Gianni knew, that he and O.B. had been 'sharing' Diana, and that he had agreed to it. Or worse, that it had been his idea. What a fool they'd made of him. His imagination circled around what he knew to be the truth, that he'd been run around first by O.B. and now by Diana, though the order was not that way, really, but O.B., Diana, O.B., and then Kaseras, though Kaseras didn't even realize it, the dumb, rich slob. At least he hadn't got the gun. That was something. But how could he know for certain what anything meant anymore, now that things had turned out as they had, and everything was as it was? Why bother anyway, why make the effort to think about it, to try to think it through, when nothing good could possibly come of it: and especially now, when the sun was turning from gold to red. This is how it was now, what he waited for. While the shadows outside the window faded and the sweet hot whiskey took effect, even as he watched, the colors and the outlines of the world about him faded, and he could begin at last to dream.

The dream began, as always in its best versions, with a feeling of motion that was not a fall but floating, a trajectory that came through him and took him as it went, so that it became him, and he it, as they moved. Its motion was neither swift nor slow, rather steady as the current of a river, a river without banks that he floated through, surely, cleanly, Icarus before the fall, or, better, Adam moving confidently along the golden path, before the apple, perfectly unblemished, unmarked by any word or deed. It was a river all in motion, but with no change, no friction or difference, like time but without a name, so that everything was outside of him—his body, too—yet it all included him in it, like the green lake with the clouds going and the blue in the water all topsy-turvy and all in motion. He moved—words are inadequate to describe it, moved like riding the horse or chasing the deer—but without the end point. Because the dream had no end. It could not have, not for him. O.B. had almost killed it, but no, that's what he found out: it was too powerful, and it couldn't end since he didn't exist apart from it but only in it, not in its substance but in its motion, so that it was perfect but never finished: he wasn't there anymore, or anywhere, but only the dream: only the dream moved and acted, not him: it had happened many times now: only the dream was real.

The dream was a river of light inside of him, pure light, as bright as the glow of the moon deep in the Wisconsin sky, dazzlingly bright, as it took him. It was surrounded by dark. Yet it held darkness in it, too, he knew that now. But as long as it moved, which now was to be forever, none of that made any difference. As long as it moved, and took him with it. Only the dream was real; and the name of the dream was....

*   *   *

"No," his mother corrected, "not Jane."

"What?" Gianni blurted. "I guess I thought that the two of you had always been in the same—"

"No," she repeated slowly. "Not Jane, just me: Jane was his. It's true, though, that you weren't encouraged to ask further. Your father had never wanted anything to do with it, given the way he felt about them Jane and Henry and even poor, pudgy little Judd—and I, well, I just didn't want to talk about it any longer. Are you at least able to see that, to see why?"

Gregory Lucente

      Gianni sat back in the chair, looking around the room where they'd sat together and talked so many times, with the same poor lighting and the blue satin couch and mahogany table, feeling that now something really had changed, and not just that O.B. had taken a turn for the worse; indeed, they didn't even talk about that, at least not at first.

      "I don't think that they even wanted us to know, your grandparents that is. We found out—or I did, anyway—in the oddest way, but probably the most understandable one, when you think about it, about how people live together day in and day out and have their own secrets, too, ones that seem in themselves big and dark and unspeakable, but then they get out in the tiniest, most unpredictable ways. It was a snowy Sunday morning in winter, and we were all in the front room, just back from church, Grandpa in the rocker and Grandma bustling about, getting things ready for cards with the Connollys, while Jane and I played with the wooden automobiles that Drew had carved for us, modeled on that fancy Phaeton he'd seen once at the fair in Minneapolis. Bless his heart, that Drew. He was so good with his hands, and well intentioned, too, with the sweetest disposition. But he just wasn't very bright. He and Grandpa were talking about Henry Stillwell's ponies, more to get a rise out of Grandma than anything else, since otherwise Grandpa didn't have all that much to say to Drew, or, I guess Drew to him—oh, they got along well, and I know that Grandpa loved Drew and would have done anything for him, and that Drew felt the same, but, as I say, Drew simply wasn't much of a....much of a thinker, I guess I mean. Anyway, they were talking about the ponies, Grandpa good and loud, too, so Grandma could hear, with that special ring to his voice because he knew perfectly well that she couldn't stand them, when somehow the topic changed to bloodlines. Then Drew was pointing at us, calling us his little daisies, like he did when he got excited, carried away I guess by Grandpa's humor, and probably just by the fact of being in the parlor all dressed up for Sunday and having conversation—of being part of it all— and his mouth must have plain outrun his thoughts, because all of a sudden he'd said something that he shouldn't have, and Grandpa's chair, which had been creaking away as he'd gone back and forth laughing and jingling his watch chain like he did when he was joking, suddenly stopped. In the silence, Drew turned bright red; Grandpa started to rock and laugh again a moment later, trying to cover things up, but I'd noticed, and he knew it, so he had to tell us something. And, like the person he was, he simply told us the truth, not then, of course, because that would have embarrassed poor Drew all the more, but later, that evening, as we sat on his lap in front of the fire that danced on the hearth. I never told him that I'd had no idea *what* the cause of that sudden, eerie silence had been, that he could have made up something about Drew or the ponies or Henry Stillwell himself or almost anything at all and neither Jane nor I would ever have known the difference. But I don't think that would have mattered, really. Once he'd started, there was no other way for him to do things, at least as he saw his lights. That was his strength, I suppose, as well as his weakness."

"And Jane?"

"Yes, he told us both...."

"No, I mean Jane and Henry, and Dad. You said...."

"Oh, yes, that. Your father couldn't stand Henry. I don't know about Jane—your father probably would never have said anything to me about her other than general grumbling, because, after all, she was my little sister. But he didn't like Henry even a bit, and he never tried to keep it a secret, either. You see, the four of us had lived together in the same house while your father was finishing law school and Henry was trying to decide which way of making money he liked best—and believe me, he had plenty of options, since he had no special training in anything and was equally mediocre at just about everything he tried his hand at. So maybe it was a matter of character, because Henry was the sort of archetypal salesman, good at nothing and, therefore, able to do or sell anything as long as he himself was nothing more than a middleman—a parasite your father would say, or leech, depending on his mood—so there was more than enough about Henry to dislike. But I prefer to think, looking back, that it wasn't only a matter of character but also one of the situation itself. None of us wanted to be stuck together as a foursome in that house—a big frame house with a huge lawn and even a garden, like they all had during and just after the war, but no house is big enough for that, believe me. We just couldn't afford anything else, any other arrangement, which was pretty much the boat that everybody found themselves in at that time. So there we were, and when O.B. arrived things got, if anything, considerably worse. There was nothing in particular, nothing that I can recall, but just a whole accumulation of little things that added up as unmitigated enmity. And I don't doubt that Henry, and maybe even Jane, felt the same, especially since Henry had been an only child, without brothers or sisters, and by then really had no family to speak of, and I think he was particularly jealous every time one or two of your aunts or uncles would drop by for an afternoon, which they did frequently after O.B. was born, since both Dominic and Aunt Fil's first husband, the one who died in that car accident, had started studying agriculture at the university by then. Anyway, after that, once we'd moved and your father had started his practice, I never liked to bring up anything about Jane and Henry and pudgy little Judd, not because of them in and of themselves but because of your father's reaction whenever I did. Those two years of misery at the outset were bad enough without paying for them in review for the rest of our lives. And of course, they—Henry—was green with envy over you two boys, and took every chance he could to show off Judd to best advantage, which wasn't easy, believe me, so we saw very little of them, thank God, in part out of deference to your father's wishes but also out of concern—mine, that is—for my own sanity."

"O.B. started to tell me something once about the guns, after the old man died," Gianni took a sip from his glass.

"I'm getting to that, don't worry. But first, I want to be sure you understand something. It may not seem of importance to you, but it is to me. Your father doesn't know everything that I'm going to tell you, and, as I said, I have no desire whatever to talk with him about any of it ever again. So please keep all of what I'm going to say between the two of us, you and me, and no one else."

He nodded immediately and she went on. "O.B. was right, of course, at least in as far as he knew about it. He didn't know everything, since we—I—was careful that no one heard so much as a word about the rest of it. Oh, as for the guns and all that, there was no way we could have kept that a secret. And it was despicable what they did. They hadn't waited more than an hour or two before they went through the closets and the den in the house on Juniper Street, even the attic. Good God, they beat the undertaker by a full day! It was Henry's doing, you can be sure of that. The whole affair was so typical of him, as though it had his stamp on it, a combination of Simon Legree and Quantrill's raiders. I'm sure he got Judd to help him—I can just see pudgy little Judd straining down those creaking attic steps, huffing and puffing under the weight of the shotguns and the boxes of shells piled across his arms, uncertain of whether to be more afraid of his father or his load. They got the old fox-skin coat, too, the one that you had on in that picture from the ice-fishing contest, if you recall, and a vintage RCA phonograph and a few other things. All of sentimental value as far as Grandma and Grandpa were concerned—even the shotguns, since by then he didn't use ten and twelve gauge any more— though I'm sure Henry turned a pretty penny on it all. That was what *he* was good at. But that wasn't the end of it, not by a long shot."

   The old woman paused for a moment to reflect, and when she went on, her voice was flatter, business-like, as though she were telling something for the first time that she wanted to get exactly right, without letting her emotions disrupt the measure of her words. As Gianni sat listening, her eyes would turn away whenever she struggled with her memory to get a name or a date correct, and he found himself wondering what her reactions must have been as she discovered, bit by bit, the disjointed pieces that she now reordered and repeated as a comprehensible whole.

   "When your Grandfather died," she began again, "he left the house, the land, whatever effects Henry and Judd hadn't carried off, and eighty thousand dollars in cash and assorted notes—a very tidy sum for a man of his time and condition. He wasn't ever just a money-man, nothing like Henry. He never let the money get in the way of his feelings, either for himself or for other people either. I know that he took a loss more than once rather than harm a neighbor who happened to be down on his luck. And he despised people who took advantage of others for a profit. But still he did all right for himself, and for us, of course. Anyway, after he died, Henry moved in and took over the management of Grandpa's affairs, all in the name of Grandma, whom he was supposedly helping out. This was all fine with your father and me, since pushing paper around had never been up our alley, and besides, we never dreamed that someone so close could be so...well, so evil, really. I was going to say greedy, but I'm too old to back away from what I can see now to be the truth of things. I suppose we should have been able to guess the sort of things that Henry was capable of, if not from knowing him before then from his performance with the guns and such after Grandpa died, but we just hadn't seen it. Maybe we didn't want to, I don't know. Anyway, Henry had two toys to fool with, the land and the cash. The house in town—they'd sold the farm several years before—was the one thing he couldn't touch, thank God, since Grandma and Drew were still living in it. But naturally the house cost money to keep up, not to mention the fact that Grandma and Drew still had to eat, though by then neither of them ate very much, and they almost never went out, unless someone came by to take them special. So in order to defray the expenses of the house, Henry sold the plot they owned next to it—"

   "The berry patch?"

   "Yes, the raspberry patch that your grandpa had put in just after they'd moved from the farm so that the loss of Grandma's berry patch and her garden would weigh less heavily on her, and she would feel at home again. After all, what did Henry care about that sort of thing? And the money from the sale of the land was just enough to permit him to protect the eighty thousand dollars."

"But there must have been a will—"

"Oh, of course there was! But it didn't say anything about who would manage—"

"No, I mean who would inherit. What was the point if Aunt Jane and Uncle Henry would have to share in the end no matter what? After all, Henry couldn't have known that Jane would die before Grandma."

"The will was quite clear, simple actually. Everything passed to Grandma, with the stipulation that at her death whatever of the estate that remained would go to Jane and me, divided equally. Of course, you're right, no one could know then that Jane would die before Grandma, but even that, in terms of the will, made no difference, since her portion was then designated as going to Judd. Henry, in his official role as manager, was well-served in any case, at least in theory. But in practice he couldn't have had any idea what would happen, that after Jane's death—given the fact that Henry moved in with that floozy secretary of his practically the next day—that after Jane's death Judd would refuse to speak to Henry, except to tell him that he never wanted to see him again if that was the way he treated the memory of his mother. Judd was angry, no denying it, and maybe he had the right to be, because Henry and his secretary had been fooling around all during the entire two years of Jane's illness, and Judd would have had to have been blind not to have known about it. It was at that point, if you recall, that Judd joined the navy, since he was a full-grown young man by then and no longer pudgy little Judd, even if he always did stay a little jowly. That whole time Henry must have been beside himself with the thought of something so precious off sailing the seven seas, without any way for him to control it from where he stood, since Kansas City isn't exactly a maritime port-of-call, and with the old alarm clock ticking away inside Grandma Britzen, who still thought, in her dotage—but bless her heart, she remained the sweetest of women—that Henry was the greatest thing since they invented peanut butter and jelly sandwiches. But none of that made any difference, you see, because Judd had the keys to the kingdom, or better, *was* the key, since without him Henry would come up completely empty. So you can see why Henry was so cheerful at Grandma Britzen's funeral, where he and Judd were finally reunited and, it seems, reconciled, to the great relief of Henry's pocketbook. There must have been at least some reconciliation between Judd and the platinum blonde, too, since when they left Crooked Falls on that cold grey afternoon I noticed it was Judd behind the wheel of the Chevy, with Anita in the front seat beside him examining her nails, and Henry ensconced in the back, and not just because that made it easier for him to count his money, you can be sure."

"But none of that is so...so...."

"So terrible? No, but I haven't told you that part—I wanted to be sure you understood the background first, the overall picture, so you could see the point of the details. The important part was what happened after Jane died—and what had already been happening before, too, from the look on her face the last time I saw her, lying in the hospital, tortured, really, more than just guilty, since she hadn't been raised to behave that way, Henry or not."

"So what exactly are you saying—"

"About the money, you mean?"

"Yes, about the money."

She took a sip of her lemon tea before going on. "Since Henry's role as manager was unofficial, there was no way for anyone to check up on him—he had no legal responsibility as executor or anything like that, because he did everything in Grandma's name and with Grandma's consent (though without her knowledge, I'm sure of that). Of the eighty thousand dollars at his disposal, only ten thousand remained on account in Crooked Falls. All the rest was put in investments and other sorts of accounts, which was perfectly normal in a situation like that. What wasn't normal was the way in which Henry did what he did. Instead of choosing investments and placing them in Grandma's or even his name, he made them in the wildest assortment of names possible, and in banks, corporations, and real estate ventures scattered across the map from here to Timbuctoo. The idea, of course, wasn't to make money for Grandma but for himself. I don't know how much Jane knew about it or exactly when she found out whatever it was she did find out, and I don't really care. It was Henry who was at the heart of things, and I know that to be the case because the real flurry of activity happened over the last year and a half of Jane's life, while she was sick and dying—too sick, if you remember, to have anything to do with matters in which she had never been trained and probably hadn't the slightest experience, because, you see, that was Henry's bailiwick."

Gianni nodded, remembering the awful whiteness of the hospital room and Aunt Jane's emaciated body, twisted by the "cure" as much as by the disease. "Then how *did* you find out?"

"After Jane died and Grandma took sick, really sick this time and not just the same old hypochondria that had kept her going all her life, we began to take a more active role in guarding her interests, your father and I. Or I should say, Ray Knoepfelmeyer, the banker in Crooked Falls (and—I must say it didn't hurt—one of my high school sweethearts), took over that role for us. By then Henry was off in Kansas City with the candidate for Miss Spearmint—Mrs., now—and Judd was, like I said, off putting his mind to sailing the seven seas. So when Grandma got sick Ray thought he should begin to tally up her account, tally and re-tally, I should say, because that was the problem: just about nothing did tally. Gradually, piece by piece, Ray learned why. At first, I guess, he didn't so much mistrust what he found as simply disbelieve it. But after a time it all became too clear to deny. Henry had spread Grandpa's—Grandma's, really I guess—money around far and wide, the point being that no one, in theory at least, would every have been able to find it all, given that this was before computers and telexes and such, and even beginning to find it meant hours and hours on the phone and literally months of correspondence. But that was just theory, nothing more, because in practice, Ray Knoepfelmeyer had two things going for him—or for us, I should say—an unblemished reputation, which apparently counted for quite a bit in that business, even if the bank was a small, local operation, and boundless energy. Once he got started, he just wouldn't stop. Slowly but surely all of Henry's chickens came home to roost. It was sad, really—and not very easy to live with, for me, I mean—that it took Jane's death to straighten it all out. That and Henry's effect on people. Because, strange as it may seem, that was really what helped Ray more than anything else: Henry. By then there were enough people that knew Henry, and, his opinion to the contrary notwithstanding, his behavior and demeanor meant that there were plenty enough people that just couldn't take him in any shape or form: to know him was to despise him, a reaction which by that time even included Judd. So, luckily enough, Ray had something extra going for him besides his own talents and gumption. Lucky, because in those years—the whole mess took quite a while to sift through—we needed all the help we could get."

"You mean help wasn't always right there? Crooked Falls is so small, you'd think people could figure out ways to get along, to help one another get along."

"You have a very glossy picture of what life is like in a small town," she smiled. "In point of fact, smaller doesn't mean better, and it doesn't mean kinder, either, or at least not necessarily. People just find different ways of getting at each other, that's all. Sometimes I think that on any given day you could take all the bad, all the evil, in Chicago or St. Louis, or New York City for that matter, and wrap it up and ship it off to a little town like Crooked Falls or New Providence and you'd still have room enough left over for packages from Detroit or maybe even Los Angeles. Oh, I suppose I'm exaggerating—but not by much. As soon as our relatives around Crooked Falls—and you know how many there are, once you start counting up the distant ones, too—found out that Grandma's illness was serious enough to start thinking about last things, and that her money had been spread around in a less than normal way—because people talk, not Ray, I don't believe, no, but the others involved, and you just can't stop them completely, any more than you can shut down human nature itself—anyway, once the relatives found out, it all seemed to strike a common chord in their collective memory, one that included, however vague or veiled, the fact that Grandpa Britzen was indeed Jane's natural father but not mine, and all of a sudden they all got very interested in things like wills and inheritance laws and legal adoptions and such. It was nasty for a time, the way things can get only in a closed arena, like the first time a stick is tossed into a snake pit, but we—I—managed to live through it."

Her face clouded over, while Gianni sat still, embarrassed and angry at the same time, but almost as quickly as her silence had come she brightened and went on, with only a trace of bitterness left to give an edge to her voice, because she appeared to have something more that she wanted to tell him now, no matter what the cost.

"Now you know the past, the way things were finally handled and the division of the estate after Grandma's death, and the reconciliation, if that's the term, between Henry and Judd, who suddenly found himself fifty thousand dollars to the good—or I guess I should say the reconciliation between Henry and Judd's bank account. Maybe that's too harsh, but probably not. And that's why I'm telling you this, what I wanted to get to. You and your brother worshipped Grandpa Britzen, I know that. But there's something else that you have to be able to see, too. There was something that he couldn't deal with, the simplest thing in the world, really, simple but not easy: time. That favorite saying of his, it was something that he never should have told to children, much less believed himself, because it's just not the case. Do you remember? It goes, 'If you live right...'"

"'...you'll never die.' That's it, isn't it?"

"Yes," she nodded. "That's the point of it. But time goes on no matter what. And the things that time brings with it are not all good, and that just by definition. Oh, Grandpa had a special way of fooling himself, but he wasn't the only one, believe me. Do you remember the picture of your Swedish greatgrandfather that I showed you when you were boys, how fine he looked in his suit and vest and his Viking's beard? If you looked closely, you could see the heavy brows over the ice-blue eyes and, closer still, the red flesh on the nose, from the drink no doubt. But the drink wasn't enough to explain the gaze. He was looking off through those hooded eyes as though he were some sort of eagle, like a god that the drink had permitted to assume his true form, and there was a twinkle there, too, like Zeus must have had just before turning into the swan. But he couldn't escape, either. You know how he ended up."

Gianni nodded.

"Because in the last analysis, he couldn't handle the notion of time any better than Grandpa Britzen, and he couldn't handle evil, either, even if in his case it came from within as well as from without, from his own passions that he just couldn't control. Good lord, O.B. was more effective as a six-year-old boy shielding you from what he seemed to see as the threat of the doctor coming to the house to give you a shot for your strep—though I always thought his protection was a little two-sided," she looked at him, "if you know what I mean, more for him than for you, in the end. But be that as it may, O.B. had a splendid left hook even then, your father had made sure of that, and poor Dr. O'Hare ended up sticking the needle in his own forearm—more effective than either of them had ever been, grown men. Because, that is what I wanted to tell you, that the inability to deal with evil is not a virtue, not if you want to live in the world, anyway. And that was the lesson Grandpa Britzen never learned, in spite of having Henry around as an ambulatory example, had he only been able to see him for what he was, see it and recognize it, and so make plans—provisions—to protect against it." She paused for a moment, stiffly, studying his face, and suddenly she seemed like a stranger to him. "Don't mistake me," she continued. "He was a wonderful man. My life, all of our lives, wouldn't have been what they've been without him. But that was his failing, what I wanted to tell you: who knows but that you might be able to learn something from it, maybe, something for yourself."

Her look remained quizzical, although Gianni hardly took notice of it, deep as he was in his own thoughts. He could see the old man riding the horse in the snow, but he had to summon the image, like a photograph produced at will and so that it has lost its magic, or that someone else shows you, a picture of something that happened somewhere else when you weren't there and that you're not a part of, with the implicit notation: you are not in this scene. He thought of the other one, and of the stories he'd heard, that his mother and Aunt Rachel and Aunt Fil had told him; of the old man rocking away night after night, and the poor, dumb, greedy Sicilian with his yard full of purple chickens. But that wasn't enough, either, he could feel that now. Because in spite of what his mother said, or what anyone said or could say, it wasn't what was outside that made a difference. He knew that, now at last, he could tell that, as he sat listening, remembering, dreaming of the hunt, the way it had been, and the overwhelming thrill of the chase through the big woods.

*　　*　　*

It all came back to him with a rush, the branches flying in front of him so that moment to moment his eyes were open to the grey sky, then blocked again, his breath coming steady, steady, then fast, as he came all at once to a dead halt and saw the stag, stock still before him in its majesty, bounding suddenly away as he resumed the chase, hurtling after. And he recalled the mix of scents, almost feeling them again at the back of his nostrils amidst the numbing snow and wet leaves, the sting of the mat of branches scraping against his cheek as he went, the taste of his own blood from the cuts, and most of all the heavy musk of the stag, as though the trees and the air and the earth itself exuded the heavy scent. In his mind he saw the ridge rising across, felt the weight of the turn, the narrow path winding down and away from him into the woods, all going backwards now in his memory, descending, pulling away as he was drawn afterwards in flight, constantly faster in pursuit, through the heavy trees and the white snow.

It came quickly to him, the challenge and the overwhelming desire to defeat it, the desire that had taken him over, head to foot, that ruled every act. He knew that force from before, knew it all too well, but he let it take him. Despite his desire, he followed the chase now as though he were at once inside and outside it, apart from it, in another time and place. He saw the trees and the path again, the white blotches leading away from the ridge and down, and his instinct made him try to stop it all, to hold up then and there, but he couldn't, following the twist into the brush and then suddenly the clearing, the branch heavy with snow hanging down from above and the blur of red, and as he felt the great unspeakable longing to do what he was going to do, he saw the stag, clearly, first in outline then full on, saw it as clearly as anything he'd ever seen in his life.

He stopped remembering then, at that moment, and went no further, because he realized what he had seen, what he hadn't wanted to know but couldn't avoid, what even at the time he had seen yet not seen, sensed yet not sensed, because of his driving need to see, instead, the stag. In his mind, he had pictured, and remembered seeing it, the blotch of red. When he recognized for certain, beyond any doubt, what he had seen, he was dumbfounded; and all at once he felt his stomach go hollow, with the same thrilling and sickening feeling as when he had been a child riding in a fast car on a hilly road. The whole of the experience—the memory and the recognition of what it meant—overwhelmed him. But it lasted only a moment. Gianni had known that the memory was there, lying in wait for him, for some time. He had sensed its presence, if only as a dark, anxious pain, better left unsounded, unexplored. He felt his jaw harden involuntarily as he looked up to find himself suddenly back in the world again, in the cold parlor across from the old woman, and, what was worse, with her smiling at him.

* * *

It was several days before they talked again. "You've thought of something?" she asked, curious, insightful, almost pixieish.

"Yes. So—yes," he admitted curtly, then blurted. "I'd seen it, the red patch of felt. His hat." However odd, he somehow felt at ease for it, now, especially with her, suddenly lighter, almost exhilarated. "So how did you know?"

"I didn't. How could I have? But I knew there was something, something going on inside. I know how you act, what you're like. Oh, don't think I haven't been watching. It's part of the job," she looked away for a second then looked back. "Up to a point at any rate."

"It's just that I wanted—needed—so much for it to be as it was, or as it seemed to be. I'd wanted it so badly that what I saw made absolutely no difference for what I wanted to see. Haven't you ever felt that way, wanted something—been set and geared for something—so bad you could taste it. Except that that's just a way of saying it because the feeling is so intense that you can't taste anything. What I wanted to see *was* what I saw, not..."

"I know." She smiled again, openly sympathetic now, and resigned. "You don't have to explain."

At once his mind changed again. "You tricked me," he said quietly.

"You'd only been fooling yourself. You, that is, and most probably O.B. Not that that was so bad. You're not so different that way, all in all. O.B. has wanted things in the past so much that he'd been able to fool himself, too. So all in all, even if I stand convicted on that one count, the charge doesn't seem so serious. Anyone, or any mother that is, would most likely have done pretty much as I did. As I say, it's part of what we do, what we are. We're supposed to see things, sense things, others don't, or can't. You should know that much, at least."

"I do now." He sat back and let the bourbon from his glass warm his throat. "Yes," he repeated, feeling the air around him go chill. "I guess I do now."

He took a moment to collect his thoughts, watching the old woman watching him, impassive now, receptive. "So neither one was enough," he said at last.

"Neither one of...?"

"I'd always thought that the first of them, Grandpa Britzen, was model enough. For me, or us, or for anyone. And then the more I learned about Grandpa Mariagrazia, the more he seemed to add to—even by way of contrast, to make up for, to go beyond— what Grandpa Britzen had taught us, or, better, I guess, shown us. Because Grandpa Britzen was that, not so much a teacher, if you take that to mean an instructor or informer, but a model, or sort of ideal you get to see in action, working itself out through a set of deeds and events, no matter how small or haphazard in and of themselves, that come together in the end in a pattern of some sort, one that can be understood, followed, imitated. So he had trouble dealing with things outside of his ken, or of his control, the distasteful things, even evil, in other people's lives that somehow crisscrossed his—"

"And the lives of those around him. Don't forget that."

"No, I haven't, believe me. But still, for that there was the second part of the lesson, the one who not only knew how to deal with the things of this world but actually seemed to take a certain relish in doing just that, if pushed, anyway, so that everything in his world—"

"Everything outside of him, you mean?"

"Yes, outside. Outside, all could be set in order—"

"Which leaves?"

"Yes, I see that now, again: which leaves whatever is inside, which is to say, what may be all, everything, that matters." He stopped to take another sip from his glass while her gaze remained fixed on him, unmoved, steady, but no longer quizzical, seemingly certain, confident.

"So, yes," he went on. "Yes, there is no model outside, nothing that is adequate. Isn't that what you've been waiting for me to say all along?"

"Yes, say, and *feel*—"

"Now, all right, yes, I can feel that. No model is complete, as long as it doesn't face whatever it is inside, and deal with it, the real power, the potential for evil, the evil rooted there, inside us," he asserted as he felt the burning sun roll away from him, and from all his worrying, into the scorched black beyond. "Nothing but us," he said bitterly, "us and our own wicked.... But no," he felt something deep within him rebel. "The whole idea is too dark, too old-fashioned. It reminds me too much of fire and—"

"Brimstone?" She smiled again.

"Well, anyway, something of the sort," he demurred, taken aback by her forthrightness.

"It may be old-fashioned, Gianni, though I must say it doesn't really seem that way to me. But even if it is, so be it. What counts isn't whether an idea, a precept, has currency or not but whether it's right or not. Otherwise being up to date isn't worth a hill of beans. What is current today amounts exactly to what will be out of fashion tomorrow and, if of no further deeper use, what the day after will be dead as a door nail. We live in the world, and we live in time: surely, by now, you've seen that, at least that. You can look at the motions of time all you like, its present as well as its past— that, if nothing else, you know very well indeed." She looked carefully at him, so intensely that for the second time that afternoon it seemed to him that he was talking with someone who had suddenly turned into a total stranger, as he for her. "But you can't run away from it forever, completely, or back into it completely, without being blinded like those poor fools who for a thrill try to watch every moment of the solar eclipse and end up never seeing the light of day again, except as shadows cast on the interior walls of their darkness, with only their memories of the world and nothing more to make their way by."

He finished the drink and set it aside. Her smile had faded now; in its place was a look he could not have described, except for the light in her eyes, which was still intense, though cool rather than hot, like the old man's in the photograph, ice-blue.

"So," she said in a tone that was friendly but clipped, a tone of conclusion, "do you want to tell me just who, or maybe better, just what, you've been looking for all these past months? Good lord, do you even know?" She sat back into her chair, her face drained of the energy with which it had glowed only moments before, as though waiting, at last, for his answer.

But the question was unfair; it didn't take very long for him to recognize that. Still, it would not go away. After all, who wouldn't have looked for a definite place to begin, a starting point that was stable and solid and dependable enough so that whatever derived from it, no matter how strangely or haphazardly, would gain at least a chance to make sense. Gianni knew that that was impossible, that trying to make sense in that way was an illusion, that all that mattered or counted wasn't the goal, the end, but the search itself, the entire ebb and flow of it: but *without* the search, how could he ever have known even that much? So by then, he had at least learned *that* if nothing else, that without a point to start from albeit only as conjecture, something to go on or, at any rate, to guess at, there wouldn't even be a void to worry about, since the very notion of an abyss meant that there was something, somewhere, that was outside the abyss, something that you could stand on and lean over from to peer into the darkness, that was firm and definite and, if merely by virtue of hope, desire, or, when all else failed, whistling in the dark, dependable. *Ergo*: What? Or, better, as the old woman herself had taken pains to insist, to make him see: Who?

Yet if even she didn't know? And she didn't, he'd come to accept that. Still, he needed something—a starting point. Without at least a place to start there couldn't be a real end, but more than that, there couldn't be anything genuinely in between, either, just doubts, betrayal, uncertainty, like Phaëthon riding his father's cart through the bright morning sky to a flash of glory and then disaster. But he didn't want to think of death now, good lord why should he when he never had before, and when the whole lesson the old woman had given him, for all its maze of twists and turns, had always had just one central point: Be. Just then he thought of O.B., rolled up in the web of tubes in the hospital bed, with the scar of his anger bouncing up and down on his face thoroughly beyond his control. Who had put that mark there, he wondered?

But no, it wasn't time to worry about that, not now, not yet, thank God. Why suffer, just to make someone else happy—anyone else—when it wouldn't do any good anyway? "Something for yourself," she had said: thanks a lot. Just what he needed. It was as bad as the old man's promise had been.

All at once he could see the stain of the red flannel, and the shock of blood again. But no, not now. Nothing he could do or say, or plan to do or say, could help now, he understood that at last. But he couldn't avoid it, either, what had drawn him to that point and then brought him up short. As he sat alone on the porch at the back of the house, looking out over the grass and into the trees that led away from the yard, hoar-grey in the ascending dusk of winter, he couldn't help but think of what Jake Arndt had told him sitting on the same sort of porch, in the same sort of twilight: "You're not the only one, you should know that. Times now, when I sit out here in the evening, I watch the hawk sweep the maples before it cuts away into the dark hanging above the trees, the dark engulfing sight and muffling sound, deepening slowly, surely, drawing everything with it into its darkness—until all of a sudden the darkness, too, is pierced by stars, cut in its turn by their bright crystals, and dispersed. But it's before that, what I wanted to tell you, with the dusk still heavy, it seems it's always at that moment, that, following the hawk, I picture the man he had been, your Grandpa, and I think: Just who was he then, and why, as the dusk falls away into night."

* * *

In the mid-morning sun—so bright against the snow of the white field that the light seemed to ricochet upwards in waves toward the trees and the sky as he drove past—Gianni turned his gaze back to the road to see the rivulets starting to glisten here and there along the pebbled shoulders in the first melt of March: false thaw, he knew, too early to last, at least in that part of Wisconsin. By the time, hours later, that he pulled up to the little white house and crossed the still matted lawn to the front porch, the sun had long since lost whatever brilliance it had had left. He'd come to let her know, so that she would hear first, and directly from him, rather than second-hand from someone else. But he should have realized from the start that the gesture, his desire for principle and order in all things, would be useless. Aunt Fil already knew, as she had always seemed to know everything first, before him or O.B. or Rachel or, indeed, anyone else, even in his childhood. Gianni was surprised, and his voice betrayed it, though he should not have been.

"But how did you know?" he said. "No one—no one ever thought he could go like—"

"I knew," she said, not asking him to come in, not even for the lemonade she most certainly had made, glancing away as though losing her voice. "I knew, that's enough." Her silhouette—as she looked away, dressed in what by then was her usual black, but her face white, almost pallid, and a freshly cut flower rising from her hand—seemed aquiline, almost delicate; but he knew the appearance to be deception itself.

"And how, you knew how as well?"

"Yes, how, more or less, all that matters...."

"By his own...."

"Yes...."

Aunt Fil's voice trailed off. They embraced, quickly, and Gianni turned to go, dreading the drive back more than the drive out, because Aunt Fil had been the easy part, he was well aware of that. Still, she hadn't known everything, he was sure, and he felt oddly relieved, as he retraced the roads to the city through the afternoon shadows, that at least he hadn't had to tell her all of the details: what the last smile had meant in the eyes beneath the white scar, and how, even after the shoulder that had been hit had infected and the arm had been taken off, he still had had enough power in the one hand left, as the nurses, supposedly watching over him with, if nothing else, professional sympathy, but mumbling all the while under their breath that he had long before run out of money to pay the surgeon's bills anyway, slept blissfully undisturbed barely two rooms away. So he'd got them, too—the old men, the one anyway, would have been proud—and Gianni smiled to himself at the thought of it as he drove the car first over the hills then through the flatlands to the day's second and last destination.

This was the hard part; he'd been aware of that from long before the day's beginning. Aunt Fil was an obligation, one he accepted with neither regret nor bitterness, if anything with a certain nostalgia for times past, for their lives together through all the summers, but Denise and the children were, well, he didn't know just what, but something else altogether, and no matter how he tried, what he thought of or dreamed about, he could not imagine what words he would find to say to her or she to him. They stood under the trees at the edge of the flower beds, dormant then, as the two children played in the yard near them in the gathering light, and they exchanged comments as though in a friendly yet sharply contested competition. It took some time before their exchange got around to what mattered.

And she: "He never could have hunted again, or done any of the other things he loved."

And he: "Maybe, maybe not. But anyway, that's beside the point. That's not what this was all about."

And she: "Which was?"

And he: "Which was—which was something like principle, or even honor, if you like."

And she: "You didn't know your brother so well after all."

And he: "Yes, all right, he was more practical..."

And she: "To say the least..."

And he: "Than that. Still, there was some of that in O.B., more than even you might have suspected. But you have to consider all the time before, in order to see that. Otherwise, he might have seemed just... just...."

And she: "What he was?"

And he: "No, you shouldn't be bitter. It was courage, what he did at the end, an act...."

And she: "To leave us like this? You can stand here in this yard and call that courage?"

And he: "No, I mean for the rest of us, not just for you and the boys but for all of us. He could have held on and just made things awful for everyone, but instead he...took his troubles with him."

And she: "Then what bothers you so?"

And he: "I just never thought it could end that way...lying there alone...and that he could leave...."

"Leave?"

"Leave us," he said quietly. "No, you're right...leave me... here...alone."

They heard a whoop and the elder of the two children came up suddenly, chasing across the dark expanse of grass. In the flush of evening light, as Gianni bent to pick the boy up, he glimpsed the white and blue blossoming in his eyes, and Gianni felt the day ending, that it was time for him to leave. He took them close one by one and for the briefest of moments grasped their arms tight with his fingers. But this was not an end, he knew that as well, any more than reflection ends. It was only that now, after everything, as he turned away the hour had come for him, too; and it was time.

* * *

O.B. is alone now without even the senseless chatter of the nurses to disturb him in the dark, all of them, he knows, asleep as usual in the room down the hall, regardless of their shifts. It's just as well, of course, since he won't have them to deal with. They deserve it anyway. The silence is so complete now that it is eerie, even the whir of those awful machines making it seem more quiet rather than less, unnatural. But then the whole place is unnatural, he's felt that from the beginning. Day one. Who could have thought then that it would turn out like this. He'd never have the pleasure of downing Kaseras or his like again, that's for sure, not anymore. Maybe that's why they took it, as his penance. But no, the idea is not amusing. And he can still feel it, anyway, so maybe it's not so thoroughly gone as it seems. Sure.

It's cold in the room now, the sheets suddenly like ice. Cold as the hearts of those creeps he had been forced by chance to deal with and who now won't let him be, not even now. No honor: bastards, all of them. But they don't have hearts anyway, only pocketbooks, cold too. Cold as ice. Still not amusing, cold. He thinks of Gianni: he can play ball with the kids, that'll make him happy. The women, the long line, one by one, not worth it. There is a noise in the hall, but it passes quickly, maybe nothing. He looks to the door again: the old man, his gaze askance, glowering, it seems, though maybe not. Then just as quickly, vanished. Cold.

Only Gianni will know, will see. So in the end he's won out after all. Not bad, kid, even for you. They got me six ways from Sunday, and nowhere left to turn. So now, it's just you.

In the darkness of the cold room O.B. reaches up. But no, get the right one at least, the left. Now, at long last. He feels the life of the tubes in his clasp, cold, as he crushes them, cold, the sudden flash, warm going hot, bright as crystal, blinding: then nothing more.